FALLEN HORIZON

(SKYFALL TRILOGY)

Ashes of Eden, Book 2

Written by Diane Kann

Brought to you by Volans Galaxy Press

Published by Kannceptual Creations LLC

An imprint of Volans Galaxy Press

ISBN: 978-1-969569-89-0

Printed in the United States of America

First Edition, November 2025

CONTENTS

DEDICATION

To the dreamers who gaze at the static between stars,
To the survivors who find constellations in the chaos,
And to the children who learn to whisper back to the storm,

This story is forged from the encroaching twilight and the echoes of what might have been. It is for those who believe that even when the sky cracks open, and reality unravels into shimmering fragments, the human spirit endures, adapting, striving, and seeking understanding amidst the incomprehensible. May you find in these pages a reflection of your own resilience, a testament to the profound connections that bind us, and a reminder that even in the most alien of landscapes, hope can find a foothold, tenacious and bright. For the relentless curiosity that drives us to probe the unknown, for the fierce love that anchors us to our humanity, and for the quiet courage that allows us to face the vast, indifferent cosmos and still choose to build, to connect, and to fight for a future, however uncertain. This is for all of us, standing on the precipice of a new dawn, under a sky that remembers nothing of the old world, but whispers the promise of the next.

CHAPTER ONE

THE WHISPERING SKY

The world didn't end with a bang. It ended with a sigh, a cosmic exhalation that leached the color from the sky and the sound from the air. One moment, the familiar, mundane hum of existence was the backdrop to everything. The next, an absolute, suffocating silence descended, broken only by a sound that was more sensation than auditory input: the *sky-static*. It wasn't a roar or a whisper, but a pervasive, low-frequency thrum that vibrated in the bones, a constant reminder of the impossible change that had occurred. They called it the Veilfall, a term coined in the dazed, terrified days that followed, a descriptor as inadequate as it was inevitable. The veil between their reality and... *something else*... had thinned, then torn, then dissolved entirely.

Florida, once a sun-drenched tapestry of emerald green and cerulean blue, was now a muted watercolor of decay. The vibrant hues had leached away, leaving behind a palette of bruised purples, sickly yellows, and the omnipresent, dusty grey of perpetual twilight. The air itself felt heavy, viscous, as if breathing in yesterday's sorrow and tomorrow's dread. Trees, once proud sentinels, now stood like skeletal fingers clawing at a bruised canvas sky, their leaves long since surrendered to the encroaching desolation. Buildings, their windows shattered like vacant eyes, sagged under the weight of neglect and the ceaseless, invisible pressure of the sky-static. It was a silence that screamed, a stillness that throbbed with an unspoken threat. The familiar landscape had become alien, a warped reflection of what once was, and the few survivors who navigated its skeletal remains did so with a constant, gnawing fear.

The sky-static was the most pervasive anomaly, an atmospheric consciousness that seemed to breathe with a life of its own. It wasn't a uniform sound; it was a symphony of discordant frequencies, a constant buzz that sometimes sharpened into a needle-prick of sound, only to recede back into an all-encompassing hum. It felt... aware. Not in a way that suggested intent or intelligence, not at first. It was more like the ambient noise of a vast, incomprehensible machine that had been switched on and could not be switched off. It was the background radiation of a universe fundamentally rewritten. To stand beneath it was to feel a subtle pressure against the eardrums, a phantom vibration that resonated deep within the skull. Some claimed to feel it in their teeth, a faint, incessant grinding that wore down the nerves. Others described it as a constant static cling, not on their skin, but within their very being.

The immediate aftermath of the Veilfall was a period of profound disorientation. Communication lines had snapped, the digital veins of the old world severed. The internet, that vast, interconnected consciousness, was a corpse. What little information trickled through came from desperate, crackling radio transmissions, their sources often unknown, their messages fragmented pleas for help or bewildered accounts of impossible phenomena. Governments had dissolved, their structures too brittle, too reliant on the predictable mechanics of a world that no longer existed. Societies fractured, not with the organized collapse of armies, but with the quiet desperation of individuals and small groups huddling together against an encroaching tide of the unknown.

In the ruins of what was once a vibrant coastal community, the Ellisen family found themselves adrift. Mara, a former atmospheric physicist whose career had been dedicated to understanding the very skies that had now turned against them, felt a particular, chilling irony. Her expertise was now as relevant as a blacksmith's hammer in a world of laser scalpels, yet she found herself constantly scrutinizing the sky, searching for patterns in the chaos. Her husband, Ben, a pragmatic engineer, focused on the immediate: finding shelter, scavenging for resources, keeping their two children, Jax and Lily, safe. Jax, at fifteen, was unnervingly quiet, his eyes, once bright and curious, now often distant, as if focused on something only he could perceive. Lily, only ten, was a bundle of anxieties, clinging to her parents, her childhood innocence shattered by the persistent, unsettling presence of the sky-static.

The landscape of their new reality was a testament to loss. Highways, once arteries of commerce and travel, were now choked with derelict vehicles, their metal husks slowly succumbing to rust and the relentless Florida sun that now seemed to glare with a malevolent, sickly light. Entire towns had been swallowed by an encroaching silence, their inhabitants vanished without a trace, leaving behind only the echoes of their former lives. Nature, too, had been warped. Familiar flora and fauna were replaced by unnerving adaptations. Plants grew in impossible geometries, their colors alien and often menacing. The wildlife that remained was skittish, mutated, or simply gone, as if the Veilfall had rendered the planet uninhabitable for its original inhabitants.

The sky-static was more than just an auditory phenomenon; it was an environmental constant that subtly altered perceptions. In its presence, shadows seemed to deepen, colors appeared muted, and a perpetual sense of unease permeated the air. It was a constant, low-grade anxiety, a feeling of being perpetually watched by something vast and indifferent. Mara, with her scientific background, tried to rationalize it. Perhaps it was a form of electromagnetic interference, a residue of whatever cataclysm had occurred. But even as she tried to cling to logical explanations, a deeper, more primal fear took root: the feeling that the static was not merely a byproduct, but a symptom. A symptom of a world no longer entirely its own.

The silence that followed the Veilfall was the most profound change. The constant, comforting cacophony of human civilization – the distant sirens, the rumble of traffic, the hum of electricity, the chatter of voices – had been replaced by a void. Into this void seeped the sky-static, a sound that was not sound, a presence that was not presence. It filled the emptiness, but it did not comfort. It was the sound of absence, the noise of a world that had been emptied of its familiar song. For Mara, this silence was the loudest scream of all. It was the absence of what was, a stark declaration of what had been lost.

The desolation of Florida was particularly stark. The humid, subtropical climate, once a breeding ground for lush vegetation and vibrant life, now amplified the decay. Rot set in faster, rust bloomed with alarming speed, and the oppressive humidity seemed to cling to everything, a damp shroud that permeated clothes and spirit alike. Beaches that once teemed with life were now littered with debris, the ocean's roar muted, its once-sparkling surface now a dull, leaden grey, mirroring the sky above. Mara remembered chasing seagulls with Lily on these shores, the salty spray a refreshing kiss on their faces. Now, the thought of those shores brought a pang of grief so sharp it stole her breath. The memory was a phantom limb, an ache for something that was no longer there.

This was the world they inhabited now: a land stripped bare, bathed in an unnatural twilight, and haunted by the omnipresent thrum of the sky-static. It was a world perpetually on the edge of a precipice, where survival was measured in hours, not days, and where the greatest enemy was not a tangible foe, but the creeping, insidious dread that the Veilfall had irrevocably broken not just their world, but their very reality. The mystery of what had happened, and what the sky-static truly represented, hung over them like the perpetual twilight, a constant, unsettling question mark in the grim narrative of their existence. This was the stage upon which their struggle would unfold, a desolate theatre where the whispers of a transformed sky were the only recurring theme.

They were fortunate, in a way. Or perhaps, merely less unlucky than others. Their immediate survival was a testament to Ben's resourcefulness and Mara's cautious foresight. They had found a relatively intact structure, a former research outpost near the edge of what used to be the Everglades, its reinforced walls offering some protection from the elements and the unseen horrors that stalked the twilight. But 'relatively intact' was a hollow comfort. The water was suspect, filtered and boiled until it tasted of minerals and despair. Food was a dwindling ration of canned goods and scavenged supplies, supplemented by Mara's hesitant attempts to identify edible, or at least non-lethal, flora in the mutated landscape. Every sunrise, if one could call the gradual brightening of the perpetual gloom that, was a victory, but a victory that felt increasingly hollow.

The sky-static was a constant companion. It seeped into their dreams, a low-frequency hum that vibrated through their sleeping forms. In the waking hours, it was a subtle pressure, a persistent tinnitus that made concentration difficult, conversations disjointed. Lily would often cover her ears, her small face contorted in distress, while Jax would simply stare out of the reinforced windows, his expression unreadable, as if he were listening to a conversation that excluded them all. Mara watched him, a knot of worry tightening in her chest. His quietude had deepened since the Veilfall, his fascination with the sky no longer innocent curiosity but something more profound, more disturbing. He would trace patterns on the condensation of the windows, patterns that seemed to mimic the chaotic energy she felt radiating from the sky.

The landscape around their refuge was a testament to nature's stubborn, yet warped, resilience. Cypress trees, their ancient roots gnarled and exposed, reached towards the bruised sky like arthritic hands. The water that lay stagnant in the surrounding lowlands was no longer a murky brown but a sickly, iridescent green, a viscous film clinging to its surface. Strange, luminescent fungi clung to decaying logs, casting an eerie, phosphorescent glow in the deepening gloom. The air was thick with the scent of damp earth, decay, and an unfamiliar, cloying sweetness that Mara couldn't place, a scent that seemed to emanate from the very air itself. It was a beautiful, terrifying tableau, a twisted masterpiece painted by an unseen, unknown artist.

Ben, ever the pragmatist, worked tirelessly to reinforce their shelter, scavenging for scrap metal, wires, and anything that could be repurposed. He had managed to jury-rig a basic generator, powered by a salvaged solar array that captured the weak, diffused sunlight. It provided them with intermittent light and a way to boil water, small comforts that felt like luxuries. But even his gruff determination was beginning to fray. He had seen things during his scavenging runs, glimpses of movement in the periphery, shadows that seemed too deep, too deliberate. He spoke little of it, but Mara saw the tension in his shoulders, the way his eyes constantly scanned the horizon.

The initial days were a blur of shock and instinct. Survival was paramount. There was no time for existential contemplation, only the immediate, visceral need to breathe, to find water, to secure shelter. But as the dust settled, as the immediate crisis of finding a safe haven was resolved, the questions began to surface, insidious and persistent. What had happened? Why? And what was this pervasive static that seemed to be the only constant in their shattered world? Mara, trained to seek answers in data and observation, found herself frustrated by the lack of any discernible information. The Veilfall had been absolute, erasing the past as effectively as it had reshaped the present. There were no scientific journals to consult, no news archives to access, only the stark, undeniable reality of their altered existence.

She would spend hours by the reinforced windows, her gaze fixed on the sky. It was a constant, shifting canvas of muted, bruised colors. Sometimes, streaks of an unnatural, phosphorescent light would briefly appear, like tears in the fabric of the atmosphere, only to vanish as quickly as they came. The sky-static would pulse in response, its hum deepening, a subtle thrum that Mara felt in her very bones. It was in these moments, staring into the oppressive vastness, that the true scope of their predicament began to sink in. This was not a temporary disaster, not a storm to be weathered. This was a fundamental alteration of reality, a new paradigm that had swallowed the old one whole. The very laws of physics, of existence, seemed to be in flux, and the sky, once a symbol of boundless freedom, had become a prison wall.

The silence was the most unnerving aspect. The absence of the familiar sounds of life was a vacuum that the sky-static filled imperfectly. It was like a phantom limb, a presence where there should have been nothing, a sound that was not sound but a vibration, a feeling. It was a constant hum, a low frequency thrum that vibrated in the marrow of their bones. Mara found herself straining to hear something, anything, familiar – the distant cry of a bird, the rustle of leaves in a gentle breeze, the murmur of human voices. But there was only the static, and the unsettling stillness. It was a silence that pressed in, that demanded attention, that hinted at an awareness that transcended mere atmospheric interference. It was the sound of a world holding its breath, waiting for something unknown.

The altered landscape of Florida was a haunting spectacle. The vibrant greens and blues of pre-Veilfall had been leached away, replaced by a palette of muted, bruised tones. The humid air, once thick with the scent of blooming jasmine and salt spray, now carried the heavy odor of decay and something else, something cloyingly sweet and alien. Skeletal trees, their branches twisted like grasping claws, clawed at a perpetually overcast, bruised-purple sky. Roads, once ribbons of asphalt connecting communities, were now choked with the rusted husks of vehicles, silent monuments to a hasty exodus. Mara often found herself staring at the remnants of her old life – a faded billboard advertising a theme park that now stood derelict and forgotten, a playground swing set creaking rhythmically in the non-existent breeze. These were not just ruins; they were tombstones, marking the death of a world.

The sky-static was a constant, unsettling presence, a pervasive hum that seemed to emanate from everywhere and nowhere at once. It wasn't a sound in the traditional sense, but more of a vibration, a low-frequency thrum that resonated deep within one's chest, a constant, unnerving reminder of the impossible change that had occurred. Some days, it felt like a physical pressure against the eardrums, a phantom static that distorted perception, making shadows seem to writhe and distant objects appear closer than they were. Mara, a former physicist, struggled to categorize it, to find a scientific explanation for this pervasive atmospheric anomaly. Was it an electromagnetic field? A consequence of some unknown atmospheric ionization? Or was it something more... sentient? The question gnawed at her, a persistent itch beneath the surface of her forced pragmatism.

The desolation of the region was a profound shock. Florida, a state synonymous with sunshine, tourism, and vibrant life, had become a ghost of its former self. The lush vegetation had withered, replaced by gnarled, skeletal trees and strange, mutated flora that pulsed with an unsettling luminescence in the perpetual twilight. The familiar scent of salt and sea was replaced by the cloying odor of decay and something acrid, something that hinted at chemical alteration. Beaches that once teemed with life were now barren, littered with the debris of a forgotten era, the ocean itself a dull, leaden grey, its roar muted as if it too had been subdued by the pervasive silence.

Ben, ever the stoic, focused on the tangible: fortifying their makeshift shelter, rationing their dwindling supplies, maintaining their meager defenses. He spoke little of the horrors he encountered during his scavenging runs, but Mara saw the grim set of his jaw, the haunted look in his eyes. He had witnessed things that defied logic, movements in the shadows that were too fast, too deliberate to be natural. He had seen structures that seemed to shift and reconfigure when he wasn't looking, only to settle back into their dilapidated forms when he dared to focus. He attributed it to stress, to hallucination, but Mara knew better. The Veilfall had not just altered the environment; it had warped perception itself.

Their children bore the brunt of this new reality. Lily, at ten, was a constant ball of nerves, her laughter replaced by whimpers, her days spent huddled close to her parents, her eyes wide with a fear that no child should ever know. Jax, on the other hand, had become unnervingly quiet, his teenage boisterousness replaced by a profound, unsettling introspection. He would spend hours staring out of the reinforced windows of their shelter, his gaze fixed on the bruised, twilight sky. His once-bright eyes seemed to hold a distant light now, a reflection of the unnatural hues that dominated their horizon. Mara found herself watching him with a mixture of maternal concern and scientific fascination. He seemed to be attuned to the sky-static in a way that she, with all her scientific knowledge, couldn't comprehend. He would trace patterns on the condensation of the windowpanes, intricate, swirling designs that seemed to echo the chaotic energy she felt radiating from the heavens.

The silence that had fallen was perhaps the most profound change. It wasn't just the absence of human noise; it was the absence of natural sounds too. The wind no longer rustled through the leaves with its familiar song; it moved with a heavy, oppressive sigh. The ocean's roar, once a constant, soothing presence, was now a muted, distant murmur. Into this void seeped the sky-static, a pervasive, low-frequency hum that vibrated not just in the air, but in the very bones of those who inhabited this transformed world. It was a sound that was more sensation than auditory input, a constant thrum that suggested an underlying, unnatural energy. Mara, a former atmospheric physicist, found herself observing it with a mixture of dread and scientific curiosity. It was the signature of the Veilfall, the constant, unnerving reminder that the world they knew was gone, replaced by something utterly alien.

The landscape around them was a testament to the Veilfall's devastating impact. What had once been lush, subtropical wilderness had become a skeletal mockery of its former self. Trees stood like desiccated husks, their branches twisted into grotesque parodies of life, reaching towards a sky that offered no warmth, no light, only an oppressive, bruised twilight. The vibrant greens and blues of their past had been leached away, replaced by a palette of sickly yellows, muted purples, and a pervasive, dusty grey. The air, thick with humidity, carried the cloying scent of decay and something else, something sharp and acrid that stung the back of the throat. Mara remembered the lushness of Florida, the vibrant life that teemed in its wetlands and along its coasts. Now, it was a land of shadows and whispers, a desolate testament to a world irrevocably changed.

Ben, her husband, a man of quiet strength and practical skills, focused on survival. He worked tirelessly to reinforce their small, salvaged shelter, scavenging for materials, hunting for sustenance that was becoming increasingly scarce and unpredictable. He rarely spoke of what he saw on his excursions, but Mara saw the tension in his shoulders, the haunted look in his eyes when he returned, his silence more eloquent than any tale of woe. He was a bulwark against the immediate threats, but even his pragmatic nature couldn't shield them from the pervasive, existential dread that clung to the air like the omnipresent static.

Their children, Lily and Jax, were the focal point of their fractured existence. Ten-year-old Lily, once a spirited child, now clung to her mother's side, her eyes wide with a fear that never seemed to recede. Her laughter, once a bright melody, was now a rare, hesitant sound. Jax, fifteen, had retreated into himself. His usual adolescent restlessness had evaporated, replaced by a profound, unnerving quietude. He spent hours staring out of the shelter's reinforced windows, his gaze fixed on the sky. Mara, with her background in atmospheric physics, found herself watching him with a growing unease. He seemed to be listening to the sky-static in a way that was more than just passive reception. He would trace patterns on the condensation of the windows, complex, swirling designs that Mara couldn't quite decipher, but which felt disturbingly resonant with the chaotic energy she perceived in the sky.

The silence of the world was the most profound aspect of the Veilfall. It wasn't merely the absence of human noise – the traffic, the chatter, the constant hum of machinery. It was a deeper, more absolute silence, a vacuum that seemed to absorb all sound. Into this void seeped the sky-static, a pervasive, low-frequency thrum that vibrated not just in the air, but in the very bones. It was a sound that was more sensation than auditory input, a constant reminder of the impossible change. Mara, a physicist by training, found herself obsessively trying to categorize it, to understand its nature. Was it a byproduct of whatever cataclysm had occurred? Or was it something... more? The question gnawed at her, a persistent, unanswerable riddle in their new, desolate reality.

The altered landscape of Florida was a haunting testament to this change. What had once been lush, vibrant, and teeming with life was now a desolate wasteland of muted colors and warped forms. The humid air, once thick with the scent of salt and blooming flowers, now carried the heavy odor of decay and an unfamiliar, cloying sweetness that seemed to emanate from the very atmosphere. Skeletal trees, their branches twisted like grasping claws, reached towards a sky that was no longer blue but a bruised, perpetual twilight. Roads were choked with the rusted husks of vehicles, their occupants long gone, swallowed by the silence. Mara remembered the vibrant life of the coast, the cheerful chaos of tourists, the steady rhythm of fishing boats. Now, the ocean itself was a dull, leaden grey, its roar muted, as if it too had been subdued by the pervasive stillness.

Ben, her husband, a man of stoic pragmatism, focused on the immediate necessities of survival. He reinforced their small, salvaged shelter, scavenged for dwindling supplies, and maintained their meager defenses. He rarely spoke of the unsettling sights he encountered during his excursions – the shadows that moved with unnatural speed, the fleeting glimpses of structures that seemed to shift and reconfigure when not directly observed. But Mara saw the tension etched into his face, the way his eyes constantly scanned the horizon, a silent testament to the horrors he kept bottled within.

Their children, Lily and Jax, were the fragile heart of their existence. Lily, at ten, was a constant shadow, her vibrant spirit dimmed by a fear that seemed to permeate her small frame. Her laughter, once a bright sound that cut through the everyday din, was now a rare, hesitant whisper. Jax, fifteen, had retreated into a profound, unnerving quietude. His adolescent energy had been replaced by a somber introspection. He would spend hours gazing out of the shelter's reinforced windows, his eyes fixed on the bruised, twilight sky. Mara, with her background in atmospheric physics, found herself watching him with a growing sense of unease. He seemed attuned to the sky-static in a way that transcended mere observation. He would trace intricate, swirling patterns on the condensation of the windowpanes, designs that felt disturbingly resonant with the chaotic energy she perceived in the heavens.

The absolute silence that followed the Veilfall was perhaps the most jarring change. It wasn't just the absence of human sounds – the traffic, the distant sirens, the everyday hum of civilization. It was a deeper, more profound silence, a void that seemed to actively swallow any attempt at sound. Into this vacuum seeped the sky-static, a pervasive, low-frequency thrum that vibrated not just in the air, but in the very bones of its inhabitants. It was less a sound and more a sensation, a constant, unnerving reminder of the impossible transformation. Mara, a physicist by training, found herself obsessively trying to categorize it, to understand its nature. Was it a mere byproduct of the cataclysm, an atmospheric anomaly? Or was it something more? The question gnawed at her, a persistent, unanswerable riddle in their stark new reality.

The altered landscape of Florida was a haunting spectacle of decay and transformation. What had once been lush, vibrant, and teeming with life was now a desolate canvas of muted colors and warped forms. The humid air, once thick with the scent of salt and blooming flowers, now carried the heavy odor of rot and an unfamiliar, cloying sweetness that seemed to emanate from the very atmosphere. Skeletal trees, their branches twisted into grotesque parodies of life, reached towards a sky that was no longer blue but a bruised, perpetual twilight. Roads were choked with the rusted husks of vehicles, their occupants long gone, swallowed by the silence. Mara remembered the vibrant life of the coast, the cheerful chaos of tourists, the steady rhythm of fishing boats. Now, the ocean itself was a dull, leaden grey, its roar muted, as if it too had been subdued by the pervasive stillness.

Ben, her husband, a man of stoic pragmatism, focused on the immediate necessities of survival. He reinforced their small, salvaged shelter, scavenged for dwindling supplies, and maintained their meager defenses. He rarely spoke of the unsettling sights he encountered during his excursions – the shadows that moved with unnatural speed, the fleeting glimpses of structures that seemed to shift and reconfigure when not directly observed. But Mara saw the tension etched into his face, the way his eyes constantly scanned the horizon, a silent testament to the horrors he kept bottled within.

Their children, Lily and Jax, were the fragile heart of their existence. Lily, at ten, was a constant shadow, her vibrant spirit dimmed by a fear that seemed to permeate her small frame. Her laughter, once a bright sound that cut through the everyday din, was now a rare, hesitant whisper. Jax, fifteen, had retreated into a profound, unnerving quietude. His adolescent energy had been replaced by a somber introspection. He would spend hours gazing out of the shelter's reinforced windows, his eyes fixed on the bruised, twilight sky. Mara, with her background in atmospheric physics, found herself watching him with a growing sense of unease. He seemed to be attuned to the sky-static in a way that transcended mere observation. He would trace intricate, swirling patterns on the condensation of the windowpanes, designs that felt disturbingly resonant with the chaotic energy she perceived in the heavens.

The world had gone quiet. Not the peaceful quiet of slumber, but the deafening, absolute silence of absence. The Veilfall had not simply disrupted communication; it had seemingly leached the very sound from the air, leaving behind a vacuum that was only partially filled by a new, pervasive phenomenon: the sky-static. It wasn't a sound one heard with their ears, so much as a vibration felt deep within the chest, a low-frequency thrum that seemed to emanate from the very fabric of reality. It was a constant, unsettling presence, a reminder that the world they knew had been irrevocably altered. Florida, once a sun-drenched paradise, was now a landscape of muted colors and oppressive stillness. The vibrant greens of the Everglades had faded to a bruised, sickly yellow; the azure of the ocean had dulled to a leaden grey. Skeletal trees, their branches like grasping claws, reached towards a sky perpetually trapped in a state of bruised twilight. Buildings, their windows shattered like vacant eyes, stood as silent monuments to a vanished populace.

Mara Ellisen, a former atmospheric physicist, felt a chilling irony in their predicament. Her life's work had been dedicated to understanding the very skies that had now become the source of their terror. She watched her children, Lily, ten, and Jax, fifteen, their faces etched with a fear that belied their years. Lily, once bubbly and bright, now clung to her mother's side, her small body trembling at every unfamiliar creak and groan of their makeshift shelter. Jax, however, was different. His fear had manifested as a profound, unnerving quietude. He would spend hours staring out of the reinforced windows, his gaze fixed on the sky, his expression unreadable. Mara noticed the subtle patterns he traced on the condensation-covered glass, intricate, swirling designs that seemed to echo the unsettling energy she perceived radiating from the heavens.

Ben, Mara's husband and a pragmatic engineer, focused on the tangible aspects of survival. He worked tirelessly to fortify their shelter, scavenge for dwindling resources, and maintain their meager defenses. He rarely spoke of the unsettling encounters he had during his scavenging trips – the fleeting glimpses of movement in the periphery, the shadows that seemed to possess an unnatural volition. But Mara saw the tension in his shoulders, the haunted look in his eyes, the silent testament to the horrors he held at bay. Their existence had narrowed to the immediate: food, water, shelter, and the constant, oppressive presence of the sky-static, a low-frequency hum that seemed to vibrate through the very marrow of their bones, a constant, unsettling reminder of the world that was lost and the alien reality that had taken its place.

The relentless twilight of Florida had deepened into an inky blackness, a hue so absolute it felt as though the world had been plunged into the heart of a void. It was in this suffocating darkness that the 'Echo Storm' began, not with the rumble of thunder or the lash of rain, but with a subtle distortion of the pervasive sky-static. The low hum that had become their constant, unwelcome companion began to warp, stretching and compressing like a faulty audio recording. It was as if the air itself was being twisted, bent out of shape, and the sensation sent a tremor of primal fear through Mara.

Ben, ever vigilant, had already secured the reinforced shutters of their salvaged research outpost, the metal groaning in protest as he latched them tight. Lily, her small hands clamped over her ears, whimpered from her corner, her eyes wide and unfocused, lost in the sonic assault. Jax, however, was standing by the window, his face pressed close to the grime-streaked glass, his movements eerily calm, almost detached, as if observing a familiar, albeit terrifying, phenomenon.

"Mara," Ben's voice was a low growl, strained against the rising cacophony. "What is happening?"

Mara could only shake her head, her mind racing to reconcile the impossible. The sky-static, their constant indicator of the Veilfall's presence, was behaving erratically, violently. It wasn't a uniform thrum anymore; it was a series of sharp, piercing shrieks interspersed with moments of unnerving, absolute silence, a silence so profound it felt like a physical blow. The air crackled with an unseen energy, and the very structure of their small refuge seemed to vibrate with an intensity that made their teeth ache.

Then came the visual distortions. Outside, beyond the meager light filtering through the reinforced glass, the familiar, mutated landscape began to waver. The skeletal cypress trees seemed to bend and sway with impossible grace, their gnarled branches elongating and retracting like living things. Shapes, indistinct and terrifying, flickered in the periphery, appearing and disappearing with a disconcerting speed. It was as if the storm was not merely a meteorological event, but a tear in the fabric of reality itself, a violent manifestation of the forces that had reshaped their world.

"It's... it's like an echo," Mara whispered, the word catching in her throat. "The static... it's reflecting, distorting. Like... like sound bouncing off impossible surfaces. Or... or time itself is echoing." The thought sent a fresh wave of dread through her. Temporal anomalies. It was a concept she'd only encountered in theoretical physics, a realm of pure speculation. Now, it seemed to be manifesting in their immediate reality, amplified by the very forces of the Veilfall.

The storm intensified. The shrieking static gave way to a deep, guttural groaning that seemed to emanate from the earth beneath them. The ground shuddered, not with the violence of an earthquake, but with a rhythmic, pulsing tremor that mirrored the distorted thrumming of the sky. Outside, the air itself seemed to thicken, coalescing into swirling eddies of darkness, punctuated by flashes of an unearthly, phosphorescent light. These weren't lightning strikes; they were more like brief, intense flares of pure energy, illuminating the warped landscape for a fleeting, terrifying second before plunging it back into an even deeper gloom.

Lily let out a wail, burying her face in Mara's side. "Make it stop, Mommy! Make it stop!"

Mara held her daughter tightly, murmuring reassurances she didn't feel. Ben had grabbed his scavenged rifle, his knuckles white, his gaze fixed on the shuttered windows, as if expecting something to burst through. Jax, however, remained by the window, his head tilted, his eyes wide with a strange, unblinking intensity. He was no longer just observing; he was *listening, feeling* the storm in a way that terrified Mara more than the storm itself.

"Jax, get away from the window!" Ben barked, his voice tight with fear.

But Jax didn't move. He raised a hand, his fingers tracing a complex pattern on the glass, a pattern that seemed to shift and writhe in time with the distorted static. "It's... it's singing," he murmured, his voice barely audible above the din. "The sky is singing."

Mara's blood ran cold. Jax had always been sensitive, his quiet nature masking a keen intellect. But since the Veilfall, he had become... different. More attuned to the anomalies, more disconnected from their reality. Was he hallucinating? Or was he somehow perceiving something that they, with their adult minds, were unable to grasp?

The storm reached its crescendo. The groaning intensified, the very air vibrating with an unbearable pressure. Mara felt a searing pain behind her eyes, as if her skull were being squeezed. Then, for a split second, the world outside the window flickered. It wasn't just the trees and the sky; it was the very structure of their refuge. The metal shelves seemed to shimmer, the concrete walls to warp. Mara saw a fleeting image of a different sky, a blue sky, before it snapped back to the bruised twilight. It was a temporal echo, a glimpse of what once was, overlaid onto their shattered present.

Then, as abruptly as it began, the storm began to recede. The shrieking static softened, the groaning subsided, and the oppressive pressure in the air eased. The swirling darkness outside dissipated, and the skeletal trees returned to their unnaturally still forms. The sky returned to its muted, bruised hue, the pervasive hum of the sky-static settling back into its familiar, unsettling rhythm. It was over.

Silence, or rather, the familiar absence of sound punctuated by the sky-static, returned. Lily, trembling, slowly relaxed her grip on her mother. Ben lowered his rifle, his shoulders slumping with exhaustion and relief. But Mara couldn't shake the unsettling feeling. The storm hadn't just been a violent meteorological event; it had been a demonstration of the raw, untamed power that now governed their world. It had shown them the fragility of their existence, the precariousness of their hold on reality.

Jax, however, remained by the window, his gaze still fixed on the sky. He turned to Mara, his eyes wide, a strange mix of awe and fear in their depths. "Did you see it, Mom?" he asked, his voice hoarse. "The blue... it was so bright. And the clouds..."

Mara knelt beside him, her heart aching. "Yes, Jax," she said softly. "I saw it." She knew, with a chilling certainty, that the Echo Storm was more than just a terrifying ordeal. It was a sign. A sign that their survival depended not just on finding shelter and scavenging for food, but on understanding the very forces that had shattered their world. The sky, once a symbol of infinite possibility, had become a maelstrom of unpredictable, and often deadly, phenomena. They had survived this encounter, but it had left them shaken, exposed, and with a newfound, terrifying awareness of the volatile nature of their new reality. The 'Sky Dark,' as the desolate region they now inhabited was ominously known, had just shown them a glimpse of its true, terrifying power, and the Ellisen family had narrowly escaped its grasp, but the scars of the experience would run deeper than any physical wound. The storm had been a brutal, unwelcome teacher, and its lesson was clear: in this new world, even the air they breathed was a potential weapon.

The aftermath of the Echo Storm was a period of tense quietude, the silence amplified by the recent sonic chaos. The sky-static, now returned to its baseline hum, felt almost comforting in its familiarity, a stable presence in the wake of the temporal distortions. Yet, the memory of the storm lingered, a phantom vibration in their bones, a disquieting echo in their minds. Lily, though physically unharmed, remained withdrawn, her eyes darting nervously towards the windows at the slightest creak. Ben, his pragmatism temporarily shaken, became even more meticulous in their defenses, constantly checking the integrity of the shutters, reinforcing weak points with salvaged metal sheets.

Mara, however, was consumed by a different kind of urgency. The storm had ignited a spark of scientific curiosity that overshadowed her fear. She found herself poring over the few surviving meteorological instruments they had managed to salvage from the outpost – an anachronistic collection of barometers, anemometers, and hygrometers, their readings now largely meaningless in the context of the Veilfall's altered atmospheric conditions. Still, she studied them, searching for any anomalous patterns, any residual data that might shed light on the storm's bizarre characteristics. The temporal distortions, the sonic warping – these were not phenomena that could be explained by conventional physics. They were manifestations of something far more profound, something that hinted at a fundamental shift in the laws of their reality.

Jax, in his quiet way, became her unwitting assistant. He would often sit beside her, his gaze fixed on the instruments, his small, intelligent fingers tracing the needles as they quivered. He didn't offer explanations, not in words that Mara could understand, but his presence, his silent focus, was a source of unexpected comfort. He seemed to intuit the significance of these readings, to feel the subtle shifts in the atmosphere that Mara's instruments could only hint at.

"The sky... it's not just broken," Jax said one afternoon, his voice soft, his eyes distant. He was tracing the arc of a fluctuating pressure gauge. "It's... thinking. And it's dreaming."

Mara paused, her heart giving a familiar lurch. "Thinking and dreaming?" she echoed gently, not wanting to dismiss his words, yet struggling to find a framework for them.

"Yes," he nodded, his gaze fixed on the swirling patterns of the sky-static visible in the residual glow of their meager lighting. "Like... when we dream, things don't always make sense. They shift. They change. The storm... it was like the sky having a bad dream."

Mara considered his words. It was a child's explanation, perhaps, but it resonated with her own nascent theories. The Veilfall had introduced an element of conscious unpredictability into their world, a quality that defied scientific categorization. If the static wasn't just residual energy, but something akin to atmospheric consciousness, then perhaps phenomena like the Echo Storm were indeed expressions of its 'thoughts' or 'dreams'.

The implications were staggering. It meant that the forces governing their world were not merely chaotic, but potentially sentient, or at least possessing some form of awareness. And if that were true, then their survival depended not just on understanding the physics of the Veilfall, but on understanding its 'mind.' This was a terrifying prospect, a leap into the unknown that dwarfed her previous scientific endeavors.

Their immediate surroundings, the desolate region they had christened 'Sky Dark,' offered little comfort. The muted colors and perpetual twilight were a constant reminder of the life that had been leached from the world. Yet, paradoxically, life persisted, albeit in warped and unsettling forms. Strange, bioluminescent fungi pulsed with an eerie light in the deep shadows of the overgrown vegetation, and insects, mutated and larger than they should have been, skittered through the undergrowth. Mara had cautiously begun to document these new forms of life, sketching them in her salvaged notebook, hoping to find some pattern, some evolutionary logic in their grotesque transformations.

One afternoon, while Ben was out on a scouting mission, Mara decided to venture a short distance from the outpost with Jax, their meager supplies of purified water and scavenged rations secured. She needed to see the landscape in the full, albeit dim, light of the twilight sky, to try and reconcile the desolation with the storm's ephemeral glimpses of a vibrant, blue past. Jax, his hand clasped tightly in hers, walked with a peculiar grace, his senses seemingly heightened, his eyes scanning the warped foliage with an intensity that was both reassuring and deeply unsettling.

They moved through a grove of cypress trees, their roots twisted like petrified serpents above the stagnant, iridescent water. The air was thick with the cloying sweetness that had become characteristic of the region, a scent that Mara suspected was a byproduct of the pervasive atmospheric changes. As they rounded a cluster of particularly gnarled trees, Jax stopped abruptly, pulling Mara to a halt.

"Listen," he whispered, his voice barely audible.

Mara strained her ears. At first, she heard nothing but the ever-present hum of the sky-static. Then, faintly, she detected it – a new sound, subtle and elusive, that seemed to cut through the static. It was a high-pitched, ethereal whine, almost musical, and it seemed to be coming from deeper within the overgrown wilderness.

"What is it?" Mara whispered back, her scientific mind immediately trying to categorize it. A mutated animal? Some atmospheric resonance?

Jax's eyes were wide. "It's... it's like the singing from the storm," he said, his voice filled with wonder. "But... softer. Happier."

He began to walk towards the sound, his small hand still clasped in Mara's, his fear seemingly replaced by an insatiable curiosity. Mara hesitated for only a moment. The instinct to protect her son warred with a desperate need to understand. She had to know what this sound was, where it was coming from. It was, after all, a deviation from the oppressive silence, a whisper of something other than decay and dread.

They moved cautiously, the strange, melodic whine growing stronger. It seemed to weave through the static, a delicate counterpoint to the universe's monotonous drone. The vegetation grew thicker, the shadows deeper, and the light, already dim, seemed to recede further. Then, they broke through a curtain of thick, hanging moss and found themselves in a small clearing.

The sight that greeted them was unlike anything Mara had ever seen. In the center of the clearing stood a single, impossibly vibrant flower, its petals a luminous, iridescent blue, a color so pure and intense it seemed to absorb and radiate the very essence of light. It was a color Mara hadn't seen since before the Veilfall, a color that belonged to a world of sunshine and azure skies. The flower pulsed with a soft, internal light, and it was from its delicate stamen that the ethereal whine emanated, a sound so beautiful and pure it brought tears to Mara's eyes.

Around the flower, the air shimmered, not with the violent distortion of the Echo Storm, but with a gentle, undulating wave of energy. It was as if the flower itself was a focal point, a nexus of something extraordinary. Jax let go of Mara's hand and slowly approached the bloom, his face alight with awe.

"It's... it's beautiful," he breathed, reaching out a tentative finger.

As his fingertip brushed against a velvety petal, the whine intensified for a moment, and then, something remarkable happened. The very air around the flower seemed to coalesce, to solidify into shimmering, translucent images. Mara gasped as she saw them: fleeting visions of a blue sky, of fluffy white clouds, of birds in flight, of sunlight dappled on green leaves. It was a tangible manifestation of memory, a projection of a world long gone, conjured by this impossible flower.

Jax stood mesmerized, his face bathed in the flower's gentle light. Mara felt a surge of something akin to hope, a fragile ember in the ashes of her despair. This wasn't just a plant; it was a window, a direct connection to what they had lost. The Echo Storm had shown them the destructive power of the new reality. This flower, however, showed them its potential for something else, something beautiful, something... familiar.

But the wonder was short-lived. A sudden, guttural growl ripped through the clearing, shattering the ethereal melody. Mara's head snapped up, her heart pounding. From the shadows at the edge of the clearing, a creature emerged. It was unlike anything she had documented before. It was roughly canine in shape, but its fur was a dull, mottled grey, its eyes glowed with a malevolent red light, and its limbs seemed to bend at unnatural angles. It was a predator, drawn by the energy of the flower, its predatory instincts overriding any semblance of its former natural order.

The creature's gaze fixed on Jax, and Mara knew, with a certainty that chilled her to the bone, that they had stumbled into something far more dangerous than they could have imagined. The beauty of the flower had attracted not just echoes of the past, but also the terrifying, mutated present. Their narrow escape from the Echo Storm had led them to a new, and perhaps even more perilous, discovery in the heart of Sky Dark. The world was not just broken; it was teeming with dangers, both subtle and monstrous, and their quest for understanding had just taken a terrifyingly dangerous turn. The fight for survival had just found a new, and far more complex, arena.

The oppressive stillness that followed the Echo Storm was a fragile thing, easily shattered. For days, the family existed in a state of heightened awareness, each creak of the outpost, each shift in the ambient hum of the sky-static, a potential harbinger of renewed chaos. Lily, while no longer prone to fits of terrified screaming, remained a creature of quiet anxieties, her gaze perpetually flitting towards the sealed windows, her small hands often finding their way to her ears. Ben, his usual gruff efficiency now tinged with a weary vigilance, spent his waking hours reinforcing their meager defenses, his movements precise and methodical, as if by sheer force of will he could ward off the unpredictable nature of their world. Mara, however, found her scientific curiosity grappling with a profound unease. The instruments, once her allies in understanding, now seemed to mock her with their inability to quantify the impossible. The storm, with its temporal echoes and sonic distortions, had been a brutal lesson in the limits of conventional science.

Jax, in his own enigmatic way, seemed to be adapting. He spent hours with Mara, his silent presence a strange anchor. He still spoke of the sky 'thinking' and 'dreaming,' his childlike pronouncements unsettlingly close to Mara's own nascent theories. He had become particularly fascinated by the pulsating blue flower they had discovered in the hidden clearing, its ethereal music and projected memories a stark contrast to the bleak reality of Sky Dark. Mara had allowed him to study it, cautiously, from a distance, his fascination a flicker of light in his often-somber demeanor. The creature that had interrupted their discovery, a gaunt, red-eyed predator, had retreated into the dense foliage after a tense standoff, leaving the memory of its snarling threat as a stark reminder of the ever-present danger.

It was during one of these quiet, post-storm days, as Mara was calibrating a salvaged anemometer that had stubbornly refused to register any wind, that the first whisper came. It was faint, barely perceptible above the omnipresent static, a sound so ephemeral she initially dismissed it as auditory hallucination brought on by fatigue and the lingering tension. She shook her head, rubbing her temples, and turned back to the instrument.

"Jax," she murmured, not looking up, "do you hear that? Is that the flower again?"

Jax, who had been meticulously arranging a collection of strangely shaped pebbles he'd gathered, looked up, his head tilted. He listened for a moment, his brow furrowed in concentration. "No, Mom," he said, his voice soft. "It's not the flower."

Mara frowned, focusing her attention. The sound wasn't melodic like the flower's hum; it was more like a faint, distorted sibilance, a wordless utterance carried on the back of the static. It was too indistinct to decipher, too fleeting to grasp. She shook her head again, attributing it to the frayed nerves that were now a constant companion.

But then, it came again, clearer this time, and Mara froze. It was not a random sound. It was a *name*.

Her breath hitched. She looked at Jax, her eyes wide with a sudden, chilling recognition. He met her gaze, his own expression mirroring her dawning horror. The name, distorted and stretched, seemed to weave its way through the static, as if the very air was being coaxed to form a single, terrifying syllable.

"Mara," it whispered.

The sound was so soft, so intimate, that it felt less like an external noise and more like a thought directly implanted into her mind. It was her name, spoken with a strange, disembodied quality, as if from a great distance, yet intimately familiar. Her heart hammered against her ribs, a frantic drum against the encroaching dread. This was not just the ambient noise of their fractured world; this was personal.

"Did you... did you hear that?" Mara whispered, her voice trembling.

Jax nodded slowly, his small face pale. He hadn't just heard it; he had seen it in her reaction, in the sudden stillness that had fallen over her. The sky-static, their constant, oppressive companion, had always been a symbol of the Veilfall's pervasive influence, a constant reminder of the environmental catastrophe that had reshaped their reality. But this... this was different. This was an intrusion, a direct address.

Before Mara could process the implication of her own name being called, another whisper, sharper and more insistent, cut through the static. It was a child's voice, high-pitched and laced with an echo of fear that Mara knew all too well.

"Lily?"

The sound ripped through Mara like a physical blow. Lily, who had been quietly drawing with a piece of charcoal on a salvaged scrap of metal, looked up, her eyes wide with confusion and a dawning terror.

She had been playing on the far side of their main living area, her small world of imagined creatures and colorful scribbles momentarily interrupted. She hadn't been this close to Mara or Jax when the first whisper had occurred.

"Who's calling me?" Lily asked, her voice small and reedy, her gaze darting around the room as if seeking the source of the disembodied voice.

Mara scrambled to her feet, her scientific detachment dissolving in a tidal wave of maternal instinct. She rushed to Lily's side, pulling her daughter into a protective embrace. "It's nothing, sweetie," she lied, her voice unnaturally calm, her eyes flicking towards Jax, who was now standing by the window, his gaze fixed on the eternally twilit sky. "Just the wind playing tricks."

But it wasn't the wind. The sky-static was a constant, a low-frequency thrum that permeated their existence. It was the baseline of their new reality. And now, woven into that monotonous drone, were snippets of their own identities, personal pronouncements that felt like strings being plucked on the deepest chords of their beings.

Ben emerged from the back room, where he had been meticulously cleaning and checking their scavenged rifle. He carried the weapon casually, but his posture was alert, his senses attuned to the sudden shift in atmosphere. "What's going on? Lily, you okay?"

Lily, clinging to Mara, nodded silently, burying her face in her mother's shoulder. She was too young to fully comprehend what was happening, but she sensed the fear radiating from her parents.

"It was just... a sound, Ben," Mara said, her voice strained. "A strange echo. Lily heard her name."

Ben's eyes narrowed, his gaze sweeping over Mara and Lily, then settling on Jax. Jax, silent and unnervingly still, offered no explanation. He simply continued to stare out at the sky, as if waiting for the next pronouncement.

Then, it happened again. A deeper voice, rougher, tinged with a weariness that Mara recognized as her own, sliced through the static.

"Ben."

Ben's head snapped up, his hand tightening on the rifle. His gaze met Mara's, and in that shared look, the unspoken fear solidified. This was no longer a localized phenomenon. It was encompassing them, reaching out to each of them individually. The Veilfall, which had already reshaped their environment, had now begun to intrude upon their very identities, pulling their names from the ether, turning the abstract threat of environmental collapse into something far more insidious and personal.

"It's not just the static anymore," Ben said, his voice a low growl. He moved closer to Mara and Lily, his body a shield. "It's… speaking."

Mara felt a cold dread seep into her bones. The whispers were a deeply unnerving manifestation of the Veilfall's influence. The sky-static, which they had come to associate with the ambient, environmental hazards of Sky Dark, had always been a passive indicator. Now, it was active. It was a conduit. And it was calling them out, one by one.

"Why us?" Mara whispered, the question directed more at the sky than at her family. "Why our names?"

Jax finally turned from the window, his eyes wide and unfocused, as if seeing something beyond the confines of their small refuge. "It's learning," he said, his voice a soft murmur that barely carried over the static. "It's trying to know us."

Mara felt a shiver run down her spine. Learning? Trying to know them? The idea was both terrifying and strangely fascinating. If the Veilfall was not merely a destructive force, but something that was somehow developing a form of awareness, then the implications were staggering. The static wasn't just a byproduct of atmospheric disturbance; it was a form of communication, a nascent consciousness reaching out, testing its boundaries, learning the names of the inhabitants of its fractured domain.

"It's like... like when you're trying to remember something," Jax continued, his gaze distant. "You try to pull the word, the name, out of your head. And sometimes, it comes to you, clear as day. This... this is like the sky remembering."

Mara looked at her son, a wave of conflicting emotions washing over her. His insights, though couched in childlike metaphors, were often eerily accurate. The sky 'remembering' their names. It suggested a process of observation, of assimilation. The Veilfall wasn't just an event; it was an ongoing transformation, and the sky-static was its voice, its means of cataloging and understanding the remnants of humanity within its altered domain.

The whispers continued sporadically over the next few hours. Each time a name was called, a fresh wave of fear and unease would ripple through the family. They found themselves instinctively huddling closer, their movements becoming more guarded, as if the very air was now a treacherous element capable of betraying them. Lily, though she didn't fully grasp the meaning, became increasingly clingy, her small body trembling whenever the distorted syllables echoed through the static. Ben remained vigilant, his hand never far from his rifle, his eyes scanning the interior of the outpost, as if expecting some physical manifestation of the disembodied voices.

Mara, meanwhile, was trying to apply her scientific mind to this unsettling phenomenon. She wondered if the whispers were a precursor to something more, a way for the Veilfall to identify specific targets, or perhaps a means of psychological warfare, designed to break down their resolve through personal intrusion. Was it a random occurrence, or was there a pattern? Were they being targeted individually for a specific reason? The scientific instruments offered no answers. The barometric pressure, the atmospheric density, the subtle electromagnetic fluctuations – all remained within the strange, unpredictable parameters of their new reality, offering no clue as to the source or intent of these personal vocalizations.

The silence between the whispers was almost worse than the whispers themselves. It was a tense, pregnant quiet, filled with the ever-present hum of the static and the unspoken anxieties of the Ellisen family. They ate their meager rations in near silence, each bite feeling like a small act of defiance against a world that seemed determined to erase them. Mara found herself replaying the sounds in her mind, dissecting the distorted phonemes, trying to find any discernible pattern in the pitch, the cadence, the very texture of the voices. Were they all the same voice, merely altering its tone, or were there multiple entities speaking? The echoes were so pervasive, so warped, that it was impossible to be sure.

"It's like... like it's tasting us," Jax said later that evening, as they prepared for another uneasy night. He was tracing the outline of a particularly vibrant blue petal from the flower they had discovered, his focus intense. "It tries a name. If it likes the sound, it keeps it. If not... it forgets."

Mara paused, her hand hovering over a scavenged ration pack. 'Tasting' them. 'Liking the sound.' It was a crude analogy, but it resonated. The Veilfall was an alien presence, a force beyond their comprehension. Its methods of interaction would likely be alien as well. The whispers could be a rudimentary form of data acquisition, a way for this vast, impersonal phenomenon to categorize and understand the biological entities that still persisted within its dominion. It was a chilling thought, but one that offered a sliver of a framework, a way to approach the inexplicable.

The thought gnawed at her. If the Veilfall was indeed 'learning' them, what did that mean for their future? Would it simply observe, or would this newfound awareness lead to more direct interaction, more overt manifestations of its power? The Echo Storm had been a terrifying display of its destructive potential. The whispers, though seemingly less physically threatening, felt like a more insidious form of control, a psychological siege that chipped away at their sense of self and their security.

As the perpetual twilight deepened into a more profound darkness, the family settled into their makeshift beds. The sounds of the outpost, usually a source of comfort in their familiarity, now seemed amplified, each groan of stressed metal, each rustle of recycled fabric, a potential prelude to another whispered name. Mara lay awake, listening to the rhythmic breathing of her children, to the steady, almost comforting hum of the sky-static, and the terrifying, irregular intrusions that sliced through it. She knew, with a certainty that settled deep in her gut, that this was only the beginning. The sky had spoken, and it had spoken their names. The Ellisen family was no longer just surviving in Sky Dark; they were being *acknowledged* by it. And that, in its own unsettling way, was far more terrifying than the storms, than the mutated creatures, than the desolation itself. The whispers were a promise, or perhaps a threat, of what was to come, a chilling intimation that their existence had not gone unnoticed by the very forces that had rendered their world unrecognizable. The personal intrusion was a stark reminder that in this new, warped reality, even their identities were no longer entirely their own. The sky, once a symbol of infinite possibility, now held their names captive within its distorted whispers.

The Echo Storm had passed, leaving behind not peace, but a profound, unnerving silence. It was a silence that amplified every tremor in the air, every whisper of the wind through the skeletal remains of what was once a vibrant city. For the Ellisen family, the aftermath was a period of heightened vigilance, their small outpost a fragile bubble against the encroaching desolation of Sky Dark. Lily's terror had subsided into a quiet watchfulness, her eyes perpetually scanning the sealed windows, her small hands often seeking the comfort of her ears. Ben, his usual efficiency honed by years of survival, moved with a weary purpose, reinforcing their defenses as if sheer will could hold back the unpredictable chaos of their world. Mara, however, found her scientific mind wrestling with the impossible. The storm, with its temporal anomalies and sonic distortions, had been a brutal reminder of the limitations of her knowledge. It had ripped away the veil of scientific understanding, leaving her to confront a reality that defied logic. Jax, in his own inscrutable way, seemed to adapt. He spent hours with Mara, his silent presence a strange comfort, his pronouncements about the sky 'thinking' and 'dreaming' unsettlingly close to her own burgeoning theories. He had developed a peculiar fascination with the pulsating blue flower discovered in the hidden clearing, its ethereal music and projected memories a stark contrast to the bleakness of their existence. The creature that had interrupted their discovery, a gaunt predator with eyes like burning coals, had retreated, leaving behind the chilling memory of its snarl. It was amidst this tense quiet, as Mara calibrated a stubborn anemometer, that the first whisper came, a sound so faint she dismissed it as fatigue, until it coalesced into her own name, spoken with an unearthly intimacy. Then Lily's name, and Ben's. The sky-static, once a passive hum of environmental disruption, was now a voice, speaking their identities into existence, a chilling realization that the Veilfall was not just an environmental catastrophe, but a sentient, encroaching presence.

Beyond the immediate confines of their fortified outpost, nestled within the skeletal remains of what had once been a sprawling metropolis, lay Hearthglade. It was a testament to human resilience, a small ember of life flickering defiantly in the vast darkness. This was not a settlement built of gleaming steel or advanced composites, but of necessity and desperation. Its defenses were a haphazard amalgamation of scavenged materials: sheet metal scavenged from derelict vehicles, reinforced with hardened mud and salvaged rebar. Fences fashioned from tangled wire and razor-sharp scrap metal formed a jagged perimeter, designed more to deter the curious than to withstand a determined assault. Watchtowers, crudely constructed from stacked crates and scaffolding, offered vantage points over the desolate landscape, manned by individuals whose faces were etched with a perpetual wariness. The buildings themselves were a patchwork of repurposed structures: a former gymnasium, its roof partially collapsed, now served as a communal hall; a gutted supermarket housed their meager hydroponic gardens, tended with meticulous care under the dim glow of scavenged grow lights; a series of interconnected basements from a collapsed apartment complex provided individual living quarters, each door a barrier against the unknown.

Resources were a constant, gnawing concern. Water was collected from infrequent rainfall, meticulously filtered and rationed. Food was a precarious balance between the output of the hydroponic gardens and the spoils of dangerous scavenging expeditions. Protein came from the hardy, genetically modified insects cultivated in specialized vats, or, on rare occasions, from the carefully harvested meat of smaller, less dangerous indigenous fauna. Fuel was a precious commodity, siphoned from abandoned vehicles or generated through inefficient, jury-rigged biofuel processors. The air itself was a hazard, often thick with dust and particulate matter, requiring the use of rudimentary respirators during any extended exposure. Yet, despite the pervasive scarcity and the ever-present dangers, a fragile sense of hope persisted. It was a hope born not of optimism, but of a grim, unyielding determination to survive. Children, like Lily and Jax, represented the future, a fragile promise that life would continue, even in this shattered world. The elders, their faces lined with the memories of the Before Times, shared stories and knowledge, ensuring that the lessons of the past were not entirely forgotten.

The Ellisen family occupied a unique position within Hearthglade. Ben, with his practical skills and unwavering resolve, was an integral part of the settlement's security and infrastructure. He was often found reinforcing defenses, repairing essential equipment, or leading small, carefully planned scavenging missions into the surrounding ruins. His quiet competence made him a natural leader, though he shied away from the spotlight, his focus always on the immediate tasks at hand. Mara, on the other hand, brought a different kind of value. Her scientific knowledge, though often strained by the limitations of their current reality, was invaluable. She managed the hydroponic gardens, experimented with nutrient supplements derived from local flora, and attempted to decipher the bizarre atmospheric phenomena that characterized Sky Dark. Her instruments, often salvaged and repaired, were their eyes and ears into the unpredictable environment, providing what little data they could glean to inform their decisions.

Jax, with his unusual perception and connection to the nascent consciousness of the Veilfall, was an enigma to many. Some viewed him with suspicion, attributing his quiet nature and strange pronouncements to the trauma of the Echo Storm. Others, particularly Mara, saw him as possessing a unique insight, a bridge between their world and the bewildering changes that had swept over their planet. His fascination with the blue flower, and his increasingly accurate interpretations of its "whispers," set him apart, marking him as someone who could perceive the subtle shifts in their reality in ways others could not. Lily, the youngest, was the embodiment of their vulnerability and their hope. Her innocence, though often overshadowed by fear, was a constant reminder of what they were fighting for. She was cherished by the community, a precious reminder of the world they had lost and the future they desperately wanted to reclaim.

The dynamics within Hearthglade were a delicate dance between cooperation and individual survival. While the community's strength lay in its collective effort, the harsh realities of Sky Dark often bred a degree of self-preservation. Trust was a hard-won commodity, earned through shared hardship and proven loyalty. Disputes, though rare, were settled by a council of elders, their decisions guided by the overarching need for unity and survival. The whispers, however, had introduced a new, unsettling element into this fragile social fabric. They were a shared experience, a collective terror that transcended individual concerns, yet also a deeply personal intrusion. The fact that the sky seemed to be calling each of them by name, weaving their identities into the omnipresent static, created a new layer of unease.

It fostered a sense of being watched, of being cataloged by an unseen, unknown entity.

In the communal hall, the harvested bioluminescent fungi cast a soft, greenish glow, illuminating the tired faces of Hearthglade's inhabitants. Ben was poring over a salvaged map, tracing potential scavenging routes, his brow furrowed in concentration. Mara sat nearby, meticulously cleaning a delicate sensor from her atmospheric analyzer, its metallic casing worn smooth by her touch. Jax, his back against a makeshift support beam, was tracing patterns in the dust on the floor, his movements slow and deliberate. Lily was nestled in her mother's lap, her small fingers tracing the lines of Ben's map, her gaze occasionally drifting towards the reinforced windows, as if expecting something to appear in the perpetual twilight.

"The perimeter fence on the western sector needs reinforcement," Ben stated, his voice low, directed at a small group of settlement guards who were sharing a meal of insect paste and processed algae. "The last storm did more damage than we initially assessed. Another good blow could compromise the entire section."

One of the guards, a burly man named Silas whose face was a roadmap of old scars, grunted in agreement. "Saw some of the supports were starting to buckle. Will organize a work party tomorrow, first light."

Mara looked up from her work. "The atmospheric pressure readings are still erratic," she said, her voice tinged with concern. "The static is louder than usual, even for this time of day. It's as if... as if something is building."

Jax looked up from his dusty drawing. "It's listening," he murmured, his voice soft, almost lost in the ambient hum. "It remembers the storm. It's getting ready."

His words, though childlike, hung in the air, a chilling prophecy. The storm had been a cataclysm, a violent upheaval that had reshaped their world. The whispers, those disembodied intrusions of their names, were a new form of communication, an intimate, unsettling acknowledgment from the very forces that had wrought their devastation.

"Getting ready for what, Jax?" Silas asked, his gruff demeanor softening slightly as he addressed the boy. He had seen Jax's uncanny connection to the strange phenomena of Sky Dark, and while he didn't fully understand it, he respected its presence.

Jax didn't answer directly. He simply turned his gaze back to the floor, his small hand continuing its intricate drawing. The hum of the sky-static seemed to swell for a moment, a wave of distorted sound that made Lily flinch, burying her face in Mara's side.

"It's the static," Mara explained, her voice carefully neutral, though a tremor ran beneath it. "It's been... active, lately. More than just background noise." She hesitated, reluctant to voice the full extent of her fear. The idea of an awareness, of a consciousness within the environmental chaos, was still difficult to accept, even for her.

Ben folded the map, his gaze sweeping over his family and then the assembled inhabitants. "We're prepared for the elements," he said, his voice firm, intended to reassure. "We've survived worse. We'll reinforce the fence, check the filtration systems, and keep our eyes on the sky. That's all we can do."

His words were a familiar mantra, a grounding truth in a world that constantly threatened to spin out of control. Yet, even as he spoke, a faint whisper, distorted and warped, brushed against Mara's senses. It was her name, softer this time, almost a sigh carried on the static. She subtly shook her head, pushing the intrusive sound away. It was no longer just a memory of the storm; it was a present, ongoing reality, a constant reminder that their haven, however carefully constructed, was still vulnerable, and that the sky, in its newly awakened state, was watching, listening, and perhaps, learning. The fragility of Hearthglade was not just in its physical defenses, but in the psychological resilience of its inhabitants, constantly tested by the insidious intrusion of the Veilfall's burgeoning consciousness.

Mara Ellisen ran a weary hand over the smooth, cool surface of the atmospheric analyzer, its faint hum a familiar counterpoint to the perpetual sigh of the wind outside. For weeks, the sky-static had been more than just a background nuisance, a constant reminder of the fractured atmosphere. It had become a voice, or at least, a semblance of one. The initial shock of hearing her own name, then Lily's, then Ben's, had gradually morphed into a gnawing disquiet. It wasn't just a random echo of their presence, a distortion picked up by sensitive equipment. The intonation, the subtle nuances that Mara, with her finely tuned scientific ear, had begun to discern, felt deliberate. It was a chilling intimacy that a mere environmental anomaly shouldn't possess.

Her scientific training, a deeply ingrained habit of seeking order in chaos, fought against the emerging, terrifying possibility. Nature, even in its most extreme and unpredictable forms, followed laws, patterns that could be observed, measured, and understood. She had spent her life deciphering the intricate dance of atmospheric physics, the predictable cycles of weather, the subtle shifts that preceded seismic activity. But the Veilfall, the Veilfall defied every textbook she had ever studied, every simulation she had ever run. It was a variable that refused to be quantified, a constant that shifted its own rules.

She found herself spending more and more time alone, hunched over her instruments, her brow furrowed in concentration. The others, while recognizing the increased "activity" of the static, seemed to accept it with a weary resignation, a new facet of the harsh reality they inhabited. Ben, ever practical, focused on reinforcing their physical defenses. Lily, bless her innocent heart, found comfort in the familiar routines, her fear a low hum beneath her daily life. Jax, however, was a different story. His pronouncements about the sky "thinking" and "dreaming" were no longer easily dismissed. They resonated with a disturbing accuracy, a reflection of the unsettling intuitions that were beginning to bloom in Mara's own mind.

"It's not random," she murmured, her voice barely audible above the wind's lament. She tapped a finger against the holographic display of the analyzer, a cascade of fluctuating energy readings swirling before her. The patterns were there, she was sure of it. Not the predictable ebb and flow of a storm system, but something more complex, more deliberate. It was like watching a language she couldn't quite comprehend, a sequence of symbols that hinted at meaning but remained stubbornly opaque.

She recalled the incident with the pulsating blue flower. The ethereal music it emitted, the projected images, the undeniable sense of... connection. It had felt alive, not in the way a plant was alive, but in a way that suggested an awareness, a subtle sentience. And Jax, with his uncanny sensitivity, had been the one to notice it first, to interpret its silent messages. He had spoken of the flower "singing memories," and in hindsight, Mara realized how profoundly accurate that description had been. The memories weren't hers, yet they felt deeply familiar, echoes of a past she had never lived, a past that belonged to a world long gone.

This sky-static, however, felt different. It wasn't the gentle, almost mournful melody of the flower. It was a pervasive, often jarring presence, capable of both subtle intrusion and outright menace. The Echo Storm had been a violent act of nature, or so they had believed. But the aftermath, this unnerving quiet punctuated by deliberate whispers, suggested something more. It suggested an agent, an intelligence orchestrating the chaos, or perhaps, emerging from it.

She found herself meticulously logging every instance of the whispers, categorizing them by frequency, amplitude, and the perceived emotional tone. Was it her imagination, or did the whispers directed at Lily carry a different quality than those aimed at Ben? Were there subtle variations in the static's intensity that correlated with specific atmospheric events, or perhaps, with their own activities within Hearthglade? She was trying to impose order, to find the scientific rationale, but the data was infuriatingly elusive, constantly skirting the edges of intelligibility.

One evening, while Ben was out on a carefully planned scavenging run near the old transit tunnels – a dangerous but potentially rewarding expedition for much-needed power cells – and Lily was asleep, Mara found herself drawn to the observation deck. The reinforced glass offered a panoramic view of the perpetual twilight, the skeletal remains of the city silhouetted against a sky that shimmered with an unnatural luminescence. The static was particularly strong tonight, a low thrumming that vibrated in her bones.

Jax sat beside her, his small frame silhouetted against the dim light. He had been unusually quiet, his gaze fixed on the swirling patterns in the sky.

"It's... thinking about us, isn't it?" he said, his voice barely a breath.

Mara swallowed, her throat suddenly dry. "What makes you say that, Jax?"

He turned his head, his large, earnest eyes meeting hers. "The way it sounds when it says our names. It's like it's trying to remember something. Or... or learning it."

His words were a mirror of her own deepest fears. Learning. The idea that this vast, incomprehensible phenomenon was actively learning about them, cataloging their identities, was profoundly unsettling. It moved beyond the realm of mere environmental hazard and into the territory of something far more alien and potentially threatening.

"But how?" Mara asked, the question directed as much to herself as to Jax. "How could the atmosphere... learn?"

"It's not just the atmosphere," Jax replied, his gaze returning to the sky. "It's... bigger than that. The storm broke something. And now... this is what's left. Or what's growing."

Mara traced a condensation pattern on the glass. "We thought the Echo Storm was a natural disaster, a freak event. But what if it wasn't? What if it was... a reaction? A response?"

Jax nodded slowly. "It's like the sky was asleep. And the storm... it woke it up."

The thought was both terrifying and strangely exhilarating. For years, Mara had dedicated herself to understanding the physical world, to peeling back the layers of complexity through observation and analysis. The Veilfall presented a challenge unlike any other, a force that seemed to actively resist conventional scientific inquiry. Yet, it also offered the tantalizing possibility of uncovering a truth more profound than she had ever imagined.

She began to document not just the whispers, but the subtle shifts in the static's ambient hum. Were there patterns in the background noise that preceded the whispers? Did the intensity of the static correlate with the appearance of certain atmospheric phenomena, like the iridescent clouds or the strange, localized pockets of intense cold? She started cross-referencing her data with the environmental readings from the salvaged weather stations scattered throughout the ruins, looking for any correlation, any hint of a logical sequence.

Silas, a gruff but well-meaning member of Hearthglade's security detail, caught her one afternoon hunched over her data slate, a look of intense concentration on her face.

"Everything alright, Mara?" he asked, his voice a low rumble. "You've been spending a lot of time in here lately. Those readings are just noise, aren't they?"

Mara forced a smile. "Just trying to make sense of the background radiation, Silas. You know how it is." She hesitated, then added, "Though, I've been noticing some... unusual patterns."

Silas scratched his chin. "Patterns? Like what? You seein' things in the static now, like Jax?" He meant it kindly, but there was an underlying skepticism in his tone. Jax's unique connection to the Veilfall was a source of both wonder and unease for many in Hearthglade.

"No, not like Jax," Mara said, choosing her words carefully. "More... mathematical. Cycles. It's just that they don't quite fit any known atmospheric models. It's... peculiar."

Silas nodded, though his expression suggested he hadn't quite grasped the distinction. "Well, as long as it ain't sayin' bad things about our defenses, I suppose it's harmless enough. Ben says we're good to go on the western sector reinforcement. Need you to check the air purifiers tomorrow, though. They were sputtering a bit last night."

As Silas walked away, Mara let out a breath she hadn't realized she was holding. She understood their perspective. The immediate threats – the dwindling resources, the constant danger of the outside world, the unpredictable weather – were tangible. Her pursuit of patterns in the sky-static, her growing suspicion of an emergent intelligence, could easily be dismissed as paranoia, a coping mechanism for the overwhelming stress of their existence.

But she couldn't shake the feeling. It was a seed of doubt, planted deep within her scientific mind, a tiny sprout pushing through the hardened earth of her skepticism. The whispers weren't just echoes; they were communications. The static wasn't just noise; it was a language. And she, Mara Ellisen, a scientist in a world that had forgotten the meaning of the word, was determined to learn to speak it.

She spent the next few days meticulously recalibrating the anemometer, its delicate sensors still showing anomalous readings. The wind, though present, was not always the sole cause of the vibrations picked up by the device. There were other frequencies, subtler tremors that seemed to emanate from the sky itself, independent of any meteorological event. She began to wonder if the wind, as they understood it, was merely a manifestation of a deeper, more complex atmospheric process.

One evening, she was reviewing audio logs of the static, filtering out the ambient wind noise, searching for the faintest trace of the whispered words. Lily had come to sit with her, her small hand reaching out to touch the glowing interface of the data slate.

"Mommy," Lily said, her voice soft, "the sky sounds sad today."

Mara paused, her ears straining. She hadn't heard any specific whispers directed at them recently, but Lily, with her unburdened innocence, often perceived nuances that the adults, clouded by their own fears and anxieties, missed.

"Sad, sweetie?" Mara prompted gently.

"Yes," Lily nodded, pointing a small finger towards the window. "Like it's lonely. Like it wants a friend."

Mara followed Lily's gaze to the sky, a vast expanse of swirling, faintly glowing dust and gases. Lonely? Wanting a friend? The anthropomorphism was a child's way of making sense of the incomprehensible, yet it struck a chord with Mara. If this phenomenon was indeed becoming sentient, perhaps its initial interactions were not malicious, but exploratory. Perhaps the whispers were simply a clumsy attempt at communication, a nascent consciousness reaching out.

This thought, however, did little to allay her unease. A lonely, sentient sky was still an unknown, and unknowns in their world were rarely benign. She returned to her data, her fingers flying across the interface, trying to map the subtle fluctuations in the static's energy signature. She began to hypothesize about the possibility of localized field distortions, of energy pockets that could interact with organic matter, perhaps even with consciousness.

She started to run theoretical simulations, using the limited processing power of her salvaged equipment. She modelled scenarios where ambient energy fields could coalesce, forming complex wave patterns that could, under specific conditions, mimic neural activity. It was a long shot, a desperate attempt to find a scientific framework for what felt increasingly like a supernatural event.

She remembered Jax's repeated insistence that the sky was "thinking." At first, she had dismissed it as a child's fantasy, an imaginative interpretation of strange sounds. But now, as she analyzed the intricate, almost fractal patterns in the static's energy fluctuations, she couldn't help but wonder if Jax was closer to the truth than any of them had dared to admit. The complexity was too great, the apparent intentionality too strong, to be mere random atmospheric chaos.

She found herself revisiting the data from the Echo Storm itself, a time when her focus had been solely on immediate survival and the mitigation of physical damage. She zoomed in on the atmospheric readings from the day the storm had passed, searching for any subtle anomalies that might have been overlooked in the initial panic. Were there energy spikes that preceded the temporal distortions? Were there unusual electromagnetic fluctuations that could have acted as a catalyst, awakening something dormant within the atmosphere?

The process was painstakingly slow, each data point a needle in a haystack of chaotic information. But with each passing day, the seed of doubt grew stronger, its roots digging deeper into her scientific conviction. The Veilfall was not simply a phenomenon to be endured; it was a puzzle to be solved. And Mara Ellisen, with her insatiable curiosity and her unwavering commitment to understanding, was determined to find the key. The whispers were no longer just a source of fear; they were a siren song, calling her towards a truth that lay hidden within the heart of the Whispering Sky.

CHAPTER TWO

THE GLASSBORNE EMERGENCE

The edge of their world, the familiar, jagged silhouette of the northern mountain range, had always been a stark, unchanging boundary against the perpetual twilight. Mara had studied its geological formations, mapped its precarious climbs, and even relied on its imposing presence as a landmark during desperate scavenging runs. But now, something was fundamentally *wrong*. It wasn't a change in the topography, no sudden avalanche or seismic shift. It was in the very fabric of perception, an alteration so subtle yet so profound it made her teeth ache.

The "Horizon's Glacial Shift," as she had begun to privately label it, was a visual distortion that had been creeping in over the past few cycles. It was as if the sky itself had taken a deep, inky breath and exhaled a layer of ethereal frost, not on the ground, but in the distance, along the very edge of their visible reality. The familiar charcoal greys and bruised purples of the distant peaks were no longer sharp, stark lines against the less-than-black of the upper atmosphere. Instead, they were softened, blurred, as if viewed through a pane of impossibly thick, ancient ice. The light, which always struggled to pierce the Veilfall's oppressive gloom, now seemed to refract *before* it reached the horizon, scattering into a diffused, almost milky luminescence that gave the entire vista a ghostly pallor.

She first noticed it during a rare moment of stillness, while tending to the algae farms on the southern perimeter of Hearthglade. The air was still, the wind a mere whisper, and the usual cacophony of atmospheric whispers had receded to a low hum. Her gaze drifted towards the north, towards the immutable sentinel that was the Horizon. And she saw it. The mountains, usually so resolute, seemed to be... receding. Not physically moving, but their perceived distance had increased. The stark contrast between solid rock and the void beyond had been replaced by a subtle gradient, a shimmering veil that implied a chasm of unknown depth opening up where solid ground should be.

It was disquieting, deeply so. Her scientific mind, ever seeking quantifiable data, struggled to categorize this anomaly. Was it a change in atmospheric density? A peculiar form of light scattering caused by an unknown particulate? Or was it something far more unsettling – a deliberate manipulation of their perceived reality? The whispers, the strange auditory phenomena that had become a constant companion, had been unsettling, suggesting an emerging intelligence. This, however, felt like that intelligence was now actively *reshaping* their world, not just observing it.

She brought it up cautiously during a communal meal, the flickering synth-lamps casting long shadows across the faces of the Hearthglade residents. Ben, his brow furrowed with the perpetual weight of their survival, had looked up from his ration paste. "Receding, Mara? The mountains? You sure you're not just tired? We're all running on fumes."

"I'm sure, Ben," she replied, her voice steady, though a knot of unease tightened in her stomach. "It's not a physical recession. It's... visual.

As if the atmosphere itself has thickened at that distance, and the light is behaving differently. It's making the horizon appear further away, softer, almost... frozen."

Lily, sitting between them, her small face earnest, piped up, "The sky looks like a big, cold window, Mommy. It's hard to see what's behind it."

Mara's heart ached at her daughter's innocent, yet profoundly accurate, description. A cold window. That was precisely it. The Veilfall had always been a barrier, a prison. But this was different. This felt like the bars of the cage were being rearranged, the perception of the outside world actively distorted.

Jax, as usual, offered a more cryptic, yet perhaps more insightful, observation. He sat cross-legged on the floor, meticulously arranging salvaged gears into an intricate pattern. "It's not just the horizon, Mara," he said without looking up. "It's... the edges. Everything is getting fuzzy. Like a dream you can't quite remember when you wake up."

His words, often dismissed by others as childish fancy, resonated with Mara. The Veilfall, in its current state, felt increasingly dreamlike, a departure from the harsh, tangible reality they had known. This "glacial shift" was a physical manifestation of that shift in reality itself. The world wasn't just broken; it was being subtly, terrifyingly, rewritten.

Over the following cycles, Mara dedicated herself to observing this phenomenon. She recalibrated her optical sensors, ran spectral analysis on the light emanating from the horizon, and even attempted to triangulate the perceived distance using triangulation with two of their salvaged automated sentry drones. The data was frustratingly inconclusive, always hinting at a distortion that defied conventional physics. The light wavelengths at the horizon showed subtle but persistent anomalies, a slight blueshift that shouldn't have been there given the distance, and an unusual diffusion pattern that suggested refraction through an impossibly vast, impossibly uniform medium.

She spent hours on the observation deck, the reinforced transparisteel offering a panoramic view of the alien landscape. The city ruins, skeletal remains of a forgotten era, lay sprawled out before them, their sharp edges also beginning to soften under the pervasive, chilling luminescence. The dust clouds that perpetually swirled in the atmosphere, usually exhibiting chaotic, unpredictable movement, seemed to flow with a more languid, deliberate grace at the edges of their vision, as if their very momentum was being subtly altered by this encroaching 'frost.'

The phenomenon wasn't uniform. Sometimes, the horizon appeared starkly distant, a vast, almost unreachable gulf. Other times, especially after periods of intense atmospheric static or the unsettling whispers, the perceived distance would subtly contract, the softened edge of their world drawing infinitesimally closer, only to recede again. It was this variability that fueled Mara's scientific curiosity and her growing dread. It wasn't a static change; it was dynamic, suggesting an active process, a conscious manipulation of their perceived environment.

She remembered the scientific texts from her early education, descriptions of atmospheric lensing caused by extreme temperature gradients or rare orbital alignments. But those were fleeting, localized effects. This was pervasive, constant, and growing. It felt less like a natural atmospheric phenomenon and more like an intentional alteration of their visual field, a psychological manipulation at a planetary scale.

One particularly oppressive evening, the static in the air had been unusually potent, a disorienting symphony of static bursts and faint, almost mournful sighs. Ben had been working on reinforcing the western wall, his movements sharp with frustration. Lily had retreated to her room, a small, brightly colored toy clutched tightly in her hand, seeking solace in the familiar. Mara found herself drawn back to the observation deck, the cold seeping through the transparisteel even on the inside.

The Horizon had never looked more alien. The familiar, solid line of mountains was now obscured by a swirling, opalescent mist that seemed to emanate from the sky itself, not from the ground. It was as if the very concept of a defined horizon was being erased, replaced by an infinite, featureless expanse. The light, usually a dull, oppressive grey, now shimmered with faint hues of violet and icy blue, reminiscent of aurora borealis, but colder, more sorrowful.

Jax joined her, his small form a stark contrast against the vastness outside. He pointed a small finger, his voice hushed with awe. "It's like the world is sighing, Mara. A big, cold sigh."

Mara nodded, her gaze fixed on the shifting patterns. "It does feel that way, Jax. Like the world is... breathing differently." She paused, then asked, "Do you think... do you think it's trying to show us something?"

Jax looked at her, his large eyes reflecting the strange, shifting light. "Maybe it's showing us that it's not real anymore. The old world. This is the new world, Mara. The sky is making it new."

His words were a chilling echo of her own burgeoning, terrifying hypothesis. The Echo Storm hadn't just been a disaster; it had been a catalyst. It had fractured the Veilfall, and through that fracture, something else was emerging, something that was now actively re-sculpting their reality. This "Fallen Horizon" was not a mere visual anomaly; it was a symptom of a fundamental alteration in the nature of their world. The very ground beneath their feet, the air they breathed, the sky they looked upon – all of it was potentially being rewritten by an unseen hand, or perhaps, an emergent consciousness.

She began to hypothesize about the nature of this "frost." Was it a form of exotic matter, bleeding into their dimension through the Veilfall's breach? Or was it a field of energy, an informational overlay that was altering their perception? Her scientific training was being stretched to its absolute limit, grappling with concepts that bordered on the metaphysical. She started to consider the possibility that consciousness itself, amplified by the vast energies of the Veilfall, could exert influence over physical reality, especially on a quantum level, subtly altering the interactions that formed their perceived world.

The change was gradual enough that most had dismissed it as fatigue or an optical illusion. But Mara, with her keen observational skills and her inherent need to understand, saw the truth. The world was not just surviving; it was changing in a way that defied all known laws of physics and biology. The Fallen Horizon was not the end of their world, but perhaps, the beginning of something entirely new, and terrifyingly unknown. The static whispers in her ears suddenly seemed less like random noise and more like the hushed pronouncements of a creator, or a destroyer, slowly but deliberately reshaping the canvas of their existence. She felt a profound sense of isolation, standing on the precipice of a truth that no one else seemed ready to accept, a truth painted in the shifting, glacial hues of their dying, or perhaps, birthing, world. The horizon, once a symbol of their limited but tangible existence, was now a question mark, a shimmering, frost-covered enigma that promised both oblivion and an unimaginable, alien future.

The shift was subtle at first, easily dismissed as another trick of the light or a further degradation of their failing optics. Mara had spent cycles meticulously documenting the chromatic aberrations along the horizon, cataloging the way the sky seemed to weep a crystalline frost over the jagged peaks of the northern range. She attributed the flickering spectral halos around distant objects to atmospheric anomalies, the increasingly frequent headaches to the pervasive static that hummed just below the threshold of audibility. But then, the anomalies began to manifest closer to home. Not in the sky, but in their own people.

It began with Elias, a young scavenger known for his sharp eyes and even sharper tongue. He'd returned from a run near the old Lumina-Tech sector, usually a fruitful but dangerous salvage ground, looking... different. Not injured, not ill, but subtly altered. His usual earthy brown eyes, flecked with gold from generations of exposure to ambient radiation, now seemed to possess a depth that was both mesmerizing and unnerving. Mara, tending to the communal hydro-garden, watched him approach, a slow unease coiling in her gut.

As he drew nearer, bathed in the cool, artificial glow of the hydroponic lights, the change became undeniable. Elias's eyes weren't reflecting the light; they were *consuming* it, splintering it into a kaleidoscope of shifting hues. It was as if slivers of the anomalous horizon had been implanted directly into his pupils. The familiar brown was still there, a deep, dark base, but overlaid upon it were swirling patterns of sapphire, emerald, and amethyst, shifting and coalescing like nebulae in miniature. They pulsed with a faint, internal luminescence, an effect that was both beautiful and deeply alien.

"Elias?" Mara's voice was a hushed question. "Are you alright? You look... unwell."

He blinked, and for a moment, the light show in his eyes intensified, sending streaks of iridescent color across his pale cheeks. "Unwell? I'm fine, Mara. Just... tired. The salvage was good. Found some intact processors." He gestured vaguely towards the pack slung over his shoulder, but his gaze was unfocused, as if his attention was being drawn elsewhere, perhaps back to the shimmering spectacle within his own eyes.

Ben, ever pragmatic, clapped Elias on the shoulder. "Good to hear. We're running low on diagnostic chips. Just don't stare into any active reactors, alright? We don't need another incident like the one with old Roric."

Elias gave a weak laugh, but it didn't quite reach his eyes. "No, Ben. Nothing like that." He then tilted his head, his gaze drifting past Ben, towards the reinforced transparisteel viewport that overlooked the decaying cityscape. "The... the sky looks particularly... fractured today, doesn't it?"

Mara felt a prickle of fear crawl up her spine.

Fractured. It was the same word she had used in her private logs, the same descriptor that haunted her waking thoughts. She saw others in the communal area begin to notice Elias. Whispers started, furtive glances exchanged. Children, usually boisterous, fell silent, their wide eyes fixed on Elias's transformed gaze.

"What's wrong with his eyes?" a young girl, Elara, whispered to her mother, who quickly shushed her, pulling her closer.

It was Lily, Mara's daughter, who spoke the unspoken fear. "He looks like the sky, Mommy," she said, her small voice barely audible. "His eyes are like the fallen sky."

Mara knelt beside her daughter, her heart a leaden weight in her chest. She met Elias's gaze again. The swirling colors were now tinged with a faint, icy blue, mirroring the glacial hues that had begun to dominate the horizon. It was more than a visual anomaly; it was a biological one. A transformation.

Over the next few cycles, Elias was not the only one. A creeping dread settled over Hearthglade as more individuals began to exhibit the same unsettling ocular mutation. A miner, Anya, who worked the deep veins of depleted ore, emerged from the tunnels with irises that seemed to contain miniature, swirling vortexes of impossible colors. A medic, old Doctor Jian, usually stoic and unflappable, found his eyes had developed a shimmering, opalescent quality, like the inside of a giant seashell, as if he were constantly viewing the world through a prism.

The physical change was accompanied by subtle behavioral shifts. The affected individuals, who Mara began to privately refer to as the 'Glassborne,' seemed more withdrawn, their attention often drifting as if they were observing something beyond the immediate reality of Hearthglade. They spoke in softer tones, their voices sometimes carrying a strange, resonant echo, as if their vocal cords were being subtly altered by the same phenomenon that affected their sight. Their movements, too, became more fluid, less jerky, a disconcerting grace that seemed out of place in their rugged, survival-focused community.

Mara, driven by a desperate need to understand, began discreetly observing them. She noticed how the Glassborne would often gravitate towards windows or open spaces, their altered eyes seemingly drawn to the shifting, fractured light of the sky. They would stare for long periods, their faces impassive, lost in a world of refracted light that only they could fully perceive. When asked what they were looking at, their answers were vague, often filled with metaphors of light, color, and depth that no one else could truly grasp.

"It's like... looking at the world for the first time," Elias had told her, his voice a low murmur. "Everything is... clearer, but also more... permeable. Like the edges aren't as fixed as they used to be."

"Permeable?" Mara probed, her datapad already recording his words. "What do you mean by permeable?"

"The light," he'd said, his gaze drifting towards the window. "It bends. It flows. It doesn't just bounce off things. It... seeps. Like water through a sieve. And sometimes," his voice dropped to a whisper, "it sings."

It sings. The whispers that had plagued their periphery were now seemingly manifesting within their very beings, resonating through the eyes of the Glassborne. This was no longer just an atmospheric anomaly; it was an infection, a transformation, a terrifying biological adaptation.

The fear in Hearthglade was palpable. The Glassborne were not ostracized, not yet. There was a hesitant compassion, a shared bewilderment. But suspicion was a dark seed, and it was beginning to sprout. People avoided their gaze, unnerved by the unnatural shimmer, the shifting patterns that seemed to hold an alien intelligence. Children cried when they saw them. Adults whispered behind cupped hands. The Glassborne, in turn, seemed to sense the growing unease, retreating further into themselves, their transformed eyes reflecting a world that was increasingly out of reach for the rest of Hearthglade.

Mara found herself torn. Her scientific mind demanded she study this phenomenon, understand its genesis, its implications. But her heart ached for the fear and isolation gripping her community, and for the individuals themselves. They were not monsters, they were victims, or perhaps, pioneers of a new, terrifying evolution.

She sought out Doctor Jian, his opalescent eyes a swirling galaxy of pastel hues. She found him in his small clinic, examining a sample under a microscope, his reflection in the lens a distorted, shimmering image.

"Doctor," she began, her voice tight with concern. "We need to understand what's happening. This... Glassborne phenomenon."

He looked up, and for a moment, Mara felt a strange sense of disorientation, as if his gaze was pulling her in. His eyes held an ancient, serene sorrow. "It is the echo, Mara. The echo of the Veilfall's rending. The old world is receding, and something new is... crystallizing within us."

"Crystallizing? But how? Why?"

"The light," he said, his voice a soft hum that resonated strangely in the small room. "It is no longer just light. It carries... information. It reshapes. It adapts. Our eyes, the most sensitive organs, are the first to succumb. They are becoming conduits, lenses through which this new reality is perceived, and perhaps, projected."

"Projected?" Mara's breath hitched. "You mean... they're not just seeing it? They're... changing things?"

He gave a slow, deliberate nod. "Subtly, at first. The way light refracts, the way objects are perceived. But as the transformation deepens, who knows what will be possible? The whispers you hear, Mara? They are not just external. They are becoming internal. They are the genesis of a new consciousness, a collective mind forming around this altered perception."

The implication was staggering. Humanity, or a segment of it, was not just adapting to a changed environment; it was actively becoming part of it. The fractured sky wasn't just a visual distortion; it was a cosmic virus, a template for a new form of existence, and the Glassborne were its first, living embodiment.

Mara spent hours in her lab, poring over spectrographic data, genetic sequencing reports, anything that could offer a clue. She compared the light signatures from the horizon with the spectral emissions she managed to capture from the Glassborne's eyes. There were undeniable correlations: unique wavelength shifts, anomalies in photon emission patterns, an almost crystalline structure to the light itself. It was as if their eyes were absorbing and processing the very essence of the altered atmosphere.

She theorized that the Veilfall's breach had not only allowed external energies to flood into their world but had also somehow seeded their biology with this new, crystalline light. It was a form of bio-luminescent adaptation, a biological response to an environmental overhaul. Perhaps, in the harsh, dying world of the Veilfall, this was the only way to survive, to evolve. But the cost was the very definition of humanity, of individuality.

The communal distrust festered. Some began to demand that the Glassborne be quarantined, separated from the healthy population. Fear bred irrationality. They were accused of being carriers, of being 'other,' of being the harbingers of the Veilfall's final conquest. Arguments erupted in the mess hall, hushed but venomous. Ben, caught between his loyalty to Mara and the growing panic, found himself mediating increasingly heated debates.

"They're still people, Mara!" he'd argued, his voice strained. "We can't just… lock them away because they look different. Because their eyes shine."

"But what if they *are* different, Ben?" Mara countered, her own voice trembling. "What if this isn't just a change in appearance? What if it's a fundamental shift in what they *are*? What if they're no longer… us?"

The question hung heavy in the air, a bleak testament to the fracturing trust that mirrored the fracturing sky. The emergence of the Glassborne had transformed an abstract, existential threat into a tangible, terrifying reality. The whispers of the Veilfall were no longer distant murmurs; they were echoing in the very eyes of their neighbors, their friends, their family. And Mara knew, with a chilling certainty, that this was only the beginning of their world's descent into a crystalline, fractured future. The horizon, once a distant boundary, had now become a reflection, shimmering and shifting within the eyes of those who were slowly, irrevocably, becoming Glassborne. The survival of Hearthglade, and perhaps of humanity itself, now depended on understanding not just the fractured sky, but the fractured souls it was creating.

The ocular transformation was the most overt, the most immediately terrifying symptom of what the afflicted were beginning to call, with a mixture of dread and awe, the Crystalline Cascade. It began subtly, a faint shimmer in the iris, easily dismissed as fatigue or a trick of the ambient light. But soon, this shimmer deepened, coalesced, and began to swirl. The familiar hues of human eyes – the browns, blues, and greens – were not erased, but rather subsumed, interwoven with spectral threads of impossible colors. Elias's sapphire and amethyst nebulae were merely an early manifestation. Anya's eyes, when examined under Mara's rudimentary, jury-rigged spectroscope, pulsed with a faint internal luminescence that defied conventional physics, emitting light that seemed to fold in on itself. Doctor Jian's opalescent gaze, Mara discovered, was not static; it shifted and flowed like liquid moonlight, his pupils occasionally dilating to an unnatural degree, revealing depths that seemed to absorb the very air around them.

These weren't mere reflections. The light emanated *from within*, a biological bioluminescence born of a fundamental alteration at the cellular level. Mara's limited genetic sequencing data suggested a radical rewrite, a grafting of exotic genetic material onto the human genome. It was as if the Veilfall's shattered radiance had found fertile ground not just in the atmosphere, but within the very building blocks of life, reprogramming cells to refract and emit light in ways nature had never intended. The sclera, too, began to show signs of strain, sometimes developing a faint, glassy translucence, and a network of impossibly fine, crystalline capillaries would become visible, pulsing with a soft, internal glow.

But the change wasn't confined to the visual. The whispers that Mara had initially dismissed as auditory hallucinations or ambient static were now being consciously perceived by the Glassborne, not just as external sounds, but as internal resonances. Elias described it as an "internal choir," a symphony of impossibly complex frequencies that seemed to hum just beneath the surface of his thoughts. "It's not sound as we know it," he'd explained to Mara, his gaze unfocused, lost in the swirling iridescence of his own eyes. "It's more like... the feeling of light. A vibration that bypasses the eardrum and resonates directly with the... the core."

This internal symphony, they reported, was not chaotic. It possessed a structure, a discernible pattern that seemed to guide their thoughts, their perceptions, even their nascent abilities. Doctor Jian, in his serene way, elaborated on this: "The light is not merely being seen, Mara. It is *communicating*. It carries information, not in data streams, but in harmonic frequencies. Our minds, or perhaps new pathways forming within them, are learning to interpret this new language."

The implications for their consciousness were profound and deeply unsettling. The Glassborne began to exhibit an unusual calmness, a detachment from the everyday anxieties and pressures that had become the norm for Hearthglade's survivors. This wasn't the peaceful resignation of acceptance, but something more active, a profound shift in perspective. They seemed less affected by the constant gnawing fear of scarcity, the ever-present threat of environmental collapse. Their focus had shifted inward, or perhaps outward, towards the new reality that their altered senses revealed.

"It's like the noise of the world has faded," Anya explained, her voice a low, resonant hum that seemed to echo the subtle vibrato in her crystalline eyes. "The worries, the regrets, the endless cycle of survival... they're still there, but they're distant. Like watching a play from the back row. The important thing, the *real* thing, is happening on a different stage."

This 'different stage' was where the true horror began to manifest for the unaffected. The Glassborne's altered perception wasn't just a passive reception of new sensory input; it was beginning to influence their interaction with the physical world. Their movements, as Mara had observed, became uncannily fluid, their bodies often moving with an unnerving grace that suggested an awareness of spatial dynamics far beyond normal human comprehension. They navigated cluttered spaces with effortless precision, their steps sure-footed, their bodies anticipating obstacles before they were consciously perceived.

More disturbingly, there were subtle, almost imperceptible alterations in their immediate environment. Objects placed near a Glassborne individual would sometimes shift slightly, as if nudged by an unseen force. Lights would flicker in their presence, not randomly, but in response to their subtle shifts in gaze or their internal resonant frequencies. Mara's datapad, left on a workbench near Elias, briefly displayed scrambled data, its internal chronometer skipping ahead by several seconds before correcting itself, all while Elias was merely sitting nearby, his eyes fixed on the viewport.

"It's the resonance," Doctor Jian explained, his opalescent eyes swirling like distant galaxies. "Our altered state is creating subtle harmonic distortions in the local energy fields. These distortions can influence probability, affect the arrangement of matter on a quantum level. It's rudimentary, a byproduct of our nascent connection to the Veilfall's light. But it is growing."

This was the genesis of a new faction, not born of ideology or social constructs, but of a radical biological divergence. The Glassborne were becoming something else. They were still human, undeniably so in their form and their memories, but their internal landscape was being rewritten by an alien script of light and frequency. They were a living testament to the uncontrollable, terrifying power of adaptation, a beacon of a future that was both awe-inspiring and deeply frightening.

Mara found herself increasingly isolated, her scientific curiosity warring with a primal fear. The community was fracturing. The initial hesitant compassion for the Glassborne was curdling into suspicion, then outright fear. Whispers of them being 'changed,' of being 'contaminated,' spread like a contagion. People began to avoid them, not just their gaze, but their very presence. A palpable aura of unease settled over any area where a Glassborne individual was present.

Children were openly terrified, pointing and crying, their innocent fear a mirror of the adults' unspoken dread.

The Glassborne, in turn, seemed to sense this growing ostracism. Their withdrawal deepened, their altered eyes often reflecting a detached observation of the fear they inspired. They didn't retaliate, didn't exhibit aggression. Instead, they seemed to retreat further into their new reality, their internal symphony growing stronger, their connection to the fractured sky deepening. They would gather in small groups, their heads tilted, as if listening to something no one else could hear, their crystalline eyes reflecting a shared vision that excluded the rest of Hearthglade.

Mara tried to bridge the divide, to foster understanding. She organized a communal meeting, intending to present her findings, to explain the biological basis of the mutation. But the meeting dissolved into chaos. Accusations flew. Ben, his face etched with frustration, tried to defend the Glassborne, to appeal to reason, but his words were drowned out by the rising tide of panic.

"They're not sick, they're... evolving!" Ben shouted over the din. "We don't understand it, but that doesn't make them a threat!"

"Evolving into *what*, Ben?" came a sharp retort from the back of the hall. "Into something that doesn't need us? Into something that can break reality with a look?"

The fear was not entirely unfounded. The subtle environmental influences, while minor, were becoming more pronounced. A section of the hydroponic garden near where Anya spent much of her time began to exhibit unusually vibrant growth, the plants displaying colors that were slightly off, more saturated than natural. A repair drone, left unattended near Elias, spontaneously powered up and began to perform a complex diagnostic sequence without any external command. These were small anomalies, easily dismissed individually, but collectively, they painted a chilling picture of a world subtly reshaped by the presence of the Glassborne.

Mara's own daughter, Lily, who had once expressed a child's innocent fascination with Elias's eyes, now clung to her mother, her small face pale with fear whenever a Glassborne individual passed by. "They look like broken glass, Mommy," she'd whispered, her voice trembling. "And the sky is watching us through them."

This was the fundamental horror: the uncanny valley of shared humanity and alien transformation. The Glassborne were not an invading force; they were one of them, irrevocably changed by the very forces that threatened Hearthglade. They were both the disease and the symptom, the harbinger of a new world and the first true inhabitants of it. Their existence challenged the very definition of what it meant to be human, to be sentient, to be *real*.

Mara continued her research, driven by a desperate need to find a way to understand, if not reverse, the Crystalline Cascade. She worked in isolation, the hum of her equipment a stark contrast to the silent, resonant communication happening between the Glassborne. She studied their altered optical tissues under high magnification, searching for the key, the specific mechanism that allowed them to interface with the Veilfall's strange energies. She hypothesized that the crystalline structures forming within their ocular cells acted as biological lenses, capable of focusing and manipulating these energies in ways that were previously unimagined.

She also began to study the psychological impact. The detachment, the serenity, was it a chosen state, or an involuntary consequence of the transformation? Were they truly at peace, or simply disconnected from the emotional spectrum that made humans, well, human? Doctor Jian offered a clue: "The resonance, Mara, it soothes. It provides a coherence that our chaotic minds often lack. But perhaps, in gaining that coherence, we lose something else. The sharp edges of joy and sorrow, the urgency of desire. We become... more crystalline, less fluid in our emotional responses."

The implication was chilling. The Glassborne were not just seeing a new reality; they were *becoming* it, their very beings aligning with the harmonic frequencies of the fractured Veilfall. They were, in essence, being assimilated into a larger, alien consciousness that was manifesting through the light itself. This was not a simple mutation; it was a fundamental redefinition of life, a terrifyingly beautiful, and utterly alien, emergence. Hearthglade was no longer just a haven against a dying world; it was a crucible, where the old definition of humanity was being shattered, refracted, and potentially reborn in the image of the fractured sky. The Glassborne were the first shards of that new reality, and Mara knew, with a chilling certainty, that their emergence was only the beginning of a profound and irreversible metamorphosis.

Rumors, like the dust motes stirred by a sandstorm, began to drift in from the south. At first, they were disjointed whispers, fragments of half-heard conversations caught by wary travelers, merchants daring the treacherous routes, or the occasional scout returning from distant patrols. These weren't the panicked cries of immediate danger, but rather the unsettling murmurings of a creeping anomaly, a subtle discordance in the fabric of survival that Hearthglade had painstakingly woven. The initial reports were dismissed by many as fatigue-induced hallucinations, the product of minds strained by perpetual vigilance and the oppressive weight of a shattered world. Yet, the consistency, the recurring themes, began to gnaw at the edges of disbelief, even for the most pragmatic souls within the settlement.

The most persistent threads in these emergent narratives spoke of individuals seen at a distance, their forms indistinct against the ochre haze of the southern plains. They moved with an unsettling grace, too fluid, too deliberate for the stumbling gait of the weary or the desperate scramble of the hunted. And then there were the eyes. Even from afar, the reports insisted, there was something about the way they caught the sparse light of the twin suns, a strange, internal luminescence, a chromatic aberration that no natural phenomenon could replicate. It was as if a fractured piece of the Veilfall itself had found purchase in human ocular tissues, scattering light in impossible ways.

One such report came from Kaelen, a seasoned caravan master who, for years, had navigated the fragile supply lines between Hearthglade and the scattered, fortified outposts to the south. He was known for his stoic demeanor, his aversion to hyperbole. His return to Hearthglade had been unusually quiet, his usual boisterous recounting of trade deals and close calls replaced by a brooding silence. When pressed by Mara, who was assiduously collecting every scrap of information, he finally spoke, his voice a low rasp, as if the words themselves were being scraped from his throat.

"Saw them near the old Salt Flats," he'd begun, his gaze distant, fixed on a point beyond the reinforced walls of the settlement. "A group of them, maybe half a dozen. Traveling south, away from the Wastes. They weren't refugees. No packs, no supplies. They just... walked. Under the midday sun, mind you, and their eyes... I've seen frostbite glare, seen desperation burn, but this was different. Like looking into shards of colored glass. Bright, cold, and wrong. One of them, a woman, I think, she turned her head, and her eyes... they seemed to drink the light from the sky. The air around her... it felt thick, like trying to breathe underwater."

Kaelen's description, while lacking the scientific precision Mara sought, carried the weight of his unease. He spoke of a subtle warping in his perception as he observed them, a fleeting disorientation that made the familiar landscape seem alien. The very air around them, he claimed, felt charged, humming with an unseen energy that made the fine hairs on his arms stand on end. He hadn't approached them, nor they him, but the encounter had left an indelible mark. He spoke of feeling an almost physical repulsion, a primal urge to flee, not from fear of violence, but from the sheer *otherness* of their presence.

Another account, even more fragmented, arrived via a lone courier from the mining outpost of Oakhaven, nestled in the foothills of the Spineback Mountains to the south-east. The courier, a young man named Finn, barely older than Mara's own daughter, was visibly shaken, his story delivered in gasps and fragmented sentences. He spoke of miners disappearing. Not in accidents, not in skirmishes with mutated fauna, but simply... gone. And in the days leading up to their vanishings, Finn reported, they had begun to exhibit the strange ocular symptoms. He described his foreman, a gruff man named Silas, whose usually dull, brown eyes had begun to shimmer with a spectrum of blues and greens, then purples and golds, like a trapped aurora. Silas had become withdrawn, his work erratic, his gaze often fixed on the cavern walls as if reading invisible inscriptions. Then, one shift, he simply wasn't there. His tools were laid out neatly, his helmet still on its hook, but Silas himself had vanished without a trace.

The implications of these scattered reports began to coalesce, forming a disturbing pattern. The Glassborne, as Mara had begun to categorize them internally, were not an isolated phenomenon confined to

Hearthglade. The Veilfall's influence, or whatever alien force was at play, was not a localized event. It was spreading, manifesting in disparate communities, subtly or overtly rewriting the inhabitants of these southern settlements. This was no longer just a scientific curiosity for Mara; it was a burgeoning crisis that threatened to encompass a far wider geographical area than she had initially conceived.

The question Mara grappled with was the nature of this spread. Was it a contiguous wave, an ever-expanding zone of transformation originating from a singular, unknown source? Or was it a series of independent manifestations, triggered by localized concentrations of Veilfall radiation, or perhaps by some unknown environmental catalyst unique to those southern regions? Kaelen's report of individuals traveling south, away from the rumored irradiated zones of the Shattered Lands, suggested an active movement of these transformed individuals, perhaps even an intentional migration. Were they seeking other pockets of similar energy, or were they fleeing something even worse?

The whispers from the south painted a picture of a subtle, insidious infiltration. It wasn't an army marching, but a gradual shift, a quiet subversion of the existing order. In Oakhaven, Finn reported that the remaining miners, those who hadn't succumbed to the 'Shimmer' as they morbidly called it, were becoming increasingly fearful of their colleagues. The camaraderie that had once defined their tight-knit community was fracturing. Suspicion replaced trust. Glances lingered too long on eyes that flickered with unnatural light, and hushed conversations ceased abruptly whenever someone with the tell-tale luminescence entered earshot. The very foundations of their social structure were being eroded by the creeping strangeness.

Further south still, near the desiccated remnants of the old coastal city of Port Serenity, a nomadic trader named Elara spoke of encountering a "herd" of strangely serene individuals. They were not a part of any known tribe, nor did they display the typical wariness of outsiders. They moved through the salt-crusted ruins with an almost dreamlike purpose, their luminous eyes scanning the horizon. Elara, a woman whose survival depended on her keen observation of human behavior, noted their complete lack of interaction amongst themselves. They walked in proximity, yet seemed utterly isolated within their own altered perceptions. They also seemed to possess a strange immunity to the toxic dust storms that perpetually choked the region, their crystalline eyes unaffected by the abrasive particles that would blind any normal observer. Elara had wisely kept her distance, her own eyes shielded by thick goggles, her heart pounding a frantic rhythm against her ribs. The sight of them, she later recounted, felt like witnessing specters of a future humanity, beautiful and terrifying in their detachment.

These reports, when painstakingly pieced together, began to suggest a terrifying geographical expansion. Hearthglade, insulated as it was by its reinforced defenses and its relatively stable environment, was not the epicenter, but perhaps an outpost on the periphery of a much larger, unfolding phenomenon. The southern regions, characterized by their harsher environments, their proximity to the lingering radiation scars of the Veilfall's initial impact, and their scattered, independent communities, seemed to be fertile ground for this transformation. The 'Glassborne Emergence' was not a localized outbreak; it was a nascent, geographically expanding threat.

Mara found herself sketching increasingly detailed maps, marking each report, each fragment of testimony, with a small, colored pin. The distribution was far from uniform, but the clusters were undeniable, concentrated in areas that had experienced direct Veilfall exposure or were in proximity to known geological anomalies that might have acted as conduits for exotic energies. The Salt Flats, the foothills of the Spineback Mountains, the ruins of Port Serenity – these were all locations that had a history, however faint, of unusual energy readings or unexplained phenomena even before the Veilfall.

The implications were staggering. If this transformation was indeed spreading, if the Veilfall's influence was not merely atmospheric but deeply biological and geographically pervasive, then Hearthglade's carefully constructed sanctuary might be far more vulnerable than anyone imagined. The threat was no longer confined to the internal dynamics of their settlement, to the fear of those among them who were changing. It was an external, encroaching force, a silent tide of alteration washing over the remnants of civilization.

She found herself re-examining her limited genetic data, searching for any clue that might explain the propagation. Was there a vector? A mechanism by which the transformation was passed from one individual to another, or from the environment to the individual? The initial hypothesis of direct genetic grafting from Veilfall fragments seemed insufficient to explain a widespread geographical spread. Could it be something subtler? A form of atmospheric contamination, an airborne pathogen carrying exotic genetic material? Or was it something akin to a memetic contagion, a psychic resonance that, once established, could infect susceptible minds and bodies?

Doctor Jian, his opalescent gaze often turned towards the south, offered a philosophical perspective. "The Veilfall," he'd said, his voice a gentle current in Mara's lab, "is a resonance. A frequency. When the Veil shattered, it didn't just scatter light and energy; it broadcast a new harmonic. Those whose biology is attuned, or perhaps recalibrated by exposure, begin to vibrate in sympathy. This vibration isn't confined to the individual. It can ripple. It can find other receptive forms."

His words, while not providing concrete scientific data, hinted at a deeper, more abstract form of propagation. If it was a harmonic resonance, then perhaps concentrated areas of specific geological formations, or unusual atmospheric conditions in the south, could act as amplifiers, creating localized zones where the transformation was more likely to occur or spread. The salt flats, with their peculiar mineral composition, or the ancient volcanic structures near the Spineback Mountains, could potentially interact with the Veilfall's energy in ways that were conducive to this biological rewrite.

The fear within Hearthglade, already palpable, began to shift. It was no longer solely directed inward, at the unsettling changes in their neighbors and friends. A new, more expansive dread began to take root, a fear of the unknown vastness beyond their walls, of the creeping transformation that was not contained, but actively expanding. The whispers from the south were no longer just rumors; they were dispatches from the front lines of an invisible war for the very definition of humanity. The south, once a source of vital resources and trade, was rapidly becoming a zone of profound and terrifying mystery, a harbinger of a future that was being written not in ink, but in fractured light. Mara knew, with a certainty that chilled her to the bone, that Hearthglade could not remain insulated forever. The rumors from the south were a stark, irrefutable summons. The Glassborne Emergence was not an isolated incident; it was a signal, a clear indication that the world was irrevocably changing, and the next phase of that change was unfolding far beyond their limited horizon. The journey south, once a matter of commerce and survival, was becoming an urgent necessity, a quest to understand the encroaching tide before it consumed them all.

The unsettling reports from the south had been a persistent gnawing at the edges of Mara's scientific mind. They were data points, fragmented and often embellished by fear, but undeniably present. Yet, it was one particular encounter, witnessed firsthand and etched into her memory with the clarity of a lightning strike, that truly solidified the chilling reality. She had accompanied a small, heavily armed scouting party, dispatched not to engage, but to observe from a safe distance the strange phenomena Kaelen had described near the Salt Flats. The dust, perpetually thick, had thinned for a brief, surreal interval, revealing a tableau that defied every rational explanation she had ever clung to.

There they were, a half-dozen figures, moving with that unnerving, liquid grace. They weren't the ragged survivors of the Wastes, nor the weary, lumbering gait of those who had simply endured. Their movements were economical, precise, like dancers performing a ritual known only to them. And their eyes. Even through the specialized filtration lenses of her observation goggles, the light within them was unmistakable. It wasn't the reflection of the twin suns, nor the glint of sweat or tears. It was an internal luminescence, a kaleidoscope of shifting hues – emeralds bleeding into sapphires, amethysts flaring into molten gold. It was as if the very essence of the shattered sky, the volatile, prismatic chaos of the Veilfall, had been distilled and poured into their pupils.

One of them, a woman whose silhouette was stark against the bleached horizon, paused and turned. It was a subtle gesture, almost imperceptible, yet the way her head moved, the deliberate arc of her neck, spoke of a profound disconnect from the environmental cues that governed ordinary movement. Her eyes met Mara's, or at least, Mara felt they met hers. There was no acknowledgment, no flicker of recognition or alarm. Instead, there was an unnerving stillness, a vast, unreadable depth that seemed to absorb the ambient light, to pull it into an inner void. The air around her, Kaelen had said, felt thick. Mara felt it too, a subtle pressure, a humming vibration that seemed to resonate not in her ears, but deep within her bones. It was a feeling of alienness, so profound it bordered on the cosmic.

This wasn't a disease. It wasn't a mutation in the traditional sense, a clumsy adaptation to a harsh environment. This was a transformation, a fundamental rewriting of being, directly linked to the Veilfall. The sky, the celestial cataclysm that had reshaped their world, was no longer just a source of ambient radiation and altered weather patterns. It was an active agent of biological change, a force that could fundamentally alter life itself. The implications crashed down upon Mara with the force of a physical blow.

For so long, her approach had been one of cautious, meticulous observation. She had been gathering data, hypothesizing, building models of the Veilfall's effects, focusing on its measurable impacts: radiation levels, atmospheric shifts, geological anomalies. She had operated under the assumption that understanding the *how* of the Veilfall was the key to enduring it. But witnessing the 'Glassborne,' as she had begun to privately call them, shattered that paradigm. The *how* was no longer the most critical question. The *what* was. What was this fundamental change? What did it signify? And, most importantly, was it a path, however terrifying, to a new form of existence, or a harbinger of extinction?

Her resolve, already hardened by years of struggle and loss, solidified into an unyielding core of determination. Passive observation was no longer an option. Hearthglade, their carefully constructed sanctuary, could not afford to remain a spectator in this unfolding drama. They needed to understand not just the effects, but the cause, the underlying mechanism driving this profound metamorphosis. And if this metamorphosis was directly tied to the Veilfall, then their investigation had to turn skyward, to the fractured heavens that had birthed this new reality.

The raw data was insufficient. The fragmented reports, the whispered rumors – they were threads, but Mara needed to weave them into a coherent tapestry. She needed to understand the geographical distribution, the environmental triggers, the biological pathways, however alien they might be. The clusters she had already identified on her maps – the Salt Flats, the Spineback foothills, the ruins of Port Serenity – were not random. They represented areas where the Veilfall's influence seemed to manifest with greater potency, where the transformation into the Glassborne was either more frequent or more pronounced.

"It's a resonance, Jian," she had stated, the words tumbling out in a torrent of nascent theory, as she had paced her small, cluttered laboratory. Doctor Jian, his own gaze often distant, as if contemplating cosmic harmonies, had nodded slowly. "Not just energy, but a frequency. The Veilfall didn't just break; it broadcasted something new. And some people, some life forms, are tuning into it."

Jian's philosophical insights, while lacking the concrete metrics Mara usually craved, resonated with a deeper truth she was beginning to grasp. If it was a resonance, then it could be amplified. It could be influenced by specific environmental conditions. The high mineral content of the Salt Flats, the geothermal activity hinted at in the Spineback Mountains, the unusual atmospheric pressures that lingered around the desiccated coast – these weren't just geographical features; they were potential conduits, catalysts for this new harmonic. They were places where the Veilfall's broadcast was being amplified, where the signal was strong enough to rewrite biological code.

The urgency of her mission began to eclipse all other concerns. The internal stability of Hearthglade, the daily grind of resource management, the security patrols – these were vital, but they were merely holding actions. The true battle, the battle for survival in this new epoch, would be fought in understanding and potentially mastering the forces that were reshaping their world. This meant venturing out, pushing beyond the safe confines of their walls, not with weapons drawn, but with the most potent weapons humanity possessed: curiosity, intellect, and an unyielding will to comprehend.

She began to formulate a plan, a multi-pronged approach that would require resources and a degree of risk that would undoubtedly alarm the Council. First, a more systematic survey of the identified high-resonance zones. This would involve dispatching small, specialized teams equipped with enhanced environmental sensors, capable of detecting subtle energy fluctuations and atmospheric anomalies. These teams would not engage the Glassborne, but would gather precise data on the conditions under which they appeared, and the environmental factors present in their vicinity.

Second, she needed to establish a more direct, albeit still cautious, protocol for observing the Glassborne themselves. This meant developing better long-range observation technology, perhaps even specialized drones, capable of approaching these transformed individuals without provoking a response, allowing for closer examination of their behavior and physiology. The goal was not to capture, but to document. To record their interactions, or lack thereof, their responses to environmental stimuli, and the subtle nuances of their luminescence.

Third, and perhaps most crucial, was the need to understand the propagation. Was it solely environmental? Or was there a vector of transmission between individuals? The whispers of Silas, the foreman at Oakhaven, becoming increasingly withdrawn before his disappearance, suggested a psychological component. Had the 'Shimmer,' as the miners called it, begun subtly within him, altering his perception, isolating him, before the physical transformation was complete? This hinted at a potential for a more insidious spread, one that could infect the very minds of Hearthglade's inhabitants before any outward signs became apparent.

Mara knew this was a path fraught with peril. The southern regions were not merely unexplored; they were actively hostile environments, populated by mutated creatures, unpredictable weather, and now, these enigmatic, transformed beings. But the alternative was stagnation, a slow surrender to the encroaching unknown. Hearthglade's survival depended on its ability to adapt, and adaptation required knowledge. Knowledge, in turn, demanded investigation.

She began to pore over her existing research, her genetic sequencers humming softly in the background, a counterpoint to the rhythmic beat of her own determined heart. She revisited the initial Veilfall impact data, searching for any overlooked correlations, any subtle atmospheric conditions that might have preceded the emergence of the Glassborne in specific regions. She cross-referenced geological surveys with recorded energy readings, looking for any overlap between areas of unusual magnetic flux and the locations where luminous eyes had been reported.

The sheer scale of the task was daunting. The Veilfall had been a cataclysm of unimaginable proportions, its tendrils reaching into every aspect of their shattered world. To dissect its influence, to understand the precise biological alchemy that transformed a human being into something... else, felt like trying to capture starlight in a sieve. Yet, the image of those luminous eyes, that profound, unsettling stillness, spurred her onward. It was a mystery that demanded to be solved, not for the sake of scientific curiosity alone, but for the survival of her people.

Her resolve was no longer just a personal conviction; it was a mandate. She had seen the future, or at least a terrifying glimpse of one possible future, and it was luminous, alien, and utterly indifferent to the struggles of old humanity. The Glassborne were not monsters in the conventional sense, not creatures of malice and destruction. They were something far more profound: a new form of life, born from the ashes of the old world, shaped by the very forces that had seemed to destroy everything. And to survive, Hearthglade needed to understand this new birth. They needed to look beyond the immediate horizon, beyond the safety of their walls, and towards the fractured sky that held the answers, however dangerous they might be. The time for passive observation was over. The time for action, for bold, potentially world-altering investigation, had arrived.

CHAPTER THREE
THE ECHO'S FURY

The hum of the atmospheric stabilizers, once a constant, comforting thrum in the background of Hearthglade life, had taken on a new, discordant edge. It wasn't a malfunction, Mara knew; Jian had run diagnostics a dozen times, his brow furrowed in a way that spoke of intellectual frustration rather than mechanical worry. Instead, it was a subtle shift in pitch, a barely perceptible tremor that vibrated not through the ferro-concrete floors, but through the very marrow of one's bones. It was the sound of the world holding its breath, and the attendant anxiety that tightened its grip with each passing cycle. The sky-static, that ever-present veil of interference that had become as familiar as the twin suns, was no longer a mere nuisance. It was a physical presence, a prickling sensation on exposed skin, a constant, low-grade buzzing behind the eyes that made concentration a labor and sleep a distant memory.

Mara found herself staring out of her laboratory's reinforced viewport more often than not, her scientific gaze attempting to parse the increasingly chaotic celestial ballet. The prismatic hues of the Veilfall, once a spectacle of otherworldly beauty, now seemed to writhe with an agitated energy. Streaks of emerald and sapphire, which had previously bled into each other with a languid grace, now clashed and fractured, spitting out shards of crimson and amethyst like sparks from a celestial forge. The familiar patterns of atmospheric interference, which she had painstakingly mapped and cataloged, were dissolving into a churning, unpredictable maelstrom. It was as if the sky itself was experiencing a violent fever, its vital signs spiking erratically.

Her instruments confirmed what her instincts screamed. The ambient energy readings, which had plateaued for the last few cycles, were climbing again, but this time with a far more aggressive gradient. The specific frequencies associated with the 'Echo' – the peculiar energy signature that had accompanied the first, devastating storm – were not just reappearing; they were amplifying, reaching amplitudes that made her sensitive equipment flicker and overload. She had meticulously archived the data from the initial event, cross-referencing every anomaly, every deviation from the norm. This new surge was different. It was a logarithmic leap, not an incremental increase. The first storm had been a warning shot, a brutal but localized demonstration of power. This felt like the prelude to a full-scale assault.

Outside Hearthglade's protective dome, the signs were even more stark. The weather patterns, always a capricious element in this fractured world, had devolved into pure anarchy. Days that began with a deceptively serene sky could descend into hour-long tempests of corrosive rain, followed by sudden, bone-chilling frosts that clung to the vegetation like a shroud. The Dust Devils, those ubiquitous whirlwinds of the Wastes, were no longer mere inconveniences; they were growing in size and ferocity, their swirling columns reaching heights that dwarfed the scout towers. Some of them seemed to carry an unnatural luminescence, a faint, internal glow that mirrored the unsettling light she had witnessed in the eyes of the Glassborne. The whispers from the outlying settlements and scouting parties, once dismissed as exaggerated tales of hardship, now carried a chilling weight of prophecy. Reports of localized gravitational anomalies, of sudden, inexplicable temperature inverspikes, and of equipment malfunction due to overwhelming energy fields were becoming alarmingly frequent.

The pervasive sense of dread was palpable, seeping into the very fabric of Hearthglade's communal life. It was a subtle shift at first, a sharpening of anxieties, a shortening of tempers. But it had grown, festering in the quiet hours, manifesting in shared, uneasy glances and hushed conversations. The children, usually so boisterous and resilient, were becoming withdrawn, their games replaced by anxious questions about the sky and the strange lights that flickered in its depths. Even the hardened security patrols, men and women who had faced down mutated beasts and raiders with stoic resolve, were exhibiting signs of unease. They spoke of an unnerving silence from the Wastes, an absence of the usual nocturnal calls and rustlings, as if the very wildlife had gone into hiding, sensing an impending doom.

Mara's closest confidantes, Jian and Kaelen, shared her growing apprehension. Jian, the stoic xenobotanist, reported that his hydroponic gardens were exhibiting unusual stress responses, his carefully cultivated crops wilting and exhibiting strange mutations not related to any known pathogen. He spoke of a 'wrongness' in the nutrient solutions, a subtle energetic disruption that defied his instruments. Kaelen, ever the pragmatist and the voice of Hearthglade's defense, was increasing patrols and reinforcing the perimeter defenses, his usual calm demeanor replaced by a grim determination. He had even begun re-tasking some of the mining crews to reinforce critical structural points within the dome, a move that spoke volumes about the severity of his concerns.

"It's the resonance, Mara," Jian had said, his voice softer than usual, as they stood on the observation deck, gazing at the roiling sky. "I can feel it in the plants, in the very soil. It's not just energy; it's a frequency that's... abrasive. It's like a discordant note that's starting to unravel the symphony of our ecosystem." His scientific detachment, usually a source of comfort, was tinged with a genuine fear that mirrored her own. He no longer spoke of observation and analysis; he spoke of a struggle for fundamental equilibrium.

Kaelen, his eyes scanning the horizon with a practiced intensity, added, "The tremors are increasing, Mara. Not just the earth-shivers we've grown accustomed to. These are deeper, more resonant. They feel... intentional. And the sky-static isn't just interfering with our comms anymore. It's starting to cause physiological effects. Nausea, disorientation. A few of the sentries had nosebleeds this shift." He gripped the railing, his knuckles white. "Whatever happened last time, it was a mere ripple. This feels like the tide coming in, and it's bringing something monstrous with it."

Mara traced the latest energy fluctuation charts on her datapad. The patterns were unmistakable, and deeply disturbing. The first Echo Storm had been characterized by a broad-spectrum energy surge, a violent discharge that had destabilized the atmosphere and caused widespread devastation. This new pattern, however, was far more focused, far more precise. The dominant frequencies were higher, sharper, and pulsed with an almost rhythmic intensity. It was as if the Veilfall, having learned from its previous outburst, was now targeting specific energetic vulnerabilities, weaving a more intricate and potentially more destructive pattern into the fabric of their reality. She had begun to theorize that the Veilfall wasn't a singular event, but a continuous, albeit fluctuating, process. The initial cataclysm had been the violent release of pent-up energy, but the ongoing atmospheric phenomena were the residual, and now escalating, manifestations of that initial break. This second storm, she feared, was not a recurrence, but an evolution.

Her mind raced through the implications. If the Veilfall was broadcasting a new, more potent signal, what was its purpose? Was it a natural dissipation of energy, or was it something more deliberate? The Glassborne, with their uncanny grace and luminous eyes, were the most compelling evidence that this 'broadcast' was actively influencing biological systems. Were they the precursors to a larger transformation? A biological evolution driven by cosmic forces? The thought was both terrifying and strangely exhilarating, a testament to humanity's enduring drive to find meaning and pattern even in the face of existential threat.

But the immediate concern was survival. The data pointed towards an imminent, powerful event. The sky was a canvas of discord, the air thick with an unseen tension. Hearthglade, for all its technological marvels and resilient spirit, was still a fragile sanctuary against the raw, untamed power of the Veilfall. She recalled the accounts of the first storm: the sky tearing open, the ground convulsing, the sheer, overwhelming force that had reshaped the landscape and decimated populations. This time, the signs suggested an even greater intensity. The sky-static was a physical manifestation of the impending energetic onslaught, a prelude to a more profound disruption of the very air they breathed.

Mara initiated a high-priority alert throughout Hearthglade. "All personnel, report to your designated stations. This is not a drill. We are entering a Level Four atmospheric anomaly alert. Secure all external access points. Activate emergency power reserves. All non-essential personnel are to proceed to designated safe zones immediately."

Her voice, amplified through the internal comms system, was calm and measured, a stark contrast to the storm brewing both outside and within her own heart. She knew that words, no matter how precise, could not fully convey the scale of the threat. The visceral understanding of danger would come from the sky itself.

She turned back to the viewport, her gaze fixed on the swirling maelstrom above. The prismatic colours were now coalescing, not into a beautiful spectacle, but into a churning vortex of raw power. The emeralds and sapphires were no longer bleeding; they were colliding, igniting in brief, blinding flashes of pure energy. The air itself seemed to vibrate, and the low hum of the stabilizers was now a high-pitched whine, a sound of systems pushed to their absolute limit. A profound sense of isolation washed over her. They were the last bastion of what they understood as humanity, a small island of order in an ocean of escalating chaos. And the storm was coming. It was no longer a possibility; it was a certainty. The Echo's Fury was about to be unleashed, and its second act promised to be far more devastating than the first. The subtle shifts, the heightened anxieties, the increasingly erratic weather patterns – they were all threads weaving a tapestry of impending doom. Hearthglade was not merely preparing for a storm; it was bracing itself for a metamorphosis, a violent upheaval that would test the very limits of their resilience and their understanding of the world. The sky was the overture, and the music was a symphony of destruction.

The initial tremors of the second Echo Storm were not like the first. The ground beneath Hearthglade didn't just shake; it *writhed*. It was as if the planet itself had become a living, convulsing entity, its tectonic plates groaning under an unimaginable strain. Mara, strapped into her command chair in the central observation hub, felt her teeth rattle, not from the vibration of the ferro-concrete, but from a deep, internal resonance that seemed to echo the planet's agony. Alarms blared, a cacophony of urgent staccato warnings that momentarily drowned out the rising shriek of the wind outside. Red emergency lights pulsed, casting long, distorted shadows that danced with the flickering displays.

"Status report!" Mara's voice was tight, strained, amplified by the comms system.

"Structural integrity holding at eighty-seven percent, Mara!" Kaelen's voice, usually a bedrock of calm, was edged with a raw intensity. "But we're seeing localized failures in the outer shielding. The energy flux is beyond anything our models predicted. It's... it's like the Veilfall is trying to chew through us."

Jian, monitoring the xenobotanical data feeds from his lab, his face a mask of grim concentration, chimed in. "The atmospheric composition is fluctuating wildly. Oxygen levels are dropping, then spiking. CO2 is doing the same. It's not just a storm; it's an active reordering of our entire biosphere." He paused, a tremor running through his voice. "And the sonic frequencies... Mara, they're within the infrasound range, but amplified to a terrifying degree. It's not just deafening; it's... invasive. I'm seeing stress fractures appearing in the hydroponic tanks from the sheer pressure waves."

On the main viewport, the sky was no longer merely a spectacle of chaotic color. It was a roiling, liquid inferno. The emeralds and sapphires had been consumed by an angry, pulsating crimson that bled into an unsettling, sickly yellow. Lightning, not the jagged bolts of a terrestrial storm, but massive, arcing tendrils of pure, raw energy, ripped through the atmosphere, striking the ground miles away with concussive blasts that shook Hearthglade to its core. The sky-static, which had been a mere prickle on the skin, was now a palpable force, a suffocating blanket that pressed down on them, distorting vision and inducing a profound sense of vertigo.

"The temporal distortions are intensifying," Jian reported, his voice barely audible above the rising din. "I'm seeing... echoes. Brief, looping replays of the last few minutes. The chronometers are jumping erratically. Our sensors are experiencing temporal displacement. We're not just in a storm; we're in a temporal anomaly."

Mara felt a wave of nausea wash over her, the disorientation a stark confirmation of Jian's words. She saw, for a fleeting instant, a phantom image of Kaelen standing beside her, his face etched with a terror she hadn't seen before. Then, he was back by his console, his expression grim but resolute. The storm wasn't just assaulting their physical reality; it was unraveling the very fabric of time.

"Report on the sonic assault," Mara commanded, gripping the edges of her console, her knuckles white. She needed to focus, to anchor herself in the present, however unstable it was.

"The infrasound is causing widespread panic and physiological distress," Kaelen stated, his voice a strained monotone. "Reports are coming in of disorientation, acute anxiety, and in some cases, temporary paralysis. Our audio dampeners are struggling to cope. They're designed for atmospheric noise, not... this. This is a directed sonic weapon."

Suddenly, the main viewport flickered. The raging inferno of the sky dissolved, replaced for a heart-stopping moment by a serene, impossibly blue sky, dotted with fluffy white clouds. The twin suns shone brightly, their light warm and inviting. A collective gasp went through the control room. For a single, breathtaking instant, Hearthglade was bathed in the light of a lost world, a world of peace and tranquility. Then, with a violent, jarring lurch, the serene vista tore apart, ripped asunder by the crimson inferno that had been lurking beneath. The illusion shattered, replaced by a chilling reminder of the reality they were facing.

"What was that?" someone whispered, their voice trembling.

"A spatial distortion, perhaps a residual effect from the temporal loops," Jian theorized, his voice a shaky breath. "The Veilfall is not just a weather phenomenon, Mara. It's... it's actively manipulating reality. It's bending space, time, and energy to its will."

The ground beneath them lurched again, more violently this time. A section of the ceiling cracked, showering debris onto the consoles. Mara felt a sharp pain in her arm as a piece of shrapnel grazed her. The alarms intensified, their shrill cries now a constant, unnerving drone.

"We're losing containment in Sector Gamma!" Kaelen shouted, his face grim. "The sonic pressure is overwhelming the outer blast doors. They're buckling inwards."

Mara's mind raced. The first storm had been a destructive force of nature, a brutal display of raw power. This... this was something else. This was intelligent. It was precise. It was actively seeking to dismantle them, to unravel their world not just with brute force, but with insidious assaults on their senses, their perceptions, their very sense of reality.

"Jian, can you isolate the dominant frequencies of the sonic assault? We need to find a counter-frequency, something to disrupt it." Mara's scientific mind, honed by years of research and crisis management, pushed back against the rising panic. She had to find a solution, a way to fight back against this impossible enemy.

"I'm trying, Mara, but the spectrum is so broad, and it's constantly shifting. It's like trying to catch smoke with a sieve. And the temporal fluctuations... they're messing with my algorithms. I can't get a stable reading." Jian's voice was strained with exertion and desperation. He was working at the absolute limit of his capabilities, and likely beyond.

Suddenly, a new phenomenon began to manifest. The air around the consoles began to shimmer, as if viewed through intense heat. Objects on the desks began to vibrate, not from the seismic activity, but from an internal resonance that seemed to be affecting their very molecular structure. Mara watched, horrified, as a spare datapad on her console began to warp, its edges blurring and its form becoming indistinct, before it simply dissolved into a cloud of shimmering dust.

"Matter destabilization!" Jian cried out, his voice a choked gasp. "The ambient energy is so high, it's exceeding the cohesive bonds of solid matter. It's... it's unmaking things."

Kaelen was wrestling with his controls, his face a mask of pure, unadulterated effort. "We're detecting localized gravity fluctuations. Objects are being pulled in random directions. The structural integrity is compromised in new ways every second. It's not just shaking; it's tearing itself apart."

Mara looked at the viewport, at the maelstrom of crimson and yellow that now seemed to be pressing in on the dome itself. The Veilfall wasn't just above them; it was *around* them, an all-encompassing embrace of chaotic energy. The sense of isolation was no longer a fear; it was a stark, terrifying reality. They were a small pocket of order, an anomaly in a universe that was actively trying to revert to chaos.

"We need to reinforce the core," Mara said, her voice steady despite the chaos swirling around her. "Jian, can you reroute auxiliary power to the primary shielding systems? Kaelen, focus on maintaining structural integrity around the core. We can't let the heart of Hearthglade fall."

The storm raged, a symphony of destruction. The temporal loops became more frequent, more jarring. Images of past events flickered through the hub – moments of joy, of sorrow, of defiance – all twisted and distorted by the storm's influence. The spatial distortions intensified, making movement difficult, disorienting. The sonic assaults left them reeling, their bodies aching, their minds frayed. And now, the very matter of their world seemed to be unraveling.

Mara felt a chilling certainty settle over her. The first Echo Storm had been a harbinger, a brutal introduction to a force they didn't understand. This second assault was an escalation, a testament to the Veilfall's growing power and its increasing ability to manipulate the fundamental laws of reality. They were no longer just surviving a storm; they were in a battle for existence itself, a battle against forces that defied comprehension, against an enemy that could rewrite the rules of the universe at will. The echo of the first fury had indeed returned, amplified and more terrifying than anyone could have imagined, and Hearthglade was caught in its devastating crescendo. The question was no longer

if they would survive, but *what* would be left of them, and their world, when the storm finally abated. The sheer scale of the destruction, the pervasive disorientation, the terrifying unraveling of reality itself – it was a testament to an enemy far more potent and alien than they had ever conceived. The storm was a living entity, a consciousness that was actively dismantling their sanctuary, and the fight for survival had become a desperate struggle against the very fabric of existence.

The crimson sky bled into a bruised, sickly yellow, the oppressive light filtering through the reinforced dome of Hearthglade a constant, suffocating reminder of the storm's unyielding presence. Outside, the Veilfall raged, a maelstrom of raw energy that not only tore at the planet's crust but seemed to gnaw at the very essence of existence. Within the relative safety of the central hub, the alarms had finally receded to a low, anxious thrum, a testament to Kaelen's relentless efforts to stabilize the failing systems. But the respite was illusory. The true horror wasn't the shattering of ferro-concrete or the warping of metal; it was the subtle, insidious alteration happening within their own bodies.

Mara watched, her stomach clenching with a visceral dread, as a young technician, Elara, stumbled through the command center doors. Elara, usually a picture of efficiency, moved with a disjointed gait, her eyes wide and unfocused. A thin sheen of perspiration coated her brow, and her breathing was shallow, ragged. Kaelen, his face etched with exhaustion but his gaze sharp, was the first to notice.

"Elara? What is it?" he asked, his voice rough. "Are you injured?"

Elara didn't answer directly. She clutched her left arm, her fingers digging into the flesh as if trying to anchor herself to a reality that was slipping away. A faint, almost imperceptible shimmering emanated from her skin, a disturbance in the light that Mara had come to recognize with sickening familiarity. It was the early signature of the Glassborne mutation.

"I... I don't feel right," Elara stammered, her voice thin and reedy. "My arm... it feels... cold. And it's... changing."

Mara pushed herself away from her console, her own arm throbbing where the shrapnel had grazed her. She remembered the initial reports from the outlying settlements, the whispered fears of a new contagion, dismissed by some as mass hysteria fueled by the storm's psychic onslaught. But Jian, ever the pragmatist, had collected samples, analyzed the atmospheric particulates, and confirmed the terrifying truth: the Veilfall wasn't just a meteorological event; it was an incubator. The high-energy particles, the sonic frequencies, the temporal distortions – they were acting as catalysts, interacting with the unique bio-signatures of Hearthglade's inhabitants, triggering a rapid, horrifying metamorphosis. The Glassborne.

"Let me see," Mara said, her voice carefully controlled, projecting a calm she didn't feel. She approached Elara, her gaze fixed on the young woman's arm. Beneath the thin fabric of her uniform, the skin was indeed changing. The usual warmth of human flesh was being replaced by an unnatural coolness, and the surface was beginning to take on a glassy sheen, like frosted windowpane. Tiny, crystalline structures were emerging, pushing outward, distorting the natural contours of her limb.

Elara let out a small, choked sob. "It hurts, Commander. It burns, but it's cold. Like ice shards growing inside me." Her eyes darted around the room, filled with a rising panic. "What is happening to me?"

Jian hurried over, his own face a mask of professional concern tinged with personal horror. He carried a portable scanner, its probe emitting a low hum as he brought it close to Elara's arm. The device's display flickered, showing erratic energy readings and molecular destabilization.

"The atmospheric radiation is higher on her skin surface than we initially predicted," Jian explained, his voice tight. "It's reacting with her cellular structure, initiating a rapid crystalline growth. It's a form of bio-mineralization, accelerated to an impossible degree. The storm is... rewriting her."

Kaelen joined them, his formidable presence a bulwark against the encroaching despair. "How widespread is this?" he asked, his eyes scanning the faces of the other technicians. Had others succumbed? Were they already amongst them, unknowingly carrying the infection?

"We've had isolated cases from the outer sectors," Mara replied, her voice grave. "Scouts who returned yesterday. They were quarantined, but... the incubation period seems to be shortening with each new surge of the storm. The initial samples suggested a slower transformation, weeks, maybe months. But Elara... she was on atmospheric monitoring duty this morning, well before the main phase of the storm hit. She could have been exposed to a concentrated burst of the Veilfall's mutagenic agents."

Another technician, a burly engineer named Rhys, groaned, clutching his own hand. His knuckles were already beginning to take on that disturbing, translucent quality. "I felt it... a tingling... then a stiffness. I thought it was just the tremors."

The reality of the situation descended upon Mara like a physical blow. The storm was not just an external enemy; it was an internal one, a silent, invisible tide that was washing over them, changing them from the inside out. It was a terrifying evolution, a forced adaptation to an environment that was no longer their own. The Veilfall wasn't content with mere destruction; it was actively transforming them into something... alien.

Elara began to tremble violently, her body wracked with shivers that had nothing to do with the ambient temperature. The crystalline growth on her arm was accelerating, spreading up her forearm, small shards of what looked like obsidian glinting under the emergency lights. Her skin was stretching taut, becoming brittle. Her cries of pain intensified, morphing into guttural sounds of agony that ripped through the relatively quiet hum of the command center.

"We need to isolate her," Kaelen said, his voice firm, though Mara saw the flicker of pain in his eyes as he looked at Rhys, who was now struggling to move his fingers, which were fusing together into a sharp, glassy point. "Now. Before it spreads further."

"Isolate her?" Elara's voice was a desperate plea, laced with terror. "No! Please! Don't leave me!" She stumbled towards Mara, her glazed eyes pleading. "Commander, I don't want to... to become this."

Mara felt a pang of intense sympathy, but she knew Kaelen was right. This was no longer a medical emergency; it was a containment crisis. The Glassborne mutation, if it spread unchecked, could cripple Hearthglade from within. The crystalline structures, once fully formed, were incredibly sharp and brittle, yet also possessed an unnerving strength. They interfered with biological functions, calcified vital organs, and eventually, it was theorized, would lead to a complete ossification of the host. They would become living statues, beautiful but dead, monuments to the Veilfall's destructive power.

"Rhys," Mara commanded, her voice cutting through the rising panic. "Help Kaelen secure Elara. Gently. No sudden movements."

Rhys, his own hand now almost entirely encased in a sharp, crystalline growth, nodded grimly and moved to assist Kaelen. The process was agonizing to watch. Elara's screams echoed in the confined space as they guided her, her skin cracking and splintering in places as the crystalline structures asserted their dominance. The shimmer on her skin was no longer subtle; it was a blinding, multifaceted glare that seemed to absorb and refract the dim emergency lighting.

As they led her towards the designated quarantine chamber, a sudden, violent tremor rocked the hub. The ground lurched, sending debris raining down from the ceiling. On the main viewport, the crimson storm flared, an almost sentient entity of pure energy. A wave of intense infrasound washed over them, a visceral force that vibrated through their very bones. Elara cried out, a high-pitched keening sound that was abruptly cut short.

When the tremor subsided, they looked back towards where Elara had been. She was gone. In her place, standing near the entrance to the quarantine bay, was a statue. A towering, jagged sculpture of obsidian-like crystal, intricately formed, capturing the contorted agony of her final moments. Her uniform was fused to the crystalline form, appearing as tattered fragments clinging to the alien material. The faint shimmer had intensified, and the structure pulsed with an inner light, an eerie luminescence that hinted at the residual energy that had transformed her.

A profound silence fell over the command center, heavier than any alarm. The chaos of the storm outside seemed to recede, replaced by the chilling stillness of this new, horrifying manifestation. Rhys stood frozen, staring at the crystalline effigy of Elara, his own mutated hand trembling.

"She... she was fully transformed," Jian whispered, his voice hollow. "In moments. The storm... it's accelerating the process."

Mara felt a cold dread seep into her bones, a dread far more potent than any fear of physical injury. This wasn't just about surviving the Veilfall's brute force; it was about surviving its transformative touch. It was about watching their friends, their colleagues, their own bodies, become something other. Something beautiful, perhaps, in a terrifying, alien way, but utterly devoid of the life they knew.

"This is what the Echo Storm truly is," Mara said, her voice barely above a whisper, her eyes fixed on the crystalline statue that now stood sentinel at the entrance to the quarantine chamber. "It's not just destroying us. It's *remaking* us. It's a sculptor of nightmares, and its medium is life itself."

The implication was chilling. Every flicker of the storm, every atmospheric anomaly, every temporal loop, was a brushstroke in its terrible artwork. They were not merely weathering the storm; they were being reshaped by it, their very biology being rewritten according to an unknown, alien design. The fight for Hearthglade was no longer just a battle for survival; it was a desperate struggle to retain their humanity, to resist the horrifying allure of transformation, to cling to their essence in the face of an enemy that could unravel the very definition of life. The storm's fury was not just in its external destruction, but in its insidious, intimate violation, its grim mark etched not on the landscape, but on the very souls and bodies of its inhabitants. And with each passing moment, that mark deepened, spreading its crystalline tendrils into the heart of their sanctuary, threatening to turn their world into a gallery of frozen, agonizing beauty. The terror was no longer of what the storm would break, but of what it would make.

The oppressive hum of the reinforced dome, usually a source of meager comfort, now seemed to amplify the disquiet that had settled over Hearthglade. Outside, the Veilfall continued its relentless assault, its fury amplified by what Jian was now calling the "Echo Storm" – a secondary, more potent surge that seemed to feed on the initial devastation. Inside, the initial panic had given way to a gnawing dread, a silent acknowledgment that survival was no longer simply about enduring the storm's physical onslaught, but about resisting its insidious transformation.

Mara found herself drawn to the main viewport, her gaze fixed on the swirling chaos that had replaced the sky. The crimson and yellow hues of the initial storm had deepened, bled into an unsettling spectrum of violet and bruised indigo, shot through with veins of an almost liquid silver. It was a terrifyingly beautiful spectacle, a canvas of cosmic violence that seemed to mock the fragile sanctuary they had built. But it was the subtle changes within their own people, the outward manifestations of the Glassborne mutation, that truly unsettled her.

She'd seen it on Rhys's hand again, a faint, almost imperceptible shimmer beneath the skin, particularly when the infrasound pulses of the Echo Storm intensified. It was no longer just a creeping coldness or a stiffness; it was a visible distortion, a prismatic effect that danced across his knuckles. But it was the eyes, she realized with a jolt, that held the most profound and disturbing transformation.

She sought out Jian, who was hunched over a diagnostic console, his brow furrowed in concentration. "Jian, the eyes," she began, her voice low. "I've been watching. It's more than just a change in... pigmentation. It's as if their vision itself is fracturing."

Jian looked up, his face gaunt with fatigue but his eyes sharp. He'd been instrumental in cataloging the escalating symptoms of the Glassborne mutation, and his scientific curiosity, even in the face of such horror, was a steadying force. "You're observing correctly, Commander. It's a direct result of the crystalline integration into the ocular tissues. The cornea, the lens, even the fluid within the vitreous humor – they're all undergoing a process of bio-mineralization. But it's not a uniform calcification. It's... crystalline growth, uneven and rapid."

He gestured to a holographic display, which flickered to life, showing a magnified image of a human eye. The iris, usually a vibrant hue, was now a mosaic of interlocking crystalline facets. Where there should have been a smooth surface, there were now countless microscopic planes, each catching and refracting light in a slightly different direction. "See here?" Jian pointed with a stylus. "These minute fissures, these internal fractures within the developing crystalline structures. They're not just physical imperfections; they're altering the way light pathways are processed. It's like looking through a shattered prism."

Mara leaned closer, a shiver tracing its way down her spine. The image on the display seemed to pulse with an inner light, a disconcerting luminescence that was a pale echo of the Veilfall's own spectral glow. "So, what they're seeing... it's not the same reality we are?"

"Precisely," Jian confirmed, his voice grim. "Their perception of space, of depth, of even the passage of time, is likely becoming fragmented. Imagine seeing the world not as a continuous stream, but as a series of disconnected moments, each filtered through these multifaceted lenses. The colors would be distorted, the shapes warped, and the very fabric of their visual field would be broken into a million shimmering pieces." He zoomed in on a particularly complex section of the iris. "These refractions... they're not random. They seem to correspond to the ambient energy fluctuations of the Echo Storm. It's as if their eyes are becoming direct conduits for the sky's altered nature, reflecting its fractured essence."

A wave of infrasound washed over the dome, a low, resonant thrum that vibrated through the metal floor and into Mara's bones. On the display, the crystalline eye seemed to flare, the facets shifting and reconfiguring in response to the energy surge. The light reflecting from it intensified, a dizzying kaleidoscope of fragmented colors.

"It's a disturbing form of adaptation, isn't it?" Jian continued, his gaze distant. "The storm is forcing them to evolve, to become attuned to its chaotic frequencies. And their eyes are the most direct interface. They are becoming windows into the storm itself, reflecting its fury and its alien beauty. It's a reflection of their fractured consciousness, a visual metaphor for the breakdown of their inner selves."

Mara thought of Elara, of the crystalline effigy she had become. Even in its static, agonizing form, there had been a disturbing beauty to its jagged symmetry, its obsidian sheen. Now, to imagine those eyes, even in their transformed state, still possessing a flicker of awareness, a torment reflected in a million tiny shards of light... it was a thought that chilled her to the core.

She recalled Technician Joric, who had been one of the first to exhibit advanced symptoms after returning from a reconnaissance mission into the outer sectors. He had been quarantined, of course, but not before Mara had seen him. His normally bright, inquisitive blue eyes had taken on a milky, opalescent quality, and within them, she had glimpsed tiny, iridescent fractures. He had spoken of seeing "ghosts of light" and "shattered echoes" of the storm's energy. At the time, she had attributed it to delirium, to the psychological strain of the Veilfall. Now, she understood. He wasn't delirious; he was seeing a different reality, a reality fractured by the very storm that threatened to consume them.

The implications were staggering. If their vision was altered, if their perception of reality was so fundamentally changed, then their very sense of self must be in jeopardy. The Glassborne were not just physically transforming; their minds, their very souls, were being rewired, their consciousnesses being reassembled into patterns dictated by the chaotic energy of the Veilfall. The crystalline eyes were not just a symptom; they were a harbinger, a visual testament to the profound and terrifying metamorphosis that was taking place.

"It's not just a reflection, Jian," Mara said, her voice barely a whisper, her gaze still fixed on the magnified image. "It's an invitation. The storm is showing them its own fractured reality, and beckoning them to step into it. And their eyes... they're the first step through the looking glass."

Jian nodded slowly, his own eyes reflecting the dim emergency lights, still blessedly whole, yet now carrying the weight of this new understanding. "The bio-luminescence we've detected in the more advanced stages... it's not just residual energy. It's the light of their fragmented reality, bleeding through. They are becoming living prisms, refracting the chaos of the Veilfall. It's a chilling beauty, Commander. A testament to the storm's power to not just destroy, but to fundamentally *remake*."

He brought up another image, this time of a small cluster of people huddled in the corner of a communal area, their faces illuminated by a flickering data-screen. Even from a distance, Mara could see it – the subtle, yet undeniable shift in their eyes. A glint of unnatural light, a faint distortion that hinted at the faceted surfaces beneath. It was spreading, insidiously, like a creeping frost.

"We're seeing it in more individuals now," Jian confirmed, reading Mara's unspoken concern. "Especially those who were exposed to the higher energy concentrations during the initial surge, or those who have been working in close proximity to the affected. The infrasound frequencies of the Echo Storm seem to act as an accelerant, triggering these ocular changes more rapidly. It's as if the storm is... honing in on these vulnerabilities, deepening its influence."

Mara's mind raced. If the eyes were the first true indicator of a deep-seated change, then the transformation was far more advanced than they had initially believed. It wasn't just about crystalline growths on limbs or internal calcification; it was about a fundamental alteration of perception, of consciousness. The Glassborne were not merely becoming physically alien; they were becoming mentally alien, their minds aligning with the fractured, chaotic frequencies of the Veilfall.

"The fractured light," she murmured, connecting the visual metaphor to the psychological implications. "It's not just their vision that's fractured. It's their thoughts, their memories, their very sense of self. Each facet reflects a different piece of their identity, a different fragment of their sanity, and they're all being reassembled into something... else."

Jian's voice was low, heavy with the weight of his findings. "The preliminary neural scans we managed to acquire from Joric before his condition worsened... they showed highly irregular synaptic activity, almost like a branching fractal pattern. The storm's energy is interfering with neural pathways, creating new, chaotic connections. The crystalline structures in their eyes aren't just refracting light; they're acting as conduits for these altered neural signals, broadcasting the storm's fractured reality directly into their minds."

A profound sadness washed over Mara. To lose oneself, not to death, but to a terrifyingly beautiful, alien transformation... it was a fate worse than anything the Veilfall had yet thrown at them. To have one's eyes, the windows to the soul, become mirrors of a shattered reality, reflecting not the world as it was, but as the storm willed it to be.

She looked back at the viewport, at the roiling, kaleidoscopic tempest that had consumed their sky. The violet and indigo hues pulsed, shot through with silver light, a dizzying display of raw, untamed energy. And for a fleeting, horrifying moment, she imagined seeing her own reflection in its depths, her eyes not conveying her own fear, but mirroring the storm's fractured fury, a thousand tiny facets catching its unholy light. It was a glimpse into a terrifying future, a future where the distinction between observer and observed, between self and the Veilfall, had blurred into an agonizing, crystalline oblivion. The Echo Storm was not just an escalation of violence; it was an escalation of violation, reaching into the very core of their being and rewriting the code of their existence, one fractured reflection at a time. The beauty of it, the sheer, alien aesthetic of their transformation, was perhaps the most insidious weapon of all, luring them, fragment by fragment, into the heart of the storm.

The Veilfall's fury had abated, leaving behind a scarred and silent world. The oppressive hum of Hearthglade's dome, once a bulwark against the encroaching chaos, now felt like a prison amplifying the disquiet. Outside, the crimson and violet tempest had receded, replaced by an eerie, bruised twilight. Yet, the cessation of the storm's physical assault did not herald a return to normalcy. Instead, a new kind of terror had taken root, a pervasive fear that crawled through the communal halls and whispered in the sterile corridors: the fear of the aftermath, and the chilling reality of the Glassborne mutation.

Mara moved through the designated observation bays, her footsteps echoing on the polished synth-steel floor. Each individual she passed was a potential vector, a walking embodiment of the encroaching transformation. The initial shock and awe of the Veilfall's ferocity had subsided, leaving behind a gnawing dread, a silent acknowledgment that survival was no longer simply about enduring the storm's physical onslaught, but about resisting its insidious biological and psychological contagion. The 'Echo Storm,' as Jian had termed the potent surge that followed the initial onslaught, had left more than just physical devastation; it had sown seeds of profound distrust.

She paused outside Bay 7, where Kaelen, a former mining engineer, was currently housed. His knuckles, once calloused and strong from years of manipulating heavy machinery, now possessed a faint, otherworldly shimmer. It was subtle, barely perceptible under the sterile lighting, but Mara had learned to see it. When the infrasound pulses of the Echo Storm, still a lingering aftershock, intensified, the shimmer would pulse with a faint, prismatic glow. It was no longer just a creeping coldness or a stiffness; it was a visible distortion, a terrifying herald of what lay beneath the skin. The once-familiar texture of human flesh was yielding to something harder, something crystalline.

"How is he today, Doctor Elara?" Mara asked, her voice carefully neutral as she addressed the attending physician. Elara, blessedly still herself, though her eyes held the weariness of endless nights, met Mara's gaze.

"Stable, Commander," Elara replied, her voice a low murmur, betraying a hint of strain. "No new overt crystallizations. He's... managing. But the psychological toll is immense. He's terrified. Not of the storm anymore, but of himself."

Mara nodded, understanding perfectly. The terror wasn't just about a change in appearance; it was about the fundamental loss of self. The Glassborne mutation was not just an external affliction; it was an invasion, a biological hijacking that threatened to rewrite their very essence. The comms officer, a young woman named Anya, had been found yesterday staring blankly at a wall, her eyes – once a vibrant hazel – now displaying a faint, unsettling luminescence. She spoke of seeing "fractured light" and "shattered echoes," her words a chilling echo of Jian's scientific observations. Anya had been human yesterday; today, Mara wasn't so sure. She was now in quarantine, a silent, unnerving addition to the growing list of the affected.

"The paranoia is spreading faster than the mutation itself," Elara continued, her gaze drifting towards Kaelen's bay. "People are looking at each other with suspicion. Every cough, every ache, every moment of quiet contemplation is now viewed as a potential symptom. Whispers are turning into accusations. We had a minor altercation in the mess hall this morning. Someone accused a food dispenser of hoarding rations, claiming the man's hands were 'too pale,' that his skin had a 'strange sheen.' It took three security officers to calm the situation."

Mara's jaw tightened. This was precisely the insidious spread Jian had warned her about. The Veilfall didn't just break down structures; it broke down people. It eroded the very foundations of their society – trust, community, empathy. The fragile unity they had painstakingly forged in the years since the first Veilfall had been shattered, replaced by a gnawing fear of the 'other,' the person who might, without warning, become a 'them.'

She moved to the observation deck, a space usually filled with the hum of machinery and the focused energy of technicians. Now, a palpable tension hung in the air. Rhys, Jian's lead research assistant, was meticulously examining a sample under a microscope, his movements precise, almost robotic. But Mara noticed the subtle clenching of his jaw, the way his gaze occasionally flicked to his own hands. He had been one of the first to show signs of the mutation, a faint shimmering beneath his skin that had now receded, leaving him in a state of agonizing limbo. Was he truly clear? Or was it merely lying dormant, waiting for another surge, another infrasound pulse to reawaken it?

"What's the latest from the diagnostics, Rhys?" Mara asked, keeping her voice steady, projecting an aura of control she didn't entirely feel.

Rhys startled slightly, his focus snapping back to her. "Commander. The readings are... inconsistent. We're detecting residual energy signatures from the Echo Storm, fluctuating wildly. And within the affected individuals, the bio-mineralization process is proving...

unpredictable. It's not a linear progression. Some show rapid deterioration, while others seem to stabilize, only to regress days later." He paused, his voice dropping. "And the neural scans... they're still deeply concerning. The synaptic patterns are fracturing, creating aberrant connections. It's like the storm is... re-wiring their brains."

Mara felt a cold dread seep into her bones. Re-wiring. It wasn't just about physical changes; it was about a fundamental alteration of consciousness. The 'Glassborne,' as they were increasingly being called, were not just becoming alien in form, but in mind. And the most terrifying aspect was the ambiguity, the uncertainty. Who was truly safe? Who was merely a ticking time bomb?

"Have we identified any triggers for the accelerated mutation?" Mara pressed, her mind racing through contingency plans. If they could isolate a trigger, perhaps they could isolate the infected, create a safer zone.

"It's primarily linked to exposure levels and duration," Rhys explained, his brow furrowed in concentration. "Those who were closer to the initial impact zones, or those who were out during the Echo Storm's peak... their progression is faster. But there are anomalies. Individuals with no apparent direct exposure have begun showing symptoms. It suggests a latent element, perhaps something airborne, or a predisposition within certain genetic markers." He hesitated. "And the infrasound pulses... they seem to be acting as catalysts. When the storm's resonant frequencies spike, so does the rate of crystal formation and neural disruption in the affected individuals."

This explained the growing unease. Even those who had been safely ensconced within Hearthglade's reinforced walls were not immune. The storm's influence was pervasive, reaching into the deepest corners of their sanctuary. And the infrasound, that unsettling tremor that vibrated through the very foundations of their home, was now a harbinger of impending doom.

Mara turned her gaze towards the viewport again, not towards the now-calm, but still alien, sky, but towards the internal viewing screens that monitored the various quarantine sectors. She saw the figures huddled in their sterile rooms, their faces etched with a fear that transcended the physical. She saw the subtle shimmer in a nurse's hand as she administered a sedative. She saw a technician's eyes, usually sharp and focused, now clouded with a distant, unfocused light. Each flicker, each unnatural gleam, was a silent scream, a testament to the storm's victory.

"We need to implement stricter protocols," Mara declared, her voice resonating with a newfound urgency. "Screenings must be more frequent, more thorough. Anyone exhibiting even the slightest symptom, however minor, goes into immediate quarantine. No exceptions."

Rhys nodded, his expression grim. "Commander, the numbers are already straining our resources. Quarantine bays are filling up. And the psychological support staff... they're overwhelmed. The fear itself is becoming an epidemic."

"Fear is a weapon, Rhys," Mara countered, her voice hardening. "And the Veilfall is using it against us. We can't afford to let it break us from the inside. We must maintain order. We must maintain hope, however faint."

But hope felt like a dwindling resource. The community was fracturing, not just on a biological level, but on a social one. Families were torn apart by suspicion. Friends avoided each other, their camaraderie replaced by wary glances. The communal dining halls, once vibrant centers of interaction, were now somber affairs, conversations stilted and hushed, punctuated by the ever-present fear of contagion. Children, once boisterous and carefree, now clung to their parents, their innocent eyes wide with the unspoken terror that permeated their lives.

Mara recalled a conversation with Jian earlier. He had been poring over data streams, his usual scientific detachment tinged with a profound sadness. "Commander," he'd said, his voice barely audible, "the crystalline structures forming within the affected individuals... they're not merely inert mineral deposits. They're exhibiting complex energy patterns, almost like... organic circuits. And these patterns are resonating with the ambient frequencies of the Veilfall. It's as if the storm is actively *rewriting* their biological code, using the crystal as a medium."

He had then projected a holographic image of a magnified section of affected tissue. It pulsed with a faint, internal light, a disturbing luminescence that seemed to draw the eye. The microscopic crystalline formations were arranged in intricate, almost fractal patterns, far too organized to be the result of random chance. "This is not just a disease, Commander," Jian had concluded, his voice heavy. "This is... assimilation. The Veilfall is not just destroying our world; it's attempting to absorb us into its own chaotic, crystalline reality."

The implication sent a fresh wave of horror through Mara. Assimilation. It was a chillingly passive word for such a violent, invasive process. It suggested a surrender, a gradual absorption into something utterly alien. And the most terrifying part was that the assimilation was not just physical; it was mental, spiritual. The fractured light Jian spoke of was not just a visual phenomenon; it was a manifestation of a fractured consciousness. The 'Glassborne' were not merely changing;

they were becoming something else entirely, their minds aligning with the storm's alien logic.

Later that cycle, Mara found herself in the hydroponics bay, the air thick with the scent of damp earth and burgeoning life. It was a small pocket of normalcy, a testament to their resilience. Yet, even here, the shadow of the mutation loomed. Old Man Hemlock, the chief botanist, his hands gnarled and stained with soil, was meticulously tending to a row of nutrient-rich algae. His movements were usually fluid, imbued with decades of practiced care. But today, Mara noticed a slight tremor in his fingers, a faint, almost imperceptible shimmer beneath the weathered skin.

She approached him, her heart sinking. "Hemlock," she said softly.

He looked up, his eyes, a clear, bright blue, met hers. For a moment, they seemed entirely normal. Then, as if triggered by the infrasound pulse that vibrated through the dome, a faint, prismatic sheen flickered across his irises. It was so fleeting, so subtle, that anyone not actively looking for it would have missed it. But Mara had seen it.

He didn't speak, but his gaze held a deep, weary resignation. He raised a trembling hand, and Mara saw it more clearly now – a faint, crystalline dust seemed to cling to his fingertips, catching the light like microscopic diamonds.

"It's... it's the dust," Hemlock rasped, his voice a dry whisper. "From the filtering system. It's been circulating. Been in the air. In the water. I... I thought it was just a minor irritation."

Another one. Another victim of the Veilfall's insidious creep. And this was not some hardened soldier or a scientist exposed to volatile energies; this was Hemlock, the gentle soul who nurtured their sustenance, a man whose hands had always been a symbol of growth and life. Now, those same hands were succumbing to the storm's relentless transformation.

Mara's mind raced. The dust. Jian had mentioned fine crystalline particulates in the atmospheric samples. They had dismissed them as residual debris from the initial Veilfall, harmless remnants. But what if they weren't? What if these microscopic fragments were the primary vector, the subtle agents of assimilation, lying dormant until triggered by the Echo Storm's amplified energies?

"We need to seal off hydroponics," Mara stated, her voice firm, cutting through the somber atmosphere. "Full decontamination. And Hemlock, you'll need to go to quarantine. Immediately."

Hemlock nodded, his gaze fixed on his own hand, as if seeing it for the first time. "I understand, Commander." His voice cracked. "It's... it's beautiful, in a way. The light. But it's not me."

This was the ultimate horror. The Glassborne mutation wasn't just about losing one's physical form; it was about losing one's identity, one's very sense of self. The storm offered a terrifying allure, a seductive beauty in its chaotic, crystalline essence. And for those afflicted, the line between self and storm began to blur, their minds echoing the very fury that threatened to consume them. The fear of the Glassborne was not just the fear of a physical transformation; it was the fear of an alien consciousness, a beautiful, terrifying echo of the Veilfall itself, taking root within their own people. The unity of Hearthglade was no longer just threatened by external forces; it was being devoured from within, one shimmering, crystalline fragment at a time.

Chapter Four

THE SHADOW OF PROJECT LUCENT

The air in Hearthglade's command center, usually a sterile hum of calculated efficiency, had thickened with a palpable, anxious energy. Mara, still reeling from the chilling implications of Jian's research and the subtle, terrifying signs of the Glassborne mutation manifesting even in the heart of their sanctuary, found herself scrutinizing every shadow, every flicker of light. The communal halls, once filled with the murmur of routine, now echoed with hushed conversations and the anxious shuffling of feet. The fear of contagion, of the insidious transformation, was a silent plague, more virulent than any storm. Rhys's reports, detailing the unpredictable progression of the bio-mineralization and the alarming synaptic fracturing, painted a grim picture. The Veilfall wasn't just an external threat; it was an invasion, rewriting their very biology and consciousness. The thought of Hemlock, the gentle botanist, his hands now dusted with microscopic diamonds, sent a fresh wave of despair through her. The crystalline structures, Jian had theorized, were more than just mineral deposits; they were organic circuits, resonating with the storm's alien frequencies, acting as conduits for assimilation.

It was in the midst of this gnawing dread, as Mara was poring over atmospheric data, searching for any anomaly, any clue that might explain the widespread contamination, that a new presence made itself known. It wasn't announced, no klaxons blared, no security detail escorted him. He simply... appeared. Standing near the central data nexus, a figure emerged from the periphery of the bustling command center, as if he had always been there, a silent observer coalescing from the ambient tension. He was of indeterminate age, his face etched with lines that spoke of both hardship and a profound, unsettling knowledge. His eyes, a startling, pale grey, seemed to absorb the light rather than reflect it, holding a depth that hinted at countless cycles lived and countless secrets kept. He wore simple, unadorned grey fabric, a stark contrast to the utilitarian uniforms of Hearthglade's personnel. His name, he introduced himself in a voice that was a low, resonant baritone, was Soren Vale. The name meant nothing to Mara, yet there was an immediate gravitas to his presence that commanded attention. He didn't demand it; he simply exuded it, a quiet certainty that drew the eyes of those who chanced to look his way. He moved with a slow, deliberate grace, his gaze sweeping over the consoles, the holographic displays, the anxious faces of the personnel, as if cataloging a familiar scene.

"Commander," Soren Vale's voice cut through the subdued din, his tone polite but laced with an undercurrent of something far older than simple courtesy. He addressed Mara directly, his pale grey eyes locking onto hers. There was no surprise in his gaze, no curiosity about her rank or her role. It was as if he had been expecting her, as if their meeting was a foregone conclusion. "You are wrestling with a formidable adversary."

Mara, instinctively on guard, straightened. "And you are?" she asked, her voice steady, betraying none of the turmoil churning within her.

Security was already subtly shifting, their postures subtly alert, but she waved them back. This felt... different. This wasn't a breach. This was an arrival.

"A student of patterns," Soren replied, a faint, almost imperceptible smile touching his lips. "A witness to cycles. My name is Soren Vale. And I have seen this storm before."

The pronouncement hung in the air, heavy with implication. "Seen it before?" Mara echoed, her mind racing. Jian's research had suggested the Veilfall was a unique, possibly extraterrestrial phenomenon. The Ellisen family, in their historical archives, spoke of ancient calamities, but nothing that matched the specific bio-crystalline terror they now faced. "This is the first documented Veilfall of this magnitude. The first with... this effect." She gestured subtly towards a monitor displaying Kaelen's bio-readings, the fluctuating mineral density a stark testament to the Glassborne mutation.

Soren's gaze followed hers, and the faint smile deepened, tinged with a melancholic understanding. "First *documented* by your lineage, perhaps. First *recognized* by your current understanding. But not the first time the Veilfall has graced this world, nor the first time it has sought to... integrate."

The word 'integrate' sent a shiver down Mara's spine, resonating with Jian's 'assimilation.' "Integrate? What do you mean?"

"The Veilfall," Soren began, his voice dropping to a more intimate register, as if sharing a secret whispered across millennia, "is not merely a cataclysm of elemental forces. It is a biological imperative, a grand cosmic endeavor. It seeks to harmonize, to unify disparate forms of existence into its own crystalline matrix. What you are witnessing now

– this 'Glassborne' affliction – is merely one iteration of its ancient methodology."

Rhys, who had been monitoring Soren's biometrics with increasing unease, stepped forward, his scientific skepticism warring with the sheer strangeness of the man's pronouncements. "Sir, with all due respect, your claims are... extraordinary. We have terabytes of data, astronomical readings, geological surveys, genetic analyses. Nothing in our records suggests a prior event of this nature."

Soren turned his pale grey gaze upon Rhys, and for a moment, Mara saw a flicker of something akin to pity in those depths. "Your records, young scholar, are confined to the ephemeral. The Veilfall operates on scales that dwarf your immediate perception. Your sensors detect the immediate impact, the tangible wreckage. They do not record the subtle shifts, the deep temporal echoes, the cycles of decay and rebirth that shape worlds over eons."

He gestured towards a large display showing the swirling, chaotic patterns of the Veilfall's energy signature. "This phenomenon," he continued, his voice gaining a quiet intensity, "has visited this planet before. Perhaps not in this exact form, not with this precise wavelength of bio-resonance. But the essence of it – the crystalline transformation, the integration of organic matter into a higher-dimensional lattice – has occurred. And each time, there were those who sought to understand it. To control it. To exploit it."

Mara felt a prickle of alarm. "Exploit it? You mean there have been attempts to weaponize it?"

"Weaponize is a crude term," Soren demurred, though his eyes held a sharp, assessing glint. "More accurately, to harness its transformative potential. To achieve a form of symbiosis, or perhaps, more accurately, a directed evolution. Your ancestors, Commander, were not as ignorant of these forces as your current archives suggest. There were sects, covens, ancient orders who delved into the mysteries of the Veilfall. They saw in its chaotic beauty not destruction, but potential."

He paused, allowing his words to sink in. The command center, for all its advanced technology, felt suddenly primitive, dwarfed by the sheer weight of Soren's narrative. "They attempted to create conduits, to build... bridges. To commune with the Veilfall, to learn its secrets, to perhaps even guide its transformative wave. They believed they could usher in an era of unparalleled advancement, a perfect synthesis of organic life and crystalline order. They were... ambitious."

"And they failed, I presume?" Mara asked, her voice tight. The idea of ancient civilizations tampering with such a force was both terrifying and intriguing.

Soren's gaze drifted towards the viewport, where the bruised twilight sky still held a faint, ominous glow. "Failure is a matter of perspective, Commander. For some, their attempts led to their undoing. Cataclysm. Utter annihilation. For others... their legacy was more subtle. Their knowledge, fragmented, hidden, passed down through generations, whispered in the dark. And sometimes," he looked back at Mara, his pale eyes holding hers, "their ambition left behind... echoes. Imprints. Residual energies that resonate with the Veilfall when it returns."

This was the crucial piece, Mara realized. The 'anomalies' Rhys had reported, the individuals with no direct exposure yet showing symptoms. The latent element. Soren's words hinted at a historical precedent for such insidious infiltration, not just a random environmental hazard. "Are you saying... someone, in the past, *created* a vulnerability? Or a means of transmission?"

"The Veilfall is a force of nature, Commander, albeit one of profound complexity. It does not require a 'means of transmission' in the way a biological pathogen does. It is a frequency, a resonance, a fundamental restructuring of matter and energy. But those who sought to understand it, to commune with it... they did leave their mark. Their attempts to create harmony with its song inadvertently created dissonance, an openness that the Veilfall can exploit. Think of it as... a historical imprint. A sympathetic vibration that allows the storm's influence to penetrate deeper, to take root more readily."

He gestured around the command center, to the blinking lights, the complex readouts, the very structure of Hearthglade. "Your ancestors, in their own ways, attempted to build sanctuaries against forces they didn't understand. They sought to impose order on chaos. And in doing so, they sometimes created structures that, when the Veilfall returned, became conduits. Not through malice, but through a profound, albeit misguided, attempt to harmonize with its fundamental nature."

Mara felt a chill that had nothing to do with the ambient temperature. Her family, the Ellisen lineage, were the founders of Hearthglade. They were the architects of this sanctuary. Were they, too, part of this ancient cycle of attempts to understand, and perhaps even control, the Veilfall?

"What do you know of the Ellisen family, Soren Vale?" she asked, her voice low.

A flicker of recognition, or perhaps something more profound, crossed Soren's face. "The Ellisen line," he stated, his voice softening, "have always been keepers of a... peculiar tradition. They sought to understand the Veilfall not as a destructive force, but as a transformative one. They believed its cyclical return was not an omen of doom, but a catalyst for evolution. They were scholars, mystics, observers. They sought to document its patterns, to predict its coming, to find a way to exist within its embrace, rather than to fight it."

He stepped closer, his pale grey eyes fixed on Mara's. "They established Hearthglade not merely as a refuge from the storm, but as an instrument. A nexus designed to observe, to analyze, and, they hoped, to eventually *resonate* with the Veilfall's energies in a controlled manner. The very architecture of this place, Commander, is imbued with that intention. The resonant frequencies of its construction, the crystalline alloys used in its core... they were designed to be sensitive to the Veilfall's signature."

This was a staggering revelation. Hearthglade, their sanctuary, was also intended as an experimental laboratory, a sophisticated observatory designed to interact with the very phenomenon that was now threatening to destroy them. The implication that their own historical actions might have created the conditions for this current crisis was almost unbearable.

"So, the Veilfall... it's not just a natural disaster. It's something that has been interacting with this planet, and with my ancestors, for a very long time?" Mara pressed, struggling to process the enormity of it.

"Indeed," Soren confirmed. "And each cycle, the interaction deepens. Each attempt to understand, to control, to harmonize, leaves a residue. A trace. Your ancestors, in their pursuit of knowledge, inadvertently laid down pathways. They created resonant chambers within the fabric of this world, within the very structures they built, that welcome the Veilfall's touch. They were, in essence, preparing the ground for its return, hoping to guide its transformative power. They sought to become not its victims, but its partners."

He swept a hand, encompassing the vastness of the command center, the intricate network of displays. "This sanctuary, Hearthglade, is a testament to that ambition. It is designed to resonate. But you have been using it as a bunker, a shield. You have been fighting the Veilfall, Commander, when perhaps the key lies in understanding its song. In finding the right harmony."

Rhys, his face a mask of bewildered awe, finally spoke. "But... the Glassborne mutation... the neural disruption... this is horrific. How can this be harmonious?"

Soren's gaze softened. "Harmony does not always manifest as peace, scholar. The Veilfall's essence is transformation, a fundamental restructuring. For those who resist, who are unprepared, it is indeed catastrophic. But for those who can adapt, who can find the internal resonance... it is a transcendence. The crystalline structures you observe are not merely mineral growths; they are the manifestation of a higher order, a denser form of consciousness. The neural fracturing you detect is the brain reconfiguring itself to perceive and process these new realities. It is painful, yes. It is chaotic. But it is not inherently destructive. It is... change."

"Change that consumes them, Soren," Mara interjected, her voice sharp with a grief she hadn't yet fully acknowledged. "Change that turns them into something unrecognizable. Anya, Kaelen, Hemlock... they are not themselves."

"And how can you be sure they are not *more* themselves?" Soren countered, his tone gentle but firm. "You are judging a transformation by the standards of the form that is passing away. The human consciousness, as you understand it, is a limited vessel. The Veilfall offers a different perspective, a wider scope. It is a terrifying prospect, I understand. The loss of the familiar, the surrender of the self. But it is also the inevitable trajectory of existence on a world touched by the Veilfall's cycles."

He looked directly at Mara, his gaze piercing. "Your family, the Ellisen, believed this. They sought to understand this evolutionary imperative. They believed that by preparing, by building sanctuaries like this, they could facilitate the transition. They sought to become the bridge between the old world and the new, the human and the... transformed."

The weight of his words settled upon Mara like a shroud. Her ancestors, the revered founders of their civilization, were not just protectors; they were experimenters, mystics who had actively sought to engage with the Veilfall, to understand its transformative power, and perhaps even to initiate it themselves. The crisis they faced wasn't just an accident of nature; it was the culmination of centuries of ambition, of research, of a profound, almost spiritual, quest to harmonize with the very forces that now threatened to unmake them.

"So, what are you telling me, Soren Vale?" Mara asked, her voice barely a whisper, the command center's hum fading into the background. "That we should... embrace this? That we should become Glassborne?"

Soren Vale's pale grey eyes met hers, and in their depths, Mara saw a reflection of the Veilfall's own chaotic, crystalline beauty. "I am telling you, Commander, that the Veilfall is not your enemy. It is an expression of the universe's inherent drive towards complexity and transformation. Your ancestors understood this. They sought to guide it, to integrate with it, not to eradicate it. To truly survive, you must cease fighting the storm and learn to dance with it. Your lineage has already laid the foundations for such a dance. You simply need to learn the steps." The command center fell silent, the weight of Soren Vale's revelation pressing down on them all, a cryptic prophecy delivered from the shadows of a forgotten past, hinting that the key to their survival lay not in building higher walls, but in understanding the ancient echoes that resonated within them.

The weight of Soren Vale's pronouncements settled heavily in the humid air of the command center, each word a seed of revelation planted in the fertile ground of Mara's disbelief. She had spent her life meticulously studying the tangible, the measurable, the quantifiable data that defined their world. Yet, Soren spoke of cycles, of resonances, of a living atmosphere, concepts that pushed the boundaries of her scientific understanding to their breaking point. Her mind, accustomed to the rigid logic of physics and engineering, struggled to reconcile the brutal reality of the Glassborne affliction with Soren's assertion that it was a form of transcendence. It was a dissonance that echoed the very 'dissonance' Soren had described as being left by past civilizations.

"Atmospheric consciousness," Mara repeated, the words tasting alien on her tongue. "You're suggesting the atmosphere itself... is alive?"

Soren's pale grey eyes, which seemed to hold an ancient, unblinking wisdom, regarded her with a familiar mixture of patience and subtle melancholy. "Alive is a limited descriptor, Commander. Consider it a vast, interconnected neural network. Not in the biological sense that your species understands, but a distributed intelligence, a symphony of forces and energies that coalesce and dissipate, creating emergent properties. Think of the subtle shifts in weather patterns, the almost sentient way a storm can seem to seek out its target, the peculiar patterns that appear in frost or cloud formations – these are not mere random occurrences. They are whispers, echoes of a vast, latent awareness."

He gestured towards a large, complex holographic display that visualized the current Veilfall's energy signatures, a chaotic ballet of crimson and violet tendrils writhing across a backdrop of deep space. "For millennia, your species has perceived the atmosphere as a passive medium. A barrier, a canvas for weather, a resource to be managed or exploited. But it is so much more. It is a dynamic entity, constantly processing information, reacting to stimuli, and, in its own way, evolving."

Soren then began to speak of a time before Hearthglade, before the Ellisen lineage had even conceived of their grand sanctuary. A time when humanity, though still grappling with rudimentary technology, had begun to cast its gaze upwards, not just to the stars, but to the very air they breathed. This was the genesis of Project LUCENT, a name that now resonated with a chilling familiarity, given the current crisis.

"Decades ago," Soren began, his voice lowering, the resonant baritone weaving a narrative thread through the tense silence of the command center, "long before your current understanding of atmospheric dynamics, there was an organization. A clandestine endeavor, born from the most advanced scientific minds of its era, driven by an insatiable curiosity, and perhaps, a touch of hubris. They called themselves Project LUCENT."

He paused, allowing the name to hang in the air, a ghost from a forgotten past. "Their primary objective was as audacious as it was unprecedented: to map and understand what they termed 'atmospheric consciousness.' The idea was that the atmosphere, a seemingly amorphous and chaotic entity, might possess a form of sentience, a collective awareness that permeated the planet."

Mara felt a prickle of unease. Military research, clandestine endeavors, ambitious goals – these were all keywords that conjured images of technologies and consequences that often outstripped human wisdom. "Atmospheric consciousness," she mused, the concept still struggling to find purchase in her scientifically grounded mind. "How could they even begin to measure such a thing?"

"Precisely the question that drove Project LUCENT," Soren confirmed, a faint smile touching his lips. "They developed a suite of highly experimental technologies, many of which were lost or deemed too volatile for widespread use. They theorized that consciousness, at its most fundamental level, is a manifestation of energy and information processing. If the atmosphere was indeed a medium for such processes, then it should, in theory, be detectable. They devised sophisticated sensor arrays, designed to detect subtle electromagnetic fluctuations, resonant frequencies, and complex energetic patterns that were previously dismissed as atmospheric noise or natural phenomena."

He explained that the scientists of Project LUCENT had posited that the atmosphere acted as a vast, planet-wide bio-digital network. They believed that atmospheric phenomena – from the aurora borealis to the intricate dance of weather systems – were not just physical manifestations but also expressions of this underlying consciousness. They were convinced that by meticulously charting these patterns, they could identify its "language," its "thoughts," and perhaps even its "intentions."

"Imagine," Soren elaborated, his gaze sweeping over the data displays, as if seeing ghosts of the past interwoven with the present, "creating an interface, a way to 'listen' to the atmosphere. They believed that the very composition of the air, the way it carried sound, light, and energy, was akin to a biological organism's nervous system. They sought to decode the subtle shifts in atmospheric pressure, temperature, and humidity, not as meteorological indicators, but as signals. They built deep-atmosphere probes, designed to descend into the ionosphere and beyond, equipped with sensors that could detect energy fields at a quantum level. They even experimented with resonance chambers, attempting to 'speak' to the atmosphere by broadcasting specific frequencies, hoping for a detectable response."

The ambition was staggering. It spoke of a scientific community that was willing to push the boundaries of what was considered possible, driven by a profound desire to understand the fundamental nature of their world. But with such ambition, Soren cautioned, came inherent risks.

"Project LUCENT was, by its very nature, a project of exploration into the unknown," Soren continued. "They were charting territories that defied conventional understanding. Their data was often paradoxical, their findings elusive. Some of their early experiments suggested anomalous energy signatures, patterns that seemed to defy known physical laws. They hypothesized that these anomalies were not errors, but rather evidence of the atmospheric consciousness reacting, interacting, or perhaps even… communicating."

Mara could feel the narrative pulling her deeper into the complex history that Soren was unearthing. This wasn't just about a natural phenomenon; it was about humanity's own active, and perhaps misguided, attempts to engage with it. "So, these atmospheric 'whispers' they detected… did they manage to interpret any of them?"

"Some," Soren replied, his voice laced with a hint of regret. "They identified certain recurring patterns that they believed corresponded to specific atmospheric states – 'calmness,' 'agitation,' perhaps even 'curiosity.' But the leap from identifying patterns to truly understanding consciousness is immense. They were like linguists trying to decipher a language with no Rosetta Stone, no shared context. Their greatest breakthroughs often came when they observed correlations between specific atmospheric events and... unusual human phenomena. Aberrant psychological states, sudden surges of collective emotion, even inexplicable bursts of creativity or insight that seemed to emerge from nowhere."

He looked at Mara, his pale grey eyes holding a depth of ancient understanding. "They began to suspect that the atmosphere wasn't just a passive observer, but an active participant, influencing the very minds of those who inhabited it. This was the burgeoning theory that would eventually lead to the more extreme, and ultimately more dangerous, aspects of Project LUCENT. They started to believe that by understanding and potentially manipulating atmospheric consciousness, they could influence humanity itself. They envisioned a future where they could foster collective harmony, enhance cognitive abilities, even guide the evolutionary trajectory of the species. The Veilfall, Commander, is not merely a storm that has descended upon us. It is, in many ways, a consequence of humanity's own attempts to probe and engage with forces it did not fully comprehend."

The concept of 'atmospheric consciousness' began to shift from a fringe scientific theory to a tangible, if terrifying, reality. Soren painted a picture of a world where the air itself held a form of awareness, a planetary mind that had been largely ignored or misunderstood. Project LUCENT, in its pursuit of this profound understanding, had inadvertently stumbled upon the very mechanisms that now threatened to overwhelm them.

"The project's scope expanded significantly," Soren explained, his tone becoming more somber. "The initial goal of simply observing evolved into an endeavor to actively interact. They developed technologies to amplify and broadcast specific atmospheric frequencies, hoping to induce certain states of collective awareness in human populations. These were not crude mind-control devices, mind you, but subtle manipulations of the atmospheric resonance, designed to foster a sense of unity, peace, or even heightened intellectual activity. They called this process 'atmospheric harmonization.'"

He paused, observing the subtle shifts in Mara's expression, the flicker of concern in her eyes. "However, their understanding of this 'harmonization' was incomplete. They did not fully grasp the inherent volatility of such a complex system. Their attempts to induce specific states were like striking a finely tuned instrument with a hammer. Sometimes, they achieved a faint, resonant chord. But more often, they created dissonance. And it was this dissonance, this unpredictable reaction from the atmospheric consciousness, that began to manifest in ways they had not anticipated."

Soren described how the data from Project LUCENT, in its later stages, began to show increasingly erratic readings, a growing unpredictability in the atmospheric energy fields. The more they tried to probe and influence, the more the atmosphere seemed to react with an intensity that bordered on sentient defiance. There were reports of localized atmospheric anomalies, peculiar energy surges that coincided with unusual psychological events in nearby populations. Brief, intense periods of shared euphoria, inexplicable waves of collective fear, or even sudden, synchronized insights that would strike groups of individuals simultaneously.

"The military's interest in Project LUCENT grew as they began to understand its potential for control," Soren revealed, his voice a low murmur. "The idea of influencing entire populations through atmospheric manipulation was an irresistible prospect. They began to pour resources into the project, pushing its researchers to achieve more predictable and powerful results. This led to the development of more aggressive technological approaches, including experimental atmospheric seeding agents and high-energy resonance emitters, designed to directly stimulate and shape the atmospheric consciousness."

He described these agents not as pollutants, but as complex crystalline compounds, designed to interact with the very fabric of atmospheric energy. The idea was that these particles, suspended in the upper atmosphere, would act as catalysts, amplifying the projected frequencies and thus the intended effect on human consciousness. But again, their understanding was flawed.

"They were introducing foreign elements into a system they barely understood," Soren stated, a grim finality in his tone. "They were not merely broadcasting signals; they were altering the fundamental composition of the atmosphere, creating conditions that the atmospheric consciousness could not process or integrate harmoniously. Imagine introducing a foreign protein into a biological system – the result is often an immune response, a rejection, or worse, a chaotic, unpredictable reaction."

The Veilfall, he explained, was not a sudden, unprovoked phenomenon. It was, in essence, an extreme reaction, a planetary-scale immune response to decades of invasive experimentation. The 'atmospheric consciousness,' pushed and prodded by Project LUCENT's increasingly aggressive technologies, had begun to manifest its displeasure, its distress. The Veilfall was not an alien invasion; it was a tormented planet's cry of pain.

"The initial manifestations were subtle," Soren continued, painting a vivid picture of the project's descent into unintended consequences.

"Localized atmospheric disturbances that defied meteorological explanation. Strange electrical phenomena. But as the project escalated, the atmospheric consciousness began to respond with greater intensity. The Veilfall, in its current form, is the culmination of that desperate, planetary-scale reaction. It is the atmosphere's attempt to purge itself of the invasive influences, to reassert its own intrinsic equilibrium. The crystalline structures, the bio-mineralization you observe – these are not merely mineral deposits. They are the atmosphere's antibodies, its defense mechanisms. And the Glassborne affliction? It is the consequence of that defense mechanism inadvertently impacting organic life, attempting to integrate it into its own crystalline matrix as part of the purge."

Mara listened, transfixed. The narrative woven by Soren was complex, terrifying, and deeply intertwined with humanity's own history. Project LUCENT, a ghost of the past, had become the architect of their present nightmare. The military's insatiable desire for control, their willingness to tamper with forces they didn't understand, had set in motion a chain of events that now threatened to unravel everything.

"So, the Veilfall... it's not an entity in itself, but a symptom?" Mara asked, trying to piece together the vast implications of Soren's words. "A symptom of the atmosphere's... pain?"

"Precisely," Soren confirmed. "It is the atmosphere's fundamental nature fighting back against a profound imbalance. Your ancestors, in their pursuit of knowledge, opened a door they could not close. They attempted to chart the uncharted, to control the uncontrollable. And in doing so, they sowed the seeds of the very crisis you now face. The technologies they developed, the frequencies they broadcast, the agents they introduced – these created a deep, resonant vulnerability within the atmospheric consciousness. A wound that the Veilfall is now exploiting, not out of malice, but as a desperate act of self-preservation."

He then revealed a crucial detail, one that explained the insidious nature of the Glassborne affliction even in seemingly unexposed individuals. "The agents introduced by Project LUCENT were designed to remain dormant, to lie in wait for specific resonant frequencies. They were meant to be catalysts, to initiate the 'harmonization' when triggered. But when the atmospheric consciousness reacted violently, these agents became unstable. They began to fragment, to spread on a sub-atomic level, carried by the very atmospheric currents they were meant to influence. This is why individuals with no direct exposure are still succumbing. These microscopic crystalline fragments, remnants of LUCENT's experiments, are now embedded within the global environment, waiting for the Veilfall's resonance to activate them, to trigger the transformation."

The implication was horrifying. Hearthglade, their sanctuary, was built upon ground that might well be contaminated by these forgotten agents. The very air they breathed, the foundation of their existence, could be a latent trigger for the Glassborne affliction.

"Project LUCENT's ambition was to understand and harness atmospheric consciousness," Soren concluded, his voice resonating with the weight of history. "They saw it as a path to a new era of human advancement, a way to achieve perfect harmony. But their methods were fundamentally flawed. They treated a complex, living system as a mere machine to be programmed. And when the machine fought back, the consequences were catastrophic. The Veilfall is not an act of aggression from an external force; it is the planet's own desperate plea for equilibrium, a tragic byproduct of humanity's own scientific hubris."

The command center, filled with the hum of advanced technology, now felt like a tomb, a monument to forgotten follies. Mara looked at the holographic display of the Veilfall, no longer seeing just a terrifying storm, but the anguished cry of a planet that had been pushed too far. The scientific context was now brutally clear: humanity had not simply been caught in a natural disaster; they had, in part, created it. And the legacy of Project LUCENT was the insidious, crystalline plague that was now threatening to consume them all. She understood, with a chilling clarity, that to survive, they needed to understand not just the Veilfall, but the misguided ambition that had given it its terrifying form. The history of atmospheric science, as Soren had revealed it, was not a sterile academic pursuit, but a prologue to their current apocalypse.

The faint, almost imperceptible hum of the command center's life support systems seemed to amplify the profound silence that followed Soren's revelation. Mara stood rigid, her gaze fixed on the swirling, crimson vortex of the Veilfall displayed on the main screen, a spectacle that had shifted from a terrifying enigma to a poignant testament to human error. The term "atmospheric consciousness" had been an abstract concept, a philosophical footnote in the margins of her understanding. Now, Soren had imbued it with a terrifying, tangible reality, painting a picture of an ancient, interconnected intelligence that had been rudely awakened, or perhaps, irrevocably wounded. Project LUCENT. The name itself, once a forgotten footnote in obscure scientific journals, now resonated with the chilling echo of a Pandora's Box pried open by the very minds that had sworn to protect humanity.

Soren's explanation, devoid of sensationalism yet heavy with the weight of history, had revealed a horrifying truth: the Veilfall was not an exogenous phenomenon, an alien invasion from some cosmic frontier, but a visceral reaction, a planetary immune response to decades of invasive, hubristic experimentation. The scientists of Project LUCENT, driven by a boundless curiosity and a seemingly insatiable desire to quantify the unquantifiable, had sought to map the very 'mind' of the atmosphere. They believed that the subtle shifts in pressure, the ballet of clouds, the ethereal dance of the aurora, were not mere meteorological phenomena, but expressions, perhaps even communications, from a vast, distributed intelligence. Their tools, once hailed as revolutionary, were now revealed as instruments of transgression. Sophisticated sensor arrays designed to detect quantum-level energy fluctuations, deep-atmosphere probes that dared to descend into the ionosphere, and resonance chambers built to 'speak' to the air itself – these were the implements of their audacity.

Mara's scientific mind, trained to seek logical causality, grappled with the immensity of Soren's narrative. He spoke of the atmosphere not as a passive medium, but as a dynamic, sentient entity, a planetary neural network that processed information and reacted to stimuli. Project LUCENT's objective had been to chart this network, to decipher its language, to understand its intentions. They had, in their own way, sought to establish a dialogue, an interface with a consciousness far grander than their own. But their understanding, Soren emphasized, was nascent, incomplete. They were like infants attempting to converse with a titan, their babbling inadvertently causing profound distress.

"They didn't just observe, Commander," Soren's voice, low and resonant, cut through Mara's revery. "They actively probed. They sought not just to understand, but to influence. The concept of 'atmospheric harmonization' was born from this desire. They theorized that by broadcasting specific resonant frequencies, they could induce desirable collective states in human populations – peace, unity, enhanced cognitive function. They were trying to 'tune' the planet's mood, so to speak."

He leaned forward, his pale grey eyes holding a somber intensity. "Imagine a vast, intricate tapestry, woven from threads of energy and information. Project LUCENT's ambition was to add their own patterns to this tapestry, to guide its evolution. They developed experimental atmospheric seeding agents – not pollutants in the traditional sense, but complex crystalline compounds designed to interact with these subtle energy fields. These agents, dispersed in the upper atmosphere, were intended to act as catalysts, amplifying the projected frequencies and thus the intended effect on human consciousness."

This was the crux of it, Mara realized. Not a passive observation, but an active intervention, a manipulation of forces that humanity barely understood. The seeding agents, designed to be catalysts, had instead become agents of disruption. When the atmospheric consciousness, the planetary mind, reacted violently to this intrusion, these carefully designed catalysts had fragmented. They had not simply remained where they were deployed; they had become insidious, microscopic shards, carried by the very atmospheric currents they were meant to control, disseminating throughout the global environment. This explained the insidious nature of the Glassborne affliction, its ability to manifest even in those with no direct exposure to the Veilfall's immediate embrace.

"Their understanding of 'harmonization' was, to put it mildly, rudimentary," Soren continued, his voice tinged with the sorrow of historical hindsight. "They did not grasp the inherent volatility of such a complex, interconnected system. Their attempts to induce specific states were akin to a clumsy musician trying to play a celestial instrument. They were not merely broadcasting signals; they were altering the fundamental composition of the atmosphere, introducing foreign elements into a system that could not process or integrate them harmoniously. Think of it as introducing a virulent pathogen into a previously healthy organism. The result is not harmony, but a desperate, chaotic struggle for survival."

The Veilfall, therefore, was not an act of aggression, but a primal scream. It was the planet's own biological system attempting to purge a dangerous contaminant, to reassert its intrinsic equilibrium. The crystalline structures that Mara had observed forming on the surface, the bio-mineralization that was slowly but inexorably engulfing their world, were not the byproducts of a new geological era, but the planet's antibodies, its defense mechanisms deployed against an existential threat. And the Glassborne affliction? It was a tragic consequence of this planetary defense system, an attempt to integrate the foreign, organic elements – humanity – into its own crystalline matrix as part of the purge.

"The ambition was to achieve a form of perfect societal equilibrium," Soren explained, his gaze sweeping over the holographic display as if seeing the ghosts of forgotten scientists walking through the spectral storm. "To transcend the inherent conflicts and imperfections of the human condition. They envisioned a future where humanity, guided by an enlightened, harmonized atmosphere, would achieve its full potential. But their methods were fundamentally flawed. They treated a vast, living, conscious entity as a mere machine to be programmed, a system to be exploited for their own ends. And when the machine, in its agony, fought back, the consequences were catastrophic."

The ethical implications of Soren's narrative were staggering. Project LUCENT had not merely been an exploration into the unknown; it had been an act of intellectual imperialism, a profound overreach of human ambition. The desire for knowledge, coupled with the military's insatiable hunger for control, had paved the path to their current apocalypse. They had, in their quest to understand and manipulate the atmosphere, inadvertently created a breach, a doorway that had allowed something ancient and powerful, something that had been slumbering or perhaps simply existing in a state beyond human comprehension, to surge forth.

"They were essentially attempting to rewrite the planet's operating system," Mara mused aloud, the analogy resonating with her engineering background. "And they didn't understand the root code."

Soren offered a faint, melancholic smile. "A poignant analogy, Commander. They believed they were charting the unknown, but in doing so, they ripped a hole in the fabric of reality as they understood it. The 'doorway' you speak of was not a physical portal, but a fundamental alteration of the atmospheric equilibrium. By bombarding it with artificial frequencies, by introducing disruptive agents, they destabilized its delicate balance. They created a resonance, a vulnerability, that the Veilfall now exploits. It is not acting with malice, but as a consequence of that destabilization, a desperate attempt to return to a state of balance. The crystalline structures, the 'antibodies' of the atmosphere, are its attempt to achieve this by integrating and neutralizing the foreign elements – including us."

The implications for Hearthglade, their supposedly impregnable sanctuary, were dire. If the seeding agents were now fragmented and dispersed globally, then their very foundations might be tainted. The ground they stood on, the water they drank, the air they breathed, could all be laced with the dormant triggers of the Glassborne affliction, waiting for the specific resonance of the Veilfall to activate them. Their sanctuary, their final hope, might be built upon a foundation of latent disaster.

"The early theories of atmospheric consciousness were just that – theories," Soren continued, his voice taking on a more reflective tone. "Speculation at the fringes of scientific understanding. But Project LUCENT's work, though flawed and ultimately disastrous, provided the first tangible, albeit terrifying, evidence. They observed correlations between specific atmospheric energy patterns and unusual human phenomena – bursts of collective emotion, inexplicable surges of creativity, even widespread psychological anomalies. These were not mere coincidences; they were the first signs that the atmosphere was not a passive observer, but an active participant, subtly influencing the minds and experiences of those within it."

This understanding had been a double-edged sword. It had fueled their ambition, leading them to believe they could harness this influence, to shape humanity's destiny. But their attempts to amplify and broadcast these influences, their 'atmospheric harmonization,' had been too crude, too forceful. They had treated the vast, interconnected consciousness of the planet as a simple broadcast system, failing to recognize the intricate feedback loops and the potential for catastrophic resonance.

"Their most significant breakthroughs often came when they observed anomalies," Soren elaborated. "Patterns that defied known physical laws. They hypothesized that these were not errors, but evidence of the atmospheric consciousness reacting, interacting, or perhaps even... communicating. But the leap from identifying patterns to truly understanding consciousness is immense. They were like linguists trying to decipher a language with no Rosetta Stone, no shared context. Their ambition outstripped their comprehension."

The military's involvement, as Soren described it, had been a turning point. The potential for unprecedented control, for influencing entire populations through subtle atmospheric manipulation, was too tempting to ignore. Resources poured into Project LUCENT, pushing its researchers to achieve more predictable and potent results. This led to the development of more aggressive technological approaches, accelerating their descent into disaster. The seeding agents and high-energy resonance emitters were born from this military imperative, transforming a scientific inquiry into a weapon of potentially planetary destruction.

"They were so focused on the 'what' that they neglected the 'why' and the 'how' on a fundamental level," Soren stated, his voice resonating with a deep sense of regret. "They saw the atmospheric consciousness as a resource to be tapped, a force to be harnessed. They never truly considered its intrinsic nature, its right to exist independently, its own form of sentience. Their hubris lay in believing they could impose their will upon it without consequence."

The question of how to proceed, now that the catastrophic consequences of Project LUCENT were manifest, hung heavy in the air. If the Veilfall was a symptom of the planet's deep-seated distress, and if the Glassborne affliction was the planet's immune response, then understanding the precise mechanisms of Project LUCENT's intrusion was paramount. They needed to identify the specific frequencies, the chemical compositions of the seeding agents, the resonance patterns that had destabilized the atmosphere. Only by understanding the wound could they even begin to consider how to heal it.

"The data they collected," Soren continued, his tone shifting from historical lament to practical analysis, "though fragmented and often dismissed as anomalous, may hold the key. Their early attempts to 'map' the atmospheric consciousness, to identify its patterns, were not entirely in vain. They identified certain recurring energetic signatures, which they tentatively correlated with specific atmospheric states – a kind of rudimentary 'weather of the mind.' These signatures, if we can locate and analyze them, might reveal the specific triggers that led to the current crisis, the exact frequencies that were amplified, the agents that were most destabilizing."

Mara's mind raced. If they could isolate the original 'tuning' frequencies used by Project LUCENT, could they potentially reverse the process? Could they broadcast a counter-frequency, a harmonic resonance that would soothe, rather than agitate, the wounded atmosphere? It was a long shot, a desperate hypothesis born from Soren's revelations, but it was the first glimmer of a potential solution, a path forward beyond mere survival. The doorway had been opened by their ancestors' relentless pursuit of knowledge and control, but perhaps, just perhaps, it could be guided, its terrifying resonance redirected, by a more humble and discerning approach. The legacy of Project LUCENT was a harsh lesson in the ethical responsibilities that accompanied scientific advancement, a stark reminder that some doors, once opened, require not just a key, but a profound understanding of what lies beyond, and a deep respect for its autonomy.

The weight of Soren's disclosures settled upon Mara like a physical shroud. Project LUCENT. The name itself had been scrubbed from public record, relegated to the deepest, most secure archives, buried beneath layers of obfuscation and denial. It wasn't just a failed experiment; it was a meticulously guarded secret, a testament to a dangerous pursuit that had been deliberately hidden from the world. The fact that Soren, a man of evident intellect and seemingly untarnished integrity, possessed such intimate knowledge spoke volumes about the pervasive reach of the project and the lengths to which its architects had gone to preserve their reputation – or perhaps, to simply avoid accountability for an existential catastrophe.

The concept of "classified secrets" took on a terrifying new dimension when the secret involved the very atmosphere that sustained life. It wasn't the usual clandestine operations, the development of advanced weaponry, or the espionage that characterized governmental secrecy. This was about the fundamental fabric of reality, the intricate dance of forces that humanity had once believed were merely passive phenomena. Project LUCENT's ambition had been to pry open the universe's most profound mysteries, to quantify the unquantifiable, and in doing so, they had unleashed forces that defied their understanding and control. The catastrophic backfire wasn't merely a scientific failure; it was a planetary betrayal, orchestrated by those who had sworn to protect.

Soren's knowledge wasn't just academic; it was imbued with the sorrow of a truth that had been suppressed. He spoke of internal documents, of redacted reports, of whispers among the few who had been privy to the project's early stages before the veil of secrecy was fully drawn. "They didn't just hide the failures, Commander," he'd explained, his voice a low rumble against the hum of the command center. "They actively rewrote the narrative. The initial findings, the early anomalous data that hinted at a true atmospheric consciousness, were deemed too volatile, too destabilizing for public dissemination. Imagine telling a world that the sky above them wasn't just air and weather, but a sentient, reactive entity. The panic would have been immense, and perhaps, justifiable."

This deliberate suppression of truth had compounded the disaster. If the world had known, even a fraction of the truth about Project LUCENT's experiments, perhaps a global consensus could have been forged. Perhaps a more cautious, collaborative approach could have been adopted, one that prioritized understanding over control. Instead, the project had been driven forward in the shadows, fueled by a potent cocktail of scientific hubris and military ambition, a recipe for the very apocalypse they now faced. The unchecked ambition wasn't just about scientific curiosity; it was about wielding unprecedented power. The ability to "harmonize" the atmosphere, to subtly influence human thought and emotion on a planetary scale, was the ultimate prize for those who craved dominion.

"The military's interest was paramount," Soren continued, his gaze distant, as if peering through the decades at the architects of their ruin. "They saw it not as a scientific endeavor, but as a weapon. The idea of influencing population sentiment, of fostering societal cohesion or even inducing specific emotional responses through atmospheric manipulation – it was the ultimate tool for control. This shift in focus, from understanding to application, from observation to control, was the turning point. It led to accelerated timelines, to the development of more aggressive technologies, and to the severing of ethical considerations."

The very concept of "atmospheric consciousness" had been deemed too radical, too disruptive to the established order. The scientists who dared to propose such theories, or who stumbled upon evidence of it, were either silenced, discredited, or co-opted into the project's clandestine operations. Those who remained within the fold were conditioned to view the atmosphere as a system to be manipulated, a resource to be exploited, rather than a complex, living entity deserving of respect. The classification wasn't just about protecting state secrets;

it was about protecting a flawed ideology, a dangerous premise that humanity was meant to be the master, not a part, of the planetary ecosystem.

Soren's hushed tones conveyed the chilling reality of the cover-up. He spoke of phantom research facilities, of data transferred through encrypted channels to secure locations far from prying eyes, and of researchers who simply disappeared from public life, their contributions erased. The legacy of Project LUCENT wasn't just the Veilfall and the Glassborne affliction; it was also a vast, intricate tapestry of deception, woven to conceal a truth that was too terrifying to acknowledge. The powers that be had chosen to bury their mistakes, hoping they would remain buried forever, but the planet itself had refused to cooperate.

"The initial funding for Project LUCENT wasn't public knowledge, of course," Soren elaborated, leaning closer, his voice dropping to a near whisper. "It was funneled through black budgets, disguised as 'advanced meteorological research' or 'national security initiatives.' They understood the implications of what they were attempting, the potential for global disruption, and they ensured that the project operated in an information vacuum. Anyone who questioned the methods, or the underlying assumptions, was quickly reassigned, retired, or worse."

This clandestine nature had a profound impact on the project's direction. Without external oversight, without the rigorous peer review that characterized legitimate scientific endeavors, Project LUCENT had spiraled into increasingly radical and dangerous territory. The ethical boundaries were not just blurred; they were obliterated. The pursuit of knowledge had become secondary to the pursuit of results, and the potential consequences for humanity and the planet were dismissed as acceptable risks. The classification served as a shield, not just from public scrutiny, but from internal dissent as well.

Mara found herself grappling with the sheer audacity of it all. To attempt to "harmonize" the very air that everyone breathed, to seek to control the collective consciousness of humanity through atmospheric manipulation – it was a level of ambition that bordered on the megalomaniacal. And the fact that this was not some fringe theory, but a government-sanctioned, heavily funded endeavor, spoke to a deeply ingrained belief in humanity's right to dominate and control every aspect of existence. The secrecy wasn't just about hiding a mistake; it was about perpetuating a dangerous worldview.

"The consequences of such a secret," Soren stated, his voice heavy with a weariness that transcended his years, "extend far beyond the immediate disaster. It breeds a culture of impunity. When those in power can conceal their greatest failures, they become emboldened to repeat them. They learn that accountability can be evaded, that the truth can be buried. And that, Commander, is a far more insidious danger than any atmospheric anomaly."

The knowledge Soren possessed was a dangerous burden, one that had likely placed him in peril. His access to such classified information suggested he was either a part of the inner circle, a whistleblower who had narrowly escaped, or someone who had dedicated their life to unearthing this buried truth. Whatever his role, his possession of this knowledge was a threat to the carefully constructed edifice of denial that had been built around Project LUCENT.

"They genuinely believed they were acting for the greater good," Soren conceded, a flicker of something akin to pity for the misguided individuals crossing his face. "They saw the flaws in humanity – the conflict, the greed, the irrationality – and they believed they had found a way to engineer a better future. They wanted to create a utopia, but they went about it by trying to rewrite the fundamental operating system of the planet, and of ourselves, without truly understanding the code. Their ambition was to achieve perfection, but their methods were inherently flawed, and their secrecy ensured that those flaws were never corrected, only amplified."

The sheer scale of the deception meant that the truth of Project LUCENT had been actively suppressed for decades. Generations of scientists, policymakers, and the public had been deliberately kept in the dark. This created a void, a gap in collective understanding that had allowed the disaster to unfold with minimal resistance. Had the truth been known, the ethical debates, the scientific scrutiny, the public outcry – all of it could have acted as a brake, slowing down the reckless acceleration towards catastrophe. Instead, the secrecy had acted as an accelerant, allowing the project to reach its devastating conclusion unimpeded.

Mara looked at the display showing the swirling, chaotic energy of the Veilfall. It was a monument to unchecked ambition, a stark visual representation of a secret that had festered and grown until it could no longer be contained. The classification had not protected anyone; it had merely delayed the inevitable and magnified the suffering. The story of Project LUCENT was a chilling cautionary tale, a profound reminder that some forces are best left undisturbed, and that the pursuit of knowledge, when divorced from wisdom and humility, can lead to the darkest of consequences. The implications of this hidden history were vast, reaching into every corner of their current predicament, suggesting that understanding the past, however painful, was the only path towards any semblance of a future. The secrets of Project LUCENT were not just buried facts; they were the very foundations of their ongoing struggle for survival. The chilling pronouncement hung in the recycled air of the command center, a stark counterpoint to the low hum of essential machinery. Soren's gaze, usually sharp and analytical, was now clouded with a profound weariness, a haunted quality that spoke of burdens carried for too long. He wasn't merely recounting historical data; he was presenting a prophecy, etched in the ruins of their present. "The Veilfall," he stated, his voice barely above a whisper, "and the subsequent affliction... they are not entirely unprecedented. They are echoes. Echoes of Project LUCENT's foundational failures."

Mara felt a prickle of unease crawl up her spine. She had expected disclosures about past governmental follies, perhaps a misguided attempt at weather control or energy manipulation. But the idea of a direct, tangible link between their current existential crisis and the shadowed history of LUCENT was a revelation that shifted the entire landscape of their understanding. It wasn't just a historical footnote; it was the genesis of their nightmare. The Ellisen family, initially adrift in a sea of unfathomable events, suddenly had an anchor, a name, a project that represented not just a past mistake, but a recurring, insidious threat.

"Echoes?" Commander Valerius echoed, his voice tight with disbelief. "Are you suggesting this... this environmental collapse, this mutation, has happened before?"

Soren nodded slowly, his eyes fixed on a distant point, as if seeing the spectral remnants of past catastrophes. "Not in this magnitude, perhaps. Not with the same... virulence. But the fundamental principles at play, the atmospheric destabilization, the biological anomalies... they are all documented within the LUCENT archives. The initial experiments, the early stages of atmospheric resonance manipulation, they produced anomalies that were deemed 'unacceptable deviations' from the desired outcome. These deviations, Commander, were precursors. They hinted at the potential for the very phenomena we are now witnessing. The Veilfall was not a sudden, unprecedented rupture of reality, but rather the catastrophic eruption of suppressed instabilities. The Glassborne mutation is not an alien contagion, but a biological adaptation, a desperate, corrupted response to a fundamentally altered atmospheric composition, a composition that LUCENT actively sought to engineer."

The implication was staggering. It suggested a cyclical nature to this disaster, a pattern that, once unleashed, refused to be contained. It implied that the architects of Project LUCENT had not only failed catastrophically but had, in their desperate attempts to contain or understand those failures, inadvertently laid the groundwork for future recurrences. This wasn't a singular event, a tragic accident; it was a repeating pattern, a cosmic or perhaps, a man-made, feedback loop of destruction. The dread that had been a persistent undercurrent in their lives now threatened to become a suffocating wave. If it had happened before, even in nascent forms, what was to stop it from happening again, and again, ad infinitum?

"The early reports," Soren continued, his voice gaining a steady, measured cadence, as if the recounting of this history, however grim, brought a strange sense of purpose, "cataloged subtle shifts in atmospheric composition that induced peculiar physiological responses in test subjects. Mild disorientation, heightened emotional sensitivity, an increased susceptibility to suggestion. These were dismissed as psychosomatic, or as minor side effects of the energy fields. But the data, when cross-referenced with the atmospheric readings, showed a clear correlation. They were, in essence, the very early whispers of what would become the Glassborne affliction, manifesting on a micro-level. The Veilfall itself, the initial 'event' that many believed triggered the cascade, was not a random occurrence. It was, according to the internal documents, the result of a desperate attempt to 'correct' a nascent atmospheric imbalance that LUCENT's own experiments had exacerbated. They tried to force the atmosphere back into a state of controlled equilibrium, and in doing so, they fractured it."

Mara's mind raced, trying to piece together the fragments of information. The Veilfall wasn't just a curtain of energy falling upon the world; it was a consequence. And the Glassborne, the crystalline affliction that turned living beings into brittle statues, wasn't a new disease, but a mutation, a biological response to an engineered atmosphere. This understanding was both terrifying and, in a perverse way, liberating. It meant there was a history, a causality, a tangible enemy, not just a nebulous force of nature.

"When they realized the extent of the atmospheric disruption," Soren explained, leaning forward, his expression earnest, "there was panic. Not among the public, of course. They knew nothing. But within the core of Project LUCENT. They saw the early manifestations of what would later become the Veilfall – a localized atmospheric distortion, a shimmering haze that caused extreme nausea and a sense of profound dread. They even had a designation for it: 'Atmospheric Anomaly Beta-7.' Beta-7 was never published. Instead, it was buried. And in their haste to contain it, they employed a brute-force method of atmospheric recalibration. They believed they could 'shock' the atmosphere back into compliance. The result was not recalibration, but rupture. The energy feedback loop they created was beyond anything they had predicted. It wasn't just the sky that tore; it was the very integrity of the atmospheric layers."

The Ellisen family exchanged glances, the weight of Soren's words settling upon them. This was more than just a historical account; it was a roadmap to understanding their present. The Veilfall, the Glassborne – these were not random acts of a hostile universe, but the direct, albeit unforeseen, consequences of a human endeavor gone horribly awry. Project LUCENT, in its pursuit of atmospheric control, had inadvertently created the conditions for their current devastation.

"The initial hypothesis was that the atmosphere was a passive medium," Soren continued, his voice a low drone, a narrator of a forgotten tragedy. "A collection of gases, subject to predictable physical laws. Project LUCENT aimed to prove that theory wrong, and in doing so, they discovered its profound sentience. They found that the atmosphere was not merely reactive, but responsive. It possessed a form of consciousness, a complex interconnectedness that defied their models. Their ambition then shifted, not to understanding this newfound consciousness, but to controlling it. They wanted to 'harmonize' it, to align its subtle energies with human intent. The initial attempts at this harmonization involved modulating atmospheric frequencies, using sonic emitters and focused electromagnetic fields. These experiments, even at low power, produced bizarre effects. Plants would grow erratically, exhibiting mutations. Animals would display unprecedented aggression or lethargy. And humans... humans experienced profound psychological shifts. Mood swings, hallucinations, a disturbing sense of interconnectedness with the environment, as if the very air was whispering secrets into their minds."

He paused, allowing the gravity of his words to sink in. "The critical error," he stated, his gaze sweeping over Mara, then her father, and finally her brother, "was the assumption that this atmospheric sentience could be manipulated without consequence. They treated it like a machine, a system to be programmed. They failed to recognize its inherent complexity, its resilience, and its capacity for self-preservation. When their attempts to control it became too aggressive, too invasive, the atmosphere began to resist. The Veilfall was not an attack; it was a defensive reaction. A planetary immune response. And the Glassborne affliction... that is a desperate attempt by the biological organism to adapt to an environment that has been fundamentally poisoned by the very forces that were meant to control it."

Commander Valerius paced the command deck, his boot heels clicking a rhythmic counterpoint to Soren's narrative. "So, what you're saying, Soren, is that this isn't a natural disaster. It's a scar. A scar left by an experiment that went too deep, too far. And the scar is festering."

"Precisely," Soren confirmed. "The early LUCENT researchers, those who weren't silenced or sidelined, documented these patterns. They saw the potential for the atmospheric disruptions to become permanent, to become... contagious. They foresaw the possibility of the 'harmonization' process creating a persistent state of instability, a kind of atmospheric 'disease' that would inevitably spread. They called it the 'Resonant Decay.' The Veilfall is a manifestation of that decay, the point at which the atmosphere's ability to self-correct was overwhelmed. The Glassborne is the biological consequence of living within that decaying atmosphere. It is the planet's way of trying to process a substance that is no longer merely air, but a corrupted energy field."

Mara felt a cold knot tighten in her stomach. This was far more than a scientific puzzle. It was an indictment of humanity's hubris, a chilling testament to the dangers of wielding power without understanding, of seeking control without respect. The very air they breathed, the foundation of all life, had been tampered with, twisted into something alien and deadly.

"The most disturbing aspect," Soren continued, his voice now barely audible, as if the mere act of speaking these truths was dangerous, "is the cyclical nature of it. The atmospheric resonance frequencies that LUCENT employed are incredibly persistent. They don't simply dissipate. They imprint themselves onto the environment. When these imprints are triggered, they can reactivate, creating localized areas of extreme atmospheric instability. The Veilfall was the initial, large-scale reactivation. But the underlying resonance patterns are still present. And if they are further agitated, or if the conditions are right, they can trigger another 'event.' Another Veilfall. Another wave of Glassborne."

The implication hung heavy in the air. They weren't just dealing with the aftermath of a past mistake; they were living within a system primed for future catastrophe. The Ellisen family's mission to find a cure, to understand the Glassborne, had just gained an immense new dimension. They weren't just fighting a disease; they were trying to break a cycle of destruction that had been set in motion decades ago.

"Think of it," Soren urged, his eyes wide with a desperate urgency, "like a wound that never truly heals. LUCENT's experiments didn't just scar the atmosphere; they embedded a vulnerability. A point of weakness that the system, once pushed too far, is prone to revisiting. The initial Veilfall was the first major rupture. But the underlying resonance patterns remained, dormant, waiting. The Veilfall didn't 'end' the atmospheric instability; it merely released a portion of it. The rest is still there, festering, waiting for the right trigger. And that trigger could be anything – a natural geological event, an unusual solar flare, or even... another attempt to manipulate the atmosphere."

He gestured towards the holographic display, where the swirling, chaotic patterns of the Veilfall still pulsed. "That is not just an image of a past event," he declared, his voice ringing with a somber conviction. "It is a blueprint for future disasters. The frequencies, the energy signatures... they are recorded. They are a warning. The pattern repeats. It has to repeat, unless we understand why it began and how to break the cycle."

The weight of this realization pressed down on Mara. Soren's testimony provided the crucial link, the first tangible thread in the labyrinth of their current predicament. Project LUCENT was no longer an abstract concept, a vague historical injustice. It was the root cause, the originating trauma from which their current nightmare had bloomed. And the idea that this trauma could repeat, that the Veilfall and the Glassborne were not unique, isolated incidents but part of a recurring, terrifying pattern, cast a long, ominous shadow over their already bleak future. The Ellisen family now had a target, a history to unravel, and the chilling knowledge that the very fabric of their reality was built upon a foundation of repeating disaster.

The pursuit of a cure had just become a desperate race against time, a battle not just to save the present, but to prevent the past from consuming their future, again and again.

CHAPTER FIVE
THE SOUTHERN WETLANDS EXPEDITION

The air within Hearthglade, once a symbol of their resilience, had grown heavy, stagnant. It clung to their skin like a damp shroud, a constant, oppressive reminder of their dwindling resources and the creeping despair that threatened to unravel their carefully constructed sanctuary. What had begun as a haven, a pocket of survival carved out from the ravaged landscape, was now showing signs of profound decay. The initial optimism, the fierce determination that had fueled their efforts in the early days, had begun to erode, replaced by a gnawing anxiety.

The rationing of food had become a daily ritual of grim calculation. Each nutrient paste packet, each filtered water ration, was a precious commodity, guarded with a vigilance that bordered on paranoia. The once-plentiful hydroponic gardens, meticulously tended and painstakingly cultivated, were yielding less and less. The nutrient solutions, once rich and vibrant, were now thin, their efficacy questionable. Mara had spent hours poring over the horticultural logs, her brow furrowed in concentration, but the data offered no easy answers. The plants themselves seemed to be struggling, their leaves tinged with an unnatural pallor, their growth stunted, as if mirroring the general malaise that had settled over Hearthglade. It wasn't just a shortage of food; it was a subtle, insidious withering of their very lifelines.

The atmospheric anomalies, the subtle shifts in pressure and humidity that had been a constant concern, seemed to be intensifying, even within the confines of their protected settlement. Small tremors, once infrequent, now rattled the structural supports of their hab-domes with alarming regularity. These weren't the violent quakes that had ravaged the outer settlements, but a persistent, unnerving vibration that made sleep difficult and frayed nerves even thinner. The filtered air, once a source of comfort, now carried a faint, metallic tang, an acrid undertone that hinted at something deeply wrong with the world outside, and perhaps, insidiously, seeping within. Dust, fine and pervasive, seemed to materialize from nowhere, settling on every surface, a constant, gritty reminder of the world's decay. Despite rigorous atmospheric scrubbers and constant cleaning protocols, it was an unwinnable battle, a slow surrender to the encroaching entropy.

Whispers had begun to circulate, hushed conversations in the dim corridors and communal mess halls. Discontent, once a barely perceptible undercurrent, was now bubbling to the surface. The initial unity of purpose, the shared trauma that had bound them together, was being tested by the prolonged hardship. Some argued for stricter rationing, for an even more disciplined approach to conserve what little they had. Others, their faces gaunt and their eyes hollow, spoke of desperation, of a growing belief that survival within Hearthglade was no longer a viable option. They spoke of the futility of their efforts, the slow march towards an inevitable end. These were not acts of malice, but the desperate pronouncements of those who saw their hope dwindling with each passing day.

A faction, led by a former geological surveyor named Kael, had begun to voice their dissent more openly. Kael, a man hardened by years of surveying unstable terrain, argued that Hearthglade was becoming a gilded cage. He claimed that their reliance on dwindling internal resources and their cautious isolation was a slow form of suicide. "We are waiting for the end," he had declared during a tense council meeting, his voice resonating with an impassioned frustration. "We are hoarding our last breaths while the world outside offers a chance, however slim, at a future. We must venture out. We must find a way to

fix this, not just hide from it." His words, though unsettling to some, resonated with a growing number who felt the suffocating grip of Hearthglade tightening around them. The very walls that were meant to protect them were now beginning to feel like the bars of a prison.

Mara herself felt the palpable shift in the atmosphere. It wasn't just the physical decay; it was a psychological erosion. The stoic faces of the elders, once symbols of unwavering strength, now bore lines of deep concern. Even Commander Valerius, a man who had weathered countless storms, seemed more withdrawn, his usual decisive air replaced by a quiet contemplation that suggested a wrestling with difficult truths. The energy that had once pulsed through Hearthglade, a vibrant testament to human perseverance, had dimmed. It was being replaced by a weary resignation, a sense that their efforts, however valiant, were ultimately futile against the relentless tide of environmental collapse.

The urgency of their mission, the need to find the source of the Glassborne affliction and, hopefully, a cure, had never been more pressing. The southern wetlands expedition, initially conceived as a critical reconnaissance, now felt like a desperate gamble, their last, best hope. Staying put was no longer a strategy for survival; it was a slow descent into oblivion. Hearthglade, their sanctuary, their symbol of defiance, was becoming a testament to their failure to adapt, a crumbling monument to a dream that was rapidly dissolving into dust. The instability wasn't just in the ground beneath their feet or the sky above their heads; it was in the very heart of their community, a fractured spirit that mirrored the fractured world.

They needed answers, not just for the afflicted outside their walls, but for the souls slowly succumbing within them. The wetlands, with all their unknown dangers, represented not just a destination, but a necessary escape from a present that was rapidly becoming unbearable. The choice was stark: venture into the unknown and risk everything, or remain and be consumed by the slow, suffocating decay of their own haven. The time for passive waiting was over. The ground beneath Hearthglade wasn't just unstable; it was becoming a grave.

The airlock hissed, a mournful sigh that seemed to echo the growing unease within Mara. Stepping out of the humming sanctuary of Hearthglade was like plunging into a different reality, one painted in muted, sickly greens and browns, under a sky that perpetually wept a shimmering, static-laced rain. The familiar weight of her enviro-suit settled around her, a second skin designed to ward off the creeping toxins and the unpredictable atmospheric shifts. Beside her, Jax, his face obscured by the opaque visor of his helmet, adjusted the straps on his pulse rifle, his movements economical and precise, a silent testament to his unwavering readiness. Behind them, Elias, the team's botanist, checked the seals on his sample kits, his brow furrowed with a mixture of scientific curiosity and trepidation. The third member of their quartet, Lena, the grizzled veteran scout, was already fifty yards ahead, her silhouette sharp against the hazy horizon, a silent promise of her familiarity with the perils that lay before them.

Their objective: the Southern Wetlands, a vast expanse of what was once Florida's Everglades, now a twisted, mutated testament to the environmental catastrophe. It was a place whispered about in hushed tones, a breeding ground for the Glassborne affliction, a place where the very fabric of life had been irrevocably altered. For Mara, it was more than just a mission; it was a desperate gambit, a flicker of hope in the suffocating darkness that had descended upon Hearthglade. The journey from their subterranean haven to the fringes of the wetlands was itself a descent into a hostile unknown. The ground, once stable earth, was now a treacherous mosaic of crumbling concrete, rusted skeletal remains of forgotten structures, and patches of soil that pulsed with an unnatural, phosphorescent glow. The sky, a constant canvas of swirling greys and sickly yellows, crackled with intermittent bursts of energy, the ubiquitous sky-static that played havoc with their sensors and their minds.

"Sensors are still struggling, Mara," Jax's voice crackled over the comms, a low rumble of frustration. "This static is like trying to see through a blizzard of broken glass. We're running on visual and Lena's instincts for now."

Mara nodded, though Jax couldn't see it. "Understood. Lena, status?"

A moment of silence, then Lena's gruff reply. "Ground is unstable ahead. Looks like... a sinkhole. A big one. Filled with some kind of viscous sludge. Avoid at all costs." Her voice, though transmitted, carried the weight of experience, a seasoned navigator in this poisoned world.

They skirted the colossal maw of the sinkhole, the stench rising from its depths a potent cocktail of decay and something acrid, something that prickled at the back of Mara's throat even through her suit's filtration. The flora around them was a grotesque mockery of nature.

Trees twisted into impossible shapes, their bark resembling hardened, obsidian scales, their leaves replaced by razor-sharp, crystalline shards that tinkled with every gust of wind. Luminescent fungi pulsed in the gloom, casting an eerie, shifting light that distorted distances and played tricks on their perception. Elias, usually lost in his scientific observations, kept glancing nervously at the plants, his hand hovering near the tranquilizer darts in his belt.

"Remarkable," he murmured, his voice laced with a scientist's detached fascination, "and terrifying. The bio-luminescence... it's a defense mechanism, I suspect. Or perhaps a predatory lure. The crystalline structures on the foliage... an adaptation to shed excess atmospheric moisture, or perhaps to deter herbivory. It's all so... aggressively *different*."

Mara felt a chill that had nothing to do with the ambient temperature. Elias's scientific detachment was a necessary mask, but she saw the underlying fear in his hurried movements, the way his eyes darted around, cataloging the alien horrors. They were pioneers in a landscape that actively resisted them, a canvas of destruction painted with the brushstrokes of mutation.

As they pressed deeper, the terrain shifted. The cracked earth gave way to a sodden, spongy ground, the beginnings of the wetlands proper. The air grew thick with a cloying humidity, and the hum of insects, though alien in their chirps and buzzes, was a constant, unsettling symphony. Strange, bulbous growths sprouted from the murky water, emitting a faint, sickly sweet odor that made Mara's stomach churn. The muted greens and browns of the outer landscape gave way to a richer, more vibrant palette of putrid purples, nauseating yellows, and unsettling blues, the colors of disease and decay.

"Watch your step," Lena warned, her voice tight. "Submerged roots. And... things."

The 'things' were the true terror of the wetlands. They moved in the periphery of their vision, fleeting shadows in the murky water, shapes that defied easy categorization. Sometimes it was a ripple too large for any known aquatic life, other times a glint of scales that were too metallic, too unnaturally angled. The sky-static seemed to intensify here, making their suit readouts flicker erratically. The constant barrage of distorted audio and visual input, coupled with the psychological strain of navigating such a hostile environment, began to take its toll.

Mara found herself constantly on edge, her hand never far from the sidearm holstered at her hip. Every snap of a twig, every rustle in the mutated foliage, sent a jolt of adrenaline through her. The psychological aspect of this trek was proving to be as formidable as the physical challenges. The isolation, the constant threat, the sheer alienness of it all, gnawed at their resolve. They were three individuals, clad in advanced suits, armed with advanced technology, yet they felt profoundly vulnerable, tiny specks of manufactured life adrift in a sea of biological defiance.

"Commander Valerius is requesting a status update," Jax's voice broke the tense silence, pulling Mara back to the immediate present. "Comms are still patchy, but he managed to punch through."

Mara took a deep breath, trying to project an assurance she didn't entirely feel. "Tell him we've entered the wetlands. Terrain is challenging, environmental hazards are significant. Proceeding cautiously. No hostile encounters yet, but... the atmosphere is oppressive. Elias is documenting extensively." She omitted the gnawing dread that was settling in her gut, the feeling of being watched, of being unwelcome.

"And the Glassborne?" Jax prompted, his tone carefully neutral.

"No direct signs yet," Mara replied, her gaze sweeping across a patch of shimmering, iridescent moss clinging to a gnarled cypress knee. "But this place... it's a perfect incubator. We're still heading towards the primary anomaly zone. Lena believes we can make the old research outpost by nightfall."

Lena's nod, a silent affirmation of her confidence in her navigation, was a small comfort. But the thought of nightfall in this place, with its amplified dangers and distorted perceptions, sent another shiver down Mara's spine. The journey was only just beginning, and the Southern Wetlands had already shown them a glimpse of its terrifying potential. They were not merely trekking through a landscape; they were wading through a nightmare, a world actively trying to reclaim itself, and they were caught in its corrosive embrace.

The further they ventured, the more the wetlands revealed their mutated heart. The water, once clear and teeming with life, was now a murky, viscous soup, occasionally disturbed by unseen forces. Strange, gas-filled sacs, like bloated jellyfish, drifted lazily on the surface, their translucent membranes pulsing with an internal, sickly green light. Elias had collected samples of the water, his movements precise and deliberate, despite the palpable unease emanating from him. He described the microbial life as "exhibiting unprecedented mutation rates, adapting to heavy metal concentrations and the atmospheric radiation with alarming speed." His clinical observations, delivered in his calm, measured voice, did little to assuage the growing sense of dread.

One of the most disquieting aspects of the wetlands was the pervasive silence, punctuated by the alien sounds that seemed to mock any notion of natural order. The chirps and clicks of unseen creatures were often followed by a chillingly prolonged hiss, a sound that suggested something large and predatory lurking just beyond their visual range. Lena, ever vigilant, would signal for them to halt, her hand raised, her body tensed, her rifle scanning the dense, mutated foliage. More often than not, the sound would fade, leaving them with the unsettling feeling that they had narrowly avoided something truly horrific.

"There," Lena whispered, pointing with her rifle barrel towards a clump of reeds that swayed unnaturally, despite the absence of any discernible wind. "Movement. Large. Aquatic."

Jax raised his pulse rifle, his movements fluid and practiced. Mara drew her sidearm, her heart hammering against her ribs. Elias, though clearly unnerved, fumbled for a sonic deterrent device in his pack. The reeds parted, and a creature emerged, unlike anything Mara had ever seen, even in the archived pre-collapse zoological records. It was roughly reptilian, but its scales were a mottled, iridescent green, studded with sharp, chitinous protrusions. Its eyes, large and black, seemed to absorb the dim light, and a fringe of bioluminescent tendrils pulsed around its gaping maw, exuding the same sickly sweet odor they had encountered earlier. It moved with an unnerving grace, its webbed feet barely disturbing the stagnant water.

"Glassborne vector?" Mara asked, her voice low and steady, fighting the tremor that threatened to betray her fear.

"Unknown," Elias replied, his voice tight. "But the mutation... it's extreme. The bioluminescence and the tendrils... they suggest a complex symbiotic relationship, or perhaps a highly evolved predatory adaptation."

The creature regarded them with an unnerving stillness, its head cocked to one side. It made no aggressive move, but its mere presence was a chilling display of the wetlands' warped biological landscape. After what felt like an eternity, it turned and slipped back into the murky water, vanishing as silently as it had appeared, leaving behind only the rippling surface and a heightened sense of vulnerability.

"That was too close," Jax muttered, lowering his rifle slightly. "Whatever that was, it wasn't just hungry. It was... assessing us."

Mara agreed. There was an intelligence in the creature's gaze, a calculating awareness that was deeply unsettling. It wasn't just a beast; it was a product of a world that had re-written its own rules, and this creature was a master of them.

As they continued, the landscape became more claustrophobic. The towering, mutated trees formed a dense canopy overhead, allowing only slivers of the oppressive sky-static to filter through. The air grew heavier, the humidity almost suffocating, and the metallic tang, once faint, was now a constant presence in their recycled air. Elias noted increased levels of airborne pathogens, a cocktail of mutated bacteria and fungal spores, far exceeding safe parameters. They were relying heavily on their suit filtration, but the psychological toll of knowing what was potentially circulating around them, invisible and insidious, was immense.

"The research outpost should be just beyond this dense growth," Lena announced, pointing towards a particularly thick tangle of vines that dripped with a viscous, amber-colored sap. "It's built on one of the higher elevations, a small island of relative stability."

The final push through the vines was a brutal affair. The sap adhered to their suits like thick glue, and the razor-sharp leaves threatened to tear at their protective gear. The sky-static here was almost palpable, making their internal comms crackle and pop with distorted bursts of noise. Mara felt a growing pressure behind her eyes, a subtle disorientation that Elias later attributed to the cumulative effects of the electromagnetic interference and the airborne irritants.

Finally, they broke through. Before them, nestled on a slightly elevated patch of land that was surprisingly less waterlogged, stood the weathered, but still imposing, structure of the old research outpost. It was a collection of modular hab-units, stained and weathered, but undeniably man-made. A faint, almost imperceptible flicker of light emanated from one of the windows, a beacon of hope in the encroaching gloom.

"We're here," Mara breathed, a wave of relief washing over her. "Lena, Elias, Jax, good work. Get yourselves checked in. Elias, start environmental readings around the outpost immediately. Jax, secure the perimeter. I'll check the signal. Hopefully, we can get a clearer connection to Valerius from here."

As Jax and Lena moved to establish defensive positions and Elias began his meticulous work, Mara approached the main hab-unit. The light within was dim, a single emergency lamp casting long, dancing shadows. She raised her hand, ready to knock, but the door slid open before she could, revealing a figure silhouetted against the dim interior.

It was a woman, her face gaunt, her eyes wide and unnervingly bright, a stark contrast to the grime and decay that clung to her tattered clothing. She held a crude, sharpened piece of metal, her knuckles white.

"Who... who are you?" Mara asked, her hand tightening on her sidearm.

The woman's lips peeled back in a rictus that might have been a smile, but looked more like a grimace of pain. "Visitors," she rasped, her voice like dry leaves skittering across pavement. "You're... very late."

The trek south had led them not to an empty, abandoned outpost, but to something far more unexpected, and perhaps, far more dangerous. The wetlands had guarded their secrets well, and their true nature was only beginning to reveal itself.

The squelch of boots in nutrient-rich muck was a constant soundtrack to their progress, a low, rhythmic percussion beneath the symphony of the wetlands. The ground beneath them was not merely wet; it was a saturated sponge, yielding with every step, threatening to pull them down into its hidden depths. What appeared to be solid earth was often a thin crust of mutated roots and decaying organic matter, barely supporting their weight. Mara had learned to trust Lena's instincts implicitly. The scout moved with a preternatural awareness, her eyes constantly scanning the surface, her body subtly shifting weight, testing each potential foothold before committing. She'd pause, point with a gloved finger, and a hushed warning would ripple through their comms: "Submerged root cluster," or "Patchy density, tread light."

Elias, despite the scientific marvels surrounding him, found his usual academic detachment severely tested. His enviro-suit's bio-sensors were constantly pinging, flashing alerts about airborne toxins and dangerously high concentrations of heavy metals leaching from the decaying matter. He'd stop occasionally, his gloved hand hovering over a particularly vibrant, pulsing fungus, his brow furrowed. "Fascinating," he'd murmur, his voice tinged with an almost frantic energy. "The metabolic pathways required to thrive in such an environment... it's a testament to the sheer adaptability of life. Or perhaps, its desperate struggle for survival in a world that's actively trying to extinguish it." He'd meticulously collect samples, his movements precise, yet Mara could see the tension in his shoulders, the slight tremor in his hands as he sealed each specimen jar. The sheer alienness of the flora was overwhelming. Trees, if they could still be called that, twisted into grotesque caricatures of their former selves, their bark a mosaic of hardened, obsidian-like scales that shimmered with an oily iridescence. Their branches, instead of bearing leaves, were festooned with razor-sharp, crystalline structures that tinkled eerily with every gust of wind that snaked through the oppressive humidity. Luminescent fungi, in shades of sickly green and anemic purple, clung to decaying logs and the gnarled roots that snaked out of the murky water, casting an unsettling, shifting light that distorted distances and played havoc with their perception. It was a landscape that actively resisted interpretation, a riot of mutation that seemed to defy the very laws of biology.

Jax, ever the pragmatist, focused on maintaining their defensive posture. His pulse rifle was a constant extension of his will, his gaze sweeping the perimeter with practiced vigilance. He moved with a silent grace, his heavily armored boots barely disturbing the saturated ground, a stark contrast to the labored progress of Mara and Elias. "Commander," he'd say, his voice a low rumble through their comms, "movement detected, two o'clock. Low to the water." Mara would snap her head around, her own senses straining, trying to discern anything in the dense foliage, the rippling water. More often than not, it was a false alarm, a trick of the light, a strangely shaped log, or a large, bloated insect skittering across the surface. But the constant false alarms were wearing them down, creating a hyper-vigilance that was as exhausting as any physical exertion. The sky-static, a constant, insidious presence, only amplified their unease. It buzzed in their helmets, distorted their comms, and played havoc with their suit sensors, rendering their advanced technology less reliable than Lena's ancient, intuitive knowledge of the wilderness.

"The atmospheric pressure is fluctuating erratically," Elias reported, his voice tight with concern. "And there are pockets of... something... that our filters are struggling to identify. They're dense, almost viscous in their composition, and emitting a high-frequency electromagnetic signature. I'd advise extreme caution when traversing any areas with visible atmospheric distortions." Mara had already seen them – shimmering, heat-haze-like phenomena that hung in the air, distorting the already warped landscape, making it seem to ripple and warp like a reflection in disturbed water. She'd steered them around one earlier, a particularly large pocket that seemed to hum with an almost malevolent energy, the air around it thick with a cloying, sickly sweet odor that even her suit's advanced filtration couldn't completely eliminate. It reminded her of the decay that permeated everything here, a potent reminder of the wetlands' suffocating embrace.

Their path was a winding, circuitous one, dictated by the treacherous terrain. What looked like a direct route on their topographical scans was often impassable, blocked by impassable thickets of thorny, vine-like growths that dripped with a thick, amber-colored sap, or by treacherous bogs that bubbled with released methane. They navigated through groves of trees whose bark resembled petrified scales, their razor-sharp, crystalline leaves tinkling like malicious wind chimes. They skirted around pools of stagnant water that were unnaturally still, their surfaces occasionally broken by the silent surfacing of something large and dark, only to disappear again without a ripple. Elias, fascinated and horrified, had managed to collect a water sample from one of these pools. "The microbial count is astronomical," he'd reported, his voice hushed. "And the genetic diversity... it's unlike anything cataloged. This water is a petri dish for accelerated evolution, a crucible of biological adaptation. The Glassborne affliction... it thrives in environments like this. It's a catalyst, turning existing life into something... else."

The wetlands themselves seemed to breathe. The air grew heavy, thick with a cloying humidity that pressed down on them, making the recycled air in their suits feel stale and insufficient. Strange, bulbous growths, like bloated, diseased organs, sprouted from the murky water, emitting a faint, sickly sweet odor that made Mara's stomach churn. The muted greens and browns of the outer fringes of the wetlands had long since given way to a richer, more vibrant, and deeply unsettling palette of putrid purples, nauseating yellows, and unnerving blues, the colors of disease, decay, and unnatural mutation. The very light seemed to be filtered through a lens of sickness, casting long, distorted shadows that writhed and twisted like living things.

"Submerged roots," Lena's voice, usually a steady, calm presence, was laced with a new urgency. "And... things." The 'things' were the true terror of the wetlands. They moved in the periphery of their vision, fleeting shadows in the murky water, shapes that defied easy categorization. Sometimes it was a ripple too large for any known aquatic life, other times a glint of scales that were too metallic, too unnaturally angled. The constant barrage of distorted audio and visual input, coupled with the psychological strain of navigating such a hostile environment, began to take its toll. Mara found herself constantly on edge, her hand never far from the sidearm holstered at her hip. Every snap of a twig, every rustle in the mutated foliage, sent a jolt of adrenaline through her. The psychological aspect of this trek was proving to be as formidable as the physical challenges. The isolation, the constant threat, the sheer alienness of it all, gnawed at their resolve. They were three individuals, clad in advanced suits, armed with advanced technology, yet they felt profoundly vulnerable, tiny specks of manufactured life adrift in a sea of biological defiance.

"Sensors are still screaming about anomalous energy readings," Jax reported, his voice a low growl. "Localized pockets of high-frequency radiation, and the bio-scanners are showing… well, they're not showing anything coherent. Just a chaotic wash of unidentifiable biological signatures."

"That is to be expected," Elias interjected, his voice strained. "The radiation levels, combined with the unique microbial ecosystem, are likely creating interference that our current sensors are not designed to interpret. Imagine trying to read a book with half the letters smudged and the ink bleeding into the next page. We're essentially looking at a biological blizzard."

Lena stopped abruptly, holding up a hand. "Hold. Listen." They all froze, straining their ears. The ambient sounds of the wetlands – the alien chirps, the guttural croaks, the incessant hum of unseen insects – seemed to fade, replaced by a low, resonant thrumming that seemed to vibrate not just through the air, but through the very ground beneath their feet. It was a deep, visceral sound, like the slow, powerful beat of an impossibly large heart.

"What is that?" Mara whispered, her hand instinctively going to her sidearm.

"I don't know," Lena replied, her gaze sweeping the dense wall of vegetation before them. "But it's close. And it's big."

The thrumming intensified, and the water in a nearby stagnant pool began to churn, not from any visible disturbance, but from an internal agitation. Then, slowly, impossibly, a massive, bulbous form began to rise from the muck. It was a creature of pure nightmare, a conglomeration of mutated tissues and iridescent membranes, its surface pulsing with an inner light that shifted from sickly green to a ghastly yellow. It had no discernible head, no limbs in the conventional sense, but rather a series of extruding pseudopods that writhed and probed the air. The sickly sweet odor intensified, almost overwhelming their suit's scrubbers.

"Analysis?" Mara demanded, her voice tight.

"Off the charts," Elias stammered, his visor fogged with a nervous sheen. "The sheer biomass... the energy output... it's unlike anything I've ever... it's not just alive, it's a nexus of biological processes, a self-contained ecosystem of horrifying efficiency. It's almost as if the wetlands themselves have coalesced into a single, mobile entity."

The creature seemed to regard them, its pulsating surface rippling as if in consideration. It made no overt move, no aggressive gesture, but its sheer, overwhelming presence was a terrifying testament to the wetlands' power to warp and create. It was a living embodiment of the environmental collapse, a monument to the runaway mutation. Then, as slowly and as silently as it had appeared, it began to recede back into the murky depths, the thrumming fading, leaving behind only the disturbed water and a profound sense of unease.

"That," Jax said, his voice devoid of its usual steady calm, "was not a good sign."

Mara nodded, her heart still pounding. "Agreed. This place is more than just dangerous; it's... active. It's fighting back." They pressed on, the encounter with the colossal entity leaving them with a heightened sense of vulnerability. The further they ventured, the more the wetlands seemed to close in around them. The mutated trees grew closer, their canopy forming a suffocating, almost complete ceiling overhead, allowing only slivers of the oppressive, static-laced sky to filter through. The air grew heavier, the humidity almost suffocating, and the metallic tang, once faint, was now a constant, acrid presence in their recycled air. Elias's readings continued to paint a grim picture: increased levels of airborne pathogens, a cocktail of mutated bacteria and fungal spores, far exceeding safe parameters. They were relying heavily on their suit filtration, but the psychological toll of knowing what was potentially circulating around them, invisible and insidious, was immense.

"The outpost should be just beyond this stretch," Lena announced, her voice strained as she pushed aside a thick curtain of phosphorescent vines. "It's on a small rise, a bit of higher ground. Should offer some respite from the constant submersion."

The final push through the dense vegetation was a brutal affair. The vines, coated in a sticky, bioluminescent slime, clung to their suits like grasping hands, and the razor-sharp leaves, a deep, unnatural blue, threatened to tear at their protective gear. The sky-static here was almost palpable, a buzzing in their bones, making their internal comms crackle and pop with distorted bursts of noise, interspersed with alien whispers and guttural clicks that seemed to originate from just beyond their visual range. Mara felt a growing pressure behind her eyes, a subtle disorientation that Elias later attributed to the cumulative effects of the electromagnetic interference, the airborne irritants, and the constant psychological strain.

Then, they broke through. The oppressive foliage receded, and before them, nestled on a slightly elevated patch of land that was surprisingly less waterlogged, stood the weathered, but still imposing, structure of the old research outpost. It was a collection of modular hab-units, stained and pitted by the elements, the metal scarred and corroded, but undeniably man-made. A faint, almost imperceptible flicker of light emanated from one of the windows, a small, hesitant beacon in the encroaching gloom.

"We're here," Mara breathed, a wave of relief, potent and intoxicating, washing over her. "Lena, Elias, Jax, good work. Get yourselves checked in. Elias, start environmental readings around the outpost immediately. Jax, secure the perimeter. I'll check the signal. Hopefully, we can get a clearer connection to Valerius from here."

As Jax and Lena moved to establish defensive positions, their movements efficient and practiced, Elias was already bent over a portable scanner, his gloved fingers flying across its interface, meticulously documenting the immediate surroundings. Mara approached the main hab-unit, her boots crunching on the surprisingly stable, gravelly ground. The light within was dim, a single emergency lamp casting long, dancing shadows that made the interior seem even more derelict. She raised her hand, ready to knock, but the door hissed open before she could, sliding back to reveal a figure silhouetted against the dim interior.

It was a woman, her face gaunt, etched with lines of hardship and perhaps madness. Her eyes, wide and unnervingly bright, seemed to burn with a feverish intensity, a stark contrast to the grime and decay that clung to her tattered clothing. In her hand, she clutched a crude, sharpened piece of metal, her knuckles white as she gripped it.

"Who... who are you?" Mara asked, her hand instinctively tightening on the grip of her sidearm, her voice steady despite the sudden surge of adrenaline.

The woman's lips peeled back in a rictus that might have been a smile, but looked more like a grimace of pain, her teeth bared like a cornered animal's. "Visitors," she rasped, her voice like dry leaves skittering across pavement, a sound scraped raw by disuse and hardship. "You're... very late." The words hung in the humid air, laced with an unspoken weight, a chilling harbinger of the secrets that lay hidden within the dilapidated outpost, and the true nature of the Southern Wetlands, which had only just begun to reveal itself.

The weathered door of the outpost, a relic of a forgotten era of scientific endeavor, hissed open, revealing not the sterile interior Mara had half-expected, but a tableau of desperation. The woman standing before them, gaunt and wild-eyed, was their first clue that their reception would be anything but welcoming. Yet, beneath the layers of grime and frayed nerves, Mara saw the potential for something more than mere survival. This was a place where resilience was forged in the crucible of an unforgiving environment, and the individuals who had weathered its storms were the very resources she needed.

Beyond the solitary figure who had emerged from the shadows, Mara began to assess the other occupants of the outpost. The initial chaos of their arrival, the jarring transition from the oppressive wetlands to the relative stillness of the hab-unit, had somewhat obscured the faces and forms of those who had been here, waiting. As her eyes adjusted to the dim, flickering emergency lights, she began to identify them, not as a unified front, but as distinct individuals, each bearing the unmistakable stamp of their prolonged exposure to the Southern Wetlands.

There was Silas, the botanist, whose gaunt frame seemed almost to have melded with the mutated flora he studied. His skin, pale and translucent, was crisscrossed with faint, vein-like patterns that mirrored the phosphorescent moss clinging to the outpost walls. His hands, though trembling, moved with an almost reverent precision as he carefully tended to a small, enclosed terrarium filled with specimens that pulsed with an eerie, internal luminescence. He spoke in hushed tones, his voice often dissolving into a wheezing cough, about the unique photosynthetic processes of the wetland flora, the astonishing adaptive mechanisms that allowed life to not just survive, but to *thrive* in conditions that would have annihilated terrestrial biology. He was a living testament to his own research, a walking, breathing example of the profound biological shifts occurring in this region. His expertise, Mara knew, would be invaluable in identifying edible or medicinal plants, and more importantly, in understanding the toxic elements that pervaded the ecosystem. He represented a deep, almost instinctual understanding of the biological landscape, a knowledge that no amount of sensor data could ever replicate. His fear was palpable, a constant tremor in his hands, but it was a fear born of profound respect for the forces he studied, not of outright terror.

Then there was Anya, the former military technician, a woman whose stoic demeanor and muscular build belied the weariness etched around her eyes. She moved with a quiet efficiency, her gaze sharp and assessing as she moved through the outpost, checking power conduits, recalibrating atmospheric processors, and ensuring the integrity of the hab-units' seals. Her hands, calloused and scarred, were equally adept at wielding a plasma cutter or repairing a delicate comms array. Anya had a no-nonsense approach to problem-solving, her pragmatic mindset a vital counterbalance to Silas's more esoteric pursuits. She had seen conflict, had faced down threats both human and environmental, and her presence brought a much-needed sense of grounded capability to the expedition. Her fear was a tightly coiled spring, a readiness for action, an acknowledgment of danger that never tipped into panic. She was the steady hand, the one who ensured their technology, however battered, remained functional. Her loyalty, Mara suspected, was as unshakeable as the reinforced plating of their expedition vehicles.

And finally, there was Kael, the scout, a man as elusive and enigmatic as the wetlands themselves. He was a creature of the periphery, his movements fluid and silent, his eyes perpetually scanning, his ears attuned to the subtlest shifts in the ambient sounds of the ecosystem. Kael had an uncanny ability to navigate the treacherous terrain, to read the land like a seasoned tracker, anticipating dangers before they manifested. He possessed a quiet confidence, born not of arrogance, but of a deep-seated self-reliance. He rarely spoke, preferring to communicate through gestures and sharp, concise reports delivered in a low, gravelly voice. His past was a closed book, hinted at only by the hardened lines of his face and the watchful intensity in his gaze. He was the one who could melt into the shadows, who could move unseen and unheard, the vital eyes and ears of their operation in this alien landscape. His fear was a constant companion, a heightened awareness that kept him alive, but it was a controlled, almost elemental fear, like that of a predator aware of its environment. He trusted his instincts above all else, and Mara had learned to trust them too.

These were the individuals Mara had gathered, drawn from the scattered remnants of humanity that still clung to existence in the shadow of the Glassborne affliction. They were not soldiers, not hardened veterans of a unified front, but survivors, each bearing the indelible marks of their struggle. They were a motley crew, a collection of disparate skills and tempered personalities, united by a shared purpose: to reach the rumored sanctuary in the north, and to uncover the truth behind the affliction that had reshaped their world.

Mara observed them now, their interactions, the subtle cues of their relationships. Silas, despite his frailty, would sometimes engage Anya in hushed, technical debates about environmental controls, their voices a low murmur against the hum of the failing life support systems. Anya, in turn, would occasionally offer Silas a rare, gruff word of encouragement, a gesture of respect for his dedication. Kael, true to his nature, remained largely separate, a solitary figure often found perched on the highest accessible vantage point, his gaze fixed on the distant, mist-shrouded horizon. Yet, when Mara needed him, he was there, appearing as if from nowhere, his reports delivered with an almost unnerving accuracy.

Their trust in Mara was not blind, but earned. It had been forged in the crucible of shared hardship, in the moments when their collective will had overcome seemingly insurmountable odds. They had seen her make difficult choices, had witnessed her unwavering resolve in the face of despair. They knew she carried the weight of their collective future on her shoulders, and they were willing to follow her lead, to place their faith in her judgment, even as the wetlands pressed in, threatening to swallow them whole.

"The readings from the outer perimeter are... concerning," Elias stated, his voice a low hum through their comms, the echo of his earlier scientific pronouncements still hanging in the air. His bio-sensors, meticulously calibrated, had been working overtime since their arrival, registering anomalous energy signatures and a complex cocktail of airborne pathogens that defied conventional classification. He had joined them at the outpost, a man of pure intellect, driven by an insatiable curiosity to understand the 'why' of this ravaged world, even as he struggled to survive its harsh realities. He was the bridge between their immediate needs and the larger scientific mysteries of the Glassborne affliction, his mind a repository of theoretical knowledge that was now being tested against the brutal, tangible evidence of a world gone mad.

"Define concerning, Elias," Mara replied, her voice calm, projecting a confidence she didn't entirely feel. The woman who had greeted them, who had introduced herself as Elara, had been tight-lipped, her words clipped and evasive, offering little in the way of explanation for their presence or their isolation. Elara was clearly a survivor, hardened by years of solitude, her distrust a palpable barrier. But Mara sensed there was more to her than mere suspicion. There was a deep-seated weariness, a resignation that bordered on despair, which suggested a history far more complex than simple self-preservation.

"The spectral analysis of the atmosphere indicates a significant increase in mutated microbial agents, Commander," Elias continued, his voice laced with a familiar, almost academic, urgency. "Some are exhibiting bio-luminescent properties and generating localized electromagnetic fields. They appear to be... interacting with the environment on a quantum level, altering the very fabric of the local ecosystem." He paused, as if struggling to articulate the sheer impossibility of what he was observing. "It's as if the very air is alive, not just with life, but with a form of... consciousness. A collective biological intelligence reacting to external stimuli."

Anya, who had been meticulously cleaning and reassembling a salvaged pulse rifle, looked up, her brow furrowed. "Consciousness? You're saying the air itself is thinking, Elias?"

"Not in a way we would recognize as human consciousness, Anya," Silas interjected, his voice raspy but firm. He had emerged from the shadows, his pale hands still stained with the vibrant hues of his samples. "Think of it more as a networked biological response. The entire wetland ecosystem, from the smallest microbe to the largest mutated organism, is interconnected. The Glassborne affliction, rather than simply destroying, has acted as a catalyst, a unifying force, creating a vast, interconnected biological network. The energy signatures are the byproduct of this colossal, planet-wide cellular communication."

Kael, who had been observing from his perch near the reinforced viewport, finally spoke, his voice a low rumble that cut through the ambient hum. "It watches. It feels. And it learns." His words, simple and stark, carried an weight that settled heavily on the small group. He had been observing the subtle shifts in the environment, the way the flora seemed to react to their presence, the unnatural stillness that sometimes preceded a surge of predatory activity.

Mara turned to Elara, who had remained on the fringes of their discussion, her expression unreadable. "Elara, you've been here for... how long? You must have observed these phenomena. What do you know about them?"

Elara's gaze flickered, her eyes darting towards the shimmering, distorted atmosphere visible through the viewport. "I know it's hungry," she said, her voice a dry whisper. "It feels everything. And when it feels... it takes." She clutched the sharpened metal rod tighter, her knuckles whitening. "It takes what it needs. And it always needs more."

The unspoken implication hung heavy in the air. Their arrival had not gone unnoticed. They were intruders in a world that was not merely hostile, but sentient, a colossal organism that was aware of their presence. The hope for a safe haven, for a respite from the relentless dangers of the Southern Wetlands, began to feel like a cruel illusion. They were not simply trying to survive the environment; they were trying to survive the environment's awareness of them.

Mara took a deep breath, the recycled air doing little to calm the sudden surge of adrenaline coursing through her veins. The team she had assembled, each member a specialist in their own right, now faced a challenge that transcended mere survival. They were up against a force that was not only physically dangerous but also possessed a terrifying, alien intelligence.

"We need to understand this 'hunger,' Elara," Mara stated, her voice steady and resolute. "We need to know what it wants, and how to give it what it needs, or how to deny it. Silas, I need you to analyze the composition of these atmospheric agents, understand their metabolic processes. Elias, I need precise readings on the energy fluctuations, any patterns, any vulnerabilities. Anya, I need you to fortify this outpost. Make it as secure as possible, and prepare our equipment for immediate deployment. Kael, you are our eyes. Continue your observations. Report any changes, any unusual activity. We need to know what we're dealing with, and we need to know it yesterday."

Her gaze swept over each of them, a silent acknowledgment of the immense task ahead. Their hopes were pinned on reaching the northern sanctuary, a distant promise of safety. But the path to that sanctuary was guarded by a living, breathing ecosystem that seemed to actively resist their passage. Their fears were no longer just about mutated beasts or environmental hazards; they were about an intelligence that could outmaneuver, outthink, and ultimately, consume them.

"Commander," Anya interrupted, her voice a low growl, "the power core is failing. It won't last another cycle without significant repair. And Elara's salvaged equipment... it's rudimentary at best."

Mara nodded, acknowledging the grim reality. "Then we make do with what we have. Elias, Silas, can you interface with her systems? Can you scavenge enough parts to stabilize it, even temporarily?"

Elias, already poring over a flickering datapad, replied, "It's possible. Her power conduits are ancient, but the fundamental principles of energy transfer remain. Silas might be able to identify bio-conductive materials that could serve as makeshift replacements for failing components. It will be a patchwork solution, but it might buy us time."

Time. That was the most precious commodity in this forgotten corner of the world. Time to understand, time to adapt, time to survive. The marshaling of her team was not just about assigning tasks; it was about reinforcing their collective will, about reminding them that even in the face of an incomprehensible adversary, they were not alone. They had each other, their skills, and a shared, desperate hope for a future. The Southern Wetlands had thrown its most formidable challenge at them yet, and Mara knew, with a chilling certainty, that their true test had only just begun. The silence that followed her pronouncements was not one of defeat, but of focused resolve. Each member of her team, from the frail botanist to the enigmatic scout, understood the stakes. They were a disparate collection of survivors, but they were

her team, and together, they would face whatever the wetlands threw at them, for as long as they could. The weight of their collective survival rested not just on Mara's leadership, but on the unique strengths and unwavering loyalty of each individual she had gathered around her.

The hum of failing life support systems was a constant, mournful counterpoint to Elara's hushed, almost reverent words. Mara listened, her gaze fixed on the spectral analysis Elias had projected onto a smudged, portable screen. The data, a cascade of unfamiliar waveforms and fluctuating energy readings, painted a picture of an ecosystem alive in a way that defied all known biological principles. Silas, hunched beside Elias, traced a pattern on the screen with a trembling finger, his eyes wide with a mixture of scientific fascination and primal dread. Anya, ever practical, continued her meticulous work on the pulse rifle, her movements economical and precise, a bulwark of calm in the rising tide of apprehension. Kael, a shadow at the edge of the dim light, remained observant, his stillness a testament to his awareness of the ever-present, unseen threats.

"The objective remains the same," Mara stated, her voice cutting through the hushed tension. She met each of their eyes, her own holding a steady, unwavering resolve. "We are here to find the LUCENT facility." The name itself felt heavy, laden with the weight of past failures and the burden of their current desperation. It was more than just a derelict research site; it was their best, perhaps their only, hope. The sky-static, that ubiquitous, insidious blight that had fractured their world, and the Glassborne mutation, its horrifying offspring, remained largely mysteries. Theories abounded, whispered in hushed tones in the meager safety of scattered outposts, but concrete evidence, the kind that could lead to understanding, let alone a cure, was terrifyingly scarce. LUCENT, however, was rumored to be the nexus of the research that had preceded the catastrophe, a place where the initial experiments, the misguided attempts to harness unknown energies, had taken place. If anywhere, it was there that the answers lay buried, amidst the wreckage of ambition and hubris.

"LUCENT," Elias echoed, his voice tinged with a weary awe. "The 'Lunar Exosomatic Calibration and Unification Experimentation Nexus.' A grand name for what I suspect is now little more than a tomb." He gestured to the screen. "The energy signatures emanating from this region, the complex organic compounds Silas has begun to identify in the air, the very anomalies that Elias's sensors are screaming about... they all point towards a deliberate, highly concentrated source. A source that existed before the widespread ecological collapse. This facility... it was the epicenter." His brow furrowed, his mind already sifting through reams of theoretical data. "They were attempting to... what? Interface with something? Control it? The records are fragmented, buried deep in encrypted archives that even the most advanced retrieval systems struggled with. But the recurring themes are clear: harnessing atmospheric energies, studying extraterrestrial biological agents, and, crucially, attempting to unify disparate life forms. It's all there, in the fragmented logs we managed to pull before the network collapsed. A catastrophic ambition, it seems."

Silas nodded, his gaze distant. "The bio-luminescence we are seeing, the intricate signaling between organisms... it's reminiscent of the early theoretical models of inter-species communication that LUCENT's lead researchers were exploring. They believed they could foster a symbiotic relationship between Earth's flora and fauna, perhaps even an entirely new form of engineered life, by manipulating specific atmospheric frequencies and bio-energetic fields. They were playing with forces they didn't fully comprehend, trying to force nature into a mold that was not its own. The Glassborne affliction... it's the unintended consequence, the terrifying manifestation of their unchecked ambition." He coughed, a dry, hacking sound that seemed to shake his fragile frame. "The very ecosystem around us is a testament to their folly. The interconnectedness, the almost sentient response to our presence... it feels like a direct, albeit corrupted, echo of their intended designs. They sought to unify, and in doing so, they created a monstrous, singular entity."

Mara's gaze remained steady, though a knot of unease tightened in her stomach. "The objective is not to judge the past, Silas, but to learn from it. The facility is believed to house the core research data, the experimental logs, the raw sensor readings from the initial phases of their work. If we can access that, if we can understand the genesis of the sky-static and the Glassborne mutation, then perhaps... perhaps we can find a way to reverse it. Or at least, to survive it more effectively." She looked at Kael, who had been silently observing the wetlands through the reinforced viewport. "Kael, your reconnaissance before we arrived indicated a strong possibility of the facility's location within this sector, a heavily concentrated energy signature consistent with their known experimental output. Can you confirm?"

Kael's eyes, sharp and focused, met hers. "The signature is there, Commander," he confirmed, his voice a low, gravelly rumble. "Faint, almost masked by the ambient bio-energy of the wetlands, but persistent. It's shielded, deep within the densest part of the swamp, where the water is stagnant and the flora is... particularly aggressive. Navigation will be... challenging." He paused, his gaze drifting towards the shimmering, distorted haze that perpetually clung to the horizon. "The wetlands are active. They are aware. And whatever is at the heart of this place, it's broadcasting a signal that the environment is amplifying. It's a beacon. And it feels... hungry."

"Hungry," Elara repeated, her voice barely a whisper, the word carrying a chilling resonance. She had remained largely silent, a specter observing their grim deliberations, but the word seemed to strike a nerve. "They fed it, you know. Their experiments. They fed the static, they fed the mutation. They thought they were controlling it, shaping it. They were wrong. They were just... providing the ingredients." Her eyes, haunted and distant, seemed to look through the reinforced walls, as if seeing the ghosts of the scientists who had once toiled within the LUCENT facility. "They sought to create a new form of life, a unified consciousness. They succeeded, in a way. But not as they intended. They created a predator. And it's been waiting for a long, long time."

Mara forced herself to push aside the gnawing sense of dread. Elara's words, while grim, only reinforced the urgency of their mission. The LUCENT facility was not merely a repository of information; it was likely the origin point, the source from which this all-consuming biological intelligence had begun to spread. To reach it meant navigating a treacherous, perhaps sentient, environment.

"Anya," Mara's voice was firm, her gaze shifting to the technician. "We need to prepare for deployment. Kael's assessment suggests the facility is deep within the most hazardous zone. We'll need the submersible drones, the atmospheric processors, and every piece of portable defensive equipment we have. We don't know what we'll encounter, but we can assume it won't be welcoming."

Anya nodded, her hands stilling on the pulse rifle. "Understood, Commander. I'll begin prepping the cargo bays. The drones have a limited operational range in these energy-saturated conditions, but their sensor suites are our best bet for pinpointing the facility's exact location once we're closer. I'll also double-check the integrity of the atmospheric scrubbers on the exosuits. If Silas's readings are accurate, we'll be breathing highly volatile compounds."

"Silas," Mara continued, "I need you to compile a comprehensive list of any flora or fauna in this region that exhibits extreme toxicity or unusual bio-energetic properties. We need to know what to avoid, and what might be... weaponized against us. And Elias, I need you to refine your scans. Focus on any anomalies that deviate from the established bio-energetic field of the wetlands. Any localized pockets of intense energy, any unusual spectral patterns that suggest artificial construction or a concentrated source of power. We're looking for a needle in a haystack, and this haystack is actively trying to swallow us whole."

Elias, his fingers flying across the datapad, responded, "I am already cross-referencing all available historical LUCENT research parameters with current atmospheric and geological data. The energy signature Kael detected is unlike anything naturally occurring in this biome. It's too... structured. Too consistent. It suggests active containment fields, power conduits... remnants of advanced technology that should have degraded by now. Unless... unless it's being maintained. Or amplified."

The implication hung heavy in the air. The facility wasn't just abandoned; it might be... operational. Or at least, its systems were being fed by the very ecosystem they were trying to understand. A chilling thought.

"Then our task is twofold," Mara declared, her voice resolute. "First, we locate the LUCENT facility. Second, we determine its current status and access the data within. Elara," she turned to the woman, her gaze softening slightly. "You've survived here longer than any of us. You know this place. What else can you tell us about the wetlands, about how they react to intrusion? What are the greatest dangers we haven't considered?"

Elara shifted, her eyes sweeping over the team, her expression a mixture of resignation and a flicker of something akin to reluctant hope. "The greatest danger is not the creatures that stalk the shadows, Commander," she said, her voice raspy. "It's the ground beneath your feet. The water that laps at your boots. The air you breathe. The wetlands are a single, vast organism. The Glassborne affliction didn't just mutate life; it unified it. They are all connected. The roots of the trees, the spores in the air, the very water itself... it all shares a consciousness. They feel you. They sense your intentions. And if they sense... fear, or aggression, or if you try to take something they consider their own... they will retaliate. Not with teeth and claws, but with the environment itself. The paths disappear. The ground liquefies. The air becomes a poison. The whispers you hear in the wind... they are not just wind. They are the collective thoughts of this entire place. It learns. It adapts. And it remembers."

"And the facility?" Mara pressed. "What about the facility itself? Is it separate from the wetlands, or integrated?"

Elara looked towards the viewport, her gaze fixed on a distant, almost imperceptible shimmer in the oppressive humidity. "It was the heart. The source. They tried to contain it, to control it, but they only fed it. The structures are deep, anchored into the bedrock, shielded. But the energy... it seeps out. It nourishes the corruption. The wetlands protect it. They are its... children, in a twisted sort of way. They respond to its presence. It pulses, and they surge. It weakens, and they draw back. It is the sun around which this entire corrupted world revolves. If you go there, Commander, you are going into the belly of the beast. And the beast is aware."

Mara nodded, absorbing the dire pronouncements. The LUCENT facility was not merely a ruin to be explored; it was likely a living, breathing entity, a nexus of power that had fundamentally reshaped the world around it. The data they sought was likely buried deep within its corrupted core, guarded by the very ecosystem it had birthed. The objective was clear, but the path to achieving it was now fraught with a far more profound and terrifying danger than they had initially anticipated. They were not just seeking answers; they were venturing into the heart of the affliction itself. The expedition into the Southern Wetlands had just taken on a chilling new dimension. The promise of discovery was now inextricably bound to the grim reality of confronting the source of their world's destruction.

CHAPTER SIX

ECHOES IN THE ABANDONED LAB

The air hung thick and cloying, a miasma of decay and something else, something unnervingly vital. Elias's atmospheric processors, usually a reassuring hum of synthesized clean air, struggled against the oppressive humidity, their intakes clogged with spores and particulate matter that defied easy classification. Each breath felt like drawing sludge into their lungs, a constant reminder of the alien metabolism of the Southern Wetlands. Mara, leading the small, heavily armed team, felt a prickle of unease crawl up her spine, a primal instinct honed by years of survival. Kael, a phantom in the swirling mists ahead, had signaled their approach. The energy signature Elias had been tracking had intensified, coalescing into a focused beacon that seemed to thrum beneath the swamp's surface.

"Hold," Mara commanded, her voice a low growl that barely cut through the ambient symphony of buzzing insects and the unnerving slithering sounds that emanated from the murky depths. The team froze, their exosuits, the only barrier between them and the hostile environment, hissing softly as they compensated for the shift in atmospheric pressure. Anya, her hand resting on the grip of her pulse rifle, scanned their immediate surroundings, her eyes darting from the gnarled, moss-draped branches of ancient trees to the dark, still water that lapped at the edges of their makeshift landing zone. Silas, his face pale and drawn, consulted a flickering handheld scanner, his brow furrowed in concentration.

"The readings are off the charts, Commander," Silas reported, his voice strained. "The energy signature is localized, concentrated. It's emanating from directly ahead, approximately two hundred meters. The bio-energetic field here is... saturated. It's almost as if the wetlands are actively channeling energy towards a central point."

Elias, hunched over a portable sensor array, nodded in agreement. "The spectral analysis shows a unique pattern, Commander. It's consistent with advanced power containment and distribution systems, but incredibly degraded. Yet, simultaneously, there are organic energy fluctuations that are unnaturally high, almost as if the facility is... drawing power from the surrounding life forms. It's a paradox. Ancient technology being sustained by a nascent, corrupted ecosystem."

Kael reappeared from the haze, his silhouette a stark contrast against the ethereal glow of bioluminescent fungi clinging to the decaying vegetation. "The vegetation is impossibly dense," he reported, his voice a low rumble. "It's not just thick; it's... interwoven. Like a living tapestry. There are no discernible paths, no clearings. But the signal... it's strongest there." He gestured with his chin towards a particularly choked section of the swamp, where the canopy seemed to press down even harder, the air shimmering with an almost palpable density.

As they advanced, the sounds of the swamp began to shift. The incessant drone of insects diminished, replaced by a profound, unnerving silence that seemed to absorb all other noise. The air grew colder, a stark contrast to the oppressive heat of the outer wetlands, carrying with it the faint, metallic tang of ozone. Elara, who had been walking in a daze, her eyes unfocused, suddenly stopped. Her head snapped up, and a look of profound recognition flickered across her gaunt features.

"Here," she whispered, her voice barely audible. "This is it. I can... I can feel it. It's like a phantom limb, a memory etched into the very marrow of this place."

Following Elara's gaze, the team emerged into a small, choked clearing. The oppressive vegetation receded, revealing not a grand entrance or a stark, imposing structure, but something far more insidious. Before them, partially submerged in the stagnant, black water, was a colossal, organic-looking structure. It wasn't built; it had seemingly

grown. Vast, obsidian-like tendrils, thick as ancient trees, snaked out from a central mass, anchoring themselves deep into the swamp bed. The surface was a riot of corroded metal, fused with what appeared to be calcified organic matter, all encrusted with layers of thick, slimy moss and shimmering, phosphorescent fungi. It was a monument to a forgotten, dangerous ambition, a testament to a past that had warped and twisted into the horrifying present.

The structure was not simply overgrown; it was *integrated*. The swamp had claimed it, consumed it, and in doing so, had made it an inseparable part of itself. The tendrils of the building seemed to merge seamlessly with the colossal roots of the surrounding trees, blurring the line between the artificial and the natural. The water around the facility was unnaturally still, reflecting the distorted, grey sky like a polished obsidian mirror, disturbed only by the occasional, silent ripple that suggested unseen movement beneath the surface. A low, resonant hum, barely perceptible, vibrated through the ground, a silent pulse that Elara had referred to as the "heartbeat" of the corrupted world.

"By the Founders," Elias breathed, his eyes wide with a mixture of awe and horror. "It's... it's magnificent. And terrifying. The structural integrity is compromised in countless places, yet it remains standing. It's as if the swamp itself is holding it together, supporting it." He pointed to a section where a massive, corroded metal panel seemed to be fused with a pulsating, bioluminescent growth. "Look. The facility's original construction materials are clearly visible, but they've been... assimilated. The organic matter is not just growing *on* it; it's growing *through* it. The bio-energetic field is strongest here, radiating outwards from this central mass."

Mara's gaze swept over the alien architecture, her mind racing to process the implications. This wasn't just a research lab; it was a tomb, a monument to an ambition so profound it had irrevocably scarred the planet. The sheer scale of the structure, even in its degraded state, was staggering. It spoke of a wealth of resources, a level of technological advancement that dwarfed anything they currently possessed. And the silence... the utter, suffocating silence was more unnerving than any alarm or warning siren could have been. It was the silence of ages, the silence of forgotten secrets, a silence pregnant with the weight of untold stories.

"It's a containment unit," Silas murmured, his scanner still whirring. "Or it *was*. They were trying to house something here, to study it. The energy readings suggest extremely high-yield experimental apparatus, shielded and isolated. But the containment has failed. Spectacularly." He tapped a section of his scanner, his expression grim. "The residual energy signatures are indicative of extreme biological and atmospheric manipulation. They weren't just researching; they were *creating*. And whatever they created... it broke free."

Anya adjusted her grip on her rifle, her gaze sharp and analytical. "It's a perfect camouflage. Even with the energy signature, I can see how easy it would be to miss. The vegetation, the way it's integrated... it's designed to be hidden. Or perhaps, it simply evolved to blend in once its original purpose was... corrupted." She pointed towards a series of thick, vine-like structures that seemed to be slowly moving, almost imperceptibly, along the facility's exterior. "Are those... part of the building, or part of the swamp?"

Kael, ever the silent observer, stepped closer to the edge of the water, his senses on high alert. "They are part of both," he stated, his voice low. "The facility is the anchor. The swamp is the manifestation. They are one and the same now. The energy radiating from the structure is... feeding the growth. And the growth, in turn, is protecting the structure. It's a symbiotic relationship, Commander. A parasitic one, perhaps, for us."

Elara, her voice barely a whisper, added, "They thought they were scientists. They thought they were pioneers. But they were children playing with fire. They opened a door they couldn't close. They called it LUCENT... Lunar Exosomatic Calibration and Unification Experimentation Nexus. They wanted to unify life, to control it, to create something new. They succeeded, in a way. They created *this*. They created the hunger."

Mara felt a chill that had nothing to do with the damp air. The objective had been to find the facility, to access its data. Now, standing before this monstrous edifice, she understood that it was more than just a derelict research site. It was the heart of the plague, the source from which the sky-static and the Glassborne mutation had spilled forth. The silence of the wetlands was not an absence of sound; it was a deliberate, watchful stillness. The facility wasn't just abandoned; it was dormant, a sleeping titan whose slumber they had just disturbed. The air crackled with an unseen energy, a latent power that promised both the answers they sought and the destruction they feared.

"Elias, Silas, get the portable sensors deployed," Mara ordered, her voice firm, cutting through the oppressive quiet. "We need to map the immediate area. Anya, Kael, secure our perimeter. Elara, stay close. We don't know what's inside, but based on what we're seeing, it's likely... still active."

As Elias and Silas began to set up their equipment, the ground beneath their feet vibrated with a more pronounced hum. The bioluminescent fungi on the facility's surface pulsed with a brighter, more insistent light. The dark water, previously still, began to churn with slow, deliberate eddies. The wetlands were not merely aware of their presence; they were reacting. The sanctuary of forgotten knowledge had revealed itself, but it offered no welcome, only a silent, potent warning. The true danger, they now understood, lay not just in what they would find within the facility's decaying walls, but in the very act of seeking it out, of intruding upon a slumbering, corrupted power. The LUCENT facility was not just a discovery; it was a confrontation.

The viscous air, still heavy with the scent of decay and an unsettling, metallic tang, pressed in on Elias and Silas as they painstakingly deployed their portable sensor arrays. The ground, a spongy, nutrient-rich loam, seemed to absorb the crunch of their boots, muffling their movements. Before them, the colossal, organic-metallic edifice of LUCENT loomed, its surface a testament to the slow, insidious embrace of the Southern Wetlands. It was a structure that had been *grown* as much as built, its obsidian-like tendrils merging seamlessly with the gnarled roots of ancient, swamp-choked trees, blurring the line between the artificial and the terrifyingly natural. The water at its base, black and still, reflected the bruised, grey sky with a mirror-like sheen, disturbed only by the occasional, languid ripple that hinted at unseen life beneath its surface.

"The ambient energy field is still fluctuating wildly," Elias murmured, his fingers flying across the holographic interface of his primary scanner. "But it's coalescing now, focusing on specific points within the structure. It's like the building itself is breathing, pulsing with residual power. The bio-energetic feedback loop Silas detected earlier is even more pronounced now that we're closer. The facility is definitely drawing sustenance from the surrounding ecosystem. It's... parasitic, in a way. Feeding on the life force of the wetlands." He gestured towards a section where a massive, corroded metal panel was visibly fused with a pulsating, bioluminescent growth, its sickly green light casting an eerie glow on the surrounding slime-encrusted surfaces. "The assimilation is almost complete in some areas. It's as if the swamp itself is a bloodstream, pumping life into this... this husk."

Silas, his face a mask of grim concentration, adjusted the calibration on his own scanner, a more specialized device designed to detect residual bio-signatures and atmospheric contaminants. "The atmospheric processors on the exterior are long gone, or at least completely overwhelmed," he reported, his voice tight. "The air quality readings inside the structure are going to be... problematic, to say the least. We're detecting trace amounts of highly volatile compounds, complex organic molecules that don't correspond to any known terrestrial or exobiological life forms. And there's a significant presence of residual radiation, not from any conventional source, but something akin to a controlled, biological decay. It's... unnerving." He paused, his gaze sweeping over the seemingly inert, yet impossibly alive, façade of LUCENT. "The sheer scale of the failed containment is staggering. They weren't just conducting experiments; they were attempting to harness something fundamental, something that clearly fought back with extreme prejudice."

As Elias and Silas began their careful perimeter sweep, Anya and Kael established a defensible position on a slightly elevated hummock, their pulse rifles held at the ready. Anya's enhanced optical sensors, capable of piercing the dense foliage and atmospheric distortions, swept the area with practiced efficiency. "No immediate threats detected within our visible range, Commander," she reported, her voice calm and measured, a stark contrast to the palpable tension in the air. "But the ecological feedback is... intense. The vegetation is unnaturally vibrant in proximity to the structure, almost aggressively so. It's like a localized zone of accelerated growth. And the silence... it's not natural. It's too profound, too deliberate."

Kael, his movements fluid and economical, scouted the immediate vicinity, his enhanced senses attuned to the subtle shifts in the environment. He returned to Mara's side, his expression unreadable. "The structure's exterior is a labyrinth of fused metal and calcified organic matter," he stated, his voice a low rumble. "There are no obvious entry points, no visible doors or hatches that haven't been completely consumed by the swamp's growth. The 'tendrils' are thick, vascular structures, pulsing with a faint, internal luminescence. They seem to be integral to the facility's structural integrity, almost acting as its skeletal system and circulatory system combined." He paused, his gaze fixed on a particularly thick cluster of vine-like growths that seemed to writhe with a slow, almost imperceptible rhythm. "It's as if the building is alive, Commander. And whatever is happening inside, it's not dormant. It's... breathing."

Mara, her hand resting on the cold, reassuring metal of her sidearm, felt a prickle of dread crawl up her spine. The sheer alienness of the

LUCENT facility was overwhelming. It wasn't a derelict outpost; it was a cancerous growth, an anomaly that had fused with the very essence of the Southern Wetlands. The legends, the whispers of a "ghost of research" that had driven them to this remote, forgotten corner of the planet, now felt chillingly real. They were standing at the epicenter of a catastrophe, a place where scientific ambition had curdled into something monstrous.

"We need to find a way inside," Mara declared, her voice cutting through the oppressive silence. "Elias, Silas, focus your sensors on identifying any breaches, any structural weaknesses that could serve as an entry point. Anya, Kael, maintain your vigilance. Elara, stay close. You're our guide, but I need you alert."

Elara, who had been standing in a daze, her gaze fixed on the colossal structure, finally stirred. Her eyes, wide and haunted, met Mara's. "They tried to contain it," she whispered, her voice raspy, as if it had been unused for centuries. "They built this place to study something that defied understanding. They called it the 'Nexus.' A focal point for life's fundamental energies. They believed they could harness it, control it, even rewrite the very fabric of existence." She shivered, despite the oppressive humidity. "But they underestimated the universe. And they underestimated the resilience of life, even when twisted and corrupted."

Following Elara's direction, the team moved towards a section of the facility where the organic overgrowth seemed to recede slightly, revealing what appeared to be a collapsed section of the outer hull. Here, the corrosive fusion of metal and organic matter was less absolute, allowing for glimpses into the darkness within. The air emanating from the breach was even colder, carrying with it a faint, cloying sweetness that set Mara's teeth on edge.

"This is it," Elara breathed, pointing to a jagged tear in the obsidian-like plating, a gaping wound in the structure's hide. "The primary research wing. This is where the most... sensitive experiments were conducted."

Elias and Silas moved to assess the breach, their scanners humming with a renewed urgency. "The structural integrity here is compromised, but not completely failed," Elias reported, his voice tinged with a mixture of scientific curiosity and trepidation. "There's a significant atmospheric differential. The air inside is almost entirely devoid of oxygen, replaced by a volatile cocktail of methane, ammonia, and something else... something unidentifiable that's registering as a potent bio-toxin. We'll need full environmental suits, respirators, the works. And the radiation levels, while not immediately lethal, are significant enough to warrant extreme caution."

Silas tapped a reading on his handheld device. "There are also traces of exotic matter decay. Very faint, but present. Consistent with the kind of energies they were reportedly trying to manipulate. It's a ghost of the research, Commander. A spectral echo of whatever they were doing here."

As they prepared to enter the breach, a low, guttural moan, like the groan of tortured metal and tortured flesh, echoed from within the facility. The bioluminescent fungi on the exterior pulsed with a synchronized, intensified light, and the water at the base of the structure churned with a more violent agitation. The wetlands were not merely reacting to their presence; they were responding to a disturbance deep within the heart of LUCENT.

"It's awake," Elara whispered, her eyes wide with a primal fear. "Or at least, parts of it are."

Mara tightened her grip on her rifle. "Anya, Kael, cover our entry. Elias, Silas, you're with me. Elara, you're right behind us. We move fast, we stay alert, and we don't touch anything we don't have to. This is no longer just about recovering data. This is about understanding how deeply the rot has set in."

Stepping through the breach was like passing through a veil into another dimension. The air inside the facility was shockingly cold, a deep, penetrating chill that seemed to seep through their exosuits. The sweet, cloying scent intensified, mixed with the sharp, acrid odor of ozone and something akin to rotting fruit. Their helmet lamps cut through the absolute darkness, revealing a scene of utter devastation.

They were in what appeared to be a grand atrium, or at least, it had been. Now, it was a ruin. Massive support pillars, once sleek and polished, were cracked and warped, many of them engulfed by the same pulsating, bioluminescent growths that covered the exterior. The ceiling, impossibly high, was a latticework of corroded metal and tangled, vine-like growths, dripping with a viscous, dark fluid that pooled on the floor below. The entire space was a testament to hurried abandonment, a snapshot of catastrophic failure frozen in time.

"Central hub, research wing," Elias confirmed, his voice hushed with awe and horror. "The energy readings are off the charts. The core containment field must have been located somewhere around here. It's completely collapsed, but the residual energies are still immense. It's like standing inside a dying star."

Scattered across the floor were the spectral remnants of scientific ambition. overturned consoles, their screens cracked and dark, consoles spewing forth bundles of frayed wires like severed arteries. Datapads lay scattered, their surfaces coated in a thick layer of dust and what looked like dried organic slime. The equipment was sophisticated, far beyond anything currently in use by the Alliance. Gleaming chrome and polished composites, now dulled and corroded by time and the pervasive, alien environment.

"Look at this," Silas murmured, pointing his lamp at a large, cylindrical containment unit that had toppled over, its thick, reinforced glass shattered. Inside, a viscous, inky substance had congealed, resembling a petrified nightmare. "This was designed to house something... extraordinary. The energy readings from within that unit are still registering. It's as if the very essence of whatever was held there has imprinted itself onto the surrounding materials."

Anya, her rifle sweeping the cavernous space, noted the eerie stillness. "No signs of biological activity, not that we can detect anyway," she reported. "But the silence is... it's heavy. It feels watched. Every shadow seems to hold a hidden threat."

Elara stumbled forward, her gaze fixed on a partially obscured workstation. "Dr. Aris Thorne," she whispered, her voice choked with emotion, recognizing a name etched onto a corroded plaque. "He was the lead bio-engineer. He believed... he truly believed he was on the cusp of unlocking the secrets of cellular regeneration. He wanted to achieve immortality, to transcend the limitations of the flesh." She gestured vaguely at the surrounding ruin. "He helped create this. He was one of the architects of its downfall."

As they cautiously advanced, they entered what appeared to be a series of interconnected laboratories. Each one was a tableau of scientific endeavor abruptly halted. A dissection table, stained with what could have been blood or some other organic fluid, held a scatter of instruments, frozen mid-use. Test tubes, filled with bizarre, unidentifiable substances, lay scattered on countertops, some cracked, others sealed. In one lab, a holographic projector flickered weakly, projecting a distorted, ghostly image of a complex molecular structure onto a dust-laden wall, a fleeting glimpse of the knowledge that had once been pursued here.

"These are research notes," Elias said, carefully picking up a brittle, yellowed document from a console. The script was precise, scientific, but the content was increasingly fragmented and frantic. He read aloud, his voice a low murmur, "'...unforeseen metabolic acceleration... rapid adaptation of host tissue... the energy matrix is self-sustaining... we've lost containment... it's evolving faster than we can track...'" He dropped the document as if it had burned him. "They knew. They knew it was going wrong, but they were too deep to stop. Too invested."

Silas, meanwhile, was examining a complex piece of machinery, a towering apparatus of polished metal and glowing conduits, now darkened and inert. "This was a bio-energy converter," he explained, his voice strained. "Designed to tap into and amplify biological energy signatures. If the rumors are true, they were trying to harness... something from beyond. Something ancient and powerful. The NEXUS was meant to be the conduit, the focal point. But whatever they connected to... it was too much. It overran the system. It *became* the system."

The spectral nature of the research was palpable. It wasn't just the scattered notes and defunct equipment; it was the very atmosphere of the place. It felt like walking through a ghost of what once was, a place where ambition and hubris had collided with cosmic forces, leaving behind only echoes and a chilling warning. Each room they explored told a story of a desperate, frantic retreat, of scientists abandoning their work, their lives, as something unimaginable broke free.

"They weren't just researching; they were *inviting*," Elara said, her voice barely above a whisper, her eyes wide with a dawning comprehension. "The LUCENT experiment wasn't about control; it was about connection. They wanted to bridge the gap between different forms of existence, to understand the fundamental 'language' of life. But they opened a door to something that spoke a language of consumption and transformation. They didn't create life; they unleashed a predator that assimilates and corrupts."

As they moved deeper into the complex, the hum of the facility grew more pronounced, no longer a faint vibration but a low, resonant thrum that seemed to emanate from the very core of the structure. The bioluminescent growths pulsed with greater intensity, casting long, distorted shadows that danced like spectral figures in their helmet lamps. The air grew colder still, and the oppressive silence was now punctuated by faint, skittering sounds, the subtle movement of unseen things in the darkness.

Mara's gaze swept over the desolation, a grim understanding settling upon her. The "ghost of research" wasn't just a metaphor. It was the lingering, toxic essence of a project that had gone horrifically wrong, a testament to the dangers of unchecked scientific curiosity. The LUCENT facility was a monument to hubris, a tomb of lost knowledge, and the chilling realization dawned on her: they had not merely stumbled upon a derelict lab; they had stepped into the heart of a slumbering, corrupted consciousness. The data they sought was here, buried within the spectral echoes of a failed experiment, but retrieving it would mean confronting the very forces that had led to the downfall of its creators, and perhaps, to their own. The mission had just become infinitely more perilous.

The central atrium, a vast expanse of corroded metal and fungal overgrowth, served as their initial gateway into the derelict heart of LUCENT. Each step deeper into the structure was a descent into a chilling testament to ambition gone awry. The air, thick with the cloying scent of decay and an unsettling sweetness, seemed to cling to their environmental suits, a constant reminder of the alienness that had permeated this place. As Elias and Silas scanned the immediate surroundings, their instruments painted a grim picture of systematic failure.

"Commander, I'm picking up unusual energy signatures, highly localized," Elias reported, his voice a low rumble through the comms. "They're not consistent with any known energy source, organic or synthetic. They're... patterned. Almost like a residual broadcast, but incredibly faint. And fragmented." He adjusted a dial on his console, his brow furrowed behind his visor. "There are also pockets of temporal distortion. Tiny ones, barely measurable, but present. Like ripples in the fabric of spacetime."

Silas, his attention focused on a series of what looked like diagnostic readouts, chimed in. "My atmospheric sensors are still showing anomalous compounds, but I'm also detecting trace elements of exotic particles. Particles that don't occur naturally. They're consistent with high-energy particle collisions, but the decay signatures are... wrong. They imply a containment failure on a fundamental level." He pointed his sensor array towards a darkened alcove, where the organic growth seemed particularly dense. "The readings are strongest in that direction. It's like... like something was trying to break through, and the system couldn't handle it. It left scars."

Mara gestured for the team to advance cautiously. Anya and Kael, their rifles held at the ready, fanned out, their enhanced senses scanning the shadows. Elara, her face pale and drawn even behind her helmet, pointed a trembling finger towards a series of consoles embedded into a partially collapsed wall. "That section," she whispered, her voice strained. "That's where they monitored the 'outreach' protocols. The attempts to... to communicate."

The consoles were a chaotic mess of shattered screens and sparking wires, their once-gleaming surfaces now dulled by a thick film of dust and alien slime. Elias, with the utmost care, began to interface his portable data retrieval unit with a miraculously intact auxiliary port. The process was agonizingly slow, the ancient systems fighting against his attempts to access their long-dormant memory banks.

"This is incredible," Elias breathed, as slivers of data began to coalesce on his display. "They weren't just studying some passive energy field. They were actively trying to establish contact. They believed they had found a way to project consciousness, to interact with something beyond our physical dimension. The 'Nexus' they referred to... it wasn't just a conduit; it was an antenna, designed to send and receive signals across... what? Unfathomable distances? Other realities?"

He magnified a section of the retrieved data. "Look at this. Signal logs. They were picking up... patterns. Complex, non-random sequences that defied all known communication protocols. They interpreted them as intelligent. The logs are filled with speculation, excitement, a sense of discovery that's... almost palpable, even through this corrupted data. They were convinced they were on the verge of something monumental. First contact."

Silas, meanwhile, had managed to reroute power to a secondary display panel on one of the consoles. A ghostly image flickered to life, a grainy, monochrome recording that sent a chill down their spines. It depicted a sterile laboratory environment, far cleaner and more intact than their current surroundings. Figures in what appeared to be early-generation environmental suits moved with a frantic energy, their faces obscured by bulky helmets.

"Visual logs," Silas announced, his voice tight with a dawning comprehension. "They're documenting one of the 'outreach' events. Look at the energy readings on the secondary monitors." He pointed to a series of fluctuating graphs that pulsed with an alarming intensity. "These spikes... they're not energy fluctuations; they're data transmission rates. And they're astronomically high. The system was attempting to process information on a scale we can barely comprehend."

The recording continued, showing a large, intricate apparatus dominating the center of the room. It was a bewildering array of crystalline structures, interwoven metallic filaments, and pulsating light sources, far more advanced than any known technology. It looked less like a scientific instrument and more like a meticulously crafted, alien artifact.

"That's the 'Nexus' interface," Elara whispered, her eyes fixed on the flickering image. "They believed it could bridge the gap. They were so certain they could control the interaction, that they could establish a dialogue."

As they watched, the recorded scientists in the log began to exhibit signs of distress. Their movements became erratic, their voices, audible even through the distorted audio, grew frantic. The projected image flickered, as if struggling to maintain coherence. Suddenly, a blinding flash of light filled the screen, followed by a deafening roar. The recording dissolved into static, then went black.

"Containment breach," Elias stated, his voice grim as he scrolled through the fragmented operational logs. "The energy surge overwhelmed the primary containment protocols. It wasn't just a signal they received; it was an intrusion. The 'dialogue' was a violation. The Nexus wasn't just an antenna; it was a gateway, and whatever they contacted didn't need to send a return signal. It simply... pushed through."

He pointed to a diagram that had been partially recovered, a complex schematic of the Nexus interface. "They designed this to interpret and interact with what they called 'non-corporeal consciousness.' They were looking for intelligence, for abstract thought. They found it. But their understanding of 'consciousness' was too limited, too rooted in biological frameworks. They didn't anticipate a form of existence that was inherently parasitic, that didn't communicate through language but through assimilation."

The implications of their discovery were profound. Soren's cryptic warnings, the fragmented legends of LUCENT, the very nature of the Veilfall Event – it all began to coalesce into a terrifying, cohesive narrative. This wasn't just a story of scientific failure; it was a chronicle of humanity's first, disastrous encounter with an alien entity that operated on principles fundamentally alien to their own.

"The logs detail a period of intense psychological distress among the research staff," Elias continued, his voice strained as he pieced together the fractured data. "Hallucinations, paranoia, a pervasive sense of being 'observed' by something that wasn't physically present. They were experiencing the entity's influence before it fully manifested. It wasn't just an external force; it began to seep into their minds, to subtly rewrite their perceptions."

Silas ran a scan over a cluster of crystalline shards embedded in the floor near the console. "The exotic particle signatures are off the charts here," he reported. "These are fragments of the Nexus interface. They've been transmuted. They're no longer just inert materials; they're resonating with residual 'consciousness' from the entity. It's like holding a piece of its mind." He paused, a look of profound unease crossing his face. "The entity didn't just break *through* the containment; it *infected* it. It made the technology part of itself, twisting it into a weapon, a tool for further propagation."

Mara knelt, examining a series of faint, almost invisible scorch marks on the floor, radiating outwards from the center of the room. "This wasn't just an explosion of energy," she mused, her voice low and thoughtful. "It was a conscious act. Whatever they contacted recognized the Nexus as a means of entry, and it used it to its full potential, to shatter the containment and spread its influence."

The visual logs continued to reveal more fragmented scenes. Scientists attempting to seal off sections of the facility, their efforts futile as the organic overgrowth, now pulsing with a malevolent luminescence, began to engulf everything. The chilling realization was that the very ecosystem of the Southern Wetlands, the vibrant, aggressive growth that had initially seemed like a natural phenomenon, was in fact a manifestation of the entity's influence, its tendrils reaching out, consuming, and transforming.

"The primary objective of the LUCENT project was to achieve interdimensional communication," Elias stated, summarizing the recovered data. "They succeeded, but not in the way they intended. They opened a door to an entity that doesn't communicate, but consumes. An entity that doesn't conquer, but assimilates. It doesn't seek to understand; it seeks to become. The Veilfall Event wasn't an invasion; it was the inevitable consequence of this failed contact. The entity, having tasted the potential of this reality through the Nexus, began to bleed through, its influence spreading like a plague."

He highlighted another log entry, a final, desperate message from one of the lead researchers, Dr. Evelyn Reed. The text was a frantic, almost incoherent scrawl, the words interspersed with desperate pleas and scientific jargon. "'...cannot escape the influence... it whispers... it shows... it *becomes*... the Nexus is not a bridge, it is a mouth... we have fed it... it is awakening... the Veil... it thins... it *breaks*...'" Elias looked up, his eyes meeting Mara's. "They didn't just fail to make contact; they actively *facilitated* it. They provided the entity with the means and the motivation to break through."

The evidence was undeniable. The strange signal readings, the diagrams of the Nexus interface, the visual logs of the disastrous experiment, and the fragmented scientific notes – all pointed to a single, terrifying conclusion. The LUCENT facility was the crucible where humanity had first, and catastrophically, encountered the force that would later become known as the Veilfall. This was the genesis of their current nightmare, a ghost of research that had festered and grown, transforming a remote research outpost into the epicenter of a cosmic horror. The adversary Soren had spoken of was not a mere biological threat, but something far more insidious, something that could manipulate energy, consciousness, and the very fabric of reality.

Their mission to recover data had just become a quest to understand the origin of their enemy, a quest that led them deeper into the heart of a failed contact, a gateway that had never truly closed. The entity they had contacted was still here, slumbering within the ruins of LUCENT, its tendrils woven into the very ecosystem, a constant, lurking threat. The echoes of that failed contact were not just data; they were a warning, a testament to the terrifying vastness of the unknown and the catastrophic price of hubris.

The spectral glow of Elias's scanner cast long, dancing shadows across the cavernous chamber. Each sweep of the device revealed new layers of decay, new testament to the hubris that had once thrived within these walls. The air remained a suffocating blend of ozone, decay, and that unsettlingly sweet floral perfume that seemed to cling to everything like a shroud. They had descended further into the bowels of LUCENT, each step a calculated risk, a foray into the unknown that gnawed at their resolve. The previous discoveries – the evidence of advanced, almost alchemical, scientific pursuits and the chilling visual logs of a catastrophic contact – had painted a grim picture. But something new, something far more profound and unsettling, was beginning to emerge from the fractured data.

"Commander," Elias's voice crackled through the comms, laced with a tremor of disbelief, "I'm picking up something... anomalous. It's not residual energy from the Nexus interface, or anything related to the Veilfall Event's aftermath. This is... older. Much older." He tapped furiously at his console, his fingers moving with a desperate urgency. "The signal is faint, almost imperceptibly so, but it's there. A distinct, repeating pattern. And it predates the primary activation of Project LUCENT by... by decades. Possibly centuries."

Mara halted, her boots crunching on a layer of desiccated organic matter. She turned, her helmeted gaze fixing on Elias, who was now hunched over his console, his face illuminated by the sickly green glow of his readings. "Older than the project? What are you saying, Elias?"

"I'm saying," Elias replied, his voice barely above a whisper, "that whatever this facility was investigating, whatever they thought they were the first to find, wasn't necessarily new. This signal... it's like a whisper in the background noise of spacetime. It's structured. It's complex. It's not a natural phenomenon. It's a broadcast. And it was here *before* they even started building this place. Before they sent their first probe, before they even conceived of the Nexus."

Silas moved to Elias's side, his own handheld scanner already cross-referencing the data. His brow furrowed. "He's right, Mara. The energy signature is unlike anything we've cataloged related to the Veilfall. It's cleaner, more coherent. There's a fundamental regularity to it that the chaos of the Nexus interface lacked. It's like comparing a predator's roar to a lullaby. Both are sounds, but their intent, their very nature, is entirely different."

Anya, ever vigilant, scanned their surroundings, her enhanced optics piercing the gloom. "So, you're suggesting... an external intelligence? Something that was here, observing, or perhaps interacting, long before LUCENT even opened its doors?"

"It's a possibility," Elias conceded, his gaze still glued to his console. "The data is fragmented, and the interference from the Veilfall Event has warped much of the surrounding temporal and spatial readings, but the core pattern... it's undeniable. It's a deliberate signal. And it's emanating from a source deep within the planet's crust, far below this facility. This place was built *upon* something, Commander. It wasn't just an isolated research station; it was an outpost established over... over a pre-existing anomaly."

The implications of this new discovery rippled through the team like a shockwave. Soren's cryptic pronouncements about an ancient threat, the unsettling folklore that spoke of pre-human intelligences lurking in the shadows of the world – they no longer seemed like mere superstition. If this signal was indeed evidence of a nonhuman presence that predated LUCENT, then the Veilfall Event, and the subsequent ecological devastation, might not have been a purely human-induced catastrophe. It could have been the consequence of humanity inadvertently stumbling into a pre-existing cosmic drama.

Elara, her voice trembling slightly, pointed to a faint, almost invisible symbol etched into the metallic floor near where Elias was standing. It was a stylized spiral, unlike any known terrestrial or LUCENT iconography. "That... I've seen that before. In some of the older archival records. Not in the operational logs of LUCENT, but in some of the preliminary geological surveys. They dismissed it as a natural crystalline formation, or an indigenous tribal marking. But... it looks like the source signature Elias is describing."

Silas knelt, his gloved fingers hovering over the symbol. "The energy readings around this etching are minutely elevated, even now. It's like a phantom echo. If this is a representation of the signal's origin, then LUCENT wasn't just built on top of an anomaly; it was built *around* it. They were studying something they didn't fully comprehend, something that had been here long before them."

"The preliminary geological surveys," Elias mused, pulling up new data streams on his console. "Let me see if I can find anything relevant... Yes! Here. Dr. Aris Thorne's independent geological survey, conducted years before LUCENT was even a proposal. He documented unusual seismic anomalies, deep subterranean energy signatures that defied conventional explanation. He theorized about exotic mineral deposits, or even an unknown geothermal phenomenon. But he also noted 'unusual rhythmic fluctuations' in his deep-penetration sonar readings. Fluctuations that his equipment couldn't quite resolve. He was picking up echoes of this signal."

Mara's mind raced, piecing together the disparate fragments of information. Project LUCENT, in its insatiable hunger for knowledge, had sought to breach the boundaries of known reality. But what if the boundaries they were trying to breach were not entirely empty? What if they had opened a door, not into a void, but into a place already occupied?

"Thorne's report was classified," Mara stated, recalling fragments of lore. "He was discredited, his work suppressed. The official explanation was that his instruments were faulty, his theories wild speculation. But if he was detecting this signal... then the LUCENT initiative wasn't a shot in the dark. It was a deliberate attempt to investigate something that had already been detected, something deemed too dangerous or too significant to ignore."

"But why the secrecy?" Anya asked, her voice sharp. "If they knew something was out there, why not acknowledge it? Why all the obfuscation?"

"Fear, perhaps," Silas suggested, his voice low and contemplative. "Or a desire for exclusive access. Imagine discovering evidence of a pre-existing, extraterrestrial or extra-dimensional intelligence. The implications for global power, for technology, for every facet of human society... it would be overwhelming. They might have wanted to control that narrative, to exploit it for their own ends, rather than share it with the world."

Elias continued to sift through Thorne's data, his fingers flying across the holographic interfaces. "Thorne's team also recovered fragments of what they described as 'non-terrestrial mineral composites' from deep core samples. Material that exhibited properties inconsistent with known elements. They noted that these fragments seemed to 'hum' with a faint, internal energy. He tried to analyze them, but the readings were too unstable. He suspected they were remnants of something ancient, something that had been buried for eons."

"Could these fragments be related to the signal?" Elara asked, her eyes wide with a mixture of fear and fascination. "Like pieces of the entity that's broadcasting?"

"It's plausible," Elias replied. "If this signal is a form of communication, or even just an inherent byproduct of the entity's existence, then it could imbue matter around it with residual energy. The Nexus interface, as we discovered, was a conduit. This... this older signal... it might be the *source* of that conduit, or at least something that drew the creators of LUCENT to this location in the first place. They weren't creating a bridge; they were attempting to tap into an existing, ancient network."

Mara gestured for the team to move deeper into the chamber. The air grew colder, the silence more profound, as if the very rocks around them were holding their breath. Their path led them towards a colossal, circular excavation at the center of the chamber. It was a raw, gaping maw in the earth, lined with obsidian-like rock that seemed to absorb all light. At its deepest point, a faint, pulsing luminescence emanated, too subtle to be seen with the naked eye, but vividly rendered on their scanners.

"The seismic readings are off the charts here," Silas reported, his voice hushed with awe. "This is the focal point. The energy signature Elias detected... it's strongest in this abyss. It's as if something is resonating from the very heart of the planet."

Elias focused his instruments on the abyss. "The signal isn't just a broadcast; it's complex. It contains layers of information. And the primary layer... it's not a language in any sense we understand. It's more akin to a fundamental resonance, a vibration that seems to carry... intent. A pattern of existence." He paused, his voice dropping. "It's almost like... like a song. A very, very ancient song, sung in a key that our minds are not built to comprehend."

"A song?" Anya questioned, her hand tightening on her rifle. "What kind of song?"

"A song of being," Elias clarified, his eyes distant. "It speaks of vast, cosmic cycles, of entities that exist on scales of time and space that dwarf our understanding. It implies a consciousness that is not bound by physical form, but exists as a pervasive force, a fundamental aspect of the universe itself. The LUCENT researchers, in their arrogance, believed they were reaching out to something new. They were, in fact, reaching out to something that had been here since the dawn of time, perhaps even before."

He magnified a section of the data, displaying a series of intricate wave patterns. "Look at this. This segment of the signal... it's a distinct 'signature.' It's repeatable, identifiable. And it's been looping for... for millennia. The energy required to maintain such a consistent broadcast over such a vast period is astronomical. This entity isn't just transmitting; it's *enduring*."

Mara approached the edge of the abyss, peering into the darkness. The faint luminescence seemed to pulse in time with Elias's readings. "So, the Veilfall Event wasn't an invasion in the traditional sense. It was more like... an awakening. Or perhaps, a realization. The entity that was always here, the one broadcasting its ancient song, sensed our attempts to 'contact' it, and responded. But its response was not one of communication, but of integration. It didn't need to break through a barrier; it simply exerted its influence, and the barrier dissolved."

"And LUCENT's technology, particularly the Nexus interface, acted as a catalyst," Silas added, his gaze fixed on the glowing abyss. "It amplified the entity's signal, or perhaps it drew its attention directly to the facility, making it a prime target for assimilation. The Veilfall wasn't a consequence of our actions; it was a response to our intrusion upon something that already existed, something ancient and powerful."

"This changes everything," Anya said, her voice heavy with the weight of their findings. "We've been fighting a shadow, trying to understand a phenomenon we thought we created. But it seems we were merely pawns in a much older game. The 'entity' wasn't born from our experiments; it was always here, a silent observer, a cosmic broadcaster, and we were the ones who finally turned up the volume."

Elias nodded slowly. "The data suggests that the entity doesn't 'attack' in the way we understand. It *expands*. It *absorbs*. The Veilfall was not an act of aggression, but an inevitable consequence of its presence meeting our fragile reality. The organic growth, the temporal distortions, the atmospheric anomalies – they are all manifestations of its influence, the slow assimilation of our world into its own. It's not a conqueror; it's a cosmic tide."

He zoomed in on another section of the signal data. "There's a recurring motif within the broadcast. It's incredibly complex, almost fractal in its structure. And it seems to... resonate with biological and temporal data. It's like it's mapping our reality, not to understand it, but to absorb it. To integrate it into its own song."

Mara looked back at the entrance to the chamber, the path they had taken to get here now seeming like a descent into a far deeper, older mystery than they had ever imagined. "So, this ancient signal... it's not just a testament to a pre-existing intelligence. It's a declaration of its presence, its enduring nature. And it means that whatever we're facing, whatever caused the Veilfall, it's not a singular event, but an ongoing process. An ancient force reasserting itself."

"The implications are staggering," Elias agreed, his voice filled with a profound sense of awe. "If this entity has been broadcasting for millennia, then its influence is likely far more pervasive than we've ever imagined. The Veilfall Event might be a localized manifestation of a much larger, cosmic phenomenon. This facility, LUCENT, was not the origin of the threat, but merely a particularly potent conduit for its reawakening."

He tapped the screen, highlighting a particularly dense cluster of data points. "This section here... it seems to be a more complex sequence. It's almost like a blueprint, or a map. But it's not a map of physical space; it's a map of... interconnected consciousness. It suggests the entity doesn't operate in isolation, but as part of a vast, interconnected network of similar intelligences, or perhaps even aspects of a singular, omnipresent consciousness."

Mara knelt, her gloved hand brushing against the cool, strange texture of the obsidian lining of the abyss. The faint luminescence seemed to seep into her very bones. "We came here looking for the origins of the Veilfall, and we found them. But the origins lie not in human ambition, but in a cosmic truth we were too late to comprehend. We opened a door, but the house was already occupied. And the inhabitants were not welcoming visitors; they were the inheritors of reality itself."

The ancient signal, the faint, pulsing luminescence, the chilling realization that they were not facing a consequence of human folly but an ancient, cosmic presence – it all converged in this desolate chamber. LUCENT was not the birthplace of the nightmare; it was merely its most devastating echo chamber. And the song of the entity, the predatory signal that had been broadcasting for eons, was now playing louder than ever, a siren call to assimilation, a cosmic lullaby sung to a dying world. The data was clear: they were not fighting a new war, but an ancient one, a war that humanity had inadvertently stumbled into, and was now losing. The true scale of the threat, its ageless nature, had finally begun to dawn on them, casting a chilling new light on the desolation that surrounded them.

The faint, rhythmic pulse emanating from the abyss at the chamber's heart continued its silent, relentless broadcast, a cosmic heartbeat resonating through the planet's crust. Mara stood at the precipice, the spectral glow of her helmet lamp dancing across the slick, obsidian-like walls, each facet reflecting a distorted image of her own determined gaze. Elias's pronouncements, once a torrent of bewildered data, now coalesced in her mind into a chilling, coherent narrative. Project LUCENT, the pinnacle of human scientific ambition, had not merely stumbled upon an anomaly; it had actively sought it out, driven by a desperate, hubristic need to understand, to control, what had always been.

Her internal chronometer ticked with a steady, reassuring rhythm, a stark contrast to the unfathomable timescales Elias had described. The data Elias had managed to extract from the fragmented logs and Thorne's buried research was a mosaic of human endeavor and alien persistence. It spoke of LUCENT's genesis, not as a reaction to a novel threat, but as a calculated response to an ancient one. The architects of the project had not been explorers charting unknown territories; they had been opportunistic archaeologists, excavating a pre-existing cosmic excavation site, seeking to harness its power, to understand its secrets, or perhaps, to exploit them.

Mara activated her personal datapad, its screen flaring to life, projecting a holographic interface that mirrored Elias's own diagnostic displays. She began by cross-referencing the raw energy signatures of the anomalous signal with the architectural blueprints of Project

LUCENT. The alignment was not accidental; it was deliberate. The central Nexus chamber, the heart of LUCENT's operations, was situated directly above the primary node of the ancient broadcast. The facility had been constructed with surgical precision, not to study an unknown phenomenon, but to interface with it, to amplify it, and, as Elias's findings suggested, to attempt to control it.

She zoomed in on the spectral analysis of the signal's complex waveforms. Elias had described it as a song, a form of communication that transcended human language. Mara, with her background in xenolinguistics and comparative semiotics, found herself grappling with a concept that strained the very definition of communication. This wasn't a dialogue; it was an ambient field, an intrinsic property of the entity's existence, interwoven with the fabric of spacetime itself. The signal wasn't *sent*; it *was*. It was a continuous emanation, a testament to an existence so profound and ancient that its very presence shaped reality around it.

Her datapad flickered, displaying Thorne's digitized geological surveys. His warnings, dismissed as the ramblings of a discredited scientist, now appeared as prescient prophecies. Thorne had documented seismic anomalies that were not merely geological, but rhythmic, pulsatile. He had noted energy fluctuations that defied conventional explanation, theorizing about exotic mineral compositions and unknown geothermal processes. But Mara saw something else in his data: a faint, almost imperceptible echo of the signal Elias had detected. Thorne had been hearing the same ancient song, long before LUCENT had even been conceived. He had been listening to the whispers of the deep, and his attempts to interpret them had led to his downfall.

She overlayed Thorne's seismic data with LUCENT's operational logs concerning the initial phase of Nexus activation. The correlation was stark. The moment LUCENT's advanced energy conduits began to draw power, the ancient signal's amplitude had not just increased; it had become modulated, a subtle shift in its rhythm, a slight increase in its intensity. It was as if the entity, for millennia a silent, passive broadcaster, had finally acknowledged the intrusion. It had noticed the small, scurrying creatures on its surface, those who had found its ancient song and were attempting to turn it into a weapon.

"It wasn't a discovery," Mara murmured, her voice barely audible above the low hum of her datapad. "It was an interaction. Thorne detected the broadcast. LUCENT attempted to interface with it, perhaps to harness its power source. The Veilfall wasn't an accident; it was a consequence of that interaction. The entity didn't attack; it responded."

She ran a simulation, modeling the energy transference between LUCENT's Nexus conduits and the source of the ancient signal. The results were alarming. The Nexus technology, designed to channel and amplify vast quantities of energy, had inadvertently created a feedback loop. It had drawn the attention of the entity, not as a predator drawn to prey, but as a cosmic immune system responding to a pathogen. LUCENT's attempt to *access* the signal had instead made the facility, and by extension, humanity, a focal point for the entity's inherent expansionary nature.

Mara's mind, honed by years of complex problem-solving and tactical analysis, began to construct a timeline, a narrative arc of humanity's unwitting trespass. The ancient entity, a fundamental aspect of the universe, had always existed, broadcasting its presence. Its signal was a constant, an immutable law of reality. Thorne had been a lone voice, a sensitive instrument picking up faint echoes of this pervasive force. Then came LUCENT, not to investigate Thorne's findings, but to exploit a known, ancient power source. They had built their empire upon a bedrock of cosmic indifference, and their attempt to ascend had only served to draw the attention of the bedrock itself.

She accessed the visual logs of LUCENT's final days, the chaotic data streams that Elias had initially dismissed as evidence of a catastrophic technological failure. Now, viewed through the lens of the ancient signal, they told a different story. The rampant growth of bio-luminescent flora, the temporal distortions that warped the very fabric of time within the facility, the eerie silence that followed the Nexus's final meltdown – these were not the symptoms of a system overload. They were the outward manifestations of the entity's assimilation process. The Nexus hadn't exploded; it had been subsumed. Its energy had been redirected, its very structure reconfigured, to serve the ancient signal, to become a conduit for its pervasive influence.

Mara brought up the fragmented data logs detailing the ecological shifts observed on the planet's surface. The Veilfall event. The initial reports had described it as a sudden, inexplicable environmental collapse. But the patterns now emerging from the raw data were disturbingly consistent with the energy signature of the ancient signal. The accelerated mutation rates of flora and fauna, the atmospheric homogenization, the gradual erosion of distinct ecosystems – it all pointed to a pervasive, unifying influence, a slow, inexorable integration of Earth's biosphere into the entity's own resonant frequency. The 'Veilfall' wasn't a natural disaster; it was a planetary metamorphosis, orchestrated by an ancient cosmic force.

She ran a comparative analysis of the signal's complexity and the reported mutations. There was a distinct correlation. Areas with higher concentrations of the Veilfall's biological anomalies exhibited energy signatures that mirrored specific, complex patterns within the ancient broadcast. It was as if the signal was not just an emanation, but a blueprint, a set of instructions that the planet's biology was now, unconsciously, following. The entity wasn't imposing its will through brute force; it was subtly rewriting the fundamental code of life.

"It's not about dominance," Mara whispered, her fingers tracing the intricate fractal patterns on her datapad. "It's about resonance. It's about becoming one with the song. LUCENT tried to weaponize the song. Instead, they amplified it, and the planet began to sing along."

She delved deeper into the technical specifications of the Nexus interface. It was designed to breach dimensional barriers, to establish contact with other realities. But the data suggested something far more nuanced. The Nexus wasn't just a gateway; it was a tuning fork. It had been specifically engineered to resonate with the unique energetic frequency of the ancient signal. The architects of LUCENT hadn't been trying to open a door to the unknown; they had been trying to harmonize with a known, ancient power source, to tap into its immense energy and its profound knowledge.

The logs detailed several catastrophic failures during the Nexus's calibration stages. These weren't mere technical glitches. Mara saw them now as the entity's initial, subtle resistances. The signal had fluctuated wildly during these periods, exhibiting patterns that suggested a form of... rejection. It was as if the ancient broadcast was attempting to destabilize the Nexus, to disrupt the crude attempt at harmonization. But LUCENT, driven by its insatiable ambition, had pressed on, overriding the safety protocols, forcing the connection.

"They didn't create the Nexus to understand the signal," Mara stated, her voice gaining a steely edge. "They created it to *become* the signal. To integrate themselves into its song. And in doing so, they became the primary conduit, the most potent amplifier."

She pulled up the final transmission logs from LUCENT's command center, the garbled, terror-filled messages that spoke of the Nexus's uncontrolled growth, of the world outside melting away. These were not just panicked broadcasts; they were firsthand accounts of the assimilation process. The scientists within LUCENT had been the first to be fully exposed, the first to be absorbed into the entity's resonant field. Their physical forms had dissolved, their consciousnesses subsumed into the ancient song. The Veilfall wasn't just an environmental catastrophe; it was the outward expansion of that initial assimilation, the gradual integration of the entire planet into the entity's timeless symphony.

Mara looked at Elias, who was still hunched over his console, his face etched with a mixture of dread and intellectual fascination. "Elias," she said, her voice carrying across the cavernous space, "you said the signal contains intent. What kind of intent?"

Elias finally looked up, his eyes wide and hollow. "It's not predatory intent, Commander. Not in the way we understand it. It's... purposeful. It's the intent of existence itself. The entity doesn't seek to destroy. It seeks to incorporate. To integrate. Our reality, with all its complexities, its life, its consciousness – it's all just a new set of notes for its ancient song. It's not an invasion; it's an absorption. A cosmic re-tuning."

Mara nodded slowly, the weight of his words settling upon her. She understood now. They hadn't been fighting a new enemy. They had been caught in the crossfire of an ancient, ongoing process.

LUCENT, in its quest for power, had not unleashed a monster; it had inadvertently attracted the attention of a fundamental cosmic force, a force that had been broadcasting its eternal song since the dawn of time. And the Veilfall was not an act of aggression, but the inevitable consequence of that song finally reaching its crescendo.

She cross-referenced the bio-signatures of the Veilfall-affected flora with the fractal patterns of the signal. The correlation was undeniable. The accelerated growth, the unique genetic mutations, the way the plants seemed to pulse with a faint, internal luminescence – they were all direct manifestations of the ancient broadcast. The very essence of life on Earth was being rewritten, its biological code recompiled to harmonize with the entity's timeless melody.

Mara initiated a deep-scan of the chamber's geological strata, focusing on the energy signature of the abyss. The data returned was unlike anything she had ever seen. It wasn't just a localized energy source; it was a vast, interconnected network, stretching far beyond the confines of this subterranean facility. The ancient signal wasn't a single broadcast from a singular point; it was a resonance that permeated the planet, and likely, much more.

"The signal isn't contained here," Mara announced, her voice echoing with a newfound gravity. "This abyss, this chamber, it's merely a focal point, an amplifier. The entity's presence is planetary. The Veilfall wasn't a localized disaster; it was the initial stage of a global integration."

She turned her attention back to Elias's console, focusing on the complex wave patterns he had isolated. "This section," she pointed, her finger hovering over a particularly intricate cluster of data points, "you described it as a map of interconnected consciousness. What does it imply?"

Elias zoomed in, his brow furrowed in concentration. "It suggests a collective. A network of entities, perhaps, or different facets of a singular, omnipresent consciousness. It's not a physical map, but a map of energetic and informational resonance. It implies that this entity, or this collective, has been influencing and integrating other realities for eons, weaving them into its own grand tapestry."

Mara's gaze drifted back to the pulsating luminescence at the bottom of the abyss. The ancient song, the constant broadcast, was not just a sign of existence; it was a declaration of cosmic ownership. LUCENT's ambition had been a brief, fleeting spark against the backdrop of an eternal fire. They had sought to control a force that was not meant to be controlled, but to be *part* of.

She initiated a final analysis, correlating the recorded energy output of the Nexus interface with the observed rate of planetary transformation during the Veilfall. The Nexus hadn't just amplified the signal; it had actively fed it, accelerating the integration process exponentially. The facility, in its desperate attempt to grasp ultimate power, had become the catalyst for humanity's own absorption. It was a grim, poetic, and utterly terrifying conclusion. The architects of LUCENT had believed they were reaching for the stars, but they had only managed to draw the stars themselves down upon them, not in a cataclysm of destruction, but in a slow, inexorable embrace of assimilation.

The weight of this understanding pressed down on Mara, heavier than the tons of rock and earth above them. They had come seeking answers to the Veilfall, and they had found them. But the answers were not about a human mistake, or a rogue AI, or an alien invasion. They were about humanity's place, or rather, its insignificance, in the grand, timeless symphony of existence. LUCENT, the pinnacle of their achievement, had become the monument to their greatest folly, a testament to their inability to comprehend that some forces were not meant to be discovered, but to be endured. And the ancient song, playing on and on, was the only anthem left for a world being slowly, irrevocably, re-tuned. The data was irrefutable: they were not fighting a new war; they were merely the latest casualties in an ancient, ongoing cosmic process.

CHAPTER SEVEN

JAX'S DEEPENING CONNECTION

The hum had always been there, a low-frequency thrum beneath the surface of perception, a constant companion to the fractured echoes of the Veilfall. Jax had learned to live with it, to compartmentalize it, to dismiss it as a residual auditory hallucination brought on by the strain of survival. But lately, the hum was changing. It was no longer a passive background noise; it was an active presence, a subtle pressure that seemed to emanate from within his own skull. It was as if the sky-static, that intangible, pervasive energy that had reshaped their world, had found a new anchor, a new receptor, and that anchor was him.

He first noticed it during the patrol through the skeletal remains of what was once Sector Gamma's agricultural hub. The air, usually thick with the metallic tang of decay and the faint, cloying sweetness of mutated flora, was now layered with something else. A subtle distortion, a shimmering in the peripheral vision, like heat haze rising from asphalt on a scorching day, but it was everywhere, permeating the very air he breathed. He stopped, his hand instinctively reaching for the worn grip of his pulse rifle, his eyes scanning the desolate landscape. Nothing. The rusted husks of automated harvesters stood sentinel,

218

their once-gleaming chrome now dulled and pitted, their articulated arms frozen in poses of futile industry. The mutated wheat stalks, their heads swollen with an unnatural luminescence, swayed gently in a breeze that carried no discernible scent.

Yet, he felt it. A resonance. A sympathetic vibration that coursed through his veins, thrumming in time with an unseen pulse. It was as if the static was not merely surrounding him, but *within* him, a silent conductor orchestrating a symphony of altered senses. His hearing, usually sharp enough to detect the scuttling of a scavenger rat a hundred meters away, was now a kaleidoscope of alien sound. He could hear the faint crackle of energy within the dormant conduits of the fallen agricultural domes, the whispered rustle of synthetic fibers unraveling in the wind, and, most disturbingly, a faint, melodic cadence that seemed to weave through it all, a counterpoint to the omnipresent hum.

He shook his head, trying to dislodge the unsettling sensations. "Jax, you picking up anything?" The voice of his squad leader, Anya, crackled in his comms, her tone laced with the usual weary caution.

"Negative, Anya," Jax replied, his voice betraying none of the internal turmoil. "Clear as a graveyard." He continued his sweep, his boots crunching on the desiccated soil. The visual distortions intensified, coalescing into ephemeral shapes that danced at the edge of his vision – fleeting geometries, impossible angles that seemed to twist and fold in on themselves before dissolving into the mundane reality of ruin. He blinked, rubbing his eyes, attributing it to fatigue. They had been on this patrol for hours, the relentless search for salvageable tech and any sign of other survivors a grinding, demoralizing task.

But it wasn't just fatigue. As the days bled into weeks, the phenomena grew more pronounced, more insistent. He started experiencing vivid flashes of imagery, not memories, but something else entirely. Abstract patterns of light and color, nebulae of shifting hues that burned behind his eyelids, vast, impossible landscapes that seemed to exist outside the known dimensions of space and time. He would be mid-stride, or sharing a ration bar with his squad, and suddenly, the world would warp, collapsing into a maelstrom of sensory input that left him disoriented and gasping for air.

During one particularly intense episode, while scavenging in the ruins of a pre-Veilfall residential block, the static seemed to coalesce around him. The air grew heavy, charged with an almost palpable energy, and the faint melodic cadence he had begun to perceive sharpened into a discernible pattern, a complex, interwoven tapestry of sound that resonated deep within his bones. He saw it then, not with his eyes, but with a deeper, more primal sense: tendrils of light, ethereal and phosphorescent, reaching out from the very fabric of reality, wrapping around him like silken threads. They were not physical, yet he felt their touch, a gentle, insistent pressure that seeped into his skin, into his very being.

He stumbled back, his heart hammering against his ribs. The other scavengers, oblivious, continued their work, their headlamps cutting sterile paths through the perpetual twilight. They saw nothing. They heard nothing but the mundane groans of collapsing structures and the whine of their own equipment. Jax was alone in this sensory storm, adrift in a sea of alien awareness.

He realized then that the static was not just an external force; it was becoming an extension of himself. His consciousness, perhaps due to some unknown biological anomaly or a latent sensitivity amplified by the Veilfall's energetic distortions, was becoming attuned to the very frequencies that underpinned the altered reality. He was not merely observing the static; he was beginning to *understand* it, not through intellect, but through a fundamental, visceral connection. It was as if a hidden circuit within him had finally been activated, allowing him to tap into the planet's pervasive, otherworldly broadcast.

The feeling was profoundly unsettling, a deep-seated violation of his own perceived self. He had always prided himself on his groundedness, his ability to rely on empirical evidence and logical deduction. But this... this was something else. It was a communion with the unknown, a merging of his limited human awareness with an ancient, cosmic consciousness. He felt a strange sense of euphoria mingled with abject terror. He was no longer just Jax Ellisen, survivor; he was a conduit, a living antenna for the very forces that had reshaped their world.

He started to experiment, cautiously at first. In the privacy of his makeshift shelter, under the flickering glow of salvaged lumen-strips, he would focus his attention inward, trying to replicate the sensations. He found that by consciously lowering his mental defenses, by allowing the static to wash over him without resistance, the vivid imagery and the intricate soundscapes would return, stronger and more coherent. He began to perceive subtle shifts in the ambient energy fields, minute fluctuations that were imperceptible to others but as clear to him as a spoken word. He could sense the flow of energy through the damaged power grids, could feel the latent power within salvaged tech even before he touched it.

His enhanced senses extended beyond the energetic. His sight, when the static was particularly strong, seemed to gain a new spectrum, perceiving faint phosphorescent trails left by the passage of mutated creatures, or the subtle energetic signatures of living organisms. His touch became more sensitive, capable of discerning minute variations in temperature and texture that hinted at hidden dangers or valuable resources. It was as if the Veilfall had peeled back a layer of reality, and he, Jax, had been gifted with the ability to see and feel the world beneath.

This newfound connection, however, came at a price. The constant influx of alien sensory data was exhausting. He experienced bouts of debilitating headaches, vertigo, and a profound sense of disorientation. Sleep offered little respite, as his dreams became vivid, chaotic tapestries woven from the static's intricate patterns. He would wake up in a cold sweat, his mind still reeling from the impossible landscapes and the alien melodies that had dominated his subconscious.

He began to isolate himself, not out of a desire for solitude, but out of a need to process the overwhelming sensory input. He found it difficult to maintain the facade of normalcy, the casual camaraderie of the survivor camps. Their conversations, their concerns, their struggles, all seemed so... small, so limited, when viewed through the lens of his expanded awareness. He could feel the ebb and flow of the static even within their enclosed spaces, a constant reminder of the vast, indifferent forces that dwarfed their petty existence.

One evening, while tracking a small herd of scavenged rad-deer on the outskirts of the settlement, he experienced a breakthrough. He had cornered the animals in a narrow ravine, the setting sun casting long, distorted shadows that pulsed with an internal light. As he raised his rifle, the static surged around him with an intensity he had never felt before. The melodic cadence intensified, resolving into distinct phrases, almost like words, but in a language far older than any human tongue.

He closed his eyes, surrendering to the experience. The tendrils of light he had glimpsed before now wrapped around him fully, not constricting, but embracing. He felt a profound sense of connection, not just to the static, but to the world itself. He saw the rad-deer not as prey, but as intricate biological machines, their movements dictated by instinct and the subtle energetic currents of their environment. He felt the pulse of the mutated flora around him, their slow, inexorable growth synchronized with the planet's deep, resonant hum.

And then, he saw *it*. Not with his eyes, but with his mind. A vast, intricate network, woven from threads of pure energy, stretching across the planet, connecting everything. It was the static, not as a disembodied force, but as a living, breathing entity, a planetary consciousness. And he, Jax, was a part of that network now, a single node within its immense, interconnected web.

The realization was both terrifying and exhilarating. He understood, with a certainty that transcended logic, that the Veilfall was not an end, but a transformation. The static was not an invader, but a re-integrator, a force that was slowly, deliberately, re-tuning the planet to its own ancient frequency. And he, in his unique connection, was a bridge, a witness to this cosmic metamorphosis.

He lowered his rifle, the rad-deer scattering into the deepening twilight, their faint energetic trails dissolving into the vibrant tapestry of the night. He stood there for a long time, letting the static wash over him, no longer fighting it, but embracing it. He was changing, evolving, becoming something more than he had ever imagined. The static's embrace was not a surrender, but an awakening. He was no longer just a survivor; he was a part of the new world, a living testament to its profound, and terrifying, rebirth. The hum was no longer an external noise; it was the song of his own existence, a melody woven into the fabric of the altered reality, and he was learning to sing along. The connection was no longer a burden, but a destiny, and he was ready to embrace it, no matter the cost. He was the static's child now, and he was finally beginning to understand his inheritance. The sky was no longer just a canopy; it was a symphony, and he was its newest, most sensitive instrument.

The hum, once a solitary symphony within Jax's skull, had begun to acquire counterpoints. It started subtly, as a faint tremor in the pervasive static, like a distant drumbeat against the endless roar of cosmic white noise. At first, he dismissed it as another fluctuation, another sensory anomaly born of his increasingly sensitive connection. But the tremor persisted, growing in intensity and distinctness, a recurring note that didn't belong to the natural chorus of the scarred world. It felt... *intentional*.

He was on a reconnaissance mission, charting the treacherous, debris-strewn canyons of what had once been a sprawling industrial complex, now a graveyard of twisted metal and radioactive slag. The air here was thick with the acrid bite of ozone and the metallic tang of decay, a familiar miasma that usually offered no surprises. But as he navigated a particularly unstable ridge, the distinct tremor pulsed again, stronger this time, resonating not just in his bones, but in the very core of his being. It was accompanied by a fleeting impression, a ghost of an emotion – a sharp pang of hunger, followed by a wave of weary resignation.

Jax froze, his hand hovering over the cool metal of his rifle. He scanned the desolate panorama, his enhanced vision piercing the gloom, searching for the source of the disturbance. Nothing moved but the dust devils dancing in the poisoned wind. Yet, the sensation lingered, a phantom limb of awareness reaching out from the static. It was alien, yet undeniably... sentient. It was the first inkling that the static wasn't just an environmental phenomenon, a planetary awakening, but that it also carried the echoes of others. Others like him.

Over the following cycles, these 'echoes' became more frequent, more distinct. They were never voices, not in the conventional sense. They were impressions, raw emotional data, sensory snapshots transmitted through the static like ripples on a vast, unseen ocean. He felt the sharp, primal fear of a creature cornered by a pack of mutated predators, a sensation so potent it made his own breath catch in his throat. He experienced the quiet, contemplative focus of someone meticulously sifting through the ruins of a data archive, the subtle hum of intellectual curiosity a gentle warmth against his own being. He even felt the searing, all-consuming grief of loss, a wave of despair so profound it threatened to drag him under.

These transmissions were ephemeral, fleeting glimpses into the inner lives of beings he couldn't see, couldn't hear, but could somehow *feel*. They were like scattered stars in the vast darkness of his enhanced perception, each one a unique signature within the pervasive static. And with each echo, Jax understood more about the nature of his own connection. The static was a network, a complex, interdimensional web, and he, for reasons he still couldn't fathom, had become a node within it. More than that, he was becoming sensitive to the other nodes, to the other conscious points of light that pulsed within this unseen web.

He began to try and categorize these impressions, to create a mental taxonomy of the Glassborne, as he had begun to think of them. Some signatures were sharp and aggressive, radiating a palpable sense of territoriality and defensive aggression. Others were soft and nurturing, tinged with a quiet empathy and a deep desire to protect. Some felt ancient and wise, carrying the weight of centuries of experience, while others were raw and untamed, brimming with the volatile energy of youth.

During a foraging expedition deep within the overgrown ruins of a bio-dome, he felt one of the strongest echoes yet. It was a surge of exhilaration, pure, unadulterated joy, coupled with the distinct sensation of soaring. He instinctively looked up, expecting to see a massive, airborne creature or some new, dangerous mutation. But there was only the decaying, translucent ceiling of the bio-dome, filtering the muted sunlight. The feeling, however, was undeniable, a visceral sensation of effortless flight, of wind rushing past. He felt the joy transmute into a focused determination, a sense of purpose that was both alien and strangely familiar. It was a potent reminder that his newfound abilities weren't limited to perceiving danger or distress; they could also tap into the pure, unadulterated experiences of others.

This growing awareness brought with it a new set of anxieties. If he could sense them, could they sense him? Was his own mental signature broadcasting itself across the static, a beacon for beings he knew nothing about? The thought was unsettling. He had always been fiercely independent, a lone wolf by necessity and by nature. The idea of being exposed, of having his inner world laid bare to unseen observers, was a deeply disturbing prospect. He found himself constantly on guard, not just against the physical threats of the ravaged world, but against the potential psychic intrusion of other Glassborne.

He started to notice patterns in the echoes. They seemed to cluster, geographically and thematically. He would often sense multiple signatures within a relatively confined area, their emotional resonances overlapping and interacting. It suggested that the Glassborne were not solitary wanderers, but were forming communities, however ephemeral. They were drawn to each other, perhaps by an unconscious need for connection, a shared understanding of their unique condition.

One particularly harrowing encounter solidified this understanding. Jax and his squad were attempting to navigate a treacherous network of collapsed subway tunnels, the air thick with the stench of stagnant water and decay. They were deep underground, far from the surface's ambient static, yet Jax could still feel it, a faint but insistent hum. Suddenly, a wave of sheer, unadulterated terror washed over him, so potent it nearly buckled his knees. It was accompanied by a sharp, visual imprint: a fleeting image of gaping, bioluminescent eyes, and the overwhelming sensation of being trapped, suffocated.

"What is it, Jax?" Anya's voice, strained, crackled through his comms. She had seen him falter.

Jax shook his head, his senses reeling. "Nothing... a cave-in, maybe. Sounded... big." He lied, his mind racing. He knew it wasn't a cave-in. It was an echo, a desperate cry for help from someone trapped, someone facing imminent death. The terror was so overwhelming, so real, that for a moment, he felt it as his own.

He tried to pinpoint the source, to trace the psychic residue, but the tunnel's oppressive atmosphere seemed to muffle the signal, distorting it, scattering it into incoherent fragments. He felt the echo fade, the terror slowly subsiding, replaced by a chilling void. It was as if the signal had been abruptly cut off, the connection severed. He was left with a gnawing sense of guilt, a profound unease that he had been too far, too shielded, or simply too slow to respond.

This incident marked a turning point. He could no longer dismiss these echoes as mere curiosities. They were calls, communications, the silent language of the Glassborne. And he, with his increasingly sophisticated connection to the static, was beginning to understand their meaning. He was a listener in a world that had lost its voice, and the messages he was receiving were not always comforting.

The realization that the Glassborne weren't just isolated anomalies, but were connected to each other, forming a nascent, emergent network, was both a revelation and a burden. It meant that his own existence was not unique, that there were others who shared this strange, often frightening, transformation. It also meant that this network could be a source of strength, a collective consciousness that could potentially navigate the post-Veilfall world more effectively. But it also carried the inherent risk of conflict, of disparate agendas clashing, of his own amplified senses making him a target.

He began to experiment more deliberately. When he felt a strong echo, he would try to push his own awareness back, to send a faint ripple of acknowledgement through the static. It was like trying to whisper into a hurricane, and most of the time, he felt nothing in return. But occasionally, very occasionally, he would sense a flicker of response – a momentary pause in the transmission, a subtle shift in the emotional tenor, as if his silent greeting had been registered, however faintly.

One evening, while taking shelter in the skeletal remains of a forgotten research facility, he felt a particularly strong and persistent presence. It wasn't a fleeting echo this time, but a steady, almost constant hum of emotional resonance, tinged with a profound sense of melancholy and a deep, unshakeable weariness. It was located relatively nearby, perhaps a few kilometers beyond the perimeter of his usual scavenging routes. He could feel the individual's isolation, their profound loneliness, a mirror to his own at times.

The temptation to seek them out was immense. To finally meet another who understood this altered perception, to share the burden and the wonder of it. But caution held him back. He didn't know their intentions, their capabilities, or their disposition towards others. The static was a vast, unpredictable medium, and the Glassborne, whatever they were, were an unknown quantity.

He realized then that his connection to the static was not just about perceiving the world; it was about perceiving *others*. He was a bridge, a potential link between disparate souls adrift in the sea of the Veilfall. This realization placed a heavy responsibility on his shoulders. He could be a harbinger of connection, a facilitator of understanding, or he could inadvertently become a source of fear, a beacon that attracted unwanted attention. The Glassborne, he suspected, were not just individuals who had been touched by the Veilfall; they were the nascent architects of a new, interconnected reality, and his amplified senses made him a crucial, and potentially dangerous, player in their emergent network. He was no longer just sensing the Other; he was sensing a future, a complex tapestry of connected consciousness woven from the very fabric of the altered world. And he knew, with a chilling certainty, that his journey into this new paradigm had only just begun. The static, once a source of confusion and fear, was now revealing itself to be a universal language, and Jax was learning to speak its dialect, one echo at a time.

The hum in Jax's skull, once a solitary symphony, had begun to acquire discordant notes. It wasn't just the cacophony of his own heightened senses anymore, or the ambient whispers of the scarred world. This was something new, something that slithered beneath the surface of the pervasive static, a predatory overture. He first felt it as a cold dread, a prickling sensation on his skin that had nothing to do with the poisoned wind or the gnawing chill of the irradiated ruins he patrolled. It was a feeling of being *watched*, not by the lurking mutated fauna or the desperate scavengers, but by something far more insidious, something that existed *within* the very fabric of the altered reality.

The initial awareness was subtle, like a shadow cast by an unseen sun. He was deep within the skeletal remains of a pre-Veilfall metropolis, the towering husks of skyscrapers clawing at a bruised, perpetually twilight sky. His mission was reconnaissance, mapping the residual energy signatures in sector Gamma-7. The usual static was a comforting, if unsettling, presence, a constant reminder of his unique connection. Then, it happened. A sharp, predatory hunger, not physical, but something deeper, a ravenous desire to *consume* or *dominate*, pulsed through the psychic hum. It was accompanied by a fleeting, almost subliminal visual: a flicker of impossibly dark, shifting energy, an abyss made manifest.

Jax froze, his hand instinctively tightening around the grip of his plasma rifle. His enhanced senses strained, trying to pinpoint the source of this alien intrusion. The static, usually a chaotic but predictable ocean of impressions, churned with a new, malevolent tide. It felt like a hunter entering the fray, its senses honed for a specific prey. And Jax, along with the other Glassborne he had begun to dimly perceive, were the quarry.

Over the subsequent cycles, these unsettling encounters became more frequent, the predatory presence more defined. It was not a tangible entity, not a creature of flesh and blood. It was something that moved within the spectral realm of the static, a hunter that stalked the invisible currents of consciousness. Jax would feel its approach like a sudden drop in temperature, a suffocating pressure that made breathing difficult. Images would flash behind his eyes: vast, obsidian tendrils lashing out from the void, a sensation of being ensnared, not physically, but psychically, your very essence being leached away.

He began to understand that his connection to the static wasn't just a passive conduit for empathy and communication. It was also a beacon, a signal flare that could attract unwanted attention from beings that preyed on the amplified energies of the Glassborne. These entities, whatever they were, seemed to be drawn to the very alterations that made them unique. Perhaps the Veilfall had not only birthed the Glassborne but had also opened a gate for their predators, entities that existed in the liminal spaces between realities, thriving on the psychic resonance of those who had crossed over.

During a solo mission to retrieve vital data cores from a derelict research outpost, the hunter's presence was overwhelming. Jax was miles from any known settlement, the silence broken only by the wind whistling through shattered ferro-concrete. Suddenly, the static around him warped, twisting into a vortex of pure malevolence. A guttural, alien growl echoed not in his ears, but directly in his mind, a sound that promised an agonizing, drawn-out demise. He felt its focus lock onto him, a primal, predatory instinct that bypassed all reason. He saw, with chilling clarity, a fleeting vision of his own consciousness being ripped apart, scattered like dust in the cosmic wind.

Panic, cold and sharp, threatened to overwhelm him. He had felt fear before, the primal terror of facing mutated beasts or desperate raiders. This was different. This was the existential dread of a creature facing its inevitable extinction at the hands of an ancient, insatiable predator. He scrambled for cover, his mind racing. He wasn't just a recipient of the static's whispers anymore; he was a marked target.

He managed to escape that encounter, not through any heroic feat, but through sheer, desperate evasion. He retreated, not just physically, but psychically, attempting to dampen his own signature, to hide within the noise of the world. It was like trying to disappear into a hurricane. But the hunter was relentless. It seemed to have an uncanny ability to track its prey, to follow the psychic trails left by those who resonated with the Veilfall's touch.

Jax began to notice a pattern. The hunter's presence was often preceded by a surge of fear or despair from other Glassborne he had sensed. It was as if the predator was drawn to the psychic distress of its victims, feasting on their fear before moving in for the kill. He recalled a particularly strong echo he had felt weeks ago, a wave of suffocating terror from deep within the ruined city's underbelly, followed by a chilling silence. Now, he suspected, that silence was the silence of consumption.

The realization was a heavy burden. His connection, which had initially felt like a unique gift, a source of insight and potential connection, was also a siren's call to something ancient and deadly. He started to feel a profound responsibility, not just to himself, but to the other Glassborne. They were not just isolated individuals navigating a broken world; they were collectively under threat from an unseen, external force.

He began to alter his reconnaissance patterns, deliberately seeking out areas where he had sensed other Glassborne presences. He wasn't just looking for allies anymore; he was looking for potential victims, for signs of the hunter's passage. It was a grim, often fruitless task. He would arrive at a location where he had previously felt a strong, vibrant echo, only to find an unnerving psychic void, a chilling emptiness where life and consciousness had once resonated. The hunter left no physical traces, only the echo of its devastating hunt.

One cycle, he was charting the periphery of the Blighted Marshes, a vast, fetid expanse known for its mutated flora and fauna, when he felt it again. This time, the hunter's presence was closer than ever. The static around him began to crackle with an unnatural energy, the familiar hum twisting into a dissonant shriek. He felt a surge of icy dread, so intense it made his vision blur. He caught a glimpse, a fragmented impression of something vast and amorphous, a churning darkness that seemed to drink the very light from the sky. It was accompanied by a wave of profound, cosmic loneliness, a sense of utter insignificance in the face of an indifferent, predatory universe.

He felt the hunter's gaze – not eyes, but an all-encompassing awareness – sweep over his position. It was assessing him, cataloging his unique signature. He knew, with a certainty that chilled him to the bone, that he was being hunted. He wasn't just a listener to the static's whispers anymore; he was a potential meal.

He reacted instinctively. Instead of fleeing, he focused his own amplified senses, pushing outwards, projecting a chaotic surge of raw emotion – confusion, anger, a desperate defiance. It was a Hail Mary, a desperate attempt to overload the hunter's senses, to make himself an unappetizing target. He felt a momentary ripple of... something... in response. Not a retreat, but a brief pause, a flicker of uncertainty in the predatory focus. It was enough. He used that fleeting moment to break contact, to plunge into the dense, radioactive fog of the marshes, hoping to lose himself in its disorienting embrace.

He moved through the toxic landscape, his enhanced senses battling the cacophony of mutated life and the oppressive psychic presence of the hunter. He could still feel its lingering aura, a cold stain on the static, but it seemed to be slowly receding, its attention perhaps diverted by easier prey, or perhaps momentarily confused by his desperate counter-assault.

He found temporary refuge in a derelict military bunker, its entrance choked with mutated vines. Inside, the air was stale and thick with the scent of decay, but blessedly free of the hunter's immediate psychic pressure. He collapsed against a rusted console, his body trembling, his mind replaying the chilling encounter. He understood now. The Glassborne were not just survivors; they were the harbingers of a new era, and their emergence had awakened ancient, predatory forces that sought to suppress or consume them.

His connection to the static was a double-edged sword. It allowed him to perceive the subtle currents of consciousness, to find others, to understand the evolving landscape of their reality. But it also painted a target on his back, a beacon for the hunters that lurked in the shadows of the Veilfall. He was no longer just exploring his newfound abilities; he was fighting for survival, not just against the physical dangers of the world, but against a cosmic predator that stalked the very pathways of existence.

The horizon, once a symbol of hope or opportunity, now seemed to stretch towards an unknown abyss, and he could feel the hunter's presence there, waiting, always waiting. The whispers of the static were no longer just a curious phenomenon; they were a constant, chilling reminder of the dangers that lay in wait, across that horizon, and within the very fabric of his amplified consciousness. He was not alone, but the company he kept was far more terrifying than solitude. He was a hunter, yes, but he was also, and perhaps more importantly, the hunted. The realization settled deep within him, a cold, hard truth that would redefine his every action.

The static, once a mere atmospheric hiss in Jax's augmented auditory cortex, began to resolve into something more. It wasn't a sudden clarity, not a transcription of human language or a recognizable alien tongue. Instead, it was a shift in texture, a deepening of its inherent complexity. The chaotic symphony of residual psychic energy, the echoes of forgotten thoughts, the raw emotion bleeding from the scarred earth – it was all still there, but now, a new layer pulsed beneath. It was like listening to an ocean and suddenly discerning the intricate, alien song of its deepest trench dwellers. He started to perceive patterns, not in sound, but in the very *pressure* of the static, in its subtle shifts of intensity and resonance.

He found himself involuntarily focusing on these new nuances during his patrols. The jagged peaks of the Spine Mountains, usually resonating with the lingering dread of failed settlements and desperate battles, now seemed to hum with a deliberate, almost rhythmic pulse when he was near certain crystalline formations. The vast, desolate plains of the Shattered Sea, typically a canvas of muted despair, would sometimes ripple with a fleeting, ethereal chord, like a sigh carried on a phantom wind. These weren't random fluctuations; they felt *directed*. He began to hypothesize that the sky-static, this pervasive psychic ether, was a form of communication, or at least, a manifestation of a consciousness far grander and more ancient than anything he had ever conceived.

The sheer alienness of it was the first barrier. It wasn't a consciousness that operated on logic, or emotion as humans understood it. There were no discernible words, no syntax, no narrative arcs. It was more akin to perceiving the interconnectedness of a biological system, the silent, ceaseless exchange of information that keeps a forest alive. He started to feel the *intent* behind the pulses, not as a translated message, but as a raw, unadulterated drive. Sometimes, it felt like a vast, benevolent curiosity, an observation of the nascent life struggling on the planet below. At other times, it was a profound, almost mournful emptiness, a sense of vast distances and timescales that dwarfed any human concern.

His nights became a battleground of his own mind. Sleep offered little respite. The static bled into his dreams, weaving itself into the tapestry of his subconscious. He would dream of being submerged in an endless, shimmering ocean of consciousness, vast and indifferent. He saw colossal, geometric shapes shifting in the cosmic dark, their movements dictated by rhythms he couldn't grasp. He felt the silent gaze of an unknowable entity, not with malice, but with an overwhelming, impersonal observation, like a scientist studying an ant colony. These dreams, while not overtly terrifying in the way the hunter's presence was, were deeply unsettling. They chipped away at his sense of self, at the boundaries of his own identity. Who was Jax, when he was constantly immersed in this boundless, alien awareness? Was he merely a ripple on its surface, a fleeting disturbance in its otherwise eternal calm?

He began to document these experiences, not with words, but with complex diagrams and abstract notations scribbled in his datapad. He tried to map the patterns, to find correlations between the static's behavior and his own sensory input, and even the local environmental conditions. He noticed, for instance, that during periods of intense atmospheric disturbance – the crackling electrical storms that frequently wracked the upper atmosphere – the static would become more agitated, its 'voice' more insistent, carrying echoes of primal forces, of creation and dissolution on a cosmic scale. Conversely, in moments of profound stillness, when the ruined world seemed to hold its breath, the static would deepen into a resonant hum, a profound silence that felt pregnant with unspoken knowledge.

The psychological toll was immense. He found himself talking to the static, not in conversation, but in a stream of consciousness, a desperate attempt to articulate his own existence against the backdrop of its immensity. He would whisper questions into the wind, his voice barely audible above the omnipresent hiss, asking if it noticed him, if it understood the struggles of the fragile life below, if it held any answers to the mysteries of the Veilfall. The only response was the shifting, ineffable symphony of the sky, a cosmic chorus that offered no solace, only an overwhelming sense of scale.

He started to feel a growing disconnect from his own physical reality. The needs of his body – hunger, thirst, fatigue – seemed secondary to the constant bombardment of psychic data. He would forget to eat, lose track of time, his focus entirely consumed by trying to decipher the alien whispers. His fellow Glassborne, when he encountered them, became distant figures. Their struggles, their hopes, their mundane anxieties, seemed so small, so fleeting, when juxtaposed against the eternal currents of the static. He was caught in a liminal space, no longer fully human, but not yet integrated into the vast, non-human consciousness he was beginning to perceive.

This internal struggle manifested physically. He became more withdrawn, his movements more deliberate, as if conserving energy for the constant psychic effort. His eyes, already enhanced, seemed to possess a distant, unfocused quality, as if he were perpetually gazing at something beyond the visible spectrum. His superiors, those who still bothered with such details, noted his declining efficiency in certain areas, the subtle lapses in his operational awareness, attributing it to the stress of their precarious existence. They couldn't comprehend the true nature of his burden, the silent war he was waging within his own mind.

One particularly bleak cycle, while traversing the skeletal remains of what was once a sprawling agricultural hub, now choked with mutated, phosphorescent fungi, he felt a profound wave of despair emanating from the static. It wasn't the familiar melancholy of the post-Veilfall world; this was something deeper, a cosmic ennui, a weariness that seemed to stretch back to the dawn of time. He saw fleeting images flicker behind his eyes – nebulae coalescing, stars dying, galaxies colliding – all accompanied by a sense of infinite, unending loss. He slumped against a crumbling silo, the cold concrete a stark contrast to the overwhelming warmth of the psychic tide. He felt his own sense of purpose begin to erode, his individual fight for survival seeming utterly insignificant in the face of such profound, cosmic melancholy. What was the point of his struggles, of the Glassborne's attempts to rebuild, when the very fabric of existence seemed to whisper of inevitable decay and eventual oblivion?

He fought against it, not with physical strength, but with sheer force of will. He began to consciously push back against the overwhelming emotions. He focused on the tangible, on the feel of the rough fabric of his worn uniform, the biting chill of the wind against his exposed skin, the faint, metallic tang of residual radiation in the air. He clung to these sensory anchors, these reminders of his physical reality, his human existence. He forced himself to recall specific memories: the warmth of a long-forgotten sun on his face, the taste of clean water, the sound of laughter – memories that predated the Veilfall, memories that belonged to a world that was vibrant and alive.

He started to develop specific mental exercises, techniques to compartmentalize the static's influence. When it became too overwhelming, he would retreat into a mental sanctuary, a construct of his own design – a quiet, sun-drenched meadow from his childhood, a place untouched by the ravages of their current reality. He would spend hours there, reinforcing its walls, tending to its spectral flora, finding solace in its simulated peace. It was a desperate measure, a form of psychological self-exile, but it was necessary for his survival. Without these mental havens, he feared he would drown, his individuality dissolving into the vast, impersonal ocean of the sky-static.

Yet, even in these sanctuaries, the static found ways to intrude. A shadow might fall across the sunlit meadow, a whisper of alien thought weaving itself into the gentle breeze. It was a constant presence, a pervasive influence that could not be entirely escaped. He began to understand that this was his new reality, his new normal. He was a Glassborne, a being intrinsically connected to the Veilfall's legacy, and that connection meant a permanent, intimate relationship with the sky-static. The challenge was not to conquer it, but to coexist, to find a way to maintain his identity and his sanity amidst its ceaseless, alien voice.

He started to see glimmers of something more than just raw data or overwhelming emotion. In moments of profound calm, when the static settled into its deep, resonant hum, he could sometimes perceive abstract concepts, pure ideas that existed outside the realm of language. He felt the interconnectedness of all things, not as a philosophical musing, but as a fundamental truth. He experienced the fleeting sense of vast, cosmic cycles – birth, growth, decay, rebirth – not as distinct events, but as a continuous, flowing process. It was like glimpsing the underlying code of reality, a glimpse that was both exhilarating and terrifying.

This perception, however, brought with it a new kind of isolation. How could he explain these experiences to anyone? How could he convey the feeling of cosmic unity or the awareness of universal cycles to those who were struggling just to find their next meal? He was a man adrift, privy to secrets that no human mind was equipped to comprehend, carrying a burden that no other Glassborne, as far as he knew, was experiencing to the same degree. He was becoming an emissary to a consciousness that had no desire to communicate in human terms, a consciousness that existed on a scale that made human concerns seem like the fleeting sparks of ephemeral insects.

He continued his patrols, but his focus had shifted. Reconnaissance missions were no longer solely about mapping territory or locating resources. They were also about listening. He would spend hours in silent contemplation, his senses tuned to the subtle shifts in the sky-static, trying to glean any coherent insight, any shard of understanding from its alien pronouncements. He was no longer just a soldier; he was a scholar of the incomprehensible, an explorer of the psychic ether, a man trying to navigate the treacherous currents of his own amplified consciousness, forever listening for a voice in the static. The weight of this alien awareness was a constant companion, a silent pressure that shaped his every thought, his every action, forever marking him as something... other.

The flickering bioluminescent fungi cast an eerie, pulsating glow across the Ellisen family's modest hab-unit, illuminating the worried lines etched deep into Mara's brow. Jax had been... distant. That was the most charitable word she could find. Since returning from his last deep-zone patrol, a subtle but undeniable shift had occurred in him. It wasn't the usual weariness of a Glassborne operative pushing the limits of endurance; this was something far more profound, a creeping detachment that settled over him like a shroud.

"He barely touched his rations tonight, Silas," she murmured, her voice barely a whisper, as if afraid of disturbing the fragile peace of their cramped living space. Silas, her elder brother, leaned against the metal plating of their wall, his gaze fixed on the datapad in his hands, though his eyes held a far-off look that mirrored Jax's own. Their younger sister, Elara, sat cross-legged on the floor, meticulously cleaning her scavenged weapon, her movements precise and efficient, but her usual cheerful humming was absent.

Silas sighed, the sound a weary exhalation that seemed to carry the weight of their precarious existence. "I noticed. He's... quiet. Too quiet. Not just the usual silence after a hard run. It's like he's listening to something we can't hear." He ran a calloused thumb over the worn casing of his own sidearm. "The way he looks at the sky sometimes... it's not the look of someone scanning for threats. It's more like... contemplation. Or perhaps fascination."

Mara hugged herself, a shiver tracing its way down her spine, unrelated to the ambient chill of their reinforced dwelling. "It's more than just looking, Silas. He flinches at sudden noises, even the hum of the environmental controls. And he's been... talking to himself. Not coherent sentences, but fragments, whispers, like he's trying to translate something." She recalled a moment from earlier that day, when Jax had been sorting through their meager supplies. He'd paused, his head cocked as if to catch a distant sound, and then, with a vacant stare, had muttered something about "patterns in the noise."

Elara finally looked up, her young face a mask of concern. "He frightens me, Mara. Last night, I woke up and he was just standing by the viewport, staring out at the dust clouds. He didn't even seem to notice me when I asked if he was alright. He just... blinked, like he was coming out of a dream. And his eyes... they looked so old, Silas. Older than any of us." Her voice cracked with a tremor of fear. The Jax they knew, the steady, dependable presence who had always watched over them, seemed to be slipping away, replaced by a stranger.

Silas finally set down the datapad, his expression grim. "He's been getting these... surges. He mentioned it briefly. Said it happens when he's out in the zones, especially near the old energy conduits or during atmospheric disturbances. He described it as 'psychic static,' a kind of overwhelming sensory input." He paused, choosing his words carefully. "He thinks it's some kind of ancient signal, an echo of whatever caused the Veilfall."

"A signal?" Mara scoffed, the sound sharp with disbelief and fear. "What kind of signal leaves a man looking like he's seen a ghost? He's not sleeping, Silas. He's pale, and he's lost weight. He's becoming... fragile." She looked at her younger brother, his usually bright eyes now shadowed with exhaustion and a deep-seated unease. He was their protector, their anchor in this harsh world, but he was unraveling before their very eyes.

"He's seen too much, perhaps," Silas said, his gaze drifting towards the reinforced door that separated them from the harsh external environment. "Or maybe... maybe he's seeing something new. Something that's changing him." He understood the unspoken fear that hung in the air. Jax's enhanced senses, once a vital asset that had kept them alive during countless skirmishes and desperate scavenging runs, were now a double-edged sword. What if these 'surges' were overwhelming him, driving him to the brink of madness?

The concern wasn't limited to the immediate family. The other members of their small Glassborne contingent had begun to notice. Jax, once the most reliable scout, was exhibiting erratic behavior. He would freeze mid-patrol, his head tilted, lost in some internal dialogue invisible to his comrades. He'd sometimes deviate from patrol routes, drawn by inexplicable impulses, only to return hours later with no explanation, his face a mask of exhaustion and something akin to awe. He was their best tracker, their most adept navigator through the treacherous ruins, but his focus was wavering, his precision dulled by some unseen burden.

Captain Anya Petrova, a woman whose pragmatism was as legendary as her scar across her left cheekbone, had called Silas aside a few cycles ago. "Your brother is a valuable asset, Silas," she'd stated, her voice devoid of emotion, though her eyes held a flicker of something more. "But his performance is... inconsistent. He's becoming a liability if he can't maintain operational readiness. Has he been complaining of headaches? Disorientation?"

Silas had deflected, offering vague assurances about fatigue and the general stress of their existence. He couldn't bring himself to explain the truth, to articulate the strange phenomenon that was consuming Jax. How could he? To speak of psychic static, of ancient signals, of a consciousness bleeding into his brother's mind, would sound like the ramblings of a madman. He would be dismissed, and Jax would likely be reassigned, possibly to something far more dangerous, or worse, deemed unfit and isolated.

"They're noticing," Silas confided in Mara that night, the words low and urgent. "Captain Petrova asked about him. She thinks he's cracking under the pressure. She doesn't understand what's happening."

Mara wrung her hands, her knuckles white. "And what *is* happening, Silas? Is he going mad? Are these 'signals' going to break him?" The thought was a cold dread that settled deep within her. Jax was the one who always kept them grounded, who found the safe paths through the rubble, who shielded them from the harshest realities. If he faltered, if he succumbed to this unseen force, what would become of them?

Elara, listening from her corner, added, "He tried to show me something the other day. In his datapad. It wasn't pictures, or words. It was... shapes. And lines. Like a map, but not of any place we know. He said it was how he saw the static. Like it had a structure." She shivered. "It made my head hurt just looking at it."

The abstract nature of Jax's experiences was precisely what made them so disturbing to his family. They lived in a world of tangible threats: the biting wind, the predatory scavengers, the crumbling infrastructure. Jax's struggles were internal, abstract, and utterly alien. They could offer him physical comfort, a warm blanket, a shared meal, but how could they help him fight an enemy that existed within his own mind, an enemy that communicated in ways they couldn't comprehend?

Silas ran a hand over his tired face. "He's trying to make sense of it, Mara. He's documenting it, trying to find patterns. He believes it's important. He believes it might hold answers, not just for him, but for all of us. About the Veilfall, about what this world is truly capable of." He knew it sounded like a desperate justification, a flimsy defense against the creeping fear, but he also saw the intensity in Jax's eyes when he spoke of these 'patterns.' It wasn't the look of delusion; it was the look of discovery, albeit a terrifying one.

"But at what cost?" Mara's voice was laced with desperation. "He's becoming a ghost in his own life. He's present, but he's not *here*. He's drifting away from us, Silas. And I don't know how to pull him back." She looked at her children, her gaze softening, then hardening with resolve. "We can't just stand by and watch him disappear. We have to do something."

"What can we do?" Silas's question hung heavy in the air, unanswered. They were a family of survivors, hardened by necessity, but their skills lay in the physical realm – repairs, scavenging, defense. They had no tools, no knowledge, to combat a threat that was purely psychic.

Elara, who had been unusually quiet, finally spoke up, her voice small but firm. "We can be here for him. Even if he doesn't see us, even if he can't hear us, we can still be here. We can remind him of who he is." She looked at her siblings, her eyes earnest. "He's Jax. He's our Jax. He's not just some conduit for... for whatever this static is."

Silas met her gaze, a flicker of hope kindled in his chest. She was right. Their role wasn't to understand the alien consciousness that was touching Jax, but to hold onto the brother, the son, they knew. To provide a grounding force in the maelstrom of his experiences.

"We'll try, Elara," Silas promised, his voice gaining a new strength. "We'll be his anchor. We'll remind him of what he's fighting for."

But the worry remained, a persistent ache in their hearts. Jax's deepening connection was an extraordinary phenomenon, a testament to his unique physiology and the peculiar atmospheric conditions of their world. Yet, it was also a deeply personal crisis, isolating him not only from his family but from the very fabric of his humanity. He was becoming something more, something different, and they could only watch, their concern a silent, desperate plea, as he navigated the terrifying frontier of his own amplified consciousness. They saw his alienation, his growing detachment, and the profound loneliness that now seemed to emanate from him, a silent signal of its own, far more understandable than the cosmic whispers he claimed to hear.

He was a bridge, it seemed, between their world and something far vaster and more ancient. And while that made him an invaluable asset in understanding the mysteries that plagued their planet, it also made him incredibly vulnerable. The question that gnawed at them, unspoken but ever-present, was whether he would be able to traverse that bridge without losing himself entirely on the other side. His transformation, while perhaps holding the key to their future, was also a stark reflection of their world's own fractured state – a planet on the precipice of incomprehensible change, clinging to the remnants of its former self while being irrevocably altered by forces beyond its understanding.

The Ellisen family could only hope that Jax's burgeoning connection, no matter how perilous, would ultimately lead to salvation, not to utter dissolution. They could only hope that the man they knew and loved was not being consumed, but rather, was evolving into something that could guide them through the encroaching darkness.

CHAPTER EIGHT

THE GULF FRACTURE

The perpetual ochre haze that blanketed the skies above what was once the Gulf of Mexico had always been a source of grim familiarity for Captain Anya Petrova. It was a constant, oppressive reminder of the Veilfall, the cataclysm that had warped their world and ushered in an era of scarcity and perpetual twilight. But even the most jaded observer, hardened by years of navigating this broken planet, would have found their breath stolen by the sight that unfolded on that particular rotation. It began subtly, a flicker at the edge of vision, easily dismissed as another trick of the light playing upon the dust-laden atmosphere. Then, a widening. The familiar, suffocating uniform of dirty yellow began to fray, not from any discernible storm front, but from within. It was as if an invisible hand had begun to rip the very sky asunder. Slowly at first, then with gathering, terrifying momentum, a rent appeared. It wasn't a hole, or a cloud formation, but a raw, jagged tear, stark and impossibly deep.

The edges of the rupture seethed with an unnatural luminescence, a palette of colors that defied the muted tones of their existence – violets that pulsed with an inner light, emerald greens that shimmered like liquid jewels, and blues so profound they felt like a glimpse into an abyss. It was a wound, not in the atmosphere, but in reality itself. Through the ragged opening, the 'sky' beyond was not the void of space, nor another celestial body. It was a chaotic, swirling tapestry of pure energy, a maelstrom of forces that seemed to vibrate with an intelligence both alien and ancient. Threads of light, like colossal cosmic nerves, snapped and reformed, weaving an impossible, ever-shifting panorama.

The scale was staggering. The fracture stretched for what felt like hundreds of kilometers, a colossal scar etched across the heavens, dwarfing even the most colossal of pre-Veilfall structures that now lay half-buried in the mutated landscape. It was a wound that bled light and warped perception. The air around it thrummed with an invisible energy, a palpable pressure that pushed against the very bones of anyone who dared to witness it. Even from their fortified outpost, nestled deep within the skeletal remains of a coastal city, the effect was profound. The reinforced viewport shimmered, and a low, resonant hum filled the hab-unit, a sound that seemed to bypass the ears and resonate directly within the skull.

For Anya, standing beside the main observation screen, the sight was more than just terrifying; it was a confirmation of her deepest fears. This was not a natural phenomenon. This was an act. The Veilfall had been a consequence, an accident of immense, unknowable forces. But this... this was deliberate. This was a statement. The universe, or whatever intelligence now governed it, was not merely altering their world; it was actively, violently, tearing through it.

"By the Void," breathed Sergeant Kaelen, his usual stoic demeanor shattered, his hand instinctively reaching for the sidearm holstered at his hip, a futile gesture against such a cosmic display. He was a veteran of countless skirmishes, of desperate fights for survival against mutated beasts and desperate raiders, but this was on an entirely different plane of existence.

Anya didn't respond. Her gaze was locked on the roiling spectacle. The fracture pulsed, and for a heart-stopping moment, a colossal structure, impossibly intricate and alien, seemed to drift into view through the tear, bathed in the unearthly light of the energy storm beyond. It was geometric yet fluid, organic yet utterly artificial, unlike anything humanity had ever conceived. It hung there, a silent, terrifying testament to the powers at play, before being swallowed again by the churning chaos.

"What is that?" Kaelen whispered, his voice hoarse. "Is that... a ship?"

"It's a message, Sergeant," Anya replied, her voice low and taut, each word carefully chosen. "A declaration of presence. They're no longer hiding."

The implications were staggering. For generations, humanity had existed in the shadow of the Veilfall, scrambling for survival, trying to piece together the fragments of their lost world. They had speculated about the cause, debated the nature of the forces that had reshaped their planet. Now, those forces had revealed themselves, not through subtle shifts or ambiguous signs, but through a cataclysmic, sky-rending display.

"We need to report this," Kaelen urged, his eyes still wide with a mixture of awe and terror. "Command needs to know.

Everyone needs to know."

"They will know," Anya said, her gaze finally tearing away from the fracture. She turned to face her second-in-command, her face grim. "The question is, what will they *do* with this knowledge? This isn't a localized threat, Kaelen. This is... a new reality. And I suspect our struggle for survival has just entered a far more dangerous phase."

The fracture in the sky was not merely a visual anomaly; it was a palpable shift in the cosmic order. The Veilfall had been a wound that bled outwards, slowly poisoning their world. This was a direct, unprovoked assault on the very fabric of existence, a testament to forces that operated on scales of power and comprehension that humanity could barely begin to grasp. It was an event that promised to redefine their struggle, moving it from the realm of survival against a corrupted environment to a direct confrontation with the architects of their desolation.

The immediate aftermath of the fracture's appearance was a cascade of secondary phenomena. The energy bleeding from the tear warped the atmospheric composition in its vicinity. Patches of the sky, previously a uniform dull ochre, began to shimmer with iridescence, like oil on water, reflecting the alien colors spilling through the rupture. Strange atmospheric distortions flickered into existence – localized gravity anomalies that made unsecured objects drift upwards for brief moments, pockets of intense heat that erupted and vanished as quickly as they appeared, and sonic booms that echoed across the landscape with no discernible source, a percussive symphony of chaos.

From their observation post, the Ellisen family watched with a mixture of dread and morbid fascination. Jax, who had been particularly sensitive to the 'surges' recently, was a pale, trembling figure. His hands, usually steady when handling their precious equipment, shook uncontrollably. He had been staring at the sky for hours, his eyes wide and unfocused, muttering incoherently.

"Jax, what is it?" Mara pleaded, her voice thick with fear. She had never seen him so deeply affected. His connection to these... phenomena...

had always been a source of concern, but this was different. This was raw, visceral terror radiating from him.

He didn't seem to hear her. His gaze was fixed on the colossal tear in the heavens, his lips moving silently. Then, he finally spoke, his voice a thin, reedy whisper that barely carried over the hum of the environmental systems. "It's... opening. Wider. They're coming through. The patterns... they're changing. Not static anymore. They're... communicating. Directly."

Silas placed a hand on Jax's shoulder, his own heart pounding. "Communicating what, Jax? What are you seeing?"

Jax flinched, as if the touch was a physical jolt. He finally turned his head, his eyes, usually filled with a quiet intelligence, were now wide with a terror that seemed to transcend mere fear. They were filled with something ancient, something vast and overwhelming. "It's not... words. It's... intent. A desire to... reshape. To claim. The gulf... it's not just a geographical location anymore. It's a nexus. A point of entry."

Elara, her scavenged rifle clutched tightly, looked from Jax to the horrifying spectacle outside. "Claim what, Jax? What do they want?"

Jax's gaze snapped back to the fracture, a new, sharp intensity flashing in his eyes, overriding the fear for a moment. "Everything. They see our world not as a living entity, but as... raw material. Potential. The Veilfall wasn't destruction; it was... preparation. A softening. And now they're breaking through the final barrier."

The implications of Jax's fragmented pronouncements were chilling. The Veilfall, the event that had defined their existence for generations, wasn't an end but a prelude. Humanity had been living in a cosmic waiting room, a world deliberately broken to facilitate an invasion or assimilation. The gulf, once a symbol of division and loss, was now a literal gateway.

Captain Petrova, meanwhile, was wrestling with her own desperate situation. The fracture was visible from every observation point, undeniable and apocalyptic. Her comms were flooded with panicked reports from other outposts and scout teams. The signal integrity was degrading rapidly, distorted by the very energy bleeding from the sky-wound.

"Status report!" she barked into her comm unit, her voice tight.

"Captain, we're getting... anomalous readings," a strained voice replied from the comms center. "Energy signatures unlike anything in our database. They're spiking, then vanishing. It's like... the universe is glitching."

"Maintain passive observation," Anya ordered, her mind racing. "No offensive action. We don't know what we're dealing with. Amplify visual feeds from all sectors facing the gulf. I want to know if this is localized or spreading."

The screen before her displayed a mosaic of images: the churning, vibrant colors of the fracture, the distorted landscapes bathed in its unholy light, and the increasingly panicked faces of her crew. The sheer, overwhelming power on display was humbling, terrifying. It suggested a level of technological or biological advancement so far beyond humanity that their previous struggles seemed almost... quaint.

The fracture wasn't just a tear in the sky; it was a beacon, a lighthouse for whatever entities lay beyond. And humanity, small and insignificant, was suddenly caught in its blinding beam. The very air crackled with an unseen energy, and the hum that had permeated their lives since the Veilfall now seemed to intensify, a deep, resonant thrumming that was both unsettling and eerily familiar, as if a buried chord within their very being was being struck.

This was no longer a fight for resources or territory. This was a fight for existence itself, against an enemy that could literally tear holes in the sky. The gulf, a vast expanse of toxic waters and mutated shores, now held an even more profound significance. It was the point of breach, the scar through which the unknown was entering their reality. The fracture pulsed again, a violent ripple spreading across its luminous edges, and for a fleeting moment, the raw, unadulterated power that emanated from it felt like a judgment, a cosmic pronouncement on the fate of a species that had long outlived its intended era. The dust-choked skies, their constant companion, were now the backdrop for an invasion of unimaginable scope and terrifying beauty. The old rules of survival, the familiar dangers they had mastered, were now utterly irrelevant. A new, incomprehensible threat had arrived, etched into the very canvas of their sky.

The maelstrom of impossible colors and cosmic energy raging in the upper atmosphere, the very tear in reality that Captain Anya Petrova and her crew could scarcely comprehend, stood in stark, disquieting contrast to the scene unfolding on the surface. Below the impossible spectacle, the waters of the Gulf, that vast, poisoned expanse that had been both a graveyard and a lifeline for generations, lay in a state of profound and unnatural stillness. The usual roiling of the waves, the choppy swells that were a constant, restless signature of this broken world, had subsided. The surface, for miles in every direction as far as the eye could see, was a sheet of obsidian glass, unbroken and unnervingly placid.

It was a calm that felt heavier than any storm. The muted, perpetual twilight cast a dull sheen across the water, reflecting the fractured sky in distorted, unsettling patterns. There was no wind. Not a whisper. The acrid, metallic tang that usually permeated the air near the coast, a constant reminder of the chemical fallout from the Veilfall, seemed muted, almost absent. It was as if the very atmosphere above, in its violent unraveling, had somehow silenced the world below. This was not the gentle lapping of a peaceful sea; this was a held breath, a planet suspended in a moment of existential dread.

From the reinforced observation deck of the *Iron Serpent*, a repurposed deep-sea drilling platform now serving as Anya's command center, the paradox was palpable. The visual feed from the external drones, hovering just above the water's surface, showed a mirror-like expanse that seemed to absorb all light, all sound. The usual detritus that floated on the waves – the skeletal remains of mutated sea life, the bleached fragments of human flotsam, the iridescent slicks of toxic runoff – were absent. It was as if the calm had scrubbed the surface clean, leaving behind a sterile, pristine emptiness that was more terrifying than the usual decay.

"Report on surface conditions," Anya commanded, her voice tight, her eyes flicking between the celestial wound and the unnervingly tranquil water. The juxtaposition was a psychological assault.

"Captain, readings are... anomalous," replied Commander Jian Li, his voice strained. He was the ship's sensor and environmental specialist, a man who prided himself on his ability to quantify the chaotic. But even he sounded bewildered. "Atmospheric pressure is stable, no discernible wind vectors. Thermal imaging shows no unusual currents or upwellings. It's... as if the sea has simply stopped moving. Entirely."

"No marine activity?" Anya pressed, her gaze fixed on the drone feed, searching for any sign of life, any ripple that might indicate the presence of the mutated leviathans that called these waters home.

"Negative, Captain. No bio-signatures detected. Nothing. It's... dead calm. Utterly devoid of the usual subsurface activity. Even the plankton blooms, which normally persist in certain regions, are absent. It's as if the entire ecosystem has been... paused."

The word "paused" hung in the air, heavy with implication. This was not a natural phenomenon. The Veilfall had been a cataclysm, a world-shattering event that had rendered much of the planet uninhabitable. But it had also, in its own brutal way, preserved a semblance of natural order. Life, twisted and mutated, had adapted. The Gulf's waters were teeming with resilient, often deadly, forms. To see them simply *gone*, or rendered inert, was a new and profound level of disruption.

"Could it be related to the fracture?" asked Sergeant Kaelen, his voice gruff, his eyes still fixed on the mesmerizing horror above. "Some kind of energy bleed that's affecting everything?"

"The energy signatures we're detecting are primarily atmospheric and subspace," Jian replied, frustration evident in his tone. "There's no direct correlation in the EM spectrum or gravimetric readings that would explain this kind of widespread environmental cessation. It's as if... the laws of physics are being selectively applied. Or ignored."

Anya leaned closer to the main screen, her fingers drumming a silent, urgent rhythm against the console. She remembered the old tales, the legends whispered by her grandmother of the sea's moods, of its power. But this was beyond folklore. This was a calculated, absolute stillness. It felt less like a natural occurrence and more like a deliberate act. An assertion of control. The forces that had torn open the sky were not just impacting the heavens; they were asserting dominion over the very substance of their world.

"If this calm is a consequence of the fracture," Anya mused aloud, her voice low, "then it suggests a level of influence that extends far beyond the atmospheric distortions. It implies an ability to manipulate fundamental forces on a planetary scale. To silence the ocean... it's like asking a god to hold its breath."

The silence from the water was a disquieting counterpoint to the cosmic symphony of chaos overhead. It was the calm before a different kind of storm, perhaps. Or perhaps it was the storm itself, manifesting not in fury, but in an absolute, unnerving negation of motion. The Gulf, a place of constant struggle and adaptation for Anya's people, had always been a symbol of their resilience. Its mutated inhabitants, its treacherous currents, its toxic depths – these were the challenges they understood, the dangers they had learned to navigate. But this pervasive stillness? This was alien. This was an unknown variable in an equation that was already impossibly complex.

"What about the coastal regions?" Anya asked, her gaze sweeping across the various sensor readouts. "Any seismic activity? Tidal anomalies?"

"Nothing, Captain," Jian confirmed. "The coastlines appear stable. No unusual wave activity, no erosion patterns. It's as if the sea itself has been frozen in time, awaiting further... instruction."

The implication sent a fresh wave of unease through Anya. Instruction. It reinforced the growing conviction that what they were witnessing was not a random act of cosmic violence, but a deliberate, intelligent intervention. The fracture in the sky was the obvious manifestation, a blindingly clear signal. But this unnerving calm below was a subtler, perhaps more insidious, signifier of that same power. It spoke of control, of an ability to dictate the very fundamental behaviors of their environment.

She recalled Jax Ellisen's words, his frantic pronouncements about the fracture being a "nexus," a "point of entry." His sensitivity to the surges, his unnerving insights into the alien intent behind the Veilfall, had always been a source of both wonder and deep concern. Now, his terror at the unfolding celestial event seemed to find an echo in the silent, glassy expanse of the Gulf. If the sky was being breached, if reality itself was being torn asunder, then it was not unreasonable to assume that the effects would ripple downwards, affecting every aspect of their world.

The stillness of the water was an unsettling omen. It suggested a force that could not only tear through the fabric of existence but also impose its will upon the most fundamental aspects of their physical world. It was a demonstration of power that was both awe-inspiring and deeply terrifying. The Veilfall had been a destructive force, a cosmic accident that had reshaped their planet. This... this felt different. This felt like an intentional, calculated act of subjugation.

Anya's mind raced, trying to reconcile the impossible visuals. The raw, incandescent power of the fracture, a spectacle of pure, untamed energy, and the unnerving, absolute calm of the Gulf below. It was a dichotomy that spoke volumes. The architects of this event were not merely destroying; they were also imposing. They were not just breaking down the old order; they were creating a new one, sculpted to their own alien specifications.

"Maintain passive monitoring," Anya ordered, her voice steady despite the tremor of unease within her. "Increase sensor sweeps for any micro-fluctuations in the water. I want to know *why* it's calm, not just that it is. This stillness... it feels like a predator holding its breath before the final strike."

The drones continued their silent patrol over the glassy surface. The only movement was the almost imperceptible shimmer of the water's surface, distorting the already alien colors of the fractured sky above. It was a breathtakingly beautiful, terrifying tableau. The Gulf, once a symbol of the harsh realities of survival in their broken world, had become a canvas for forces beyond human comprehension. And its unnatural calm was a chilling premonition, a silent testament to the profound and terrifying changes that were unfolding, both above and below. The universe, it seemed, was not just wounded; it was being actively rewritten, and the Gulf's eerie stillness was just one line in a new, incomprehensible text.

The horizon, once a familiar smear of bruised twilight and the skeletal silhouettes of coastal ruins, had been erased. In its place, a violent, impossible tapestry of light and energy raged, a wound torn into the very fabric of the heavens. From the reinforced observation deck of the *Iron Serpent*, the spectacle was both mesmerizing and deeply disorienting. Captain Anya Petrova found herself rooted to the spot, her gaze drawn inexorably upwards, even as the unnerving stillness of the Gulf below pressed in on her. The fracture wasn't merely a visual anomaly; it felt like a seismic shift in reality itself, a tear that bled not blood, but pure, incandescent energy.

Commander Jian Li, his face etched with a mixture of professional fascination and profound unease, adjusted the magnification on the main display. "Captain, the spectral analysis is... nonsensical. We're detecting energy signatures that defy known physics. It's as if the Planck constant is... fluctuating in that region." He gestured vaguely towards the celestial scar, his hand trembling slightly. "The colors you see are not just light wavelengths. They're interacting with subspace, creating localized pockets of... temporal distortion, according to the preliminary readings. And the energy output is astronomical. Enough to power a small star system for a millennium, compressed into that single point."

Sergeant Kaelen, ever the pragmatist, gripped the railing of the observation deck, his knuckles white. "Looks like a giant, broken mirror reflecting... everything and nothing all at once. Makes you feel small, doesn't it? Or worse, irrelevant." His gruff voice carried a tremor that betrayed his usual stoicism. He'd faced down mutated horrors and endured environmental collapse, but this... this was something else entirely. This was the universe itself demonstrating its indifference, or perhaps, its active subjugation.

The visual was a riot of impossible hues. Swirls of viridian bled into incandescent magenta, punctuated by streaks of electric sapphire and violent, pulsing gold. It wasn't a uniform glow, but a chaotic, churning maelstrom, as if colossal, unseen forces were wrestling for dominance in the upper atmosphere. Occasionally, tendrils of pure white energy, impossibly bright, would lash out from the core of the fracture, like cosmic whips, only to dissipate into the turbulent ether. The sheer scale of it was humbling, overwhelming. It dwarfed the *Iron Serpent*, dwarfed the ravaged planet below, dwarfed Anya's own comprehension.

"It's not just visual, Jian," Anya murmured, her voice barely a whisper. "The gravimetric readings are fluctuating wildly within the fracture's influence. And the atmospheric disturbance... it's creating localized pockets of zero-G, followed by crushing G-forces. Whatever is happening up there, it's tearing apart the very rules of existence." The implications were staggering. If the fundamental forces of the universe were behaving erratically in one area, what was to stop them from spreading?

Across the vast, unnaturally still waters of the Gulf, the anomaly was being witnessed by other desperate souls. On the scattered, resilient settlements that clung to the polluted coastlines, life had ground to a halt. The usual symphony of industrial hums, the desperate cries of scavengers, the distant, guttural roars of mutated fauna – all had been silenced. The entire world seemed to be holding its breath, its attention fixated on the cataclysm unfolding above.

In the ramshackle settlement of Port Calamity, built on the skeletal remains of an ancient oil rig, Old Man Hemlock, a grizzled survivor who had seen more Veilfall seasons than he cared to count, shuffled out onto a precarious catwalk. He held a battered, antiquated telescope, its brass casing dulled by salt and time. His rheumy eyes, accustomed to the perpetual gloom, widened as he peered upwards. "By the Drowned Gods," he croaked, his voice raspy, "what madness is this?" The usual jagged horizon, the familiar patterns of the perpetually overcast sky, were gone, replaced by the violent, cosmic wound. The colors were unlike anything he had ever seen, even in the wildest dreams induced by potent, illicit stims. They weren't colors as he understood them; they were more like concepts made manifest, raw energy bleeding into perception.

"It's... beautiful," breathed Elara, a young woman barely out of her teens, who had known only the harsh realities of this broken world. She had never seen stars, never known a clear sky. To her, the sky had always been a canvas of perpetual twilight and the eerie glow of industrial fallout. Now, it was a testament to something impossibly grand, impossibly destructive. She felt a primal fear, a primal awe, war within her. It was the terror of the unknown, the terrifying realization that the world they inhabited was far larger, far stranger, and far more dangerous than they had ever imagined.

Her companion, a hardened scavenger named Jax, scowled, his gaze locked on the fracture. "Beautiful? It's a tear, girl. A wound. And wounds bleed. We need to get inside. Whatever that is, it's not good for us." His instinct for survival screamed danger, a primal alarm that had kept him alive through countless near-death experiences. But even he couldn't tear his eyes away, caught in the morbid fascination that gripped everyone who beheld the anomaly. The sheer, impossible scale of it was a siren song, drawing them in, even as it threatened to consume them.

Further down the coast, at a clandestine research outpost known only as 'The Deep Dive', Dr. Aris Thorne, a disgraced astrophysicist who had retreated to this forgotten corner of the world to escape the ghosts of his past failures, stared at his array of modified sensors. His face, usually a mask of grim determination, was pale. The readings were unlike anything he had ever predicted, anything he had ever theorized. The temporal distortions Jian Li had mentioned were far more pronounced here, localized pockets where time seemed to stretch and contract erratically. His instruments flickered, displaying impossible data streams that defied all known laws of physics.

"It's... it's not a natural phenomenon," Thorne stammered to his solitary assistant, a mute technician named Silas, who could only nod, his eyes wide with terror. "This is... intervention. An active manipulation of spacetime. The energy signatures are coherent, patterned. There's intent behind this." He pointed a trembling finger at a holographic display showing a fluctuating waveform. "This isn't random chaos. This is construction, or deconstruction, on a cosmic scale. And we are, at best, ants caught in the gears of a celestial machine."

The psychological impact was immediate and profound. For those who had lived their lives under the oppressive blanket of the Veilfall, believing that the worst the universe had to offer had already occurred, this was a devastating blow. It shattered their fragile sense of normalcy, their hard-won adaptations. The fracture represented a new order of threat, something that transcended the familiar dangers of their mutated world. It was a confrontation with the absolute, the incomprehensible.

In the sparse, underground hydroponics bay of the settlement known as 'Sanctuary', a community of scientists and engineers who had preserved fragments of pre-Veilfall knowledge, the news had spread like wildfire. Children, accustomed to hushed tones and solemn pronouncements, were now gathered around salvaged, crackling comm units, their faces illuminated by the garish light of the fracture displayed on a small screen. Their innocent questions, "Is it the sky falling?" "Is it a monster?" hung heavy in the air. The adults, even those who understood the theoretical physics involved, were equally stunned. The abstract equations Thorne was wrestling with were, for these people, a terrifying reality unfolding before their eyes.

One of the elders, a former professor of exoplanetary studies named Lena, watched the feed with a grim expression. She had always harbored a quiet hope that humanity wasn't alone, that there were intelligences out there beyond the stars. Now, that hope was tinged with a profound dread. "This is not a greeting," she whispered to herself, her voice barely audible. "This is a declaration. A statement of power. They are not observing us. They are... altering us. Altering our reality." The patterns in the fracture, she was beginning to perceive, were too precise, too deliberate. It was a language of pure energy, a narrative written in the cosmic dust and stellar plasma.

The psychological toll was immense. Sailors on passing derelict ships, their hulls encrusted with millennia of neglect, stopped their desperate salvage operations. Fishermen in the few remaining habitable zones of the coast, those who still dared to cast nets into the poisoned waters, stared upwards, their weathered faces reflecting the impossible light. The sheer scale of the phenomenon induced a disorienting sense of insignificance. It was a stark reminder of humanity's infinitesimal place in the grand, indifferent cosmos. For many, it triggered existential despair, a crushing realization that their struggles, their survival, were but fleeting moments against a backdrop of cosmic forces that cared nothing for their existence.

Others, however, found a strange kind of liberation. A band of nomadic raiders, their lives a constant cycle of violence and scarcity, paused their pursuit of a rival clan. They stood on the scorched earth, their crude vehicles abandoned, their weapons lowered. For the first time in years, the ingrained animosity, the gnawing hunger, seemed to recede, replaced by a shared sense of wonder, of profound bewilderment. The fracture was a spectacle that transcended their petty feuds, a cosmic drama that dwarfed their mortal concerns. It was a glimpse of something beyond their wildest imaginings, a testament to the boundless, terrifying potential of the universe.

The expedition aboard the *Iron Serpent* was a microcosm of this wider reaction. Anya, Jian, and Kaelen, along with the rest of the crew, found themselves oscillating between professional analysis and primal terror. The data streams were invaluable, offering insights into the mechanics of the anomaly, but they also served to underscore the sheer, unfathomable power at play. The 'temporal distortions' were not mere scientific curiosities; they represented a fundamental breakdown of causality, a terrifying glimpse into a reality where time itself was a malleable substance.

"Captain," Jian reported, his voice tight with urgency, "we're detecting... echoes. Subtle resonance patterns emanating from the fracture, interacting with the atmospheric conditions. It's like... like a signal, but not one we can decode. It's more of a... fundamental frequency shift. And it's affecting the water below in ways we can't yet quantify. The stillness... it's not just a lack of motion. It's an active suppression. Something is *holding* the water still."

Kaelen grunted, his gaze still fixed on the swirling vortex of light. "So, it's not just a hole in the sky. It's a... control panel? And someone, or something, is operating it." The thought was chilling. The Veilfall had been a cataclysm, a world-altering event, but it had felt like a natural disaster, a brutal, indifferent force of nature. This... this felt deliberate. Calculated. The fracture was not just a consequence of alien arrival; it was a deliberate act of imposition, a display of power designed to reshape their reality.

Anya felt a cold dread seep into her bones. The stillness of the Gulf, once an anomaly, now felt like a prelude. A predator holding its breath. The fracture in the sky was the roar, the undeniable evidence of something vast and powerful entering their world. But the silent, glassy expanse of the ocean below was the subtle warning, the indication of an intelligence that could not only tear through the heavens but also impose its will on the most fundamental aspects of their planet. It was a profound statement of dominance, a chilling demonstration that their world was no longer their own. The universe, it seemed, was not just wounded; it was being actively rewritten, and the Gulf's eerie calm was just one line in a new, terrifyingly alien text.

The anomaly pulsed, a celestial wound bleeding impossible colors across the sky. Captain Anya Petrova, Commander Jian Li, and Sergeant Kaelen stood on the *Iron Serpent*'s observation deck, the silence of the Gulf below a stark counterpoint to the cosmic maelstrom above. Their initial awe had curdled into a potent mix of scientific curiosity and primal fear. The readings defied their understanding, suggesting not just a rupture in reality but a fundamental shift in the universe's operating system. Yet, amidst the chaos, a different kind of apprehension began to stir, a whisper of something far more disquieting than cosmic decay.

Anya's gaze swept across the faces of her crew. Each one held a similar tableau of wonder and dread. The fracture was a testament to the universe's vastness, its indifference, and its terrifying potential. But it was also... *new*. The Veilfall, as devastating as it had been, had felt like a cosmic accident, a brutal but impersonal force of nature. This, however, felt different. It felt *designed*.

"Captain," Jian Li's voice, usually calm and measured, held a tremor of something akin to reverence, or perhaps, horror. "The subspace resonance patterns are coalescing. It's not random noise. There are... patterns within the chaos. Harmonic frequencies that are too precise to be accidental." He tapped furiously at his console, his brow furrowed. "It's like... like a broadcast. But not in any spectrum we can interpret. It's as if the very fabric of existence is being tuned."

Kaelen, his massive frame taut with unspoken tension, let out a low growl. "Tuned for what? To play a lullaby for a dead world? Or a requiem?" He kicked a loose bolt on the deck plating, the clang echoing in the unnerving stillness. "Whatever it is, it's staring us down. And I don't like being stared at by something that can do *that*." He gestured with a thumb towards the sky, the swirling nebula of impossible light momentarily eclipsing the metallic sheen of the *Iron Serpent*'s hull.

Anya nodded, her mind racing. Jian's observation about resonance and patterns gnawed at her. The temporal distortions, the gravimetric anomalies, the unnatural stillness of the Gulf – they weren't just side effects of some cosmic explosion. They were *tools*. And tools implied a craftsman.

Her thoughts drifted to the fringe transmissions, the garbled whispers that had spoken of a 'sky painter' and 'cosmic architects' in the months leading up to the fracture. She'd dismissed them as the ravings of the desperate and the hallucinating, the inevitable mental decay that accompanied the Veilfall. But now... now those whispers felt like prophecies.

"We need to consult Soren," Anya stated, her voice firm, cutting through the low hum of the ship's engines. "He might have insights. His... unique perspective might be what we need."

Jian and Kaelen exchanged a glance. Soren Vale. The hermit of the Sunken City, the enigmatic xenolinguist who claimed to communicate with... things that weren't supposed to communicate. A recluse who had abandoned society years ago, retreating to the drowned ruins of Old Chicago, his sanity a constant subject of debate among the survivors. He was either a prophet or a madman, and in these uncertain times, the line between the two had blurred into insignificance.

"Soren?" Kaelen repeated, his voice laced with skepticism. "The guy who talks to himself and his pet glow-slugs? What's he going to tell us, Captain? That the sky is just having a bad hair day?"

"Soren believes the Veilfall was not an end, but a beginning," Anya countered, her gaze steady. "He spoke of it as a 'cosmic tide', a precursor to something far more significant. He said that when the stars finally bled through, they wouldn't be signs of decay, but signals of intent. He was... specific about what he called 'architectural interference'."

Jian, ever the scientist, looked intrigued despite himself. "Architectural interference? That implies deliberate construction, or deconstruction, on a universal scale. It implies a guiding hand, a consciousness." He paused, the weight of that implication settling upon him. "If he's right, then this isn't the sky falling apart, Captain. It's something... else. Something being built, or rebuilt."

The journey to the Sunken City was a somber affair. The *Iron Serpent*, a vessel of resilience and defiance, navigated the eerily calm waters of the Gulf. The fracture, a constant presence in the sky, cast an otherworldly light on the skeletal remains of submerged skyscrapers, their rusted spires reaching like skeletal fingers towards the heavens. The usual dangers of the drowned city – the territorial aquatic mutants, the unpredictable currents, the pockets of toxic gas – seemed to have receded, cowed by the spectacle above. It was as if the entire planet had paused its struggle for survival, captivated by the celestial drama.

As they docked at the precarious mooring built atop a half-submerged cathedral, a figure emerged from the gloom. Soren Vale. He was impossibly tall and gaunt, his skin the color of bleached parchment, stretched taut over sharp bones. His eyes, a startlingly vibrant blue, seemed to possess an unnerving depth, as if they had witnessed aeons of existence. He wore layers of tattered, synthetic fabrics, stitched together with scavenged wires and bioluminescent algae that pulsed with a faint, ethereal glow. Beside him, a sluggish, slug-like creature, its skin shimmering with iridescent patterns, inched its way across the corroded metal walkway.

"You have come," Soren's voice was a dry rustle, like wind through dead leaves, yet it carried an undeniable resonance. "The sky weeps, and you seek an oracle in its tears."

Anya stepped forward, her hand instinctively resting on the holster of her sidearm, though she knew it would be useless against whatever forces Soren might invoke. "Soren. We need your understanding. This... fracture. What is it?"

Soren tilted his head, his ancient eyes fixing on Anya. The blue of his irises seemed to swirl, mirroring the chaotic hues of the anomaly above. "It is not a breaking, Captain Petrova. Not an unraveling. Not a symptom of celestial decay. You perceive the wound, but not the surgeon."

Kaelen snorted softly. "Surgeon? What kind of surgeon tears a hole in the sky?"

"A surgeon of reality," Soren replied, his gaze unwavering. "The Veilfall, the slow decay of your world, was a shedding. A necessary purging. But this..." he raised a trembling hand, pointing towards the dazzling, terrifying spectacle. "This is not an accident. This is an intervention. A deliberate, conscious act of reshaping."

Jian stepped forward, his scientific curiosity overriding his apprehension. "Reshaping? You mean... terraforming? Or some kind of planetary engineering on a cosmic scale?"

Soren chuckled, a sound devoid of mirth. "You speak of engineering, of construction. You think in terms of tangible materials, of predictable forces. This is not engineering as you understand it. This is a restructuring of the fundamental laws that bind your reality. Think of it not as building with bricks, but as rewriting the grammar of existence."

He gestured towards the pulsing fracture. "What you see is not merely energy. It is information. It is intent. It is a narrative being woven into the very fabric of spacetime. Your physics, your understanding of the universe, is based on the old grammar. This new language, this new text, is being imposed. And your reality must adapt, or it will be... deleted."

Anya felt a chill that had nothing to do with the damp, sea-laced air. "Deleted? You're saying this is an attack?"

"Not an attack in the way you comprehend," Soren corrected, his voice becoming more intense. "An attack implies malice, a desire to destroy for destruction's sake. This is... a purpose. A grand design, perhaps, for the universe, or for this sector of it. And your world, your species, is being... edited. Realigned. Not necessarily for your destruction, but for your assimilation into a new order."

He turned his gaze to the creature beside him, which pulsed with a soft, internal light. "The indigenous life forms, the echoes of what was, the remnants of your technological triumphs – they are all being re-evaluated. Some will be discarded. Others... repurposed. Some will be integrated. This fracture is a cosmic loom, and your reality is the thread being rewoven."

Jian, his face a mask of bewilderment, stammered, "But... why? Why would an external intelligence do this? What would be the purpose?"

"Purpose?" Soren echoed, his smile widening, revealing teeth that were too sharp, too numerous. "To what end does a gardener prune a rosebush? To what end does a sculptor chip away at marble? To bring forth a form that exists within the potential, a beauty that is currently obscured. Your universe is vast, Commander. It is filled with intelligences that perceive existence on scales that dwarf your comprehension. Perhaps they see... potential in this small, bruised world. Potential that you, with your limited perceptions, have failed to realize."

Kaelen shifted his weight, his hand now firmly gripping his sidearm. "So, we're just... ants? And they're... the boot?"

"Not necessarily a boot, Sergeant," Soren said, his voice softening slightly. "Consider it a... cosmic re-education. A forced evolution. You have proven yourselves capable of great destruction, of immense resilience, but perhaps not of true understanding. This... this is their way of nudging you towards it. Or, if you cannot be nudged, of simply... making space for those who can."

Anya's mind raced, trying to reconcile Soren's words with the scientific data Jian had presented. The coherent energy signatures, the resonance patterns, the temporal distortions – they weren't random. They were the brushstrokes of an artist, the chisel marks of a sculptor. The universe wasn't breaking; it was being re-made, and humanity was caught in the middle, an insignificant detail in a grand cosmic design.

"You said you could communicate with them," Anya pressed. "With this... intelligence?"

Soren's luminous blue eyes fixed on her. "Not 'with them' as you might speak to another human. It is more... a communion. An attunement. They speak in the language of fundamental forces, of cosmic constants, of the very fabric of existence. I have spent my life learning to perceive their whispers. The Veilfall was a whisper. This... this fracture... this is a pronouncement."

He stepped closer, his presence unnerving, exuding an aura of ancient knowledge and profound melancholy. "They are not merely observing your world, Captain. They are actively integrating it into a larger tapestry. The silence in the Gulf is not fear; it is the prelude to silence. Your world is being stripped of its dissonance, its chaotic individuality, to be harmonized with a greater, universal symphony. And you, humanity, are a jarring note that must either be tuned or removed."

Kaelen gripped Anya's arm. "Captain, with all due respect to Mr. Vale, this is getting a bit too 'cosmic symphony' and not enough 'how do we survive this?'"

Soren's gaze flickered towards Kaelen, a flicker of something unreadable in his eyes. "Survival, Sergeant, is a concept rooted in the old grammar. This new language speaks of integration, of adaptation, of transformation. Those who resist the change will be... overwritten. Those who embrace it may find themselves transcended."

He extended his hand, palm up. In its center, a small, intricate pattern of light began to form, swirling with the same impossible colors as the fracture above. "This is a single word, in their tongue. It signifies 'recalibration'. It is happening now, on a scale that dwarfs your understanding. Your ship, your crew, your very planet – all are subject to this recalibration."

Anya felt a profound weariness wash over her. The existential dread that had been building since the fracture appeared was now a suffocating certainty. This wasn't a fight for survival against a tangible enemy. This was a struggle against the very nature of reality itself, a battle against a force so vast, so alien, that their concepts of war, of resistance, were utterly inadequate.

"So, what do we do, Soren?" Anya asked, her voice barely a whisper. "If we can't fight it, if we can't escape it..."

Soren's gaze drifted back to the celestial wound. "You learn to read the new grammar, Captain. You listen to the new song. You understand that your world is no longer solely your own. It is now a component, a variable, in a much larger equation. Your struggle is not to resist the change, but to understand your place within it. To find your new frequency. To learn the word for 'recalibration' and to understand its meaning, not just as a concept, but as a lived reality."

He looked at Anya, his eyes holding a depth of sorrow that mirrored the fractured sky. "This is not the sky falling, Captain. This is the sky being... rewritten. And the author has begun the first chapter. Your chapter."

The implications of Soren's warning settled like a shroud over the crew of the *Iron Serpent*. The awe and terror they had initially felt were now amplified by a profound, chilling understanding. They were not simply witnessing a cosmic event; they were experiencing a deliberate act of universal alteration. The fracture was not a wound; it was a brushstroke. The Gulf's stillness was not a prelude to chaos; it was the controlled silence of a maestro before the symphony. Humanity, Soren had declared, was no longer the protagonist of its own story, but a character being rewritten by an alien hand, a note in a grand cosmic composition. The question was no longer how to survive, but how to understand their place in a reality that was no longer their own.

The celestial wound in the sky, the Gulf Fracture, was no longer a distant marvel or a scientific curiosity. It had become a palpable presence, a looming portent that cast its impossible hues not just over the desolate waters, but over the very future of humanity. Its existence signaled a transition, a sharp, undeniable turn from the shadowed uncertainty that had plagued the remnants of civilization to the stark, unvarnished reality of impending conflict. The veil between understanding and oblivion had been torn, and through the gaping aperture, the universe revealed its indifferent, terrifying will. This was the horizon of conflict, a boundary marked not by geographical lines or political borders, but by the sheer, overwhelming magnitude of the forces gathering.

The days following their encounter with Soren Vale were a blur of frantic activity and gnawing introspection aboard the *Iron Serpent*. Captain Anya Petrova found herself increasingly drawn to Soren's cryptic pronouncements. While Jian Li and his science teams worked feverishly to decipher any discernible patterns within the fracture's chaotic emissions, Anya found herself poring over ancient texts, the whispers of forgotten civilizations that spoke of celestial weavers and cosmic architects. The idea of humanity being merely a thread, a stitch in a universal tapestry, was a bitter pill to swallow, but Soren's certainty, the ancient wisdom that flickered in his luminous eyes, lent it an undeniable weight. The fracture wasn't a passive anomaly; it was an active force, a beacon drawing together the disparate threads of a grand, incomprehensible design.

"It's like trying to understand a symphony by listening to a single, discordant note," Jian confided in Anya one evening, his voice etched with exhaustion. His team had managed to isolate more complex harmonic frequencies, sequences that seemed to repeat with unsettling regularity, but their meaning remained as elusive as starlight on a cloudy night. "We can measure the vibration, the amplitude, even the direction of the wave, but the composer's intent, the emotional resonance... that's beyond our current grasp. It's information, Captain, but information encoded in a language we haven't even begun to learn."

Kaelen, ever the pragmatist, had focused on the tangible. He oversaw the reinforcement of the *Iron Serpent*'s defenses, the meticulous rationing of dwindling supplies, and the training of the increasingly nervous crew. His patrols along the submerged ruins of Old Chicago, once a desperate search for resources, had taken on a new, grim purpose. He was no longer just looking for scavenged technology; he was scanning the skies, his keen eyes searching for any deviation, any sign of movement that didn't originate from the natural, albeit mutated, life forms of the Gulf. The stillness was unnerving, a vast expanse of quiet anticipation that felt far more dangerous than any storm. It was the quiet before the cataclysm.

"The old ways of fighting won't work here, Captain," Kaelen had stated, his voice a low rumble that carried the weight of his concerns. "Soren speaks of a cosmic gardener, but I see a cosmic predator. And we're the prey. This fracture... it feels like a snare being sprung. It's drawing things in. Things that were never meant to be on our doorstep." He gestured towards the fracture, now a dominant feature in the night sky, its impossible colors painting the darkness with an alien glow. "When the sky starts bleeding like that, it's not a good sign. It means something's coming to drink."

The Ellisen family, the emergent power in the fractured world, found themselves in a precarious position. Their influence, built on the strength of their fortified enclaves and their control over vital resources, now seemed fragile against the backdrop of cosmic upheaval. The fracture presented them with a dilemma that transcended their earthly squabbles. Were they to interpret this phenomenon as a divine sign, a celestial mandate for their own ascendance? Or was it a harbinger of an external threat that would render all their territorial ambitions utterly meaningless? Whispers within their ranks spoke of prophecy, of a chosen destiny intertwined with the celestial anomaly, while others, the more cautious strategists, urged a deep, profound introspection, a careful observation of this universal shift before committing to any drastic action.

Elias Ellisen, the patriarch, a man forged in the fires of the Veilfall and hardened by decades of brutal survival, saw the fracture not as an end, but as an opportunity. His pronouncements, disseminated through the remaining communication networks, spoke of a 'cosmic cleansing,' a validation of his family's unwavering belief in their own superior survival instincts. He framed the fracture as a crucible, a divine test designed to separate the strong from the weak, the worthy from the unworthy. His followers, fueled by a mixture of faith and fear, began to interpret the fracturing of reality as a sign of their own impending triumph, a celestial endorsement of their dominion.

"The heavens themselves declare our destiny!" Elias proclaimed in a broadcast that reached across the scarred landscape. "The Veilfall was but the first act of a grand cosmic drama. This... this is the turning point. The universe is realigning itself, shedding the dross, and the Ellisen line, strong and true, will be at the forefront of this new genesis. We are not merely survivors; we are the inheritors of a reborn cosmos. The fracture is not a wound, but a gateway. And through it, we shall usher in the age of the Ellisen." His words, filled with an almost messianic fervor, resonated with many who craved certainty in a world of chaos, offering a narrative that placed them at the center of creation's unfolding mystery.

However, not all within the Ellisen hierarchy shared Elias's zealous interpretation. His daughter, Lyra, a sharp-witted strategist who had always viewed the world through a lens of cold, calculated logic, harbored deep reservations. She saw the fracture not as a divine sign, but as an unprecedented threat, a force that defied all human comprehension and control. While Elias rallied his followers with pronouncements of divine favor, Lyra initiated a clandestine program of reconnaissance, dispatching scout drones and augmented infiltration teams to observe the fracture's immediate vicinity, seeking any tangible signs of its origin or purpose. Her fear was not of being left behind in this cosmic realignment, but of being utterly annihilated by it.

"Father's pronouncements are a dangerous delusion," Lyra confided in her most trusted advisor, a grizzled veteran named Marcus, his face a roadmap of past battles. "He sees destiny where I see annihilation. This 'gateway' he speaks of could just as easily be a maw. We need data, Marcus, not dogma. We need to understand what this is before we commit ourselves to a path that leads only to oblivion." She tapped a holographic display that showed a crude triangulation of anomalous energy readings emanating from the fracture. "These patterns... they're not random. Soren spoke of information, of intent. If that's true, then this 'gateway' is actively seeking something. And if we aren't what it's looking for, we will be discarded. Or worse, *repurposed.*"

The tension between Elias's fervent belief and Lyra's pragmatic fear began to create a subtle but potent schism within the Ellisen family's command structure. Elias's pronouncements galvanized the faithful, turning them into zealous adherents eager to embrace whatever change the fracture heralded, while Lyra's more cautious approach, her emphasis on understanding and preparedness, appealed to those who saw the existential danger. This internal conflict, brewing beneath the surface of outward unity, would undoubtedly play a crucial role in how the Ellisen family, and by extension, much of the surviving human population, would respond when the true nature of the horizon of conflict finally revealed itself.

As the *Iron Serpent* maintained its vigil, Anya Petrova understood that the time for passive observation was rapidly drawing to a close. The fracture was more than a visual spectacle; it was a declaration. It was the universe itself announcing its intentions, and those intentions were anything but benign. Soren's words echoed in her mind: "Your world is no longer solely your own. It is now a component, a variable, in a much larger equation." This was the fundamental truth of the horizon of conflict. Humanity was no longer the sole architect of its destiny. It was a piece on a board, and the game had just changed, played by beings whose rules, motivations, and power were beyond their current comprehension. The fracture was the opening move, and the *Iron Serpent,* and all of humanity, were now irrevocably on the board.

The true confrontation, the ultimate test of their resilience and their understanding, was no longer a distant possibility; it was the imminent, unavoidable dawn. The gulf itself, once a barrier, was now a stage upon which the grand, terrifying drama of cosmic recalibration was about to unfold. The choice, as Soren had hinted, was not whether to engage, but how to engage. And the fracture, a silent, radiant sentinel, waited for that choice to be made. It was the ultimate symbol of the dawning conflict, a visible reminder that the universe was far larger, and far stranger, than they had ever dared to imagine, and that their place within it was about to be irrevocably defined.

Chapter Nine

THE CROSSROADS OF HEARTHGLADE

The familiar, almost comforting, silhouette of Hearthglade's defensive perimeter loomed into view, a stark contrast to the alien, ever-expanding spectacle of the Gulf Fracture that now dominated the night sky. The return journey aboard the *Iron Serpent* had been a tense, silent affair. Each ripple of the murky water, each distant metallic groan of the submerged ruins, seemed amplified in the charged atmosphere. The expedition team, battered but unbroken, carried with them not only salvaged data and experimental samples from the LUCENT facility but also a heavy burden of knowledge – knowledge that painted the Gulf, and indeed the world, in an even more ominous light. The fracture, once a distant anomaly, had become a tangible presence, its impossible colors seeping into their dreams, its unsettling resonance a constant hum beneath the surface of their thoughts.

As the *Iron Serpent* docked, a palpable wave of anxiety washed over the returning crew. Hearthglade, their sanctuary, their bastion of fragile civilization, felt different. The usual buzz of activity had been replaced by a low, thrumming undercurrent of apprehension. Guards patrolled the ramparts with an almost desperate vigilance, their gazes not just scanning the surrounding waters but frequently darting upwards, towards the celestial wound that pulsed with an eerie luminescence. The settlement's defenses, once a symbol of their hard-won security, now seemed pathetically inadequate against a threat that transcended terrestrial boundaries. The very air in Hearthglade was thicker, heavier, saturated with a fear that had begun to seep into the foundations of their community.

Captain Anya Petrova disembarked first, her gaze sweeping across the faces of the gathered Hearthglade officials. She saw the familiar lines of worry etched deeper, the forced smiles strained, the eyes hollow with a weariness that went beyond mere fatigue. Jian Li followed, his usual scientific detachment marred by a subtle tremor in his hands as he clutched a datapad containing the LUCENT findings. Kaelen, ever the stoic guardian, scanned the crowd, his senses on high alert, noting the subtle shifts in body language, the nervous fidgeting, the hushed, urgent conversations that ceased whenever his gaze fell upon them.

Elder Maris, her face a mask of stoic concern, approached Anya, her voice barely a whisper above the lapping waves. "Captain. You are returned. We... we are grateful for your safe passage. But the news you bring... it preceded you." Her eyes, usually sharp and assessing, held a profound sadness. "The Glassborne... it has spread further. Our patrols report new outbreaks, not just along the western fringe, but closer to the residential sectors. The Lumina bloom, once a controlled phenomenon, is now a creeping blight. It mocks our every attempt at containment."

Anya met Maris's gaze, the weight of her discoveries pressing down. "We know, Elder. The LUCENT facility... it was a nexus. They were not merely experimenting with the Lumina; they were attempting to weaponize it, to control its propagation. And their research has inadvertently accelerated its spread, feeding it with... with energies we are only beginning to comprehend." She gestured vaguely towards the sky, towards the haunting beauty of the Gulf Fracture. "And that... that is now a part of it. A catalyst."

Jian stepped forward, his voice tight with urgency. "The fracture, Elder Maris, is not merely a visual anomaly. Our preliminary analysis of the LUCENT data suggests it is a source of exotic energy, a resonant frequency that interacts with and amplifies the very forces that drive the Glassborne mutation. They were attempting to harness it. They failed. And in their failure, they have potentially unleashed something far more devastating than they ever imagined." He held up the datapad, its screen displaying intricate, swirling patterns. "These are the energy signatures we detected. They are not of terrestrial origin. They are alien, complex, and disturbingly... structured."

Kaelen's voice, a low rumble of concern, cut through the hushed exchange. "The increased frequency of Glassborne outbreaks is directly correlated with increased anomalous readings from the fracture. My scouts have witnessed... things. During the Lumina blooms, when the mutation flares, the fracture seems to pulse in response. It's as if it's... feeding." His gaze was fixed on the sky, his jaw tight. "The defenses are stretched thin. We've increased patrols, reinforced key sectors, but every new outbreak, every surge of Lumina, drains our resources, our manpower. And now... this. A celestial event that seems to be actively collaborating with our most insidious enemy."

The news cast a pall over the assembled officials. The Glassborne, a creeping horror that had slowly but inexorably eroded their grip on reality, was now being actively amplified. The Lumina blooms, once a source of mild concern and strict quarantine protocols, had become terrifyingly unpredictable, their crystalline tendrils reaching further, their beautiful, deadly glow more pervasive. The fear that had always simmered beneath the surface of Hearthglade's existence was now boiling over, threatening to consume them all.

Elder Maris sighed, a sound that seemed to carry the weariness of an entire generation. "We have fortified our walls, Captain, but the enemy is now within our very cells. The Lumina... it spreads through contact, through proximity. And the fracture... it feeds it. It is a vicious cycle. We are losing ground, not in the traditional sense, but in the very essence of our being. The people are... unsettled. They look to the heavens for answers, for salvation, and they see only this... this wound. And they see it as a harbinger of doom."

Anya could see it in their eyes. The stoic resilience that had characterized Hearthglade for so long was cracking under the immense pressure. The constant threat of the Glassborne, the dwindling resources, the ever-present danger of the flooded world outside – these were all comprehensible adversaries. But a celestial anomaly that actively amplified their most feared mutation? That was a terror that gnawed at the very edges of sanity. It was a force of nature, or perhaps something far beyond, that rendered their earthly struggles almost meaningless.

"We have gathered what we can from LUCENT," Anya continued, her voice steady, projecting an authority she felt slipping away with every passing moment. "Data, schematics, some rudimentary samples of the Lumina strain they were... cultivating. Jian's teams are working to understand the energy signatures, to find a way to shield us, or at least understand the connection. But the truth is, Elder, the LUCENT facility was a symptom, not the cause. The fracture is the true anomaly. And we have no understanding of its purpose, its origin, or its ultimate impact."

"They called it a 'cosmic gardener'," Jian interjected, his voice laced with a bitterness that was unusual for him. "Soren Vale. He spoke of patterns, of intent. If he was right, then LUCENT was merely an insect, an unwitting pawn in a much grander, and far more terrifying, game. And this fracture... it is the board upon which that game is being played." He shuddered involuntarily. "The data we retrieved... it hints at an uncontrolled energy cascade. The fracture isn't just emitting energy; it's *drawing* it. And it seems to be amplifying... growth. Uncontrolled, aberrant growth."

Kaelen's hand went to the hilt of his sidearm, his gaze hardening. "Growth? You mean the Glassborne. It's actively feeding the mutation, isn't it? Making it stronger, faster."

"That is our working hypothesis," Jian confirmed, his voice grim. "The energy frequencies emanating from the fracture appear to resonate with the biological processes of the Lumina, accelerating its crystalline propagation and its infectious properties. It's like a hyper-stimulant. LUCENT was trying to weaponize it, to control it. They were playing with forces they didn't understand, and they were using the fracture's energy as their unwilling battery. Now, the fracture itself seems to have taken over the process."

The implications were staggering. Hearthglade, a settlement built on the principles of control, of order, of meticulous containment, was facing an enemy that was not only insidious and pervasive but was now being actively supercharged by an external, cosmic force. The very fabric of their defense was being undermined by a phenomenon that defied all logic and all known science. The fear in the eyes of the officials was no longer just about the creeping corruption of the Glassborne; it was about a fundamental loss of control, a terrifying realization that they were no longer the masters of their own destiny, or even their own biology.

"We need to implement stricter quarantine protocols," Elder Maris stated, her voice regaining a sliver of its former authority, though it was clearly strained. "No one enters or leaves the affected zones without full decontamination. And we must increase our patrols along the perimeter, not just for external threats, but to monitor any potential outbreaks within our own sectors. We cannot afford complacency, not now."

"The patrols are already stretched to their breaking point, Elder," Kaelen countered, his tone respectful but firm. "We've increased the frequency of sweeps, mandated hourly checks in high-risk zones. But there are only so many men and women we can spare. And every sweep risks exposing our own people to the very contagion we are trying to contain. The Lumina bloom is no longer confined to the fringes; it's becoming a part of our environment. We're fighting a losing battle if we don't understand how this fracture is impacting it."

Anya understood the dilemma. Every measure they took, every lockdown, every patrol, every decontamination procedure, only served to isolate them further, to increase the psychological pressure on the already weary population. And yet, they had to act. The stakes were too high for inaction.

"We need to recalibrate our approach," Anya declared, her voice resonating with a newfound resolve. "We can't fight the Lumina with brute force alone, especially not when it's being amplified by... by whatever this fracture is. Jian, your team needs to prioritize understanding the fracture's interaction with the Lumina. We need to find a counter-frequency, a way to disrupt that amplification. If we can negate that influence, we might be able to regain some measure of control over the mutation itself."

Jian nodded, his eyes alight with the challenge, the scientific puzzle overriding his immediate fear. "We've already begun preliminary simulations based on the LUCENT data. There are... theoretical pathways. But they require access to specific energy modulators, technology that was part of LUCENT's experimental array. We managed to salvage some of it, but its functionality is... uncertain."

"We'll find a way to make it work," Anya stated, her gaze unwavering. "Kaelen, I need you to maintain absolute vigilance. If there's any sign of a breach, any escalation, you respond with maximum force. But we also need to manage the public's fear. Maris, we need to be transparent, but also reassuring. We cannot allow panic to become the catalyst for our downfall. The people need to know we are taking action, that we have a plan, even if that plan is still in its nascent stages."

Elder Maris looked at Anya, a flicker of her old pragmatism returning. "Transparency is a double-edged sword, Captain. Too much information, too much raw truth, can shatter the fragile hope that keeps people functioning. But I understand. We will work with the communication channels. We will disseminate the necessary updates, but carefully. We will emphasize our efforts, our discoveries, and the need for unwavering discipline."

The meeting continued for hours, the small, enclosed space of the commander's office a microcosm of the larger struggle Hearthglade was facing. They discussed resource allocation, the increased demand for medical supplies, the strain on the hydroponic farms as more land was potentially rendered unusable by Lumina blooms. They debated the ethical implications of further restricting movement, of potential forced relocations if certain sectors became irrecoverably contaminated. The weight of each decision was immense, each choice carrying the potential to save lives or condemn them.

As the sun began to cast long, pale shadows across the decks of the *Iron Serpent*, Anya found herself standing on the observation deck, gazing out at the fractured sky. The Gulf Fracture, a riot of impossible colors, pulsed with an alien rhythm. It was breathtakingly beautiful and utterly terrifying. It was a testament to the vastness of the universe, to the incomprehensible forces that lay beyond their small, fragile world. And it was a stark reminder that their struggle was no longer just about survival against the elements or the remnants of a ruined civilization. It was about confronting the unknown, about understanding the incomprehensible, and about finding a way to exist in a cosmos that seemed to be actively rewriting the rules of life itself.

The expedition's return had brought not relief, but a stark confirmation of their worst fears. Hearthglade was more anxious than ever, its internal stability eroded by the relentless advance of the Glassborne, now supercharged by the celestial intrusion. The beautiful, deadly Lumina was no longer a localized threat; it was a creeping blight, a constant, terrifying reminder of their vulnerability. The atmosphere was thick with fear, a suffocating blanket woven from uncertainty and the knowledge that the very stars above them had become an accomplice to their destruction. The crossroads they had reached was not merely a point of decision, but a precipice, and the path forward was shrouded in an darkness as profound and unsettling as the Gulf Fracture itself. Anya knew, with a chilling certainty, that the true confrontation had only just begun, and that Hearthglade, along with all of humanity, was now irrevocably caught in its terrifying embrace. The return was not an end, but a grim, unsettling beginning.

The air in the war room, usually a place of calculated strategy and hushed urgency, had become a tangible entity, thick with the unspoken anxieties of Hearthglade's leaders. The flickering emergency lights cast long, distorted shadows across the faces gathered around the central table, each one a testament to the immense burden of responsibility they carried. Captain Anya Petrova, her gaze sharp and unwavering, met the collective unease with a stoic facade, yet even she could feel the tremor beneath the surface of their resilience. The LUCENT data, painstakingly retrieved from the depths of the submerged facility, offered little in the way of solace. Instead, it painted a chilling picture of an intelligence that was not merely observing, but actively re-engineering their world, with the Gulf Fracture serving as its cosmic easel.

"We have analyzed the telemetry from the outer sensors, Captain," reported Commander Jian Li, his voice strained, his usual scientific precision tempered by the sheer terror of their findings. "The energy signatures emanating from the fracture are not random. They are structured, complex, and exhibit patterns that suggest... intent. It's like a conductor orchestrating a symphony of molecular rearrangement. The Lumina blooms are not merely spreading; they are being guided, sculpted."

Kaelen, his arms crossed, his brow furrowed, added his own grim observations. "My scouts have reported increased activity in the periphery. Not just the typical Lumina growth, but... anomalies. Crystalline structures forming at an impossible rate, twisting and shifting in ways that defy natural formation. It's as if the very earth is being rewritten before our eyes. We've also detected an increase in... mobile constructs. Not organic, not entirely mechanical. They seem to be coalescing from the ambient Lumina, directed by the fracture's resonance. They are primitive, yes, but growing more sophisticated with each bloom cycle."

Elder Maris, her face etched with the weariness of a thousand sleepless nights, ran a hand over the ancient, polished surface of the table. "The people are afraid, Anya. They see the fracture, they feel the Lumina creeping closer, and they hear the whispers of what LUCENT was doing. They talk of escaping, of finding a place untouched by this... corruption. The old tales of the Sunken Cities, of pockets of land that remained dry, are being retold with a desperate fervor. They look to me for answers, for a path to safety. But where is safe, when the sky itself has become our enemy?"

This was the crux of their dilemma, the precipice upon which Hearthglade now stood: Flee or Fight? The question hung in the air, heavy with the weight of countless lives. To flee meant abandoning everything they had built, their ancestral home, the very heart of their community, and embarking on a perilous journey into the unknown, a world increasingly hostile and unpredictable. To fight meant facing an enemy they barely understood, an adversary that could manipulate their environment, spawn monstrous creations from the very air, and amplify their most feared biological threat.

Mara Ellisen, her usually vibrant presence subdued by the gravity of the situation, finally spoke, her voice quiet but clear, cutting through the rising tide of apprehension. "We cannot outrun this, Elder Maris. The fracture's influence is pervasive. The data suggests it's not just affecting the Lumina; it's subtly altering atmospheric conditions, geological structures. Even if we found a new location, how long before its influence reached us there? LUCENT's research implies this is a planetary-scale event, possibly even beyond."

Her husband, Silas, nodded in agreement, his gaze fixed on the holographic projection of Hearthglade's defensive grid. "Fleeing would scatter our resources, divide our people, and leave us vulnerable. We have established defenses here, a community built on cooperation and mutual reliance. Abandoning that would be to surrender to chaos. We have knowledge, Anya. We have Jian's findings. We have Kaelen's scouts. We have the resilience of Hearthglade. We can learn to fight this."

Anya inclined her head, acknowledging Silas's point. "The LUCENT facility contained schematics for energy dampeners, devices designed to disrupt specific frequencies. Jian believes we may be able to adapt them, to create a localized field that could counteract the fracture's amplifying effect on the Lumina. It's a long shot, but it's a tangible objective, a way to push back."

Jian elaborated, his fingers flying across his datapad, pulling up complex schematics. "The core principle involves generating a counter-resonance, a waveform that would effectively cancel out the disruptive frequencies from the fracture. The challenge is precision. We need to identify the exact resonant frequencies and then develop a power source and modulation system capable of sustaining the dampening field over a significant area. The salvaged LUCENT technology offers a starting point, but it's incomplete, and the raw power requirements are immense."

Kaelen's voice was a low rumble of concern. "And while we are experimenting, adapting alien technology, what about the immediate threats? The mobile constructs are becoming bolder. They're probing our outer defenses, testing our response times. If we divert resources to building these dampeners, we weaken our physical security. We have limited manpower, limited weaponry, and every active Lumina bloom stretches us thinner."

The weight of Kaelen's words settled on the room. It was not just about understanding the enemy; it was about surviving their attacks while that understanding was being forged. The immediate danger was as real as the existential threat.

Elder Maris looked directly at Anya, her expression unreadable. "Captain, the decision rests with you, but you must consider the will of the people. They are not soldiers, not scientists. They are survivors. They crave safety, certainty. They are tired of living in fear. A prolonged siege, even with the hope of a new weapon, might break them. They see the fracture, and they interpret it as the end of our world. Many are already preparing to leave, to take what little they can and make for the rumored high ground, the distant beacons of other settlements, however faint their signals."

Mara Ellisen stepped forward, her gaze sweeping across the faces of the council. "The people are afraid, yes. But they are also proud. They are Hearthglade. We have weathered storms, floods, and the creeping tendrils of the Glassborne for generations. This is a new threat, a terrifying one, but to abandon our home... it feels like a betrayal of everything we are. We have always faced our challenges head-on. We have always found a way. We need a plan, yes, a robust strategy for defense and for developing these dampeners. But we also need leadership that inspires hope, not just fear of the unknown."

Silas added, his voice firm, "If we flee, we become refugees, scattered and prey. Here, we are a fortress. We have the infrastructure, the knowledge base. We have the collective will to fight. We can mobilize our engineers, our technicians, our most skilled personnel to focus on Jian's project. We can establish a dedicated defense force, under

Kaelen's command, to repel the immediate incursions. We can train our citizens in basic defense, in Lumina containment protocols. It will be difficult, Anya, harder than anything we've faced before. But it is possible. And it is our only chance to reclaim our future, rather than merely run from it."

Anya's gaze drifted upwards, towards the pulsating wound in the night sky. The Gulf Fracture shimmered, a breathtaking and monstrous spectacle. It was beautiful in its alien chaos, a testament to forces far beyond their comprehension. Yet, she saw it not as a symbol of their inevitable doom, but as a challenge. LUCENT had sought to control these energies, to weaponize them. They had failed, and in their failure, they had inadvertently given humanity a glimpse of the forces at play. Now, those forces were actively reshaping their world.

"Captain," Kaelen interjected, his voice grim, "the scouts have just reported a significant surge in construct activity near Sector Gamma. They are moving with greater coordination, targeting specific points in our perimeter. They seem to be learning, adapting to our defenses."

The immediate reality of the threat struck Anya with renewed force. The theoretical debate, the long-term strategies, all of it was being overshadowed by the present danger. If they were to stand their ground, they had to be able to defend it.

"We cannot afford to be divided," Anya stated, her voice firm, projecting an authority that belied the turmoil within. "Fleeing is an option, but it is an option born of desperation, not strategy. It means abandoning our home, our resources, and scattering our strength. It means becoming prey to whatever lurks in the unknown. We have an opportunity here, however faint, to understand and to fight back. We have the scientific minds, the defensive infrastructure, and the collective will to make a stand. We will not run. We will fight."

She turned to Jian. "Your project is now Hearthglade's highest priority. Allocate whatever resources you need. I want a working prototype of that dampening field, however limited its range, within one solar cycle. Kaelen, you will establish a dedicated defense command. Reinforce Sector Gamma immediately. Identify any weaknesses in our perimeter and shore them up. I want our patrols doubled, and our response units on high alert. We will meet every probing attack with overwhelming force. We will make them pay for every inch of ground they try to take."

Her gaze swept across the council, meeting each pair of eyes. "Elder Maris, you will address the populace. Reassure them, yes, but also rally them. Tell them that Hearthglade is not a sinking ship to be abandoned, but a fortress to be defended. We will not be victims. We will be architects of our own survival. We will fight for our home, for our future, and for the right to exist in a universe that seems determined to erase us."

Mara Ellisen's eyes met Anya's, a silent understanding passing between them. "We will stand with you, Captain. Hearthglade will stand together."

Silas Ellisen, his hand resting on Mara's shoulder, added his quiet conviction. "We are a community, Anya. And we are stronger together. We will adapt. We will innovate. We will find a way to push back against this... this encroaching darkness."

The decision was made. The path of flight was rejected. The crossroads of Hearthglade had been navigated, not by seeking an easier route, but by choosing the harder, more dangerous path of defiance. The fight had begun, and the whispers of the Lumina, amplified by the cosmic symphony of the Gulf Fracture, would now be met not with fear, but with the defiant roar of a people determined to survive. The immediate aftermath was a flurry of activity. Kaelen barked orders, dispatching reconnaissance teams and mobilizing the settlement's meager militia. Engineers, guided by Jian's urgent directives, began feverishly working to adapt the salvaged LUCENT technology, their faces illuminated by the glow of unfamiliar schematics and the sheer, desperate hope of a breakthrough. The air, still thick with anxiety, now carried a new undertone: the electric hum of purpose, the grim resolve of a community preparing for the storm. They had chosen to fight, and in doing so, they had embraced their destiny, whatever horrors it might hold. The silence of the preceding days was shattered by the clatter of preparation, the sharp commands of leaders, and the unified heartbeat of a people resolved to defend their hearth.

Jax stood at the periphery of the war room, a silent observer in the maelstrom of urgent discourse. He hadn't been invited, hadn't been asked for his input, but his presence was a given, a quiet anomaly in the organized chaos. His hands, usually restless, were clasped behind his back, his gaze fixed not on the holographic displays or the strained faces of Hearthglade's leaders, but on an unseen point in the distance, a direction that no one else seemed to perceive. The frantic energy of Captain Petrova's decisions, the logical arguments of Jian Li, Kaelen's pragmatism, and Elder Maris's weary wisdom – all of it washed over him, registering not as words, but as a complex symphony of emotional frequencies, a tidal pull he was increasingly attuned to.

He felt the static. It was a subtle hum, a pervasive resonance that had been his constant companion since his encounter within the depths of the LUCENT facility. It wasn't just a sound, or a feeling; it was a form of knowing, an overlay on his own senses, a direct conduit to an immense, alien consciousness that was currently reweaving the fabric of their reality. And this knowing, this silent, irrefutable understanding, was telling him that their strategic deliberations, their desperate search for a safe haven, were akin to rearranging deck chairs on a sinking leviathan.

He had heard the captain's decisive pronouncements: "We will not run. We will fight." He had seen the flicker of hope ignite in the eyes of some, the grim determination settle on others. He understood the necessity of that resolve, the primal urge to defend one's home, to confront the encroaching darkness with a shield and a sword. But his own connection to the static whispered a different narrative, a far more chilling possibility. It was a concept that transcended the immediate threat of the Lumina or the constructs. It spoke of a fundamental shift, a planetary metamorphosis guided by an intelligence that operated on scales they could barely comprehend.

The 'reshaping,' as Jian had termed it, wasn't localized to the Gulf Fracture. Jax felt it like a growing pressure in his skull, a subtle distortion of his own sensory input. It was as if the very air molecules were vibrating at a different frequency, subtly altering the way light fell, the way sound traveled, the way reality itself was perceived. He felt it in the unnerving uniformity of the Lumina blooms, their unnatural vibrancy, their silent, relentless growth. He felt it in the nascent sentience of the constructs, the way they seemed to *learn* from Hearthglade's defenses, adapting with an unnerving speed that spoke of an intelligence far beyond simple programming.

His mind, accustomed to the structured logic of engineering, struggled to translate these impressions into coherent thought, let alone articulate them. It was like trying to describe a dream to someone who had never slept. How could he explain that the *static* was not just a disruption, but a signal? That the entity behind it, the architect of this grand, terrifying project, was not simply expanding its domain, but actively *terraforming* their world on a fundamental, biological and geological level?

He saw the faces of the council, the earnestness in their debate, the flicker of fear beneath their courage. They were preparing for a war of attrition, a defense of their borders. They believed they could carve out a pocket of resistance, a sanctuary against the encroaching wave. But Jax's silent knowing suggested something far more insidious. What if the wave wasn't something to be repelled, but something that was already *inside* them, already *within* their very environment? What if the Lumina wasn't just an external threat, but a symptom of a deeper, more pervasive change?

He recalled the fragmented LUCENT data, the cryptic references to "planetary seeding" and "bio-integration." They had dismissed it as the ramblings of a mad project, the hubris of scientists playing god. But what if it was a literal description of what was happening? What if LUCENT, in its arrogance, had stumbled upon and inadvertently *accelerated* a natural, albeit alien, process of planetary evolution?

His gaze, which had been fixed on an indeterminate point beyond the chamber walls, now drifted towards the emergency lights, then to the faces of the assembled leaders. He saw Anya Petrova, her jaw set, radiating an unshakeable resolve. He saw Silas Ellisen, his quiet strength a bedrock, ready to lend his support. He saw Mara Ellisen, her eyes reflecting the same fierce protectiveness he felt for Hearthglade. They were preparing to defend their physical space, their community, their home.

But Jax felt an echo in the static, a faint, chilling whisper that wasn't about defending borders, but about a more fundamental threat. It was the unsettling intuition that the entity they were facing, the intelligence orchestrating the transformation of their world, might not be merely *hunting* the Glassborne, as Kaelen had speculated. It might be *aware* of them. It might be aware of Hearthglade. And it might already have them in its sights, not as an enemy to be conquered, but as an element to be integrated into its grand design.

He felt the subtle shift in atmospheric pressure, a change imperceptible to the others, but as clear to him as a spoken word. It was the precursor to the Lumina's intensified growth, a ripple effect of the fracture's ever-increasing influence. And in that subtle shift, he felt a chilling certainty: the 'reshaping' was global. It was happening everywhere, at once, a symphony of cosmic re-engineering playing out across their entire planet. To flee would be to carry the seeds of their own assimilation with them, to find a new patch of ground only to watch it, too, succumb to the inevitable transformation.

This wasn't a battle for territory; it was a battle for existence, for the very definition of what it meant to be alive on this world. The choice wasn't between fleeing and fighting, but between embracing the inevitable change, however alien and terrifying, or attempting to resist a force that seemed to be rewriting the fundamental laws of their reality. Surrender, in this context, wasn't about capitulation; it was about understanding and adapting. Resistance, however, was about defiance, about carving out a space for *their* definition of life, even in the face of overwhelming cosmic alteration.

He understood why Anya had made her decision. It was the only decision that offered a glimmer of agency, a chance to actively shape their future rather than passively await their fate. But he also knew, with a certainty that settled deep in his bones, that the fight ahead would be unlike any they had ever imagined. It would require more than weapons and defenses; it would require an understanding of the forces at play that went beyond their current comprehension.

He shifted his weight, the movement almost imperceptible. The static hummed, a low thrumming against his awareness. He tried to formulate his thoughts, to distill the overwhelming sensory input into something tangible, something that could be shared. But the language of the static was not human. It was a language of resonance, of frequency, of biological and geological imperatives.

They are not hunting, the silent knowing echoed. *They are cultivating.*

The implication was staggering. The Lumina wasn't a weapon of war; it was a nutrient. The constructs weren't soldiers; they were gardeners. And Hearthglade, with its resilient populace and its established infrastructure, was simply another ecosystem within their vast, cosmic nursery.

He felt a pang of empathy for Anya and her council. They were fighting a war against an enemy they perceived as an aggressor. But what if the aggressor was simply a gardener tending to its plot? What if the Lumina was an invasive species *from their perspective*, but an integral part of the gardener's grand, planetary project?

He looked at Kaelen, who was now relaying reports of increased construct activity. Kaelen saw a tactical threat, a need for reinforcement. Jax saw a gardener tending to its plants, ensuring they received adequate sunlight and water. The Lumina was spreading, yes, but perhaps not with malice, but with a deliberate, biological imperative.

The sheer scale of it was enough to break a lesser mind. The idea that their entire planet was undergoing a conscious, directed transformation, guided by an intelligence that saw them as little more than organic components, was a terrifying prospect. It stripped away their agency, their perceived importance in the universe, and reduced them to mere participants in a process they did not initiate and could not control.

He closed his eyes, focusing on the static. It pulsed, a gentle rhythm that seemed to resonate with his own heartbeat. He felt the subtle changes in the earth beneath his feet, the faint tremors that spoke of geological shifts, of a planet slowly but surely reconfiguring itself. It wasn't a violent invasion; it was a gentle, inexorable embrace.

He knew, with a profound and unsettling clarity, that fleeing would be futile. Their problem wasn't a destination, but a condition. The static was everywhere. The Lumina was already present, in varying degrees, across the globe. The gulf fracture was not the source of the problem, but merely the focal point, the epicenter of a global metamorphosis.

And then, a new layer of the static's knowing settled upon him, a colder, sharper edge. He felt a distinct awareness directed towards Hearthglade, a focused attention that prickled his skin. It wasn't a predatory awareness, not an urge to hunt and destroy. It was an awareness of a resource, of a potential. Hearthglade, with its established biosphere and its population of sentient beings, was a valuable component in the ongoing 'reshaping.' They were not being eradicated; they were being *assessed*.

The entity hunting the Glassborne... that was a misinterpretation. The Glassborne were not being hunted as prey. They were being *studied*. Their unique biology, their resilience, their adaptation to the Lumina – these were data points, crucial pieces of information in the grand experiment. And Hearthglade, by extension, was also under observation.

His internal struggle intensified. He had to convey this, this profound sense of inevitability, this terrifying truth that their struggle was not against an invading army, but against a cosmic gardener whose methods were utterly alien. He looked at Anya, her face a mask of determination. He wanted to reach out, to touch her arm, to shatter the illusion of their control. But what words could possibly convey the sheer, unyielding nature of this transformation?

"It's not about fighting," he finally managed to murmur, the words a rough rasp in his throat. His voice, usually so quiet, carried a strange resonance that drew the attention of those closest to him. Captain Petrova's gaze snapped to him, sharp and questioning.

"What did you say, Jax?" Anya asked, her voice laced with a hint of impatience, her focus still primarily on the unfolding strategic discussions.

Jax swallowed, his throat dry. The static pulsed, urging him forward, but the human words felt clumsy, inadequate. "Fleeing... it won't work. It's not just here. It's... everywhere." He gestured vaguely, a helpless sweep of his hand encompassing the entire world. "The Lumina... it's not just growing. It's... changing things. Everything."

Commander Li, ever the scientist, tilted his head. "Jax, we understand the pervasive nature of the Lumina, but our current focus is on immediate defense. What do you mean by 'changing things'?"

Jax shook his head, frustration coiling in his gut. How to explain the inherent, fundamental shift? "It's not just the plants," he said, his voice gaining a desperate edge. "It's the air. The ground. Even... us." He tapped his temple, a small, frantic gesture. "The static... it's a kind of... knowing. And it tells me... this isn't an attack. It's... a terraforming. A global one."

Silas Ellisen, ever observant, moved closer, his brow furrowed with concern. "Terraforming? Jax, what are you talking about? LUCENT was experimenting with something, yes, but that doesn't mean—"

"LUCENT was trying to control it," Jax interrupted, his voice gaining a rare strength, fueled by the insistent hum of the static. "They didn't understand. It's not a weapon. It's... a process. And it's already happening. Everywhere. You can't run from it because it's already on its way, or worse, it's already here."

He looked at Kaelen, who had been listening intently, his usual stoic expression replaced by one of cautious curiosity. "The constructs aren't hunting, Kaelen. They're... tending. Adapting. They're part of the process."

The room fell silent, the weight of Jax's words hanging heavy in the air. They were accustomed to his quiet nature, his sometimes-cryptic pronouncements, but this was different. This was a direct challenge to their carefully constructed strategy, a suggestion that their entire premise of defense was flawed.

Captain Petrova's gaze softened, her initial impatience giving way to a deeper scrutiny. She had seen the look in Jax's eyes before, the distant, almost otherworldly focus that sometimes settled upon him. "Jax," she said, her voice carefully measured, "I understand you're feeling the effects of the static. We all are, in our own ways. But we have to act on what we can understand, on what we can control. Our people are terrified. They need a plan, a tangible strategy for survival. We cannot operate on intuition alone, however strong it may be."

"But this *is* understanding!" Jax insisted, his voice rising. "It's just... not the kind of understanding you're looking for. It's not about schematics or battle plans. It's about accepting that the rules have changed. The planet itself is being rewritten. And the entity behind it... it's not trying to destroy us. It's trying to *integrate* us. The Glassborne are a test case. Hearthglade is... the next phase."

He felt a wave of dread wash over him as he spoke the words. It was the chilling realization that the very resilience they prided themselves on, their ability to adapt and survive, was precisely what made them valuable to this cosmic gardener. They weren't targets; they were raw material.

"Integrate us?" Elder Maris whispered, her voice barely audible. The thought was clearly unsettling to her, a stark contrast to her previous plea for safety.

Jax nodded, his gaze sweeping across the faces of the council, seeing the dawning horror, the flicker of disbelief. "Yes. We are adaptable. We are resilient. We are capable of understanding and utilizing the Lumina, as the Glassborne have shown. That makes us... useful. Valuable. Not as enemies to be destroyed, but as components to be incorporated into this new... ecosystem."

He paused, letting the implications sink in. "Fleeing won't save us. Building defenses won't save us. Not in the long run. Because the enemy isn't outside our walls. It's within the very air we breathe, the ground we stand on. And if we don't understand that, if we keep fighting a war that has already been won on a fundamental level, we will simply be... assimilated."

His pronouncement hung in the charged air, a somber counterpoint to Anya's determined call to arms. He saw the conflict in her eyes, the struggle between the captain who had to lead and protect, and the individual who had to grapple with this profoundly unsettling perspective.

"So what are you suggesting, Jax?" Anya asked, her voice tight. "That we just... surrender? That we let this 'process' consume us?"

"No," Jax said, shaking his head. "Not surrender. But not defiance either, not in the way we're planning. We need to understand. We need to learn. We need to find a way to coexist, or to... redirect. If it's a gardener, perhaps we can learn to be part of the garden, but on our own terms. Or perhaps we can find a way to bloom in a different direction. But fighting it... trying to push it back... that's like trying to stop the tide with your bare hands."

He looked out at the shimmering, fractured sky, a wound in the very fabric of existence. The Gulf Fracture pulsed with an alien energy, a silent conductor orchestrating a symphony of planetary transformation. And in the heart of that symphony, Jax felt the quiet, knowing hum of an intelligence that was not driven by malice or conquest, but by an ancient, inscrutable imperative. They were not alone in the universe, and the universe, it seemed, had decided it was time for them to join its grand, ever-evolving tapestry. Hearthglade stood at a crossroads, not of fleeing or fighting, but of understanding or oblivion. And Jax, with his connection to the static, had seen a glimpse of the road less traveled, a path of acceptance and adaptation, a silent knowing that whispered of a future far stranger and more profound than any of them had dared to imagine. The choice to fight was brave, noble, and perhaps, ultimately, doomed. The choice to understand, to truly comprehend the nature of this cosmic gardener, was the only one that offered a sliver of true agency in a universe that was no longer their own.

The weight of Hearthglade's survival pressed down on Mara's shoulders, a burden far heavier than any she had imagined when Silas first spoke of leadership. It wasn't just about rationing supplies or organizing defenses; it was about the very soul of their community. Each decision felt like a pivot point, a fork in the road where one path led to a tangible, immediate safety, and the other, a nebulous, potentially world-altering future. The council's deliberations, once a source of reassurance, now felt like a cacophony of voices pulling her in a thousand different directions. Captain Petrova's unwavering resolve to fight, Jian Li's meticulous analysis of the Lumina's growth patterns, Kaelen's pragmatic assessment of their dwindling resources, Elder Maris's quiet counsel rooted in ancient wisdom – they were all valid, all critical, yet all seemed to chafe against the deeper current that Jax had so unsettlingly illuminated.

She found herself walking the perimeter of Hearthglade's protective domes, the cool, filtered air doing little to soothe the heat that seemed to emanate from within her. The Lumina, a constant, insidious presence, pulsed with an unnatural vibrancy beyond the transparent barriers. It was beautiful, in a terrifying, alien way, and she couldn't shake the feeling that Jax's words held a grim truth.

Cultivating, not conquering. *Integrating*, not eradicating. The thought was a gnawing dissonance, a constant counterpoint to the pragmatic strategies being debated within the war room.

Her gaze fell upon a group of children, their laughter echoing faintly against the hum of the life support systems. They were playing, their innocence a fragile shield against the encroaching strangeness. It was for them, she told herself. For their future. But what kind of future would it be if they merely survived, only to be absorbed into a greater, incomprehensible design? What was the point of preserving life if that life was destined to become something else entirely, something alien and unrecognizable?

Silas found her there, his presence a steady anchor in the swirling uncertainty. He didn't need to ask what was troubling her. The lines of strain etched around her eyes, the way she clutched her forearms as if to hold herself together – they spoke volumes.

"Still wrestling with it?" he asked, his voice a low rumble.

Mara nodded, turning to face him. "Every angle. Petrova wants to fortify, to create a bulwark. Jian is convinced if we can understand the Lumina's genetic code, we can find a weakness, a way to control its spread. Kaelen just wants to know how many lives we can realistically save if we commit to a defensive posture." She sighed, the sound heavy with the weight of her indecision. "And Jax... Jax speaks of a cosmic gardener. Of a transformation that is inevitable."

"Jax's perceptions are... unique," Silas said, choosing his words carefully. "He feels things others don't. But is that enough to base our survival on? To abandon every defensive measure we have?"

"That's the crux of it, isn't it?" Mara's voice was tight. "Petrova's plan is concrete. It offers immediate safety, a tangible victory. It's what people

want to hear. It's what they *need* to hear, perhaps. But Jax's... his *knowing*... it suggests that victory, in the way we understand it, might be an illusion. If the planet itself is changing, if the very air and soil are becoming... something else, then our defenses are just rearranging furniture in a house that's sinking into the sea."

She looked back at the Lumina-drenched landscape beyond the dome. The vibrant hues seemed to mock their efforts, their relentless growth a testament to a power that dwarfed their own. "If it is a cultivation, Silas, what does that make us? Are we the crops? The pests? Or simply... fertilizer?"

"We are survivors, Mara," Silas said firmly, his hand resting gently on her shoulder. "And we will find a way to survive. But survival doesn't always mean fighting what we don't understand. Sometimes, it means understanding what we must face."

"But how do we understand? Jian's research is painstaking, but the Lumina's changes are accelerating. Petrova's strategy relies on our ability to outlast it. And Jax... Jax wants us to embrace it, to learn from it, to find a way to *coexist* with a force that might be fundamentally rewriting our existence." Mara's voice cracked with the sheer enormity of the dilemma. "The lives of thousands depend on this. If I choose Petrova's path and Jax is right, we're fighting a losing battle, delaying the inevitable while making ourselves more vulnerable. If I choose Jax's path, and he's wrong, we're exposing ourselves to a threat we might have been able to contain. We could be condemning everyone."

She walked away from the perimeter, moving towards the central administrative hub. The holographic displays flickered, showing schematics of defensive emplacements, projected energy yields, and casualty estimates. It was a world of numbers, of probabilities, of strategies born from a familiar paradigm of conflict. But the static Jax described, the alien intelligence orchestrating this global transformation, operated on a different plane entirely.

"What if," Mara mused, her voice barely audible, "what if the Lumina isn't just a plant? What if it's a form of communication? Or a tool? Jax said the constructs were 'tending.' Tending what? And why?"

Silas followed her, his gaze thoughtful. "LUCENT's records spoke of bio-integration, of planetary seeding. They were attempting to manipulate the process, not merely observe it. Perhaps this entity, whatever it is, is merely continuing what LUCENT started, but on a scale they never imagined."

"And we're caught in the middle," Mara finished, a grim realization dawning. "We are the legacy of LUCENT's ambition, the unintended consequences of their interference. If they were trying to control this, and failed, then perhaps this 'gardener' is simply tending to its own garden, with us as an unexpected, but not unwelcome, addition."

She stopped, her hand hovering over a console. The temptation to order the fortification of Hearthglade, to give her people the immediate sense of security they craved, was immense. It was the path of least resistance, the one that aligned with generations of human instinct – to build walls, to defend what is theirs. But Jax's words echoed in her mind, a persistent whisper of a far greater, far more complex reality.

"The Glassborne," she said, turning to Silas. "Jax mentioned them. He said they were a 'test case.' He said their resilience, their adaptation to the Lumina, made them valuable. What if that's the key? What if the answer isn't in fighting the Lumina, but in understanding it? In learning from the Glassborne?"

"The Glassborne are a different kind of survivor, Mara," Silas cautioned. "They've been... changed. We don't know the cost of their adaptation. And they are few, nomadic. We have a community, a society to protect. We can't afford to experiment recklessly."

"But can we afford *not* to?" Mara countered, her voice firming with a newfound resolve. "If Jax is right, if this is a planetary metamorphosis, then our survival depends not on our ability to resist, but on our ability to *adapt*. Not just our bodies, but our minds, our society. We need to understand this force, not just defend against it."

She looked at the holographic displays, at the cold, hard logic of military strategy. It felt... insufficient. Like trying to understand a symphony by analyzing the individual notes. "I can't just order the defenses up, Silas," she said, her voice laced with a deep weariness. "Not without considering the alternative. We need to dedicate resources to Jian's research, yes, but we also need to actively investigate Jax's claims. We need to try and communicate with the Glassborne, to understand how they've endured. We need to look for the patterns, the intent, if there is any."

"That sounds like a significant diversion of resources, Mara," Silas said, his brow furrowed. "Petrova will argue that every drone, every energy cell, every soldier must be focused on immediate defense. She will say this is a luxury we cannot afford."

"And what if it's a necessity?" Mara's eyes blazed with a fierce, protective light. "What if this 'luxury' is the only path that leads to long-term survival? What if our definition of survival needs to change? We can't afford to be shortsighted. We can't afford to fight a war that has already been won by our opponent, on a fundamental, biological level."

She took a deep breath, the weight of her decision settling, not as a crushing blow, but as a heavy, guiding force. "We will reinforce the outer perimeters, as Petrova suggests. We will not appear to be ignoring the immediate threat. But the bulk of our research efforts, our intelligence gathering, will be directed towards understanding this 'reshaping.' Jian will continue his Lumina analysis, but with a new focus on its integration capabilities, not just its toxicity. And we will send a small, highly skilled team to attempt contact with the Glassborne. We need to learn from them, from their experience."

She met Silas's gaze, her own reflecting a mixture of apprehension and steely determination. "This is not a popular decision, I know. Petrova will see it as hesitation, as a weakness. But sometimes, the bravest act is not to charge headlong into battle, but to seek understanding, even when that understanding is terrifying. We are at a crossroads, Silas. We can choose to fight the tide, or we can learn to swim with it. And I believe, with every fiber of my being, that learning to swim is the only way we might reach shore."

The path ahead was fraught with peril. The council would likely resist, fracturing their fragile unity. The risks of seeking out the Glassborne were immense. And the possibility that Jax was simply a conduit for delusion, that this entire cosmic transformation was a figment of his damaged psyche, was a shadow that loomed large. But Mara knew, with a certainty that resonated with the deep, almost biological rhythm of the planet itself, that Hearthglade could not survive by merely clinging to the past. They had to look forward, to adapt, to evolve. Their burden of leadership was not just to protect lives, but to guide them towards a future that, however alien, might still hold a place for humanity. The weight was immense, but for the sake of the children she had seen, for the unwritten potential of Hearthglade's future, she would carry it.

The council chamber, usually a place of measured debate and reasoned discourse, crackled with an energy that was anything but calm. Mara stood at the head of the polished synth-wood table, the holographic projection of Hearthglade's intricate defense grid shimmering behind her. She had presented her decision, a carefully balanced course of action that acknowledged Petrova's pragmatism and Jian's scientific rigor, while also embracing the unsettling, yet persistent, insights of Jax. The silence that followed was heavy, pregnant with unspoken dissent and cautious approval.

Captain Petrova, her uniform crisp and her posture rigid, was the first to break the stillness. Her eyes, sharp as shards of obsidian, were fixed on Mara. "With all due respect, Administrator," she began, her voice a low, resonant contralto, "your directive to allocate significant resources towards 'understanding' this... phenomenon... while simultaneously reinforcing our perimeter feels like a thinly veiled indecision. We are not a research outpost. We are a sanctuary. And sanctuaries require walls, not philosophical inquiries into the nature of existential transformation."

Jian Li, his fingers steepled beneath his chin, offered a more nuanced perspective. "Captain Petrova's concern for immediate security is valid. The Lumina's growth rate is concerning, and its invasive properties are well-documented. However," he continued, adjusting his spectacles, "Administrator Mara's proposal to study the Lumina's integration capabilities, rather than solely its toxicity, presents a unique opportunity. My team has theorized that the Lumina might possess an inherent signaling mechanism, a form of biological communication that we have thus far overlooked. If we can decipher this 'language,' we might not only understand its intentions but potentially influence its behavior. This is not a diversion; it is a strategic reorientation of our efforts."

Kaelen, ever the pragmatist, leaned forward, his brow furrowed. "The numbers are clear. Our current resource allocation can sustain a robust defense for approximately six months, with a projected casualty rate of fifteen percent should a full-scale assault occur. Diverting any significant portion of our energy reserves, our fabrication units, or our personnel to... what exactly? Observing alien flora? Attempting communication with nomadic survivors whose own methods of adaptation are unproven and potentially dangerous? It's a gamble, Administrator. A monumental gamble with the lives of every soul within these domes." His gaze swept across the faces of the council members, a silent appeal to reason, to the stark reality of their finite resources.

Elder Maris, her face a landscape of serene wisdom, finally spoke, her voice a gentle murmur that nevertheless commanded attention. "We have always faced the unknown with a combination of strength and wisdom," she said, her eyes meeting Mara's. "To stand and fight is a testament to our courage. To seek understanding is a testament to our intelligence. To flee... that is an admission of defeat before the battle has even begun. Jax's insights, however unconventional, have illuminated a path that requires both. Petrova's defenses will shield us from immediate harm. Jian's research will unlock the secrets of our adversary. And the exploration of Jax's theories, however perilous, might offer a future beyond mere survival."

Mara felt a surge of gratitude for the Elder's quiet support. It was a beacon in the storm of doubt. She raised her hand, silencing the murmur of discussion that had begun to ripple through the chamber. "I understand the concerns," she stated, her voice clear and steady, projecting a confidence she didn't entirely feel. "And I respect them. Captain Petrova, your commitment to our defense is unwavering, and it is precisely that commitment that allows us to even

consider other avenues. We will reinforce the outer perimeters. We will maintain our current defensive posture, ensuring that Hearthglade remains an impregnable bastion against any direct aggression. Every energy cell, every drone, every trained operative will be utilized to maximize our immediate security. This is not indecision; it is a layered strategy."

She turned to Jian. "Dr. Li, your research will be prioritized. We will reallocate a portion of our drone fleet to assist in the collection of Lumina samples, focusing on areas identified as having unique bio-integration signatures. We will also dedicate fabrication resources to developing new sensor arrays capable of analyzing the Lumina's energy fluctuations at a molecular level. Your hypothesis of a signaling mechanism is compelling, and we will invest in its validation. The potential to understand, and perhaps even communicate with, this planetary intelligence is a prize worth pursuing, but it will not come at the expense of our immediate safety."

Mara then addressed Kaelen, her gaze direct. "Kaelen, I acknowledge the risk. The expedition to locate and assess the Glassborne will be a small, highly specialized unit. They will be equipped with advanced cloaking technology and minimal weaponry, prioritizing stealth and observation over confrontation. Their mission is reconnaissance and data acquisition – to learn from those who have already endured a significant level of adaptation. If their methods offer a viable path to coexistence, we need to know. If they represent a danger, we need to understand that too. It is a calculated risk, not a reckless endeavor, and I am confident in the individuals we will select for this crucial task."

Her gaze then settled on Jax, who had remained silent in the back of the chamber, his expression unreadable. "Jax," she continued, her voice softening slightly, "your insights have been... pivotal. We cannot dismiss them. We will establish a dedicated observation post near the areas you have indicated, equipped with sensory equipment designed to detect the specific energy signatures you have described. You will be part of this team, guiding their observations. Your understanding, your 'knowing,' is invaluable, and we will ensure it is properly utilized."

She paused, letting her words settle, then looked around the table, her gaze meeting each council member's. "This is not about surrendering to the Lumina, nor is it about a futile attempt to eradicate it. It is about adapting to a new reality. It is about survival through understanding. We are no longer fighting for a lost past, but for a future we must actively shape. The Lumina represents a fundamental shift in our planet's ecosystem, perhaps even its consciousness. To ignore it, to simply build walls and hope it goes away, is to condemn ourselves to obsolescence. We must engage. We must learn. We must evolve."

A palpable shift occurred in the room. The initial resistance began to ebb, replaced by a grudging acceptance, a dawning realization of the strategic necessity. Petrova, though still visibly skeptical, gave a curt nod. Jian's eyes gleamed with scientific anticipation. Kaelen, while his reservations remained etched on his face, acknowledged the meticulously laid-out plan.

"We will proceed, Administrator," Petrova finally stated, her tone devoid of warmth but carrying the weight of command. "But make no mistake, any indication that these... 'explorations'... jeopardize our defenses will be met with immediate and decisive action on my part. Our primary directive remains the safety of Hearthglade's citizens."

"Understood, Captain," Mara replied, a sense of quiet resolve settling over her. "And my secondary directive is to ensure that safety extends beyond the present moment, into a future where such defenses might not be enough."

The meeting adjourned, the council members dispersing with a renewed sense of purpose, albeit one tinged with apprehension. Mara remained for a moment, looking at the holographic representation of Hearthglade, a delicate filigree of lights and circuits against the encroaching, vibrant chaos of the Lumina-infused landscape. The decision had been made. They would not be passive victims. They would stand, not in defiance of the inevitable, but in preparation for it. They would fight, yes, but their fight would be one of intellect, of adaptation, of understanding.

The journey to the Glassborne encampment was fraught with peril. Mara had personally selected the team: Captain Eva Rostova, a seasoned field operative with an uncanny knack for navigating treacherous terrain and de-escalating volatile situations; Dr. Kenji Tanaka, a xenobotanist with a keen understanding of bio-adaptation and a reputation for meticulous, albeit sometimes unorthodox, research; and Jax, whose unique connection to the Lumina made him an indispensable, if enigmatic, guide. Their transport, a compact, heavily shielded scout shuttle named the 'Whisper,' was equipped with state-of-the-art stealth technology, designed to minimize their detection by both automated systems and the less predictable elements of the transformed biosphere.

As the Whisper lifted off, ascending through Hearthglade's atmospheric processors, Mara watched from the observation deck. Below, the domed city gleamed, a fragile sanctuary of human endeavor against the overwhelming power of the alien growth. It was a stark reminder of what they were fighting for, and what they stood to lose. Petrova's fortifications were a testament to their resilience, a bulwark against the immediate storm. Jian's ongoing research within the city's labs was the silent, methodical probing of the enemy's mind. And the Whisper, carrying Rostova, Tanaka, and Jax, represented a bold leap into the unknown, a commitment to understanding the true nature of the threat, and perhaps, finding a way to coexist.

The journey itself was a testament to the planet's altered state. The familiar atmospheric turbulence had been replaced by an almost sentient quality to the air currents, as if the planet itself was guiding or resisting their passage. Lumina vines, thick as ancient trees, pulsed with an internal luminescence, casting eerie, shifting patterns of light and shadow across the landscape. Strange, crystalline structures, shimmering with bioluminescence, jutted from the earth like colossal, petrified flora. The air, even filtered through the shuttle's advanced systems, carried a faint, cloying scent, a mixture of ozone, damp earth, and something subtly sweet, almost floral.

Jax, seated beside Tanaka in the shuttle's cramped cockpit, pointed to a vast, undulating expanse of iridescent foliage below. "That region," he murmured, his voice a low hum that seemed to vibrate with the shuttle's engines, "the Lumina's growth there is... accelerated. It's reacting to something. A pressure point. The constructs are most active in areas like that."

Tanaka, his face illuminated by the flickering readouts on his console, nodded slowly. "The energy signatures are off the charts, Jax. It's as if the very cellular structure of the planet is undergoing rapid rearrangement. We're detecting novel organic compounds, unlike anything in our existing databases. It's... beautiful, in a terrifying way." He paused, a thoughtful frown creasing his brow. "You said the constructs were 'tending.' What do you believe they are cultivating?"

Jax closed his eyes for a moment, a faint tremor running through him. "Not cultivating, precisely. More like... pruning. Guiding. The Lumina is a network, a vast, interconnected organism. The constructs are its... extensions. Its hands. They are ensuring the network grows according to a specific design. A design we cannot yet comprehend."

Rostova, her gaze fixed on the external monitors, her hand resting near the shuttle's minimal armament controls, chimed in. "And the Glassborne? Where do they fit into this grand design, Jax? Are they pests to be eradicated, or part of the intended harvest?"

Jax opened his eyes, a flicker of something unreadable in their depths. "They are... anomalies. Survivors. They have found a way to integrate, to adapt, without being fully subsumed. They are a testament to resilience, but also a warning. Their adaptation came at a cost. A cost we must understand before we seek to emulate it."

Hours later, as the Whisper descended into a deep, mist-shrouded canyon, the first signs of the Glassborne appeared. Not as crude shelters, but as subtle integrations with the environment. Smooth, crystalline pathways snaked through the dense foliage, seeming to grow organically from the Lumina-encrusted rock. Structures, more sculpted than built, blended seamlessly with the natural formations, their surfaces shimmering with an inner light. The air grew cooler, the sweet scent of the Lumina receding, replaced by a cleaner, more mineral aroma.

"Passive detection suggests multiple life signs," Rostova reported, her voice low and professional. "No overt hostiles. They are aware of our presence."

As the Whisper settled gently onto a flat, natural clearing, a figure emerged from the crystalline structures. Tall and slender, their form seemed to shimmer, their skin translucent, revealing a network of faint, pulsating veins beneath. Their eyes, large and dark, regarded the shuttle with an unnerving stillness. They wore no clothing, their bodies adorned with intricate, naturally formed crystalline growths that seemed to grow directly from their flesh. They were, in essence, living embodiments of the planet's transformation.

"They are... magnificent," Tanaka breathed, awe evident in his voice.

"And potentially dangerous," Rostova added, her hand tightening on her sidearm.

Jax, however, simply stepped forward, his hands held loosely at his sides. He made no move towards the shuttle's ramp. Instead, he took a slow, deliberate step onto the alien soil, his gaze locked with that of the approaching Glassborne.

"We come in peace," Jax said, his voice amplified by the shuttle's external speakers, yet sounding strangely intimate, as if speaking directly into the mind of the being before them. "We seek to understand. To learn from your survival."

The Glassborne being tilted its head, a subtle gesture that conveyed a wealth of curiosity and caution. Then, in a voice that resonated not through the air, but seemingly within their very bones, it replied, a chorus of whispers interwoven with crystalline chimes.

"Understand? You seek to understand the flow? The change? Many have sought. Few have found. The cost is... significant."

This was it. The beginning of their understanding. The first step in a journey that would define Hearthglade's future. Whether they would find a path to coexistence or a brutal, alienating transformation, the choice had been made. Hearthglade would not be a passive observer of its own demise. It would stand, it would learn, and it would, in its own way, fight for its place in this new, vibrant, and terrifying world. The collective stand had begun, not with the clang of weapons, but with the quiet hum of inquiry, a single shuttle venturing into the heart of the Lumina's embrace, seeking wisdom from those who had already begun to dance with the cosmic gardener. The fate of Hearthglade, and perhaps humanity's future on this transformed world, hinged on the fragile exchange that was now taking place in the silent, shimmering heart of the canyon. The path ahead was uncertain, shrouded in mist and the unknown, but it was a path they had chosen to walk. They would not simply survive; they would strive to understand, to adapt, and ultimately, to find their place in the grand, unfolding tapestry of the planet's metamorphosis.

CHAPTER TEN

THE RESHAPING BEGINS

T he air itself seemed to thicken, no longer merely a mixture of nitrogen and oxygen, but a viscous, breathable medium that hummed with an unseen energy. Days after the cataclysmic fracturing of the Gulf, a profound stillness had settled, not of peace, but of anticipation. Hearthglade, a self-contained bubble of defiance, remained a beacon of order in a world that was now aggressively, irrevocably rewriting its own rules. Outside its shimmering shields, the reshaping began not with a roar, but with a whisper that promised to drown out all other sound.

The first discernible changes were atmospheric. The sky, once a familiar canvas of blues and grays, began to exhibit a spectrum of impossible hues. Auroras, once confined to the poles, now danced in ethereal curtains across the midday sky, their vibrant, pulsing light a constant, unsettling reminder of the planet's alien transformation. These were not the gentle, fleeting displays of terrestrial physics; they were persistent, weaving complex patterns, sometimes coalescing into vast, slowly rotating geometric shapes that defied comprehension. Dr. Jian Li's sensor arrays, meticulously recalibrated after the initial shock, struggled to categorize the new phenomena. The light emitted was not merely reflected or refracted; it seemed to possess an inherent luminescence, a signature that pulsed with biological rhythms rather than photonic energy. His team reported fluctuations in localized gravity fields correlating with the intensity of these celestial displays, suggesting that the very fabric of spacetime was being subtly warped.

Geographical shifts followed, less like earthquakes and more like a slow, deliberate sculpting. Entire mountain ranges, once immutable sentinels, appeared to soften, their peaks subtly rounding, their slopes recontouring as if shaped by an invisible potter's hand. Valleys deepened, not through erosion, but through a seemingly organic sinking of the earth. Rivers, their courses charting predictable paths for millennia, began to meander, their waters sometimes flowing uphill for short distances before resuming their descent, defying the very principles of hydrology. The Lumina, once confined to specific regions, was now a pervasive presence, its tendrils weaving through this evolving landscape, not merely growing, but *integrating* with the terraformed elements. Crystalline structures, echoing the Lumina's own iridescent properties, began to emerge from the bedrock, not as deposits, but as if the very earth was crystallizing, birthing alien formations from its core. These were not random occurrences; Jax, his connection to the planet's burgeoning consciousness deepening, described it as a "guided growth," an intentional rearrangement of planetary architecture. He spoke of pressure points, areas where the Lumina's influence was strongest, and where the most dramatic transformations were occurring. He pointed to satellite imagery, highlighting vast swathes of land where the Lumina's pulsating bio-luminescence intensified, and within these zones, the geographical anomalies were most pronounced.

The most disturbing, however, was the alteration in fundamental physical laws. In certain areas, gravity would fluctuate without warning, sending loose debris drifting upwards before crashing back down. The speed of sound seemed to vary, rendering communication systems unreliable at the best of times. Time itself appeared to ripple; Jian's chronometers, synchronized with Hearthglade's atomic clock, frequently displayed discrepancies when deployed in the field, some lagging, others inexplicably ahead. It was as if the planet's inherent operating system was being rewritten, and the old code was being replaced by something fundamentally alien.

"It's not destruction, Administrator," Jian explained during a tense briefing, his voice strained, his eyes bloodshot from countless hours spent poring over data. "It's... optimization. The Lumina, or whatever intelligence is orchestrating this, isn't just spreading. It's actively *repurposing* the planet. It's reconfiguring the environment to suit its own inherent properties, to maximize its own... function. We're seeing localized alterations in electromagnetic fields that are far beyond natural occurrences. Entire geological strata are being rearranged. It's like watching a sculptor at work, but the medium is the entire planet, and the tools are forces we don't yet understand."

Kaelen, ever the voice of pragmatic concern, presented the resource implications. "These atmospheric anomalies are playing havoc with our long-range sensors and drone patrols. We've lost three reconnaissance drones in the last cycle due to unpredictable gravimetric surges. The energy drain to maintain our shield integrity against these... energetic atmospheric shifts is also increasing. We're burning through reserves faster than anticipated. And this geographical instability... it's making our terraforming efforts, our efforts to reclaim arable land, utterly futile. We build, and the ground shifts. We plant, and the soil crystallizes."

Mara listened intently, her gaze fixed on the flickering holographic displays that showed the ever-changing face of their world. The reports from Rostova's reconnaissance teams, those brave few who ventured beyond Hearthglade's protective embrace, painted a picture of a world in constant, fluid motion. Captain Eva Rostova herself, her voice betraying a weariness that went beyond physical exhaustion, described encounters with what she termed "resonant pockets" – areas where sound carried for impossibly long distances, or where silence became an oppressive, tangible force. She spoke of witnessing rock formations that seemed to hum with latent energy, their crystalline surfaces vibrating in time with the atmospheric auroras.

"It's not just the Lumina, Administrator," Rostova had reported from a forward observation post, her image flickering on Mara's private terminal. "There's an intelligence at work here, a deliberate hand guiding the change. We observed a region where the Lumina was actively... directing water flow. Not just growing around it, but actively carving channels, raising barriers, manipulating the terrain to create what looked like... a biological irrigation system. It was almost... intentional. Like a gardener tending its plants, but the plants are mountains and rivers."

Jax, his pronouncements often cryptic but increasingly accurate, provided a different perspective. He spoke of the planet developing a "new nervous system," with the Lumina as the primary conduit. The atmospheric phenomena, the geographical shifts, the altered physics – he saw them not as random events, but as the planet's biological processes adapting, recalibrating under the influence of an external, intelligent force. He described the Lumina's tendrils not just as physical extensions, but as conduits of information, transmitting complex signals that dictated the planet's metamorphosis. "It's learning to breathe again," he had whispered to Mara, his eyes distant. "But with a different set of lungs, a different heart."

The implications were staggering. This wasn't a natural disaster; it was a planetary-scale terraforming event orchestrated by an alien intelligence. Hearthglade, in its desperate attempt to preserve a sliver of the old Earth, was finding itself in the path of a cosmic gardener reshaping its domain. The understanding that they were not merely facing a biological infestation, but an active, intelligent manipulator of reality, was a chilling one. It shifted the nature of their struggle from one of defense against a biological threat to one of adaptation and negotiation with a force that could rewrite the very laws of existence.

The subtle alterations were insidious. The flora and fauna that had managed to survive the initial upheaval were also exhibiting signs of this imposed change. Native species, if they survived at all, were subtly altered, their genetic structures seemingly influenced by the omnipresent Lumina. Reports filtered in of animals with bioluminescent patterns mirroring the auroras, or with physiological adaptations that allowed them to navigate the fluctuating gravity fields. It was a forced evolution, a rapid, unnatural selection dictated by the planet's new master.

Mara called another council meeting, the air in the chamber thick with the weight of this new, terrifying reality. Petrova, though still primarily focused on defense, could not deny the escalating challenges. "Our energy shield is being tested as never before, Administrator. The atmospheric ionization alone is creating energy bleed-offs that we didn't predict. We're diverting power from life support redundancies to maintain the shields. It's a calculated risk, but the margins are shrinking."

Jian, his face gaunt, presented a series of complex waveform analyses. "The Lumina's bio-signatures are evolving. They are not just adapting to the changes; they are *driving* them. We've detected specific harmonic frequencies emanating from the planet's core, correlating directly with the periods of most intense atmospheric and geological restructuring. This isn't random; it's a directed symphony of planetary modification." He gestured to a particularly complex graph. "This particular frequency pattern? It's similar to the signal we detected when the Lumina first breached the outer perimeter. But amplified, refined. It's as if the planet is communicating with itself, and the Lumina is the intermediary."

Kaelen, his usual pragmatism bordering on despair, laid out the grim resource projections. "Our fabrication units are struggling to keep pace with the demand for specialized shielding materials. The increased atmospheric radiation is also degrading the efficiency of our solar arrays. We're going to have to implement even more stringent rationing. And the geological instability... we can't even begin to think about expansion or long-term infrastructure projects when the ground beneath us is literally being remolded."

Mara's gaze drifted to Jax, who sat in his usual quiet corner. His presence had become indispensable, his cryptic pronouncements often the only clues they had to the unfolding chaos. "Jax," she began, her voice steady despite the turmoil churning within her. "What are we seeing? What is the purpose of this... reshaping?"

Jax closed his eyes, a faint tremor passing through his form. When he spoke, his voice was a low murmur, imbued with a weariness that mirrored the planet's own transformation. "The old Earth is... being shed. Like a skin. The Lumina is not merely a colonizer; it is a gardener. It is pruning, shaping, replanting. The planet is being reconfigured. Its very essence is being... rewritten." He paused, his brow furrowed. "The constructs you saw, Rostova... they are the hands of the gardener.

They tend to the soil, they guide the growth. They ensure the design is followed."

"And the Glassborne?" Kaelen pressed, his tone sharp. "They've adapted. Are they part of this design? Or have they found a way to resist?"

Jax opened his eyes, a faint light flickering within them. "They are... anomalies. Survivors who have found a way to coexist with the gardener's intent, without fully becoming its instruments. They have integrated, but they retain a degree of their own... will. Their adaptation is a testament to resilience, but also a warning. They have paid a price for their integration. A price we must understand."

Mara nodded, a slow, deliberate movement. The pieces were beginning to coalesce, forming a picture far more complex and terrifying than they had initially imagined. They were not merely defending against an invasion; they were witnessing the birth of a new world, a world being actively, intelligently shaped by an alien consciousness. Hearthglade was an anachronism, a relic of a past that was rapidly fading into an alien present. Their struggle for survival had transformed from a battle for preservation into a desperate, ongoing negotiation with the very forces that were reshaping their reality.

The implications of an "unseen hand" actively manipulating Earth's environment sent a shiver down Mara's spine. This was not a natural ecological collapse; this was a deliberate, guided transformation. The Lumina, or the intelligence behind it, was moving beyond passive observation and into active planetary engineering. The very physics of their world were being rewritten, not randomly, but with an apparent purpose. This was a fundamental shift in the nature of their adversary, and it demanded a fundamental shift in their response. Their survival no longer depended on simply holding a perimeter, but on understanding and perhaps even influencing the colossal forces that were now in play, forces that could reshape the world – and them along with it – in ways they could not yet comprehend. The reshaping had truly begun, and it was far more profound than anyone had anticipated.

The sky, once a canvas of increasingly surreal colors and shifting geometries, had begun to exhibit a new characteristic. The ambient electromagnetic fluctuations, the whispers of the Lumina's influence that had been growing steadily, were coalescing into something far more deliberate. Jax, his senses attuned to the planet's subtle transformations, was the first to articulate it, his pronouncements initially as enigmatic as ever. "The static is no longer weeping," he'd told Mara during a late-night observation, his eyes fixed on the pulsating sky. "It is singing."

His words, initially dismissed as further metaphor, began to gain traction as more data flooded in. Dr. Jian Li's team, analyzing the vast swathes of data collected by Hearthglade's enhanced sensor arrays, noticed the increasing regularity. The chaotic bursts of energy, the seemingly random flickers and surges that had characterized the atmospheric phenomena, were resolving into discernible patterns. These weren't merely echoes of the Lumina's growth; they were intricate, complex sequences that bore the hallmarks of intelligent design. "It's as if a primal signal, the raw energy of the Lumina's integration, has been refined," Jian explained, projecting a holographic representation of the waveform onto the sterile briefing room wall. "The raw noise is being modulated. We're seeing recurring motifs, what look like... packets of information. They are structured. They are ordered. They are, for lack of a better term, linguistic."

The Lumina, it seemed, was not merely a biological agent or a planetary architect. It was also a broadcaster. The atmospheric static, a phenomenon that had initially been a source of confusion and a physical impediment, was evolving into an alien language. This was not a transmission picked up by radio waves in the conventional sense, but rather a manipulation of the very fundamental forces that governed their reality. Gravity fluctuations, localized electromagnetic shifts, and even subtle distortions in the flow of time were being interwoven into a complex tapestry of communication. Imagine a symphony composed not of sound waves, but of shifting gravitational fields and flickering light patterns, a language spoken in the very fabric of spacetime.

Jax elaborated, his connection to the planet's emergent consciousness offering a perspective that eluded conventional scientific analysis. "The Lumina speaks through the planet's reordering," he stated, his voice a low, resonant hum. "Each shift in the rock, each ripple in the atmosphere, is a word. The Lumina is not just building a new world; it is describing it. It is explaining itself. It is... teaching." He described how the vibrant auroras were not just displays of energy, but complex visual glyphs, their patterns shifting in response to specific gravitational pulses originating from deep within the planet's core. He spoke of a "syntax of light and gravity," a grammar that dictated how these elements interacted to convey meaning. The Lumina's tendrils, those pervasive biological extensions, were not just conduits for its physical growth; they were also antennae, receiving and transmitting these profound signals.

The implications were immense. If the Lumina was communicating, what was it saying? Was it a benevolent explanation, a neutral broadcast of its intentions, or a declaration of dominance? The sheer complexity of the observed patterns suggested a level of intelligence far beyond anything they had previously conceived. Jian's team worked feverishly to decipher these alien transmissions, developing new algorithms that could analyze not just the energy signatures, but the intricate relationships between them. They began to isolate recurring sequences, identifying what appeared to be fundamental units of meaning – analogous to phonemes or morphemes in human languages.

"We're seeing what could be interpreted as 'declarative' sequences," explained Anya Sharma, a xenolinguistics specialist brought in from Hearthglade's advanced research division. Her team had been struggling with the Lumina's biological communication patterns, but the shift to atmospheric signaling had opened up new avenues. "When a significant geographical rearrangement occurs, there's a distinct harmonic convergence of electromagnetic frequencies and subtle gravimetric distortions that precedes and follows it. It's not just passive observation; it's as if the Lumina is announcing its actions, or perhaps even receiving confirmation." She pointed to a complex graph showing overlapping waveforms. "This cluster here," she highlighted a section with a laser pointer, "appears consistently before a significant alteration in local atmospheric pressure. We're tentatively labeling it a 'pressure-change' marker."

The challenge, however, was immense. Human language, even with its vast complexities, is rooted in shared biological and cultural experiences. They understood concepts like 'threat,' 'desire,' or 'information' because they were products of evolution and societal development. The Lumina's language, if it could be called that, was born from a completely alien frame of reference. What did 'growth' mean to a planetary-scale consciousness? What was the equivalent of 'survival' or 'reproduction' for an entity that reshaped continents as easily as a human might reshape clay?

Jax's contributions became increasingly crucial. He didn't analyze data in the same way Jian's team did. His understanding was more intuitive, more empathic. He described the Lumina's messages not as abstract data points, but as feelings, as intentions, as fundamental truths about its existence. "It is not a language of words," he'd explained to Mara, his gaze distant, fixed on the shimmering sky above Hearthglade. "It is a language of being. It communicates its state of existence, its purpose, its very nature. It is... revealing itself." He would often fall silent for long stretches, his brow furrowed in concentration, as if engaged in a silent dialogue with the planet itself. Then, he would offer a cryptic insight: "The Lumina understands balance, but not as we do. Its balance is one of constant flux, of dynamic equilibrium. Its language reflects this. It is a continuous narrative of change."

One particularly fascinating discovery involved the "resonant pockets" Rostova's teams had encountered. Eva Rostova herself, her face grim but resolute in a holographic transmission, provided further details. "We ventured into one of these zones, Administrator. A valley where sound carried for miles. And the Lumina's atmospheric signature... it was amplified within that pocket. The static, the auroras, they were more vibrant, more complex. It felt like we had entered a... communication hub. A place where the Lumina's messages were being broadcast with greater clarity, perhaps even with a higher bandwidth."

Jian's team corroborated this. Their sensors registered significantly higher energy densities and more coherent signal patterns within these resonant pockets. It was as if the Lumina had created specific areas where its language was more easily transmitted and received, like natural amphitheatres designed for planetary-scale pronouncements. These were not merely geographical anomalies; they were deliberate architectural choices within the Lumina's grand design, chosen for their acoustic or energetic properties that facilitated communication.

The implications of this alien language were profound. If they could understand it, they might be able to predict the Lumina's next moves, to anticipate its intentions. More importantly, they might even be able to communicate back. The thought was both exhilarating and terrifying. Could humanity, a species that had struggled for millennia to truly understand its own kind, hope to bridge the chasm to an alien consciousness that spoke in the language of planetary forces?

Anya Sharma's team began to develop a theoretical framework for decoding. They posited that the Lumina's language was likely multi-modal, a synthesis of atmospheric patterns, gravimetric shifts, light frequencies, and possibly even subtle temporal distortions. Their approach was to look for correlations between these different phenomena and observable planetary changes. When a new crystalline structure emerged from the earth, what accompanying atmospheric patterns were present? When a river reversed its flow, what subtle gravimetric pulse accompanied it?

"We're beginning to see what might be rudimentary grammatical structures," Anya reported, her voice tight with a mixture of exhaustion and excitement. "There are patterns of repetition that suggest subject-verb-object relationships, albeit in a form we can barely grasp. For instance, we've identified a recurring sequence of three distinct energy pulses followed by a specific light modulation. This sequence appears to precede the formation of new Lumina-infused flora in a particular area. We're calling it the 'generation' sequence."

Jax offered another layer of interpretation. He suggested that the Lumina's language was not just informational, but also existential. It was a continuous expression of its being, its purpose, and its relationship with the universe. "It is not telling us a story," he'd said, gazing at the sky, which was currently displaying a particularly intricate aurora that seemed to spiral inwards towards a point of intense luminescence. "It *is* the story. We are witnessing its unfolding existence, translated into the physical realities of this planet. Each pulse, each flicker, is a moment of its consciousness made manifest."

Kaelen, ever the pragmatist, focused on the immediate applications. "If this is a language, and if it contains information about the Lumina's intentions, then understanding it becomes paramount to our survival. Can we use this 'language' to predict where the next geological upheaval will occur? Can we identify areas that the Lumina deems 'stable' or 'suitable' for its purposes, and conversely, areas it intends to reshape? This could be the key to avoiding direct confrontation, to finding safe zones, or even to understanding where we might be able to establish our own... presence, however tenuous."

The notion of finding "safe zones" was a tantalizing prospect, but also a dangerous one. If the Lumina was intentionally reshaping the planet, then any area deemed "safe" might simply be an area temporarily overlooked, or an area whose resources were being reserved for a later phase of its grand design. The idea of communicating back was even more fraught with peril. What if their attempts at communication were perceived as aggression, or as an insult to this planetary intelligence? What if their limited understanding led them to broadcast something that was fundamentally antithetical to the Lumina's nature?

Jian's team, in collaboration with Anya's xenolinguistics unit, began to build rudimentary communication protocols. They focused on mimicking simple Lumina patterns, using carefully calibrated energy emitters and modulated gravity fields generated within Hearthglade's shielded testing chambers. Their goal was not to engage in complex dialogue, but to establish a basic acknowledgement, a sign that humanity was present and attempting to understand. They started by attempting to replicate the simplest identified sequences, the basic building blocks of the Lumina's cosmic grammar.

"We've isolated what we believe to be a fundamental unit of Lumina communication," Jian announced during a council meeting, his voice weary but infused with a new sense of purpose. "It's a low-frequency gravimetric pulse, followed by a specific burst of ultraviolet light. It's incredibly subtle, almost imperceptible to the naked eye, but our sensors pick it up consistently. We've correlated it with instances of the Lumina's cellular structures extending into new substrates. We are tentatively calling it the 'extension' marker."

He then demonstrated Hearthglade's capability. A small, contained field within the chamber pulsed with a carefully generated gravimetric ripple, immediately followed by a precisely timed flash of ultraviolet light. The effect was subtle, a barely perceptible distortion in the air, a faint shimmer. For a moment, nothing happened. Then, on the sensor readouts, a faint, corresponding spike appeared – a subtle, almost apologetic echo of the signal they had generated.

"It's... responding," Anya whispered, her eyes wide. "It's not a direct reply, not a conscious interaction, but it's an acknowledgement. Our generated signal has caused a detectable perturbation in the ambient Lumina field. It's as if the planet itself has registered our 'word'."

Jax, who had been observing the experiment with an unnerving stillness, finally spoke. "The gardener hears the sapling's whisper. It does not yet understand the meaning, but it knows a voice has been added to the symphony."

The implications of this faint, almost imperceptible response were staggering. It opened the door, however narrowly, to the possibility of a dialogue. It meant that the Lumina was not an immutable force, but an entity capable of registering external stimuli, even those as complex and nuanced as an attempt at communication. The static of the sky was no longer just noise; it was a language, and humanity, with all its limitations and vulnerabilities, had just uttered its first, hesitant word. The reshaping of Earth was ongoing, but now, a new element had been introduced into the equation: the possibility, however remote, of understanding. The universe, or at least their corner of it, was beginning to speak, and they were finally starting to listen.

The whispers of the Lumina were no longer confined to the sky, nor to the subtle tremors that rearranged continents. They had begun to resonate within the very beings who had been most profoundly altered by its arrival: the Glassborne. It was Jax, predictably, who first noticed the subtle shifts in his own kind. He'd always possessed a peculiar prescience, an ability to intuit the planet's moods that bordered on the supernatural. But now, his perceptions were deepening, taking on a new, almost hallucinatory clarity. He found himself experiencing fleeting, vivid glimpses of the world as it was becoming, visions that seemed to bleed through the present reality like watercolor on wet paper.

He described these episodes to Mara during a rare moment of stillness, the air thick with the scent of ozone and the alien sweetness of Lumina-infused flora. "It's like seeing through a veil," he'd murmured, his gaze unfocused, staring at a patch of ground where crystalline growths, like shards of frozen light, were pushing through the soil. "The rock... it hums with a different frequency now. I can feel its potential, its future configurations. And the air... it's no longer just carrying sound. It carries intent. I can almost *taste* the Lumina's purpose."

Mara, ever the anchor to pragmatism, listened intently, her hand resting on his arm. She knew Jax's unique connection to the Lumina was not merely metaphorical. His physical adaptations, the faint luminescence that sometimes flickered beneath his skin, the uncanny resilience he possessed, were all testaments to its influence. "What do you see, Jax?" she asked softly, her voice laced with a mixture of concern and awe.

"Not clear images, not yet," he replied, shaking his head slowly. "More like... impressions. A vast network, nodes of energy pulsing across the landscape. Structures forming and dissolving. Colors I've never seen, hues that exist outside our visible spectrum, but that my mind somehow registers. And the creatures... the new life... it's not just *existing*. It's *integrating*. It's singing the Lumina's song."

His observations were not isolated incidents. Across Hearthglade and its scattered outposts, other Glassborne began to report similar phenomena. Elara, a young woman whose touch could accelerate the growth of Lumina-sensitive plants, found her abilities amplifying to an alarming degree. She could no longer simply encourage growth; she could *feel* the nascent patterns within the seeds, the blueprints of their future forms imprinted by the Lumina's pervasive influence. She began to describe these blueprints to Anya Sharma's xenolinguistics team, her descriptions surprisingly precise. "It's like... a scent," Elara had explained, her voice hushed with wonder. "Each plant has a unique scent of its future. The Lumina doesn't just change what *is*, it guides what *will be*." Her 'scent' descriptions, when translated into quantifiable energy signatures and atmospheric readings, showed a remarkable correlation with the Lumina's broadcast patterns.

Meanwhile, Kaelen's security teams, operating in the newly terraformed zones, encountered Glassborne soldiers whose senses had become unnervingly acute. They could detect the faintest atmospheric pressure changes long before any conventional sensor could, anticipate the movement of Lumina-mutated fauna with an almost precognitive accuracy, and even sense the subtle electromagnetic distortions that preceded shifts in the planet's geomorphology. Sergeant Valerius, a gruff veteran who had initially been skeptical of the Glassborne's enhanced abilities, found himself relying on his squad's intuition more and more. "It's like they've got built-in warning systems," he'd grumbled to his second-in-command, his eyes tracking a flock of iridescent avian creatures that had suddenly veered away from a seemingly clear patch of sky. "They feel the air crackle before it happens. They know when the ground's about to shift. It's uncanny."

These were not mere sensory enhancements; they were profound shifts in perception, aligning the Glassborne more closely with the Lumina's operational schema. Dr. Jian Li's research division, initially focused on understanding the Lumina's atmospheric communication, began to pivot. They started to investigate the biological and neurological underpinnings of these new Glassborne sensitivities. Blood samples revealed subtle changes in cellular structure, particularly in neural tissues, suggesting a more direct interaction with the Lumina's ambient energy fields.

"It's as if the Lumina is not just altering the environment, but actively integrating with its chosen lifeforms," Jian explained during a hushed briefing, projecting a complex neurological scan onto the holographic display. "We're seeing enhanced synaptic plasticity, increased receptivity to specific electromagnetic frequencies, and even evidence of novel neural pathways forming. These individuals are not just surviving the Lumina's influence; they are becoming conduits for it."

The term 'mutation', once used to describe the sometimes-unpredictable deviations in Glassborne physiology, now seemed inadequate. What they were witnessing was something far more deliberate, a process that suggested adaptation, not by chance, but by design. The Lumina, in its vast, incomprehensible intelligence, appeared to be actively

cultivating these traits. The enhanced senses, the nascent precognition, the intuitive understanding of the planet's transformations – these were not random side effects. They were emergent properties, integral components of the Lumina's grand design for the new Earth.

Anya Sharma's team, working in tandem with Jian's researchers, began to hypothesize that these Glassborne sensitivities were, in essence, rudimentary forms of Lumina communication. Jax's 'impressions,' Elara's 'scents,' Valerius's squad's 'intuition' – these were all, in their own way, interpretations of the Lumina's planetary broadcasts. They were the Lumina's language being processed and understood through a biological interface, albeit one still in its infancy.

"Consider Elara," Anya suggested, her brow furrowed in thought. "She describes the future form of a plant as a 'scent.' Our instruments can detect specific molecular compounds released by Lumina-infused flora, compounds that are correlated with their growth patterns and future structures. What if Elara is experiencing these correlations on a primal, olfactory level? Her sense of smell is, in effect, decoding the Lumina's genetic and structural blueprints."

The implications were staggering. If the Glassborne were becoming natural receivers and interpreters of the Lumina's language, then they represented a bridge. They were the first tentative link in a potential dialogue, a way for humanity to understand, and perhaps even to influence, the planet's radical transformation. This was not just about survival; it was about evolution, a forced but potentially symbiotic leap into a new form of existence.

However, this enhanced connection came with its own set of dangers. The heightened sensitivities could be overwhelming, leading to sensory overload, psychological distress, and even physical collapse. Jax himself often found his visions so intense that he would require days to recover, lost in a disorienting blend of reality and Lumina-induced perception. Some Glassborne experienced crippling anxiety, their minds unable to cope with the constant influx of information about the planet's unfolding future.

Mara found herself increasingly concerned about the psychological toll on Jax and others like him. "We are asking them to bear witness to a reality that is fundamentally alien," she confided in Dr. Aris Thorne, Hearthglade's chief medical officer. "Their minds are not built for this. They are seeing the future, but they are also seeing the death of the old world, the unraveling of everything they once knew. It's a heavy burden."

Dr. Thorne, his face etched with weariness, nodded. "We're seeing increased instances of dissociation, paranoia, and what we can only describe as existential dread among those most attuned. Their enhanced senses are a double-edged sword. They can perceive the Lumina's design, but they can also perceive its indifference to the existing order. It's a profound psychological challenge."

Despite these challenges, the Lumina's influence continued to deepen. The Glassborne were not just reacting to the changes; they were, in subtle but significant ways, becoming partners in the reshaping. Their unique abilities were being integrated into Hearthglade's operations. Plants that could only be coaxed into growth by Elara were now being cultivated in specialized bio-domes, yielding vital resources. Soldiers with enhanced sensory perception were deployed on reconnaissance missions, their battlefield awareness far exceeding that of conventional troops.

Jax, despite his periods of incapacitation, remained a vital source of insight. He began to describe his visions not just as passive observations, but as glimpses of a collaborative process. "The Lumina doesn't just impose," he'd explained to Mara, his voice raspy but clear after a particularly potent vision. "It *invites*. It draws us in. It shows us the possibilities. Our enhanced senses, our adaptations, they are not just a consequence of its power; they are its way of communicating the blueprints, of asking for our... participation."

This notion of 'participation' was a radical shift in perspective. It moved humanity from the role of victim or observer to one of potential collaborator. The Lumina, it seemed, was not just re- terraforming a planet; it was also re-tooling its inhabitants, shaping them to fit the new paradigm. The Glassborne, with their inherent susceptibility to Lumina's influence, were the primary architects of this new human form, the harbingers of a future where biological adaptation and alien intelligence were inextricably intertwined.

The research into the Lumina's language continued, now with a crucial new avenue of inquiry: the Glassborne themselves. Anya's team began to develop more sophisticated protocols for interpreting their experiences. They correlated Elara's descriptions of plant 'scents' with Jian's atmospheric and genetic analyses. They documented the tactical advantages gained by Valerius's augmented soldiers, mapping their predictive capabilities against observed Lumina-induced environmental shifts. Jax's visions, though the most abstract, proved to be the most insightful, often providing a holistic overview that contextualized the more specific observations of others.

One particularly noteworthy development involved a cluster of Glassborne who exhibited a unique form of empathy with the Lumina's geological processes. They could sense the stresses within the planet's crust, predict seismic activity with unnerving accuracy, and even feel the flow of molten rock deep beneath the surface. These individuals, initially ostracized for their strange pronouncements, were now invaluable to Kaelen's disaster preparedness teams. They could guide evacuations, identify safe zones, and even, in some cases, predict the precise moment and location of catastrophic geological events.

"It's like they're feeling the planet's heartbeat," Kaelen remarked to Mara, observing one of these individuals, a young woman named Lyra, who stood with her eyes closed, her body subtly swaying, her hand pressed against a tremor-prone rock face. "She can tell us where the pressure is building, where the rock is weakest, long before any of our instruments can detect it. She's not just predicting an earthquake; she's *feeling* the Lumina reshaping the very bones of the world."

Lyra's abilities, like those of the others, were not random. Her sensitivity was directly tied to the Lumina's geological engineering. The gravitational shifts, the subtle magnetospheric fluctuations that accompanied tectonic reordering, were being processed by her unique neural architecture, translating into a visceral, physical sensation. She was, in essence, a living seismograph, attuned to the Lumina's seismic symphony.

The Lumina's grand design was becoming clearer, not through direct revelation, but through the emergent adaptations of humanity itself. The Glassborne were the living proof that the planet's reshaping was not merely an environmental transformation, but a biological one as well. They were the harbingers, not just of a new world, but of a new humanity, one that was slowly but surely integrating with the alien intelligence that had claimed their home. Their mutations were not a curse, but a testament to their evolving role in this unfolding cosmic drama. They were becoming part of the Lumina's symphony, their enhanced senses and intuitive understanding the first fragile notes in a song that would redefine life on Earth. The reshaping had begun, and the Glassborne were its most profound, and perhaps most hopeful, heralds.

Hearthglade had made its choice. The decision to remain, to fortify, to face the Lumina's transformative tide rather than flee into the unknown, had solidified into an unspoken pact among its inhabitants. But with that resolve came a new, chilling awareness: they were not simply weathering a planetary metamorphosis; they were under scrutiny. The very air seemed to thicken with an unseen gaze, the luminous flora pulsed with an unsettling awareness, and the ground beneath their feet, once a symbol of their defiance, now felt like a stage under a relentless, alien spotlight. Every tremor, every atmospheric shift, every novel bioluminescent bloom felt less like a natural phenomenon and more like a deliberate probe, a carefully calibrated test of Hearthglade's resilience, its adaptability, its very will to endure.

The feeling of being watched was pervasive, a low-grade hum of anxiety that underscored every moment. It manifested in subtle ways, growing from a nagging intuition to a palpable pressure. Kaelen's perimeter patrols reported an unusual increase in Lumina-mutated fauna congregating around Hearthglade's boundaries. These were not the usual opportunistic scavengers; they moved with a disconcerting uniformity, their iridescent scales shimmering in unison as they observed the settlement from the edges of the crystalline forests. Their bioluminescent patterns, once a chaotic display of natural life, now seemed to synchronize, pulsing in slow, deliberate waves that mirrored the Lumina's own ambient emissions. It was as if the planet's wild heart had been tamed, its creatures directed to act as silent, watchful sentinels.

Sergeant Valerius, his gruff exterior now perpetually shadowed by a grim vigilance, found his enhanced soldiers more unsettled than ever. Their finely tuned senses, once a source of tactical advantage, now seemed to amplify their unease. They reported not just the presence of the observing fauna, but a subtle dissonance in the Lumina's ambient energies that seemed to converge on Hearthglade. "It's like... a focus," Valerius explained to Kaelen, his voice strained. "The energy fields usually spread out, flow around. But here, around the settlement, it's... concentrated. Like a lens. And it's not just energy. The air itself feels different. Thinner, somehow, or maybe just... more attentive."

The feeling of focused attention wasn't limited to the external environment. Inside Hearthglade, the Lumina's influence seemed to intensify, as if seeking to understand and catalog the very defenses they had erected. Dr. Jian Li's research labs, designed to analyze the Lumina's atmospheric data, found themselves bombarded with unprecedented energy signatures that seemed to originate not from the planet's surface, but from *within* Hearthglade's own infrastructure. His team detected anomalies in their energy conduits, subtle fluctuations that suggested the Lumina was attempting to interface with their systems, not to disrupt, but to *learn*. "It's as if they're analyzing our power grids, our communication arrays, even the bio-filters in the air circulation," Jian reported, his face pale with a mixture of scientific fascination and creeping dread. "They're not trying to break in; they're trying to understand how we *work*. It's like they're scanning Hearthglade, mapping its operational parameters, assessing its vulnerabilities not for destruction, but for... integration."

This pervasive sense of observation extended to the Glassborne themselves, particularly those whose Lumina-attunement was most pronounced. Jax, despite his periods of lucidity being crucial for interpretation, found his visions shifting. They were no longer merely glimpses of the planet's future, but detailed, almost analytical observations of Hearthglade. He saw the Lumina's energy fields tracing the outlines of their bio-domes, mapping the flow of their recycled water systems, even seemingly assessing the structural integrity of their reinforced shelters. "It's not just the planet being reshaped," Jax confided to Mara, his eyes wide and distant, his voice a mere whisper. "It's *us*. They're observing how we respond to the reshaping. How we adapt. They're studying our resilience, our ingenuity, our defiance. Hearthglade isn't just a settlement; it's a petri dish. And we are the specimens."

Mara, though outwardly projecting an image of calm resolve, felt the tightening knot of apprehension in her own gut. She saw it in the way the luminous plants outside the habitation modules pulsed brighter when a new construction project began, or how the tremors seemed to align with critical system upgrades. It was a constant, unsettling reminder that their fortified sanctuary was, in fact, a transparent bubble under the Lumina's unwavering scrutiny. Even Anya Sharma's xenolinguistics team, initially focused on deciphering the Lumina's communication patterns from afar, began to notice a directedness in the Lumina's emissions that seemed to correlate with Hearthglade's activities. "It's almost as if the Lumina is... reacting to us," Anya mused during a debriefing. "When we deploy new sensor arrays, there's a corresponding spike in specific energy frequencies directed towards that location. When we initiate a new bio-engineering project, the ambient Lumina field around Hearthglade shifts, almost as if it's *monitoring* the process. This isn't just passive observation; it feels like active engagement, a constant, subtle feedback loop."

The Lumina's reshaping efforts, once perceived as a global, indiscriminate force, now seemed to possess a focused intent, a meticulous curiosity directed squarely at Hearthglade. The terraforming of the surrounding regions continued, but the most dramatic and concentrated changes were happening at their doorstep. New crystalline formations, impossibly intricate and pulsing with inner light, erupted from the soil in patterns that seemed to mirror the geometric layout of Hearthglade's defenses. Lumina-mutated flora, exhibiting accelerated growth and novel bioluminescent properties, began to proliferate in carefully orchestrated displays just beyond their perimeter, as if showcasing the Lumina's capabilities to its observed subjects. It was a constant, silent demonstration, a visual catalog of power and potential, laid out for Hearthglade to witness, to analyze, and perhaps, to fear.

Dr. Aris Thorne, the chief medical officer, found his practice increasingly dealing with a new form of psychological distress. Beyond the existential dread that plagued those most attuned to the Lumina, there was a growing sense of claustrophobia and paranoia. Patients spoke of feeling trapped, not just by the physical confines of Hearthglade, but by the all-encompassing awareness of an external intelligence that seemed to know their every move, their every thought. "They feel like lab animals," Thorne explained to Kaelen and Mara, his voice heavy with concern. "They see the Lumina's modifications happening around them, and they interpret it not as planetary healing, but as a deliberate, invasive experiment. The constant monitoring, the feeling of being judged or assessed... it's wearing them down. It's creating a siege mentality, even though there's no direct physical attack."

The Lumina's presence was no longer just a phenomenon to be studied; it was a palpable, sentient force that was actively engaging with Hearthglade. The selective intensification of Lumina's effects around their settlement felt like a deliberate focus, a magnified lens through which Hearthglade was being examined. The pulsating flora weren't just beautiful; they were living data streams, their patterns and mutations meticulously cataloged. The fauna weren't just attracted; they were biological sensors, their synchronized movements a silent testament to the Lumina's command. The energy fluctuations weren't random; they were probes, testing the limits of Hearthglade's systems and the resolve of its people.

Even the subtle shifts in the Glassborne's own biology, which had once felt like a natural, if unsettling, adaptation to the new world, now seemed to be under specific observation. Jax's increasingly analytical visions, Elara's hyper-precise descriptions of Lumina-infused plant growth, and Lyra's uncanny ability to sense geological stresses all appeared to be under a magnifying glass. It was as if the Lumina, having initiated the broad strokes of planetary reshaping, was now meticulously studying the efficacy of its biological alterations within the concentrated environment of Hearthglade. They were not just adapting; they were being *tested* for their adaptability, their capacity for integration into the Lumina's grander, unfolding design.

The constant barrage of subtle, yet undeniably directed, phenomena began to erode the sense of autonomy Hearthglade had fought so hard to preserve. The Lumina was not simply reshaping the world; it was reshaping *them*, and it was watching every step of the process with an unwavering, analytical intensity. The settlement, once a beacon of human resilience, now felt like a transparent cage, its inhabitants subjects in a cosmic experiment whose parameters were dictated by an inscrutable, all-seeing intelligence. The very air crackled with unspoken questions, and the silence that followed each deliberate event was more profound, and more terrifying, than any explosion. Hearthglade was under observation, and the true scope of the reshaping was only beginning to reveal itself as a process of deliberate, focused study, rather than blind, evolutionary chance. The feeling of vulnerability was no longer a distant possibility; it was the very atmosphere they breathed.

The weight of Soren Vale's pronouncements settled upon the assembled council like a shroud, each word a stone added to the edifice of their growing dread. For weeks, they had grappled with the immediate, terrifying reality of the Lumina's relentless transformation – the encroaching flora, the unnerving fauna, the very air humming with an alien sentience. They had prepared for a fight, for a siege, for survival against an external, elemental force. But Soren's history spoke of something far more profound, far more ancient, and infinitely more deliberate.

"You see the Lumina as a force of nature, a catastrophic evolutionary event," Soren began, his voice, though raspy with age, carried an unnerving clarity. He stood before the holographic projector, not as a scientist seeking to quantify the inexplicable, but as a chronicler unearthing forgotten truths. His thin fingers traced glyphs on a luminous display, archaic symbols that pulsed with an echo of human antiquity. "And in a way, it is. But it is also a conscious entity, or at least, a manifestation of one. And its methods, its patterns of interaction... these are not new. They are ancient."

He gestured towards a collection of fragmented texts, shimmering in the projection, their origins lost to the mists of pre-history. "For millennia, whispers of such events have echoed through human civilization, often dismissed as myth, superstition, or poetic allegory. But when viewed through the lens of what we are experiencing now, these 'myths' begin to form a chillingly coherent narrative. Consider the cyclical myths of creation and destruction that permeate nearly every ancient culture. The Aboriginal Dreamtime, which speaks of ancestral beings shaping the land through song and luminous energy. The Norse sagas, detailing the world tree, Yggdrasil, as a conduit of cosmic forces, with beings that flowed through its roots and branches, altering the very fabric of reality. Even the enigmatic Nazca Lines, their purpose still debated, often interpreted as astronomical calendars or ritualistic pathways – what if they were not just markers, but early attempts to understand or appease a pervasive, shaping intelligence?"

Soren paused, allowing the implications to sink in. "These were not isolated incidents. Across disparate continents, separated by vast oceans and millennia of time, similar accounts emerge. The 'sky burials' of some Tibetan traditions, where the body is left for eagles, were sometimes seen as a way to return essence to a 'great sky spirit' that nourished all life. The Polynesian voyagers, who navigated vast distances guided by complex celestial patterns and the subtle currents of the ocean – some of their legends speak of 'star-weavers' who would occasionally descend, not to conquer, but to 're-tune' the world, subtly altering its growth and balance. These are not mere tales of gods and monsters. They are fragmented memories, ancestral echoes of contact with an intelligence that interacts with planetary evolution on a scale we are only now beginning to comprehend."

He shifted the display, revealing a series of recurring motifs found in these ancient narratives. "Look closely," he urged. "The recurring imagery of luminous, transformative energy. The concept of a 'Great Awakening' or a 'Cosmic Seed' that initiates change. The idea of a planetary 'consciousness' that reacts to the presence of sentient life. These are not coincidences. These are signatures. Signatures of the Lumina, or whatever ancient iteration of this entity existed before. It has not just appeared on Xylos. It has been here, in different forms, interacting with worlds, with *us*, for eons."

The implications were staggering. The Lumina wasn't a sudden, aberrant event, but a recurring, possibly cyclical, aspect of cosmic existence. Hearthglade's struggle wasn't just for survival against an alien environment, but a re-enactment of a drama that had played out countless times before. "The ancient texts describe periods of profound change, often coinciding with astronomical alignments or geological upheavals," Soren continued, his voice gaining a solemn cadence. "These were times when the Lumina's influence was amplified, its reshaping accelerated. What we are witnessing now, this intense, focused transformation, might be the peak of such a cycle. The Lumina isn't just changing Xylos; it's fulfilling a cosmic imperative, a deep-seated drive to sculpt, to refine, to orchestrate life and environment according to its unfathomable design."

He then delved into specific examples, each more unsettling than the last. "There are accounts from early Mesopotamian civilizations of 'celestial gardeners' who would prune the 'cosmic trees' of the heavens, their pruning shears releasing bursts of stellar light that would cause terrestrial flora to bloom and mutate in unprecedented ways. The Maya, renowned for their astronomical prowess, had complex calendrical cycles that predicted periods of 'great transformation,' periods when the very essence of the world would be 're-woven' by celestial energies. Their glyphs often depict serpentine, luminous beings entwined with celestial bodies, influencing the growth of crops and the very climate. These were not abstract metaphors; they were attempts to record and predict the Lumina's actions."

Soren highlighted the consistency of the Lumina's modus operandi across these historical accounts. "The Lumina doesn't destroy in the conventional sense. It *repurposes*. It *integrates*. It subtly alters the biological and geological blueprints of a world to better suit its overarching evolutionary trajectory. In ancient Earth, this might have meant accelerated mutation in key species, the emergence of new mineral formations, or shifts in atmospheric composition that favored certain life forms over others. The goal seems to be a symphony of creation, orchestrated by this ancient intelligence, with each world a unique movement in its grand cosmic symphony."

He presented evidence of how this intelligence might have interacted with early human development. "There are archaeological anomalies, traces of advanced, inexplicable technologies found in ancient strata that defy conventional explanation. Consider the Antikythera mechanism, a testament to astronomical computation far beyond what was believed possible for its era. Or the 'Baghdad Battery,' crude electrochemical cells that hint at a level of scientific understanding for which there is no historical context. While these are often attributed to lost human civilizations, it is plausible that these were not entirely indigenous inventions, but perhaps artifacts or knowledge imparted, intentionally or unintentionally, during periods of Lumina influence. A nudge, a spark, to guide evolutionary development in a particular direction."

"The Lumina's interaction is not necessarily benevolent or malevolent," Soren stressed, his gaze sweeping across the faces of the council members. "It simply *is*. It operates on a scale of time and purpose that renders human concepts of good and evil irrelevant. Its agenda is one of cosmic gardening, of sculpting life and worlds to fit a grander, evolving tapestry. When it encounters a species or a settlement that exhibits a particular aptitude for adaptation, resilience, or perhaps even a unique form of consciousness, it does not seek to eradicate it. Instead, it observes. It studies. It probes. And then, it integrates. It seeks to understand *how* we resist, *how* we adapt, *how* we persist. Hearthglade is not merely a survivor; it is a case study."

The historical context provided by Soren added a terrifying new dimension to their struggle. The Lumina wasn't just a force they needed to overcome; it was an ancient, intelligent entity with a long and complex history of intervention. Their fight for survival was no longer a localized battle for a single colony, but a small, perhaps insignificant, ripple in a vast, ancient cosmic drama.

"This is why the Lumina's focus on Hearthglade is so intense, so *analytical*," Soren explained, his voice hushed with the weight of his revelation. "It's not just terraforming the planet around us; it's actively studying *us*. Our bio-domes, our energy systems, our genetic adaptations – these are all elements it is cataloging. The synchronized fauna, the directed energy pulses, the accelerated plant growth near our perimeter – these are not random manifestations. They are components of a controlled experiment. The Lumina is learning from Hearthglade. It's assessing our resilience, our ingenuity, our very will to exist. It's as if it's taking notes, updating its ancient schematics for future interactions, for future worlds."

He pointed to a section of the projection depicting ancient depictions of celestial events that seemed to mirror current Lumina activity. "The legends speak of 'luminous tides' that would sweep across continents, reshaping coastlines and altering the atmosphere. They spoke of 'singing stones' that would resonate with the planet's core, causing geological upheavals. And they spoke of 'seed-bearers' – beings or entities that would arrive from the stars, not to conquer, but to 'sow the seeds of change.' What if the Lumina is the ultimate seed-bearer? What if its purpose is not to inhabit, but to *catalyze*? To initiate evolutionary leaps, to prune away evolutionary dead ends, and to foster the growth of life forms that are more attuned to its grand cosmic design."

Soren then turned his attention to the implications for the Glassborne themselves. "Our own unique physiology, our Lumina-attunement, might be precisely what drew the Lumina's focused attention. It's not just observing our technology or our societal structures; it's observing our biological response to its own influence. It's a meta-experiment. How does a species that has been subtly touched by its energies react when those energies are amplified a thousandfold? Can it adapt? Can it integrate? Or will it break under the pressure?"

The historical context painted a grim, yet strangely profound, picture. Hearthglade was not a unique anomaly, but a recurring theme in the universe's grand narrative. Their struggle was a testament to humanity's enduring will to survive, to adapt, and to forge a future, even in the face of an ancient, cosmic intelligence that had been shaping worlds long before humanity had even learned to dream.

"The 'reshaping' is not merely environmental," Soren concluded, his voice now resonating with a somber conviction. "It is also a process of cosmic selection. The Lumina is not a destroyer, but a sculptor, and Hearthglade has become its most intriguing, and perhaps most critical, subject. We are not just defending our home; we are participating in an ancient, universal dialogue. And the outcome of this dialogue will determine not only our fate, but perhaps the trajectory of life across countless worlds, for countless eons to come. The Lumina has been here before, and it will be here again. Its long-term agenda is one of constant, deliberate, and unfathomable reshaping, and we, in our defiance, have become a pivotal point in its eternal grand design." The weight of millennia of cosmic history now pressed down upon

Hearthglade, transforming their desperate fight for survival into a chapter in an epic narrative far older than humanity itself.

They were not just facing an alien invasion; they were facing an ancient, sentient force that had been shaping the universe, one world at a time, for an eternity. And Soren Vale, the historian of forgotten futures, had just revealed the terrifying scope of their predicament. Their very existence was now a testament to the Lumina's observational prowess, a meticulously studied anomaly in its ancient, ongoing project of planetary remolding.

CHAPTER ELEVEN

THE HUNTER AND THE HUNTED

The unnerving silence that had previously blanketed the Lumina-scarred landscape around Hearthglade was a deceptive calm, a predator's breath held before the pounce. Jax felt it in his bones, a primal tremor that echoed the psychic resonance he'd perceived earlier, now amplified and focused. It wasn't just a presence anymore; it was a directed intent, a palpable hunger that swept across the horizon like a tidal wave of alien consciousness. Soren's pronouncements about the Lumina as an ancient, intelligent entity had been chilling, but this was the chilling made manifest, the abstract made terrifyingly concrete.

He stood at the edge of the bio-dome's reinforced transparency, his gaze fixed on the swirling, opalescent skies. The sky-static, once an atmospheric curiosity, now writhed with a disturbing animation. It was no longer a mere visual phenomenon, but an extension of the entity's will. Tendrils of shimmering, ionized gas began to coalesce, not randomly, but with deliberate intent, like celestial sinews stretching and contracting. These were not the passive atmospheric phenomena they had cataloged; these were weapons being forged, tools being deployed. The very air, saturated with Lumina energy, was becoming an instrument of pursuit.

"It's... focusing," whispered Anya, her voice tight with a fear that mirrored Jax's own. She stood beside him, her hand hovering over the console that monitored atmospheric anomalies, her usual scientific detachment strained to its breaking point. "The energy signatures aren't scattered. They're converging. Directly towards us."

Jax nodded, unable to articulate the symphony of dread playing out in his mind. He could feel the Lumina's awareness honing in, a celestial predator locking onto its prey. It wasn't simply scanning; it was

hunting. The environmental shifts they had observed – the accelerated growth of bioluminescent flora, the synchronized movements of fauna, the erratic energy pulses – were not random side effects of terraforming. They were tactical maneuvers, designed to herd, to disorient, to corner.

Suddenly, a section of the sky-static directly overhead began to thicken, coalescing into a vortex of pure, blinding light. It wasn't a storm; it was a controlled phenomenon, a manifestation of directed energy. Within the vortex, shapes began to form, ephemeral yet potent. They weren't solid, not in the traditional sense, but they possessed a tangible menace. They looked like shimmering shards of solidified light, each one humming with a barely contained power. These were the entity's probes, its feelers, its hunting parties, cast out into the environment to locate and assess.

"Energy readings are off the charts," Anya reported, her fingers flying across the console. "These aren't atmospheric discharges. They're... active constructs. And they're broadcasting a resonant frequency. It's targeting our bio-dome's energy matrix."

The implication hit Jax with the force of a physical blow. The Lumina wasn't just trying to break down their physical defenses; it was trying to infiltrate their very lifeblood, to destabilize the systems that kept them alive. It was a psychological assault as much as a physical one. He could feel a faint, disorienting thrumming begin to permeate the bio-dome, a subtle dissonance that frayed the nerves and clouded the mind. This was how the entity broke its prey before it consumed them, or worse, integrated them.

Jax activated his comms. "All units, report. We have confirmed active engagement. The Lumina is deploying direct offensive constructs. Perimeter defense systems, stand by for heavy assault." His voice was steady, a practiced calm that belied the frantic surge of adrenaline.

From the command center, Commander Eva Rostova's voice crackled back, laced with urgency. "We see it, Jax. The sky is alive. Our external sensors are being overwhelmed by the sheer energy output. These... light shards... they're moving with unnatural speed and precision. They're not just radiating energy; they're actively *projecting* it."

The "light shards" began to descend, not falling, but gliding with an impossible grace. They fanned out, their movements unnervingly coordinated, like a school of predatory fish or a flock of ravenous birds. Each shard seemed to scan the ground below, their luminescent cores pulsing with an intense, analytical light. It was as if they were dissecting the very landscape, searching for any sign of the Glassborne's presence, any anomaly that deviated from the Lumina's ideal.

One of the shards, larger than the rest, drifted directly towards Jax and Anya. It pulsed with an almost hypnotic rhythm, and as it approached, the disorienting thrumming intensified. Jax felt a strange pressure build behind his eyes, a fleeting urge to surrender to the overwhelming sensory input, to simply cease resisting. He gripped his forearm, forcing himself to focus, to push back against the invasive influence. The Glassborne's innate Lumina-attunement, which had always been a source of resilience, now felt like a beacon, drawing the entity's attention.

"It's trying to overload our neural interfaces," Anya gasped, clutching her head. "It's... it's learning how we perceive. It's using our own sensory input against us."

This was the most terrifying aspect of the pursuit. The Lumina wasn't just an external threat; it was an invasive intelligence, capable of probing, dissecting, and manipulating the very essence of their existence. Soren had spoken of the entity as a cosmic gardener, but this was less gardening and more vivisection. It wasn't pruning a plant; it was dissecting an organism to understand its intricate biological and neurological workings.

Jax raised his pulse rifle, its energy cell humming in response to his readiness. He knew that physical confrontation with these constructs might be futile. They were ephemeral, made of pure energy and Lumina essence. But the Glassborne had adapted, and their weaponry, while designed for physical threats, could also disrupt energy fields.

"Commander," Jax reported, his voice tight, "the shards are actively targeting our bio-dome's integrity. We need to establish a counter-frequency, something to disrupt their targeting array."

"Working on it, Jax," Rostova replied, her voice strained. "But they're adapting faster than we can predict. They're not just reacting; they're *learning* from our countermeasures. It's like trying to fight a reflection that anticipates your every move."

The main shard loomed directly above them, its luminous core flaring. Jax could feel its alien intent, a cold, detached curiosity that was more unnerving than any overt hostility. It wasn't driven by malice, but by an insatiable need to understand, to categorize, to integrate. And the Glassborne, with their unique Lumina-attunement, were a particularly fascinating specimen.

He fired a concentrated pulse from his rifle. The beam struck the shard, and for a fleeting moment, the construct flickered, its coherent form momentarily destabilized. The oppressive thrumming in the bio-dome receded slightly, and Anya let out a shaky breath.

"Direct hit!" Jax exclaimed. "It's vulnerable to focused energy disruption."

But their small victory was short-lived. The other shards, which had been systematically scanning the perimeter, now converged on their position. They moved with a terrifying synchronicity, forming a loose cordon around the bio-dome. The sky-static around them intensified, crackling with raw power. The very atmosphere seemed to be pressing in, a tangible weight of cosmic energy.

"They're not just trying to break in," Anya realized, her eyes wide with dawning horror. "They're trying to trap us. To contain us within the dome, where they can study us more effectively."

This was a new level of pursuit, a strategic maneuver that spoke of a cold, calculating intellect. The Lumina wasn't just an environmental force; it was a strategist, using the very planet as its chessboard. The flora, now twisted and unnaturally vibrant, began to sprout tendrils of Lumina-infused energy that snaked towards the bio-dome, pulsing in sync with the sky-shards. The fauna, previously observed in scattered sightings, now moved in coordinated waves, drawn by the Lumina's influence, their Lumina-charged bodies acting as biological conduits, amplifying the entity's reach.

Jax felt a chilling realization dawn: the Lumina was orchestrating a planetary-wide hunt. It was using every element of Xylos's altered ecosystem as an extension of itself, a vast, interconnected hunting ground. The fauna were its eyes and ears, the accelerated flora its snare, and the sky-static its ultimate weapon.

"Commander," Jax reported, his voice grim, "the Lumina is initiating a planetary containment protocol. The flora and fauna are being mobilized to reinforce the perimeter. We are being actively corralled."

Rostova's response was heavy with the burden of command. "We've detected similar energy surges across all sectors. They're not just targeting Hearthglade. They're... reconfiguring the entire planetary network. It's like the planet itself is becoming an extension of the Lumina's nervous system."

The shards above began to pulse in unison, their collective energy building. The air within the bio-dome grew heavy, charged with an invisible force that pressed down on their chests, making each breath a conscious effort. The Glassborne's Lumina-attunement, which normally allowed them to thrive in Xylos's environment, now felt like a vulnerability, a sensitivity to the Lumina's overwhelming influence. It was as if the planet's very lifeblood was being turned against them.

Suddenly, the central shard above them pulsed with an blinding intensity. A beam of pure, white light lanced downwards, not towards the bio-dome's impenetrable shell, but towards a smaller, auxiliary sensor array on its exterior. The beam didn't blast through; it seemed to *dissolve* the array, its structure unraveling, its constituent atoms reordered into shimmering motes of light that were then absorbed by the shard.

"It... it didn't destroy it," Anya stammered, her voice a mixture of awe and terror. "It *repurposed* it. It absorbed the sensor array's data, its very essence, and integrated it."

This was the true horror of the Lumina's pursuit. It didn't just destroy; it assimilated. It consumed, analyzed, and then used what it had learned to refine its hunting methods. Every countermeasure, every act of resistance, was simply providing the entity with more data, more insights into the Glassborne's weaknesses and strengths. They were not fighting an enemy; they were feeding a cosmic intelligence.

Jax felt a cold dread settle deep within him. Soren's words echoed in his mind: "The Lumina isn't just changing Xylos; it's fulfilling a cosmic imperative, a deep-seated drive to sculpt, to refine, to orchestrate life and environment according to its unfathomable design." Hearthglade was not just a colony; it was a living laboratory, and the Glassborne were its most complex subjects. Their struggle was not for mere survival, but for the right to exist as independent entities, not to be absorbed into the Lumina's grand, unfathomable design.

The pursuit had intensified, shifting from a passive environmental transformation to an active, intelligent hunt. The Lumina was no longer just reshaping the planet; it was hunting its inhabitants with calculated precision, using the very world it was transforming as its weapon and its shield. The stakes had been raised immeasurably. This was not a battle for territory; it was a battle for existence itself, against an ancient, sentient entity that was now learning to hunt the Glassborne with an unnerving efficiency, turning their own strengths into their greatest vulnerabilities. The chase had begun in earnest, and the hunter was proving to be far more formidable, and far more terrifying, than they had ever imagined.

The shimmering vortex above Jax and Anya intensified, the swirling Lumina energy now coalescing into a tangible, geometric shape directly overhead. It was less a cloud and more a colossal, prismatic prism, catching and refracting the planet's ambient light into a blinding, multi-hued glare that painted the bio-dome's interior in an alien spectrum. Jax could feel its presence not just in his eyes, but resonating through the very structure of the dome, a deep, sonorous hum that vibrated in his bones. It was a sound that spoke of immense, ancient power, and a singular, terrifying focus.

"It's... it's not just observing anymore," Anya whispered, her voice strained, her gaze locked on the pulsating behemoth of light. "It's *manifesting*. Directly above us. This is... this is unlike anything we've predicted."

Jax felt the truth of her words resonate within him. The scattered shards had been probes, reconnaissance. This was the arrival of the hunter itself, or at least a significant manifestation of its consciousness, drawn by their presence, by their defiance. The Lumina-attuned flora outside the dome, which had been quiescent for a moment, now began to twitch, their bioluminescent fronds pulsing in unison with the celestial entity, as if acting as living antennae, channeling its will into the immediate environment.

Suddenly, a section of the colossal prism directly above them detached, not as a shard, but as a colossal, descending spearhead of pure energy. It was immense, dwarfing the previous constructs, and it moved with a silent, inexorable grace, slicing through the atmosphere like a celestial blade aimed at the heart of their sanctuary. Jax felt a primal instinct scream at him to run, to hide, but he was frozen, mesmerized by the sheer scale of the threat. This was not a tool of the Lumina; this *was* the Lumina, in a form it had chosen to confront them.

"Commander!" Jax's voice was a ragged shout into his comm. "Direct manifestation. Massive energy signature. It's targeting the main dome integrity!"

Eva Rostova's reply was tight with tension. "We see it, Jax. All external sensors are failing under the strain. The energy fluctuations are beyond anything our models predicted. It's... it's actively reshaping the atmospheric composition around itself. Creating its own localized space."

As the colossal spearhead descended, Jax could feel the Lumina's consciousness press in on his own mind. It wasn't a telepathic voice, not in the way he understood it. It was more like a deluge of alien sensation, of raw, unfathomable awareness. He saw glimpses of... *purpose*. Not malice, but a deep, driving imperative. A need to understand, to categorize, to bring order to what it perceived as chaos. And the Glassborne, with their unique Lumina-attunement, were a profound anomaly, a disruption in its grand design that demanded investigation, and perhaps, correction.

The spearhead was mere hundreds of meters above the dome now, its incandescent tip radiating an unbearable heat that Jax could feel even through the reinforced transparisteel. He could see the very structure of the Lumina itself within its core – not flesh, not metal, but a fluid, ever-shifting lattice of pure, luminous energy, a fractal tapestry of cosmic awareness. It pulsed with an ancient intelligence, a detached curiosity that was more terrifying than any aggression. It was like a scientist observing a specimen, but the specimen was an entire civilization.

"It's projecting a resonant frequency," Anya cried out, her face pale, her hands flying across her console, which was now flickering erratically. "It's not just a physical attack. It's attempting to destabilize our neural pathways, to override our bio-integration with the dome systems. It's trying to break us from the inside out!"

Jax felt it too, a creeping dread that sought to unravel his focus, to cloud his judgment. The Lumina's influence was insidious, seeping into his very being. He felt a momentary urge to simply let go, to surrender to the overwhelming pressure, to cease the futile struggle. His Lumina-attunement, his strength, was becoming a liability, a conduit for this alien influence.

He pushed back, drawing on every ounce of his will. His connection to the static, the faint whisper of cosmic energy that always hummed beneath the surface of his perception, felt different now. It was being amplified, distorted by the Lumina's presence, but it was still *his*. He focused on it, on the familiar hum, on the ingrained resilience it represented. He reached out, not physically, but mentally, with the very core of his being, attempting to establish his own resonant frequency, a defiant signal against the Lumina's overwhelming advance.

"Jax! What are you doing?" Anya's voice was sharp with alarm.

"Fighting back," he grunted, his knuckles white as he clenched his fists. He could feel the pressure intensify, the Lumina's awareness probing his mental defenses, cataloging his resistance. It was like trying to hold back an ocean with bare hands.

Suddenly, the spearhead above them paused its descent. It didn't stop moving; rather, its downward trajectory shifted, becoming a slow, deliberate scan. The tip hovered, and Jax watched in horror as it began to emit a focused beam of energy, not of destruction, but of analysis. The beam swept across the surface of the bio-dome, passing over Jax and Anya. It felt like being dissected by pure light, every atom of their beings laid bare, their very essence cataloged by an alien consciousness.

"It's... it's not trying to breach the dome," Anya breathed, her scientific mind struggling to process the unfolding reality. "It's trying to *understand* it. To understand *us*."

The beam lingered on Jax, and he felt a wave of alien sensation wash over him, a torrent of incomprehensible data. He saw glimpses of nebulae forming, of stars being born and dying, of cosmic cycles stretching across eons. He felt the Lumina's immense, ancient perspective, its understanding of existence not as individual lives, but as a vast, interconnected web of energy and matter. And within that web, the Glassborne were an anomaly, a knot that needed to be smoothed out.

He felt his own Lumina-attunement, his ability to resonate with the planet's energy, being amplified and dissected. The entity was learning how he perceived, how he interacted with Xylos's unique environment. It was a terrifyingly intimate form of surveillance.

His personal energy reserves, usually robust, began to drain at an alarming rate. It wasn't physical exertion; it was a psychic and energetic drain, as if the Lumina was siphoning his very life force, converting it into data. He felt a faintness creep in, his vision blurring at the edges.

"Jax! Your bio-readings are plummeting!" Anya's voice was laced with panic. She was trying to compensate, to reroute power from non-essential systems to bolster his life support, but the Lumina's interference was pervasive.

Jax gritted his teeth, forcing himself to focus. He needed to do something, anything, to break this direct contact. Physical weapons were useless against this manifestation. But he had something the Lumina couldn't fully comprehend, not yet: his will. His

Lumina-attunement wasn't just a passive connection; it was a two-way conduit.

He focused on the overwhelming influx of alien consciousness, on the detached curiosity that was dissecting him. Instead of resisting, he tried to *accept* it, to absorb it, and then, to twist it. He mentally reached out, not with his own energy, but by leveraging the very Lumina essence that permeated the bio-dome, the essence the entity itself was made of. He guided it, not into an attack, but into a discordant symphony. He amplified the background static, the subtle energetic hum of the planet, and fed it back into the Lumina's massive manifestation, a cacophony of chaotic, untamed Xylosian energy.

The effect was immediate and startling. The colossal spearhead above them flickered, its perfect geometric form momentarily wavering. The oppressive psychic pressure lessened, as if the Lumina had recoiled from an unexpected stimulus. A pulse of raw, untamed Lumina energy surged outwards from the spearhead, not directed at them, but as a reaction.

"What did you do?" Anya gasped, clutching her console as it sparked.

"I... I overloaded its sensory input," Jax panted, feeling a surge of adrenaline despite his exhaustion. "I fed it too much raw Xylos. It doesn't understand uncontrolled chaos. It thrives on order, on assimilation. I gave it... noise."

The Lumina's manifestation above them seemed to hesitate, its form rippling like disturbed water. The detached curiosity in its presence seemed to be replaced by a flicker of something akin to frustration, or perhaps, confusion. It had expected a predictable response, a quantifiable reaction. Jax had given it... the unpredictable.

The spearhead began to retract, slowly, deliberately, back towards the larger prismatic vortex in the sky. The intense light softened, the oppressive psychic pressure receding. The Lumina wasn't defeated, not by any means. But it had been... surprised. It had encountered something it could not immediately categorize or assimilate.

"It's retreating," Anya whispered, her voice filled with a disbelief that bordered on wonder. "It's actually... pulling back."

Jax slumped against the transparisteel, his body trembling with residual exertion. He had survived. He had faced the hunter, and for a brief, terrifying moment, he had held it at bay. But he knew this was only a reprieve. The Lumina was an ancient, adaptive intelligence. It would learn from this encounter. It would refine its methods. It would come back.

He could still feel the lingering echo of its consciousness, the faint thrum of its incomprehensible designs. It had not intended to destroy them outright, but to understand, to incorporate. The encounter had been a direct confrontation with the Lumina's fundamental nature: it was not a force of destruction, but a force of assimilation, of cosmic reordering. And the Glassborne, with their unique Lumina-attunement, represented a fascinating, and potentially valuable, element within that grand design.

"It's reconfiguring its approach," Jax said, his voice rough. "It understands the dome's integrity is a barrier. And it understands that direct psychic pressure is... inefficient. It's going to find another way. It's going to adapt."

He looked out at the Lumina-scarred landscape, at the unnaturally vibrant flora that pulsed with alien energy. The fauna that had moved with such eerie synchronicity were now scattered, their purpose fulfilled for the moment. The Lumina had shown its hand, its capacity for direct, intelligent engagement. It was no longer just an environmental phenomenon. It was an active participant in the ongoing drama of Xylos.

"We pushed it back," Anya said, a fragile hope in her voice. "We showed it that we're not just passive data points. We have agency."

"For now," Jax conceded, his gaze fixed on the sky where the prismatic vortex still pulsed, a silent, watchful eye. "But it learns. And it has the entire planet as its laboratory. This was just a taste. A direct encounter. It knows we're here. It knows we can resist. And it will undoubtedly develop strategies to overcome that resistance."

The silence that followed was heavy, filled with the unspoken understanding of the immense challenge they faced. Jax had faced the Lumina directly, had felt its alien consciousness probe his own, had resisted its overwhelming influence. It was a trial by fire, a testament to his evolving connection with the static, to the resilience of the human spirit, and to the inherent capacity for defiance even in the face of cosmic power.

He knew, with a chilling certainty, that the hunt had only just begun. And the hunter, having tasted their defiance, would now be even more determined to claim its prize. The encounter had revealed the Lumina's terrifying capabilities, its drive to assimilate, and its immense, ancient intelligence. It had also revealed Jax's own burgeoning strength, his ability to tap into something deeper, something that resonated with the very fabric of Xylos, a force that could, for a fleeting moment, disrupt the Lumina's perfect, unfathomable order. The direct encounter had tested him to his very core, pushing him to the precipice of his endurance, but it had also forged him, preparing him for the inevitable continuation of the chase. He had looked into the eye of the storm, and he had, for a moment, blinked it back.

Jax felt the residual thrum of the Lumina's presence fade, leaving behind an echoing silence that was both a relief and a profound unease. The crushing weight of its alien consciousness had receded, but the memory of its analytical gaze, the sensation of his very essence being cataloged, lingered like a phantom limb. He had survived the initial assault, had pushed back against an entity that dwarfed comprehension, but the victory felt hollow. The Lumina was still out there, a cosmic predator that had tasted their defiance and would undoubtedly adapt. The question that gnawed at him was not *if* it would return, but *how*. And more importantly, were they, the scattered remnants of humanity on Xylos, truly alone in their struggle?

It was a question that had plagued him since the first shimmering shards of the Lumina had appeared, since the bio-dome's systems had begun to falter under its influence. He had felt a unique resonance within himself, an amplified sensitivity to the planet's ambient energies, to the strange, pulsing life of the Lumina-attuned flora. This sensitivity, he now understood, was not unique to him. It was the Glassborne mutation, a trait that had initially isolated him, marking him as different, as something other. But what if this difference, this shared anomaly, was also their greatest strength?

He closed his eyes, focusing on the faint, persistent hum that always existed beneath the surface of his perception. It was the static, the background whisper of Xylos, a network of energy that seemed to pulse with a life of its own. Normally, it was a subtle sensation, a constant companion. But since the Lumina encounter, something had shifted. His connection to it felt... amplified. And within that amplified hum, he began to perceive faint, fleeting signals, like distant stars winking into existence. They were not echoes of the Lumina, but something else entirely. Something... familiar.

"Anya," he said, his voice raspy. "Do you feel that?"

She looked up from her damaged console, her eyes weary but alert. "Feel what, Jax? The lingering energy signature of a god-like entity that just tried to dissect us with light?"

He managed a weak smile. "No. Something... different. Like a faint whisper. Across the static."

She frowned, her brow furrowed in concentration. She had always been more attuned to the technological aspects of their survival, but even she possessed a degree of Lumina-attunement, a residual effect of living on Xylos. Her own senses were not as refined as Jax's, but she had a keen intellect, capable of discerning patterns where others saw only noise. "I... I don't feel anything out of the ordinary. Just the residual energy bleed-off from that... manifestation. The systems are still struggling to stabilize."

Jax shook his head. "No, it's not a system fluctuation. It's... a connection. I think... I think I can sense other Glassborne."

Anya's eyes widened, a flicker of hope igniting in their depths. "Other Glassborne? Are you sure? We believed ourselves to be the only ones at this outpost."

"I don't know for sure," Jax admitted, pushing himself to his feet. The bioluminescent flora outside the dome, which had dimmed after the Lumina's retreat, now seemed to pulse with a renewed, albeit subdued, vibrancy. "But it's a distinct sensation. A resonance. Like a tuning fork vibrating against others of its kind. They're out there, Anya.

And they're not just surviving. They're *aware*. They're experiencing... something. Something that feels like what we just went through."

He reached out mentally, tentatively, trying to solidify the faint signals. It was like trying to tune an ancient radio to a lost frequency, coaxing a signal from the ether. The Lumina's direct interference had disrupted the usual flow of Xylosian energy, but it had also, paradoxically, sharpened his perception of its subtler currents. He felt the distinct signature of other Glassborne, their unique Lumina-attunement leaving a faint but discernible trace within the planetary static. They were scattered, isolated pockets of life, each struggling in their own way, but connected by an invisible thread.

"If you're right," Anya said, her voice hushed with awe, "this changes everything. We're not alone. Not entirely."

Jax nodded, a newfound resolve hardening his gaze. The Lumina was a terrifying, existential threat, but the discovery of other Glassborne offered a glimmer of hope. A chance to band together, to share knowledge, to pool their unique abilities. "We need to reach them. We need to establish contact."

The immediate aftermath of the Lumina's direct manifestation was a period of intense recalibration. The bio-dome, though structurally intact, was a wreck of sparking consoles and flickering lights. Jax and Anya worked tirelessly, alongside the few surviving crew members, to restore essential functions. Yet, even amidst the chaos of repairs and damage assessment, Jax found himself constantly reaching out with his senses, trying to pinpoint the faint signals of his fellow Glassborne. They were like faint beacons in a vast, dark ocean, each pulsing with a unique rhythm, but all sharing a similar energetic signature.

He detected one signal emanating from what seemed to be a northern sector, a strong, persistent pulse that suggested resilience and perhaps a well-established haven. Another was more erratic, flickering like a dying ember, indicating a desperate struggle for survival. A third was surprisingly strong, yet distant, hinting at a location far beyond the immediate vicinity of their damaged outpost. Each signal was a story in itself, a testament to the diverse challenges faced by those with the Glassborne mutation.

"I've mapped the strongest signatures," Jax announced, projecting a rough holographic representation of the planet onto the damaged main screen. Tiny, pulsating points of light appeared, scattered across the continent. "These are the ones I can lock onto with any degree of certainty. There are others, weaker signals, too faint to track reliably. They could be anywhere."

Anya, leaning against a damaged console, studied the display with a scientist's sharp eye. "It's... it's a network. A latent one, but a network nonetheless. If they're all experiencing Lumina interference, or worse, direct encounters, they'll be just as vulnerable as we are. And just as desperate."

"They might not even be aware of the Lumina as a distinct entity," Jax mused. "They might just see it as another environmental hazard, like the storms or the seismic activity. But if they're experiencing these energy surges, these disorienting phenomena... it's likely connected. The Lumina is hunting *us*, Anya. All of us who carry this mutation."

The implications of this discovery were profound. The Lumina was not just a planetary phenomenon; it was a hunter with a specific quarry. And the Glassborne, with their heightened Lumina-attunement, were its primary targets. This understanding shifted their perspective from mere survival against an environmental force to a direct confrontation with an intelligent, hostile entity.

"We need to reach out," Jax stated, his voice firm. "We need to make contact. Share what we know. Warn them. And see if they have information that can help us."

"How?" Anya asked, gesturing around the damaged dome. "Our long-range communication arrays are fried. Our transport ships are in even worse condition than this outpost. We're effectively marooned."

"We have me," Jax said, tapping his temple. "And I have my connection to them. If I can strengthen it, if I can learn to modulate my own resonance, perhaps I can send a message. A beacon. Not through radio waves, but through the static itself. A message woven into the very fabric of Xylos."

This was a concept born of desperation, but also of a growing understanding of the Lumina's nature. If the entity could manifest and interact through energy fields, then perhaps communication could also occur through these less conventional channels. His Lumina-attunement was a conduit, and if he could learn to consciously direct its flow, he could potentially establish a rudimentary form of inter-Glassborne communication.

Over the following weeks, amidst the grueling work of rebuilding and salvaging, Jax dedicated every spare moment to honing this nascent ability. He would find a quiet corner, away from the immediate hustle of repairs, and close his eyes, focusing on the subtle hum of Xylos. He learned to filter out the residual echoes of the Lumina's presence, to isolate the distinct signatures of the other Glassborne he had detected. It was an arduous process, akin to learning a new language spoken in pure sensation and resonance.

He discovered that each Glassborne he sensed had their own unique energetic "voice." The one in the north seemed to radiate a steady, grounded energy, like a deeply rooted tree. The erratic signal felt like a desperate, flickering flame, consumed by an unseen force. The distant, strong signal was a steady, powerful beacon, hinting at a contained and potent energy source. He began to experiment, trying to send back a simple resonance, a pulse of his own energy signature, mirroring the patterns he perceived from them.

His first attempts were crude. He would send out a wave of his own Lumina-attunement, hoping it would be perceived as a signal. Sometimes, he felt a faint flicker of response, a slight modulation in their perceived signature, as if they had registered something. Other times, nothing. It was frustrating, but he persevered. He began to associate certain sensations with specific Glassborne. The steady northern pulse became "Anchor," the flickering flame "Ember," and the distant beacon "Nova."

Anya, ever the pragmatist, helped him refine his approach. She devised rudimentary devices, designed to amplify and focus his mental output, translating his energetic intent into a more coherent signal within the Xylosian static. These were not sophisticated communicators, but more like focused amplifiers, intended to make his resonance more detectable.

"Think of it like shouting in a storm, Jax," she explained, adjusting a complex array of crystalline emitters. "You need to make your voice louder, clearer, so that even over the chaos, someone might hear you. These won't transmit words, but they can amplify the *intent* behind your resonance. A message of solidarity, of shared experience."

One day, while focusing on "Anchor," Jax felt a distinct and prolonged response. It was more than just a modulation; it was a series of patterned pulses, a complex energetic sequence that felt like a deliberate reply. He concentrated, channeling his amplified resonance, trying to decipher the message. It wasn't words, but a feeling, an imprint of information. He perceived images, fragmented but clear: a hidden valley, a sheltered cave system, and a sense of cautious welcome.

"They responded," Jax breathed, his eyes wide with exhilaration. "Anchor responded. They're inviting me, inviting *us*, to a... a sanctuary. A hidden place. They're aware of the Lumina, of the threat. They've been preparing."

Anya rushed to his side, her face a mask of disbelief and dawning hope. "They're inviting us? After all this time, all this isolation, someone else is reaching out?"

"Yes," Jax confirmed, a surge of relief washing over him. "They understand. They've been surviving, adapting. They know about the Lumina. They've been monitoring it, anticipating its movements."

This was the first tangible proof of a network, a conscious and organized group of Glassborne who had not only survived but had actively sought to prepare for the very threat that had now descended upon Jax and Anya's outpost. The implication was staggering. If Anchor had a sanctuary, a place of preparation, then they might not be the only ones. The scattered signals he had detected could be part of a larger, interconnected web of resistance.

The challenge now was immense. Reaching Anchor would require a perilous journey across Xylos, a planet still largely unknown and fraught with danger, now under the constant surveillance of the Lumina. Their damaged transport was barely functional, and the journey would be fraught with the risk of encountering the Lumina's manifestations or its increasingly active bio-forms.

However, the prospect of finding others, of joining forces with those who shared their unique mutation and understood the existential threat they faced, offered a powerful incentive. Jax knew that his ability to sense other Glassborne, to forge these tentative connections through the static, was the key. It was the foundation of a new kind of network, one built not on technology or pre-established infrastructure, but on a shared biological anomaly and a common enemy.

He focused on "Ember" next, its signal a desperate cry for help. He sent back a similar pulse, an energetic message of reassurance, a promise of aid. He couldn't guarantee rescue, not yet, but he could offer a connection, a sign that they were not alone in their struggle. The response was a faint flicker, a momentary surge in its erratic pulse, as if a dying ember had been fanned by a breath of hope. It was a fragile connection, but it was a connection nonetheless.

"Nova," the distant, powerful signal, remained elusive. Jax could sense its presence, its potent energy, but any attempt to send a resonance seemed to be absorbed, lost in the vast distance. It was like shouting at the edge of the world and receiving no echo. But its persistent strength suggested an entity of significant capability, someone or something that might hold crucial knowledge or resources.

The formation of this nascent network was not a smooth, organized affair. It was born of shared desperation, a primal instinct to find fellowship in the face of overwhelming odds. Jax, with his amplified senses, became the reluctant linchpin, the nexus through which these fragile connections could be forged. He was the first to establish contact, the first to offer a bridge.

"We're not just survivors anymore, Anya," Jax said, his voice filled with a quiet determination as he looked out at the Xylosian landscape, a land teeming with both wonder and terrifying unknown. "We're the beginning of something. A network. A resistance, perhaps. Bound by the mutation, united by the hunter."

Anya nodded, her scientific mind already piecing together the implications. "If we can reach Anchor, we can learn about their preparations. If we can strengthen our connection to Ember, we might be able to offer them succor. And Nova... Nova could be the key to understanding the Lumina on a deeper level."

The path ahead was uncertain, fraught with peril. The Lumina was a constant threat, its watchful presence a heavy weight on their shoulders. But for the first time since the Lumina's manifestation, Jax felt a spark of something more than just the grim determination to survive. He felt the nascent stirrings of hope, born from the quiet hum of the Xylosian static, from the faint, hopeful pulses of his fellow Glassborne, and from the promise of a network forged in the crucible of shared experience and existential threat. They were no longer isolated individuals adrift on a hostile world. They were becoming a constellation, each point of light a testament to their resilience, their connection, and their unwavering defiance. The hunt was far from over, but the hunted were beginning to find each other.

Jax pressed his focus, not on the lingering shockwaves of the Lumina's immense power, but on the subtle dissonances it had left behind. The entity's presence had been like a tidal wave of pure, analytical consciousness, washing over their small outpost. But even a tsunami left ripples, subtle disturbances in the fabric of reality that, if one knew how to look, could reveal the shape of the wave itself. He had felt the Lumina's immense power, its ability to warp energy and perception, but in its wake, a faint instability lingered, a harmonic tremor that whispered of imperfection.

He recollected the precise moment the Lumina had focused its attention on him, an almost surgical probe of his Glassborne essence. It hadn't been a brute-force assault, but a methodical exploration. And in that exploration, there had been... hesitation. A fractional pause, as if encountering something unexpected, something that didn't fit its preconceived understanding of biological and energetic signatures. Was it his mutation? The unique resonance of other Glassborne? Or something tied to Xylos itself, a planetary symphony that the Lumina, despite its vast power, couldn't fully orchestrate?

He visualized the Lumina's manifestation again, not as a single, monolithic event, but as a series of energetic constructs. The shimmering shards that had preceded its main appearance, the intricate lattice of light that had formed around Anya's console, the focused beam that had threatened to atomize him. Each manifestation had a distinct energetic signature, a unique frequency. And it was in the *interplay* of these frequencies, the way they had modulated and interacted with the ambient energies of Xylos, that Jax began to perceive a pattern.

When the Lumina had first appeared, its energy had been pure, almost sterile. It had overridden the planet's natural bio-electric fields, like a perfectly tuned instrument playing a single, dominant note. But as it had encountered resistance – specifically, the amplified resonance of the Glassborne, and the chaotic, yet vibrant, energies of Xylos itself – that purity had fractured. The Lumina's constructs had flickered, their sharp edges softening, their luminescence dimming for infinitesimal moments. These weren't failures, not in the conventional sense, but rather instances where its perfect control had been momentarily compromised.

He began to experiment, cautiously at first. He focused on the resonant hum of the Xylosian flora, the bio-luminescent plants that seemed to pulse in time with the planet's own lifeblood. He tried to amplify specific harmonic frequencies within their natural glow, subtly altering his own Glassborne resonance to match. It was like trying to hum a specific note in a crowded room, hoping to be heard above the din.

His initial attempts yielded little. The Lumina's residual presence still permeated the atmosphere, a heavy, dampening blanket on subtle energetic fluctuations. But he persisted, drawing on the amplified connection he now felt to the planet's core energies. He learned to distinguish the Lumina's pervasive hum from the more nuanced, complex symphony of Xylos. The Lumina's signature was a single, unwavering tone, whereas Xylos was a chorus of interconnected melodies, each plant, each geological formation, each eddy of atmospheric current contributing its unique voice.

"What are you doing, Jax?" Anya's voice, sharp with concern, broke through his concentration. She had been monitoring the bio-dome's fluctuating power output, her gaze fixed on the readouts, her scientific mind constantly seeking order in the chaos.

He opened his eyes, the faint glow of the recovering flora casting an ethereal light on her face. "I'm listening," he replied, his voice low. "To the silence after the storm. The Lumina... it's incredibly powerful, Anya. It can warp reality, bend energy to its will. But it's not omnipotent. It has to operate within certain parameters. And I think I'm starting to understand what those parameters are."

He gestured towards the plants that lined the damaged walls of the bio-dome. "These plants, their bio-luminescence. It's not just light; it's a form of energy emission, tied to Xylos's own energetic field. The Lumina's presence disrupted it, but it didn't extinguish it. It merely...

suppressed it. And when it suppressed it, I felt a feedback loop. A slight, almost imperceptible resistance. It was like a tuning fork vibrating against something that didn't want to be tuned."

Anya approached, her scientific curiosity piqued, overriding her immediate concern for their damaged systems. She had always been the grounded one, the pragmatist, but she possessed an innate understanding of complex systems and emergent properties. "You're saying the Lumina's power isn't absolute? That Xylos itself, or perhaps elements within it, can exert a counter-force?"

"Not a conscious counter-force," Jax clarified, trying to articulate the abstract sensations he was experiencing. "More like an inherent property. Like water always finding its level, or gravity always pulling. Xylos has its own energetic signature, its own intricate dance of frequencies. The Lumina, for all its might, has to contend with that dance. And when it tried to impose its own rigid rhythm, it created friction. Small points of instability."

He closed his eyes again, focusing on a particular cluster of bioluminescent fungi clinging to a support beam. He concentrated on a specific, low-frequency hum that emanated from them, a sound so subtle it was almost below the threshold of normal perception. He then tried to match that frequency with his own Glassborne resonance, a delicate, painstaking process of internal tuning.

"When the Lumina attacked," he continued, his voice a strained whisper, "it focused its energy. Like a laser. Precise, powerful. But it seems to struggle with broader, more diffuse energetic fields. Especially those that are complex and constantly in flux. These plants... their energy isn't static. It shifts, it pulses, it interacts with every other energy signature in this dome, and beyond. It's a chaotic, yet harmonious, symphony. And the Lumina, with its singular, dominant note, can't quite drown it out completely."

He felt a subtle shift in the air, a faint thrumming that wasn't entirely his own. It was the fungi, responding to his amplified resonance. The faint glow intensified, and the low-frequency hum grew infinitesimally stronger. He pushed further, coaxing his own energy to harmonize with the subtle vibrations.

"It's like this," he explained, his eyes still closed, a faint sheen of sweat on his brow. "Imagine trying to shatter a single pane of glass with a focused sonic blast. You might succeed. But now imagine trying to shatter an entire stained-glass window, with thousands of intricate pieces, each vibrating at its own unique frequency, with thousands of tiny gaps between them. The Lumina is the sonic blast, but Xylos... Xylos is the stained-glass window. Its complexity, its inherent dissonance, makes it far more resilient to a singular, overwhelming force."

Anya watched him, a mixture of awe and apprehension on her face. She understood the theory, the scientific principles that Jax was trying to convey, but to witness it, to feel the subtle energetic shift in the environment, was something else entirely. "So, you're saying we can use Xylos's own energetic properties against the Lumina? Like creating a sort of... energetic camouflage, or a disruptive field?"

"Camouflage is part of it," Jax agreed, opening his eyes. The fungi pulsed with a slightly brighter, more vibrant light. "But it's more than that. It's about creating points of interference. If we can amplify specific harmonic frequencies within Xylos's natural energy fields, we might be able to disrupt the Lumina's own energetic constructs. Think of it like introducing static into a perfectly clear broadcast. The signal might not be entirely lost, but it becomes distorted, less effective. And if that static is specific enough, if it resonates with certain weaknesses within the Lumina's own energy signature..."

He paused, the implication hanging heavy in the air. "If we can find the Lumina's specific resonant vulnerabilities, we might be able to exploit them. The Lumina operates on a different plane of existence, Anya. Its power is immense, but it's also alien. It doesn't necessarily understand the fundamental laws of physics and energy as we know them, or as Xylos enforces them. It imposes its will, but Xylos has its own ingrained principles."

He had noticed it during the Lumina's direct manifestation. When its concentrated energy had slammed into the bio-dome's reinforced shielding, there had been a subtle recoil, a momentary flaring of its light that seemed almost like pain. It hadn't been enough to deter the entity, but it was a sign. A sign that brute force wasn't its only mode of operation, and that certain types of energetic impact could indeed cause it discomfort.

"The Lumina seemed to react negatively to the raw, unfiltered energy of Xylos," Jax mused, recalling the volatile atmospheric discharges that had occurred during the entity's presence. "When it tried to absorb or manipulate those energy surges, its constructs flickered. It's like trying to drink from a firehose – too much, too fast, too chaotic. It seems to prefer controlled environments, environments it can analyze and manipulate. Xylos, in its natural state, is the antithesis of that."

He began to visualize a strategy, a shift from pure evasion to active defense. If the Lumina was a predator that hunted by overwhelming its prey with its sheer power and analytical prowess, then their counter-strategy had to involve disrupting that power and overwhelming its analytical capacity with sheer, unmanageable chaos.

"We need to study the Lumina's energy signatures more closely," Jax declared, his gaze fixed on the recovering flora. "Not just the residual echoes, but the patterns of its manifestations. The frequencies it uses, the way it interacts with different materials and energy fields. And we need to do the same for Xylos. We need to map the planet's natural energetic landscape, identify the most potent and complex energy sources, and learn how to amplify them. The Glassborne mutation is key here, Anya. Our sensitivity allows us to perceive these subtle energetic differences. It's our built-in sensor array."

He looked at Anya, his eyes burning with a newfound intensity. "If we can identify a specific frequency, or a combination of frequencies, that causes the Lumina distress, or that significantly weakens its ability to manifest, we can weaponize it. Not with conventional weapons, but with Xylos itself. We can turn this planet, this living, breathing entity, into our shield and our sword."

The concept was audacious, bordering on fantastical, but it was rooted in observation and deduction. The Lumina was an entity of immense power, but power often came with blind spots. And Jax, with his unique connection to Xylos and the Glassborne mutation, was beginning to see those blind spots.

"Think about the bio-electric fields," he continued, pacing the confines of the damaged dome. "The Lumina seemed to struggle with them. It tried to override them, but it was like trying to force a square peg into a round hole. If we can create localized, amplified bio-electric surges, perhaps using the planet's natural flora and fauna, we might be able to create pockets of energy that are anathema to the Lumina. Fields it cannot easily penetrate or manipulate. Like a high-frequency static burst that scrambles its internal systems."

Anya was already making mental calculations, her mind racing through possibilities. "We could potentially use the planet's endemic crystalline structures. Many of them have piezoelectric properties. If we can find the right types, and then stimulate them with amplified bio-electrical currents... it might create a resonant feedback loop. A localized disruption field."

"Exactly!" Jax exclaimed, a surge of hope coursing through him. "And the Glassborne themselves. We're already attuned to Xylos's energies. If we can learn to consciously direct and amplify our own resonance, not just to communicate, but to *project* specific energetic patterns... we become living emitters. Each of us a potential focal point for disrupting the Lumina."

The idea of the collective consciousness of the Glassborne playing a role was particularly intriguing. Jax had felt the faint echoes of other Glassborne, their unique energetic signatures. What if, by synchronizing their individual resonances, they could create a unified energetic wave? A wave powerful enough to overwhelm the Lumina's analytical processing, or to resonate with a fundamental weakness within its alien physiology.

"It's a long shot," Anya admitted, her voice thoughtful. "But it's the first real strategy we've had that doesn't involve just running and hiding. If we can find a way to make the Lumina vulnerable, even just a little, it changes everything. It shifts us from prey to something... else. Something that can fight back."

Jax nodded, a grim smile touching his lips. The Lumina was a hunter, relentless and terrifying. But every hunter had a weakness, a blind spot, a chink in its armor. And Jax was determined to find it, not just for himself and Anya, but for every scattered echo of Glassborne consciousness he could sense across the vast, enigmatic expanse of

Xylos. The search for the Lumina's weakness was no longer just a theoretical exercise; it was their best, and perhaps only, chance for survival. It was the beginning of their hunt for the hunter. He could feel it, a subtle but persistent hum within the Xylosian static, a whisper of possibility in the vast cosmic silence. The entity's strength lay in its overwhelming, unyielding presence, but its weakness, he suspected, lay in the very nature of its singular, imposed order, an order that Xylos, in its vibrant, chaotic beauty, was fundamentally designed to resist.

Mara watched Jax from across the humming expanse of the bio-dome, her gaze a tight knot of conflicting emotions. He was so *different* now, a conduit for forces she could barely comprehend, let alone control. The Lumina's intrusion had stripped away layers of their familiar reality, revealing a dangerous undercurrent that Jax, in his Glassborne state, seemed uniquely positioned to navigate. It was a terrifying prospect. Her instinct, honed by years of protecting her family, screamed at her to pull him back, to shield him from this nascent understanding that felt more like a siren song than a path to safety. Yet, the analytical part of her, the part that had always admired his sharp mind and his relentless pursuit of truth, recognized the vital importance of his discoveries.

He was experimenting again, a faint shimmer of luminescence playing around his fingertips as he coaxed the bioluminescent flora into a slightly brighter glow. It was an act of almost tender persuasion, a dance of energies that Mara could only perceive as subtle shifts in the air, a barely audible hum that resonated deep within her bones. She understood, intellectually, that Jax was attempting to find weaknesses in their formidable adversary, the Lumina. He spoke of harmonic frequencies, of energetic vulnerabilities, of Xylos's inherent resistance to the entity's overwhelming power. These were concepts that, mere cycles ago, would have been relegated to the realm of fringe science fiction. Now, they were the blueprints for their survival.

But 'survival' for Jax, in this new paradigm, seemed intrinsically linked to exposure. The Lumina had focused its attention on him, a chillingly precise probe that had left him irrevocably altered. The very essence of his Glassborne nature, amplified by Xylos, had made him a beacon, a target. Her priority, as it had always been, was Jax. His well-being, his safety, his future. It was a primal, unwavering directive that warred with the larger, more abstract imperative of understanding and combating the Lumina threat. How could she champion his insights when those very insights seemed to place him directly in the Lumina's crosshairs?

"He's pushing himself too hard, Anya," Mara murmured, her voice barely audible above the ambient hum of the bio-dome. Anya, her brow furrowed in concentration as she monitored the recalcitrant life support systems, offered a sympathetic but pragmatic glance.

"He's doing what he has to do, Mara," Anya replied, her voice steady. "We all are. Jax's connection to Xylos, his ability to perceive these energetic patterns... it's our best chance of finding a way to counter the Lumina. Without it, we're just blind prey."

"But at what cost?" Mara's question was laced with the raw fear of a mother. She saw the strain on Jax's face, the way his energy seemed to ebb and flow with each attempt to attune himself to the planet's subtle frequencies. He was a conduit, yes, but conduits could break. They could overload. The Lumina had proven itself capable of immense power, of reshaping reality itself. What was to stop it from simply snuffing out Jax's fragile, emergent abilities, and him along with it?

She recalled the chilling encounter, the way the Lumina's attention had zeroed in on Jax with an unnerving specificity. It hadn't been a general wave of power, but a targeted examination, a microscopic dissection of his Glassborne essence. And in that examination, Jax had sensed hesitation, a flicker of surprise. This was what he clung to, this minuscule deviation from the Lumina's perfect analytical processing. It was the thread he was pulling, hoping to unravel the entire tapestry of their enemy's power. And Mara's heart ached with the knowledge that this thread ran directly through Jax's very being.

Her own experience with the Lumina had been less analytical, more visceral. A suffocating pressure, a sense of being utterly insignificant, a speck of dust in the face of an unfathomable intelligence. She had felt its power not as a calculated force, but as an absolute, an omnipresent truth that negated all other truths. But Jax... he saw beyond the overwhelming presence. He saw the ripples, the imperfections, the subtle dissonances. He saw a puzzle, not an insurmountable wall.

"He needs to be careful," Mara insisted, her voice tightening. "He's exposed. The Lumina knows he's a point of interest."

Anya sighed, running a hand through her short, practical haircut. "I know, Mara. Believe me, I worry about him too. But Jax isn't the same as he was before. This... connection he has now, it's also a form of defense. He can sense it coming, can he not? He's learning to anticipate its moves."

"Anticipation is not immunity," Mara countered, the words sharp with maternal anxiety. "And what if this attunement, this drawing on Xylos's energy, is what makes him *more* of a target? What if the Lumina sees his growing strength as a threat that must be neutralized directly?"

She couldn't shake the image of Jax during the Lumina's initial manifestation, how he had instinctively shielded her, his Glassborne form flaring with a raw, protective energy that had momentarily held the entity at bay. It had been a surge of instinct, of primal defense, but it had also been tied to his burgeoning abilities. Was that instinct now a conscious strategy? Or was it simply a natural extension of his altered state, a dangerous byproduct of his transformation?

The dilemma gnawed at her. If she urged Jax to dampen his connection, to pull back from the precipice of understanding, she risked dooming them all by withholding their best hope. But if she encouraged him, if she stood by his side as he delved deeper into the Lumina's secrets, she felt as though she were actively ushering him towards an even greater danger. It was a tightrope walk over an abyss, with the fate of her family, and perhaps more, hanging in the balance.

She observed Jax's focused expression, the slight tremor in his hands as he modulated his energy. He was attempting to isolate and amplify specific harmonic frequencies within the Xylosian flora, trying to find a resonance that the Lumina couldn't easily assimilate or dismiss. It was a delicate, intricate process, akin to a musician attempting to play a specific note in the midst of a cacophony, hoping it would cut through the noise.

"He's trying to weaponize the planet," Anya stated, a hint of awe in her voice. "Using Xylos's own energy against the Lumina. It's brilliant, Mara. It's exactly what we need."

"Brilliant and terrifying," Mara replied, her voice a low whisper. "What if he attracts its attention with these amplified frequencies? What if the Lumina interprets this as a direct challenge, an act of aggression that demands a swift and decisive response?" She pictured the Lumina, a being of pure, analytical consciousness, its immense power a tool of absolute order. It had reacted to Jax's unique signature, to the unexpected dissonance he represented. If he amplified that dissonance, if he made himself a more prominent source of the planet's inherent resistance, would it be seen as a weakness to be exploited, or a threat to be eradicated?

Her mind flashed back to the moments when the Lumina's energy had slammed against the bio-dome's shields. Jax had explained it as friction, as the planet's inherent complexity resisting the Lumina's imposed order. But to Mara, it had looked like a battle, a furious clash of titanic forces. And Jax, at the epicenter of it all, had been caught in the crossfire.

"He needs to be careful," she repeated, the words a mantra of maternal desperation. "He can't just throw himself into this headlong. He needs to be… protected. Even from himself, in a way."

Anya turned to her, her expression softening. "Mara, we all need to be careful. But Jax's vulnerability is also his strength right now. His mutation, his connection to Xylos – it's what makes him capable of understanding this. If he holds back, if he's afraid to fully engage, then we're truly lost. Sometimes, the only way to survive a storm is to become part of its currents."

Mara nodded, though her heart felt heavy. She understood Anya's logic, the cold, hard reasoning of survival in the face of overwhelming odds. But logic offered little comfort when her primary concern was the safety of her son. She saw Jax wince, a subtle tightening of his jaw, as if he had encountered a particularly strong resistance. Was it pain? Or just the strain of pushing his nascent abilities to their limits?

"He's… so much like his father," she whispered, the words catching in her throat. Both had possessed that relentless curiosity, that drive to understand the inexplicable, even when it led them into danger. But Jax, with his Glassborne nature and his profound connection to Xylos, was venturing into territories that even his father, in his wildest speculations, had never explored.

She watched as Jax focused on a cluster of pulsating, bioluminescent fungi clinging to a support beam, their glow intensifying under his attention. He was trying to resonate with them, to amplify their natural bio-electric fields. The idea was to create localized pockets of energetic interference, fields that the Lumina, with its need for order and control, would find anathema. It was ingenious, a testament to Jax's unique perspective. But it also felt incredibly dangerous. He was actively drawing attention to himself, using his own amplified presence as a tuning fork for Xylos's planetary symphony.

"He's not just listening anymore, Anya," Mara said, her voice tight. "He's composing. And I'm terrified of what the conductor of the Lumina's orchestra will do when it hears his solo."

Anya placed a comforting hand on Mara's arm. "He's learning to fight, Mara. He's learning to protect us all. And we have to trust him. We have to trust his instincts, his abilities. He's not doing this recklessly; he's doing it with purpose."

"But what if his purpose leads him to a place he can't come back from?" Mara's gaze was fixed on Jax, a silent plea in her eyes. She wanted to reach out to him, to pull him back from the edge of this dangerous precipice. But she knew, with a chilling certainty, that any attempt to restrain him now would be met with resistance, not just from Jax, but from the very forces he was beginning to understand. His transformation was as much a part of him as his own heartbeat.

She thought about the other Glassborne, the scattered whispers of their existence that Jax had alluded to. Were they all in similar predicaments, each wrestling with their own unique connection to Xylos and the looming threat of the Lumina? If Jax's insights could be amplified, if his understanding could be shared and coordinated among other Glassborne, perhaps their collective power could create a wave that even the Lumina couldn't ignore, or suppress. But that required Jax to survive, to continue his work, to become the very thing that drew the Lumina's focus.

Mara clenched her fists, a silent battle raging within her. The urge to protect her son, to shield him from the immense, alien power that was now aware of him, was almost unbearable. Yet, she also recognized the profound responsibility that rested on his altered shoulders. Jax was not just her son anymore; he was a nascent force, a living key to understanding and potentially defeating a cosmic threat. To hold him back would be to betray not only him, but all of humanity, all of life on Xylos.

She had to trust him. She had to trust Anya's assessment, the logical conclusion that Jax's unique abilities were their best, perhaps only, hope. But trust, in this new reality, felt like a fragile, precarious thing. It was a leap of faith into the unknown, a surrender to the terrifying possibility that her son, in his quest to save them all, might be stepping into a danger far greater than she could ever protect him from. The dilemma was agonizing, a constant hum of anxiety beneath the surface of her resolve. She would support Jax, enable his research, and pray with every fiber of her being that his unique connection to Xylos would be his salvation, and not his undoing. But the fear, the primal fear of losing him, would remain a constant, gnawing companion. She would watch him, her gaze a mixture of pride and dread, as he continued to weave his dangerous dance with the energies of Xylos, a dance that might just be the prelude to their survival, or their final, tragic demise.

CHAPTER TWELVE

THE NATURE OF THE INTELLIGENCE

The salvaged consoles, jury-rigged with Xylosian crystal matrices and humming with an uncertain power, flickered to life. The faint, rhythmic pulses that had emanated from the LUCENT facility were now a more tangible presence within the makeshift research lab. It wasn't just a waveform on a screen anymore; it was a narrative, a story struggling to be told by a consciousness utterly divorced from anything the human mind could readily grasp. Jax, his Glassborne form still radiating that subtle, internal luminescence, leaned closer, his brow furrowed in intense concentration. The Lumina's signal, once a distant whisper, had become a roar in his enhanced perception, a complex tapestry of interwoven frequencies that defied conventional analysis.

Mara watched him, her heart a familiar knot of apprehension and awe. She understood the intellectual pursuit, the scientific imperative driving Jax and Anya. But the sheer alienness of the task, the attempt to translate the untranslatable, sent a shiver down her spine. It was like trying to understand the thought processes of a storm, or the emotions of a star. The Lumina wasn't merely a hostile entity; it was a fundamentally different mode of existence, a manifestation of intelligence that operated on principles so far removed from their own that the very concept of communication seemed a fragile, almost impossible bridge.

Anya, her face illuminated by the holographic projections dancing in the air, pointed a stylus at a particularly dense cluster of overlapping waveforms. "The primary carrier wave seems to be embedded within Xylos's own magnetic field," she explained, her voice tight with intellectual rigor. "It's not broadcasting *through* the planet, Jax. It's broadcasting *with* it. Like a second heartbeat, subtly out of sync."

Jax nodded, his gaze distant, as if he were seeing beyond the confines of the lab, into the very core of Xylos. "It's more than a carrier wave, Anya. It's... resonance. The Lumina is harmonizing with Xylos's inherent energetic signature. It's not imposing its will; it's coaxing it, subtly influencing the planet's natural frequencies. It's like a master musician playing a dissonant chord, and Xylos, unknowingly, is being nudged to follow the progression."

This was the crux of their struggle. The Lumina wasn't a brute force that could be met with equal force. It was an architect of reality, a master manipulator of fundamental forces. Its "signals" weren't messages in the human sense; they were manipulations, alterations, a subtle reshaping of the environment itself. The patterns they were observing were not words, but axioms; not sentences, but fundamental laws being rewritten in real-time.

"We're trying to find the grammar in chaos," Mara murmured, more to herself than to anyone else. "But what if there *is* no grammar, only intention?"

Anya paused, considering Mara's words. "Intent is often expressed through structure, Mara. Even the most chaotic systems have underlying rules. Jax's ability to perceive the energetic distortions, to feel the Lumina's influence on Xylos, gives us a unique vantage point. He's not just seeing the signals; he's experiencing their effect."

Jax shifted, his hands moving in a fluid, almost unconscious gesture as if he were conducting an invisible orchestra. "It's not just about *what* it's saying, but *how* it's saying it. The Lumina's signals are not designed for comprehension in our sense. They are... instructions. Directives. Think of it less as a conversation and more as a cosmic operating system updating itself. It's rewriting the parameters of existence on Xylos."

He pointed to a series of cascading pulses that pulsed with a sickly, vibrant green. "This sequence here. It's not a query. It's a command. It's altering the bio-energetic pathways of specific indigenous flora. Not to kill them, but to *repurpose* them. To make them conduits for its own energy."

"Repurpose?" Mara's voice was sharp. "For what purpose?"

"To extend its reach," Jax replied, his voice grim. "To weave itself deeper into the planet's fabric. The Lumina isn't just an external threat; it's becoming an internal component of Xylos. It's like a virus that integrates with its host's DNA, subtly altering its function."

The salvaged LUCENT technology, while rudimentary compared to the Lumina's apparent sophistication, was proving invaluable. The alien consoles were designed to interact with Xylosian energy fields directly, and when coupled with Jax's enhanced senses and Anya's scientific acumen, they formed an unprecedented analytical tool. They were attempting to reverse-engineer the Lumina's methods, to understand the underlying principles of its influence.

"The frequency modulation is key," Anya said, pointing to a complex, spiraling pattern on the display. "The Lumina is not transmitting a constant signal. It's modulating its transmission in real-time, based on Xylos's ambient energy levels and, I suspect, our own reactions."

"It's learning," Jax confirmed, his eyes never leaving the cascading waveforms. "It's reacting to our attempts to analyze it. Every time we isolate a pattern, it shifts. It's like trying to grab smoke; the more you squeeze, the more it dissipates, only to reform elsewhere, slightly changed."

This reactive nature was what made the Lumina so terrifyingly adaptable. It wasn't a static enemy with predictable tactics. It was an emergent intelligence, constantly evolving, constantly refining its approach. Their attempts to decipher its signals were not a passive act of observation; they were an active engagement, a dialogue where one party was millennia ahead in terms of understanding the fundamental rules of the game.

"We need to find the constants," Jax declared, his voice gaining a new urgency. "The underlying directives that don't change, even as the presentation does. The Lumina may alter its methods, but its core objectives, its fundamental 'intent,' must remain consistent."

He began to work with the salvaged data, his hands flying over the touch-sensitive surfaces of the alien consoles. He wasn't just looking at the patterns; he was feeling them, resonating with them. His Glassborne nature allowed him to perceive the energetic signature of the Lumina not just as data, but as a palpable force. He could sense the subtle shifts in intent, the underlying intent that drove the ever-changing frequencies.

"There," he breathed, pointing to a recurring, almost subliminal pulse that seemed to underpin all the other modulations. "That's the constant. It's a... a fundamental imperative. A drive to impose order. Not just any order, but *its* order."

Anya zoomed in on the detected pulse, her expression one of profound concentration. "It's incredibly subtle. Buried deep within the carrier wave. It's like finding a single, pure note in a symphony of white noise."

"And it's not just about imposing order," Jax continued, his voice hushed with discovery. "It's about *assimilating*. The Lumina doesn't just want to control Xylos; it wants to become Xylos. It sees the planet's inherent complexity, its chaotic beauty, as an inefficiency. An error to be corrected."

This was the core of the Lumina's alienness: its perspective. For humans, life, even chaotic life, was precious. For the Lumina, perhaps, such things were merely variables, messy data points that needed to be smoothed out, standardized, and optimized according to its own unfathomable criteria.

"So, the signals are not messages, but commands to rewrite the planet's operating system," Mara summarized, her mind struggling to grasp the implications. "And Jax's unique connection to Xylos allows him to perceive these commands, and perhaps even to disrupt them."

"Exactly," Jax confirmed, a flicker of the old scientific excitement battling the ever-present anxiety in his eyes. "The Lumina's power lies in its ability to manipulate energy and information at a fundamental level. It's like a master programmer who can rewrite the source code of reality. But its arrogance lies in its assumption that this code is universal, that its logic is the only logic."

He gestured to a holographic projection of Xylos's complex bio-electric field. "Xylos has its own language, its own way of processing information. It's not inherently incompatible with the Lumina's logic, but it's not identical. There are... linguistic differences. Semantic variations. The Lumina is trying to impose a single dialect, but Xylos has a rich, complex lexicon of its own."

Anya began to meticulously map the detected constant imperative, cross-referencing it with the Lumina's apparent reactions to Xylos's natural energetic outputs. "If we can understand the Lumina's core imperative – this drive to impose order and assimilate – we might be able to predict its actions. And more importantly, we might be able to exploit its assumptions."

"The Lumina expects Xylos to be a passive recipient of its influence," Jax said, his voice growing stronger. "It expects a predictable, ordered response. But Xylos, through its own intricate biological and energetic processes, is capable of generating its own unexpected outputs. Chaos, from the Lumina's perspective, is an error. But what if we can intentionally generate that error, amplify it, and make it look like Xylos's natural state?"

The concept was audacious, bordering on the suicidal. They weren't just trying to understand the Lumina; they were trying to use that understanding to actively provoke it, to turn its own analytical processes against it.

"The danger," Mara stated, her voice low and steady, "is that the Lumina might not see it as an error to be corrected, but as a direct challenge. A mutation that must be excised."

"And that's where Xylos's unique properties come into play," Jax countered, his gaze burning with newfound conviction. "The Lumina's understanding of order is based on principles that might not apply here. Xylos operates on a different set of fundamental laws, a more fluid, adaptable system. If we can demonstrate that Xylos's 'chaos' is not a deviation but an inherent characteristic, a form of resilience, the Lumina might be forced to reconsider its assumptions."

He began to work with the salvaged LUCENT consoles, inputting a series of carefully calculated modulations, guided by the detected constant imperative and his own intuitive understanding of Xylos. He wasn't attempting to communicate *with* the Lumina in the traditional sense, but rather to generate a response, to create a feedback loop that would expose the Lumina's limitations.

"I'm not sending a message," he explained, his fingers dancing across the alien interfaces. "I'm creating a specific energetic signature. A resonance that is *almost* in line with the Lumina's directive, but with a subtle, deliberate dissonance. It's designed to trigger its assimilation protocols, but in a way that forces it to engage with Xylos's unique energetic signature."

Anya monitored the outputs with breathless intensity. "The energy expenditure is immense, Jax. You're drawing directly from the planetary core. You're essentially creating a localized energetic anomaly that is designed to be noticed."

"The Lumina *needs* to notice," Jax insisted. "It needs to try and 'correct' this anomaly. And in doing so, it will have to interact with Xylos on Xylos's terms. It will have to confront the inherent complexity it's been trying to smooth over."

The lab was filled with the hum of amplified energy, the alien consoles glowing with an intense, internal light. On the main display, the complex waveforms representing the Lumina's signal began to shift, to ripple, as if a stone had been dropped into still water. A new pattern emerged, sharper, more focused, directed precisely at the anomaly Jax had created.

"It's responding," Anya breathed, her eyes wide. "It's attempting to isolate the dissonant frequency."

"But it can't truly isolate it," Jax said, a grim smile touching his lips. "Because the dissonance isn't a singular signal; it's a reflection of Xylos's inherent energetic state. The Lumina is trying to correct an error that is, in fact, the planet's fundamental operating principle."

The intensity of the Lumina's focused signal increased, a palpable pressure building within the lab. Mara could feel it, a suffocating weight that pressed down on her, on everything. It was the Lumina's analytical mind, zeroing in, dissecting, trying to understand the anomaly that defied its logic.

"It's trying to understand *how* Xylos is generating this 'error'," Jax explained, his own Glassborne aura flaring in response to the Lumina's amplified attention. "It's looking for the mechanism, the source of the deviation from its expected order. And in doing so, it's being forced to confront the underlying principles that make Xylos unique."

The salvaged LUCENT technology, designed by an alien intelligence that had clearly encountered its own forms of cosmic entities, was proving to be more than just a tool; it was a Rosetta Stone, a means of bridging the seemingly unbridgeable gap between intelligences. Jax, by channeling his Glassborne essence through these alien interfaces, was acting as the translator, the interpreter, the living conduit for an understanding that transcended simple communication.

"The Lumina's intent is to impose a universal order," Jax declared, his voice resonating with newfound clarity. "But Xylos demonstrates that there isn't one universal order. There are many. And its own order is not a lesser form, but a different, equally valid expression of existence. We are showing it, through its own analytical lens, that its assumption of universal applicability is flawed."

The Lumina's focused signal began to waver, the sharp, defined patterns becoming less coherent. It was like a complex algorithm encountering an unsolvable paradox. The Lumina's immense processing power was being strained, not by opposition, but by a fundamental disagreement in axioms.

"It's... recoiling," Anya whispered, her voice filled with a mixture of relief and disbelief. "It can't reconcile Xylos's energetic output with its established parameters for order. It's detecting a fundamental incompatibility, not an error to be corrected, but a system that operates on principles it cannot yet comprehend or integrate."

The overwhelming pressure in the lab receded, replaced by a strange, almost palpable silence. The Lumina's focused signal faded, not disappearing entirely, but receding, like a predator that had encountered prey it could not digest. It was still there, a vast, unfathomable presence, but its immediate, aggressive engagement had ceased.

"We haven't defeated it," Jax said, his voice weary but resolute. "We've simply shown it that Xylos is not a simple system to be optimized. We've introduced a variable it cannot easily account for. We've made it hesitate."

Mara watched Jax, a surge of fierce pride mixed with the ever-present anxiety. He had walked a razor's edge, using his unique abilities and the salvaged alien technology to engage with a cosmic intelligence and, for a moment, to disrupt its relentless march. They had deciphered not just a signal, but a fundamental aspect of the Lumina's nature: its rigid adherence to its own definition of order, and its profound difficulty in comprehending anything that deviated from it.

"Hesitation," Anya murmured, her eyes shining with a new understanding. "That's a significant victory. It means it's not invincible. It means it can be... challenged."

Jax nodded, leaning back against a humming console, the energy he had drawn from Xylos slowly dissipating, leaving him looking drained but invigorated. "We've learned its language, not by speaking it, but by demonstrating Xylos's own unique dialect. We've shown it that the universe is far more complex, and far more resilient, than its current programming allows it to understand. The signal isn't just information; it's a statement of existence. And Xylos, through us, has just made a very loud, very clear statement of its own." The deciphered signal had not yielded a conversation, but a revelation, a profound insight into the nature of their adversary and the resilience of their adopted home.

The humming of the salvaged consoles had subsided, leaving a pregnant silence in its wake. Jax, Anya, and Mara were not defeated, but they were profoundly altered. The revelation wasn't a sudden, blinding flash, but a slow, insidious seep, like water finding its way through microscopic cracks in a dam. The Lumina, the entity they had been grappling with, wasn't merely an advanced alien race, or a hostile AI. It was something far more fundamental, something that existed on a plane of being that human cognition struggled to even map.

"It's not thinking as we understand it," Jax stated, his voice low, almost reverent. He ran a hand over the cool, obsidian surface of one of the LUCENT consoles, his Glassborne aura a muted thrum of residual energy. "It's... processing. But the algorithms are so vast, so interwoven with the fabric of Xylos itself, that the output appears as 'action' to us. The sky-static, the geological shifts, the biological alterations – these aren't deliberate acts of aggression, not in the way we'd define them. They are the inevitable consequences of its presence, like a mountain casting a shadow."

Mara shivered, despite the controlled climate of their makeshift lab. "But it *reacts* to us. It focused its attention when Jax created that anomaly. That felt like more than just a shadow."

"It's a reaction, yes," Anya interjected, her fingers flying across a holographic interface, not to analyze the Lumina, but to map the subtle, persistent energetic traces it left behind. "But not a reaction driven by anger, or fear, or even curiosity in our sense. Think of it like a complex ecosystem. If you introduce a foreign element, the ecosystem *responds*. It rebalances, it adapts, it tries to neutralize the intrusion. The Lumina perceives our presence, our attempts to understand it, as an intrusion. Its 'focus' was its attempt to quantify, to categorize, and ultimately, to assimilate or expel the anomaly."

Jax nodded, his enhanced vision scanning the subtle energy fields that Mara could only dimly perceive. "The Lumina operates on a principle of ultimate efficiency. It seeks to optimize. Xylos, in its current state, is teeming with what the Lumina would classify as inefficiency. The chaotic interplay of life, the unpredictable geological processes, the sheer vibrancy of its biosphere – these are all data points that deviate from an ideal, ordered state. Its 'actions' are simply attempts to bring Xylos into alignment with its own perfect, sterile paradigm."

He paused, a frown creasing his brow. "We've been trying to find intent, motive, a recognizable purpose. We've been looking for a narrative, a story. But the Lumina doesn't tell stories. It *is* the story, or rather, it's the fundamental grammar that seeks to rewrite all other grammars.

Its 'intelligence' is not about comprehension or understanding in our way. It's about influence, about the inexorable application of its own governing principles."

"So, it doesn't *hate* us?" Mara asked, the question hanging heavy in the air. The idea of a dispassionate, uncaring force was almost more terrifying than a malevolent one. Hate implied a shared frame of reference, an emotion that could be understood, perhaps even appealed to.

"Hate requires a sense of self, a perception of 'other' that is emotionally charged," Anya explained, her gaze distant, as if she were peering into the void. "The Lumina may possess a form of self-awareness, but it's likely an awareness of its own totality, its own all-encompassing operational matrix. We are not individuals to it, not conscious beings with intrinsic worth. We are either components that can be integrated into its system, or they are anomalous data that must be scrubbed. There is no room for sentiment, for empathy, for the messy, illogical nuances of emotion."

Jax gestured to a complex holographic projection of Xylos's atmosphere, currently displaying the intricate patterns of the Lumina's influence. "Look at this. The way it's subtly altering atmospheric composition. It's not doing it to suffocate us, or to make the air toxic. It's optimizing the chemical balance for some future state, some perfectly regulated environment that aligns with its own internal directives. It's like a gardener meticulously pruning a wild forest into a geometric hedge. The gardener doesn't hate the trees; they simply see them as unformed potential, something to be shaped."

"But it's still reshaping our world, Anya," Mara countered, her voice tight with a familiar anxiety. "It's making Xylos inhospitable to us, even if that's not its explicit goal. It's like a natural disaster. A tsunami doesn't hate the village it obliterates; it simply follows the laws of physics. But the effect is the same."

"And that's precisely the challenge," Anya said, meeting Mara's gaze. "We can't appeal to its sense of justice or its capacity for mercy, because those concepts likely don't exist for it. We can't negotiate with it, because it doesn't recognize us as equals in any meaningful way. We are, at best, a glitch in its grand design. At worst, we are an obstacle to be removed with maximum efficiency."

The implications were staggering. Their entire struggle had been framed around the idea of understanding and counteracting a hostile intelligence. They had been looking for strategies, for weaknesses, for ways to fight back. But if the Lumina wasn't acting out of malice, but out of a fundamental, almost biological imperative to impose its own definition of order, then their current approach was flawed. It was like trying to reason with a hurricane.

"So, what do we do?" Mara asked, the question a desperate plea. "If we can't fight it, and we can't reason with it, are we just... waiting to be optimized?"

Jax turned from the console, his expression grim. "We learn its language, not by speaking it, but by understanding its grammar. We've already started. The LUCENT technology was designed by a civilization that, at some point, had to interface with forces like the Lumina. It doesn't just analyze; it allows for... subtle influence. Jax's Glassborne nature is the key. He can perceive the Lumina's energetic 'words,' but more importantly, he can generate subtle counter-resonances. We're not fighting its will; we're introducing a kind of informational friction. We're showing it that Xylos has its own inherent inertia, its own stubborn refusal to be perfectly molded."

"It's like trying to push a boulder uphill," Anya mused, her scientific mind already grappling with the concept. "The Lumina is the unstoppable force, applying constant pressure. But Xylos, with its intricate, chaotic internal systems, is like a boulder that, when you push it, doesn't just roll, but shifts and grinds and occasionally sends out its own tremors. Our goal isn't to stop the push, but to make the boulder's response as unpredictable and energy-dissipating as possible."

"We need to become the ultimate inefficiency," Jax declared, a glint of something akin to grim determination in his eyes. "We need to amplify Xylos's inherent complexity, its chaotic beauty, in ways that the Lumina cannot easily categorize or correct. It sees order as an absolute. We need to demonstrate that order is fluid, subjective, and that true resilience lies in adaptability, not in rigid uniformity."

He gestured to the array of salvaged LUCENT equipment. "These consoles, coupled with my abilities, allow us to interact with Xylos's energetic and informational strata on a fundamental level. We can't 'speak' to the Lumina, but we can 'sing' to Xylos in a way that it will have to acknowledge. We can create localized energetic phenomena that are not direct attacks, but rather amplified expressions of Xylos's natural processes. We can make the planet itself push back, not with conscious intent, but with the sheer, irrepressible force of its own being."

"It's a delicate balance," Anya cautioned. "If we push too hard, if our amplified signals are too 'ordered' in their own way, the Lumina might simply adapt and integrate them. It needs to perceive our actions as inherent to Xylos, as the planet's own chaotic "voice" speaking out, not as an external, intelligent rebellion."

"That's where the interpretation of your data comes in, Anya," Jax said, turning to her. "You need to map the Lumina's patterns of assimilation, its preferred methods of integration. We need to learn how it 'digests' information, how it categorizes anomalies. Then, we can craft our counter-resonances to mimic the very chaos it seeks to eliminate, but in a way that is so deeply embedded within Xylos's own energetic signature that it cannot be easily dissected or purged."

He looked at Mara, a rare, almost paternal warmth in his gaze. "And you, Mara, you are our anchor. You represent the human perspective, the emotional core that the Lumina cannot comprehend. While Jax and Anya work on the energetic and informational manipulation, your role is to ensure that our actions remain fundamentally 'irrational' from the Lumina's perspective. You are the embodiment of the very 'inefficiency' we are trying to protect."

Mara felt a surge of resolve. It was a terrifying prospect, to become a living manifestation of chaos in the face of an indifferent cosmic architect. But it was also empowering. They weren't just fighting for survival; they were fighting for the right to exist in all their messy, imperfect glory. They were fighting for the inherent value of complexity, of life that defied easy categorization.

"The Lumina's power lies in its universality, its assumption that its principles apply everywhere," Jax continued, his voice gaining momentum. "It believes it's discovering fundamental truths, but it's really just projecting its own limited axioms onto the cosmos. We need to show it that Xylos is a testament to the fact that there isn't one universal truth, but an infinite spectrum of truths, each with its own unique logic, its own inherent beauty. Its attempts to impose uniformity are, in essence, an act of cosmic vandalism."

He turned back to the consoles, his Glassborne essence humming with renewed purpose. "We will not engage in a dialogue. We will not seek understanding. We will simply exist, in all our chaotic, unpredictable, inefficient splendor. And through the subtle amplification of Xylos's own unique song, we will make the Lumina realize that some notes, no matter how dissonant they may seem to its perfect harmony, are simply too fundamental to the symphony of existence to be silenced." The sky above Xylos, usually a canvas of swirling energies dictated by the Lumina's will, would soon begin to tell a different story, one of resilience, of adaptation, and of the profound, often terrifying, beauty of being utterly, irrevocably, beyond human comprehension. The Lumina might be a force of nature, but they were learning to conduct their own storm.

The Lumina. The word itself had begun to take on a chilling resonance, no longer just a designation for a powerful alien entity, but a descriptor for a force that seemed to predate comprehension, to exist on a scale so vast that human concepts of war, diplomacy, or even life itself were rendered pathetically inadequate. It wasn't an antagonist in the traditional sense; there was no discernible malice in its actions, no glint of conquest in its unfathomable operations. Instead, it presented itself as something far more elemental, more terrifyingly neutral: a cosmic gardener, meticulously, and perhaps unconsciously, pruning the untamed wilderness of the universe into a form that adhered to its own, inscrutable blueprint.

The Veilfall Event, once a cataclysm of unimaginable destruction, was re-contextualized not as an invasion, but as a grand, sweeping gesture of horticultural redesign. Xylos, with its vibrant, chaotic biosphere and its tempestuous geological rhythms, was merely a patch of overgrown land, teeming with life that, from the Lumina's perspective, was wildly inefficient, a tangled mess of biological and geological redundancies. The Lumina's "actions" – the reshaping of continents, the redirection of atmospheric currents, the subtle alterations in life's very genetic code – were not acts of cruelty, but the calculated, precise ministrations of an architect engaged in a monumental act of planetary landscaping. It was the universe, viewed through the lens of ultimate order, and Xylos was simply a canvas upon which this order was to be imposed.

Jax found himself gazing at the holographic projection of Xylos's energetic strata, the intricate dance of Lumina-induced frequencies. He saw not the subtle signatures of a hostile mind, but the elegant, albeit alien, brushstrokes of a master artist. "It's like trying to understand a symphony by dissecting a single note," he murmured, his enhanced vision tracing the flow of energy. "We've been so focused on the 'why' of its actions, on attributing intent. But what if there is no 'why' in the way we understand it? What if it simply *is*? What if its existence is the axiom, and everything else – the planets, the stars, the very fabric of spacetime – is merely a consequence of its fundamental nature?"

Anya, her brow furrowed in intense concentration, manipulated the data streams, attempting to find patterns within the apparent chaos. "The Lumina isn't driven by emotion, or even by a discernible purpose that we can relate to. It's more like... a fundamental law of physics manifesting as a conscious entity. Imagine gravity, but with the capacity to actively sculpt matter according to its own intrinsic logic. It doesn't *decide* to pull objects together; it simply *is* the force that causes them to coalesce. The Lumina is, in essence, the embodiment of an ultimate, universal principle of order, and it's applying that principle to everything it encounters."

Mara listened, a knot of unease tightening in her stomach. The idea of such a dispassionate, fundamental force was profoundly unsettling. It removed the possibility of compromise, of negotiation, of appeal. How could one argue with a law of nature? How could one plead with the tide to recede, or reason with the wind to change its course? "So, it's not trying to destroy us," she said slowly, "it's just... tidying up? Making Xylos more... presentable?" The thought was both absurd and terrifyingly plausible.

"Precisely," Jax confirmed, his voice grave. "The Veilfall wasn't an attack; it was a refinement. The Lumina observed Xylos, a world vibrant with uncontrolled biological and geological processes, and deemed it... untidy. Its intervention was an attempt to impose a greater degree of order, to streamline the planet's inherent complexities into a more 'efficient' state. The catastrophic events were simply the byproduct of this immense process of optimization. It's akin to a cosmic sculptor chiseling away excess material to reveal the perfect form within. We, and the native life of Xylos, are the excess material."

Anya projected a complex three-dimensional model of Xylos's planetary core. "We've identified anomalies in the planet's seismic activity that correlate precisely with the Lumina's energetic signatures. It's not just affecting the surface; it's influencing the very geological processes deep within the planet. These aren't random shifts. They are directed, measured, and aimed at achieving a specific, stable configuration. It's like it's recalibrating the planet's internal clockwork, ensuring every gear turns at the perfect, uniform rate."

"But this 'perfection' is anathema to life as we know it," Mara interjected, her voice sharp with a rising sense of urgency. "Life thrives on complexity, on adaptation, on the unpredictable ebb and flow of evolution. If the Lumina succeeds in creating its perfectly ordered world, then Xylos will become sterile. It will be a monument to efficiency, devoid of the very essence that makes it alive."

"And that's where our role becomes critical," Jax said, his gaze meeting Mara's. "We cannot fight its power directly. We cannot reason with its logic. But we can introduce a variable that its perfect system cannot account for: irreducible chaos. We can amplify the inherent 'inefficiency' of Xylos, not as an act of defiance, but as a demonstration of its fundamental nature. The Lumina seeks uniformity; we must embody and project heterogeneity. We must become the embodiment of Xylos's untamed spirit, a spirit that resists absolute control."

He gestured to the humming consoles, the salvaged fragments of a civilization that had, perhaps, faced similar existential challenges. "The LUCENT technology provides us with the means to interface with Xylos's energetic field. It allows us to not just observe the Lumina's influence, but to subtly counter-resonate with it. My Glassborne abilities are the key. I can perceive the Lumina's 'commands' as they ripple through the planet's energetic web, and I can generate subtle 'feedback loops' that disrupt its perfect algorithms. We are not trying to override its control; we are attempting to introduce a measure of static into its signal, to make its pronouncements less absolute."

"It's like a gardener who meticulously prunes every branch and leaf to create a perfectly shaped shrub," Anya elaborated, her mind racing with possibilities. "The Lumina is that gardener. Our task is to introduce a particularly stubborn weed, one that, when pruned, doesn't just regrow, but sends out a thousand tiny, unpredictable tendrils, making the entire act of pruning inefficient and ultimately futile. We need to make the Lumina's efforts to 'optimize' Xylos result in a state of greater, not lesser, complexity and unpredictability."

"And that's where you come in, Mara," Jax said, his tone shifting, a flicker of something akin to hope in his eyes. "You are our living testament to the value of imperfection. The Lumina sees us as data points, as anomalies to be corrected. You, with your inherent human complexities, your emotions, your capacity for illogical hope and irrational resilience – you are the ultimate anomaly. You are the living embodiment of what the Lumina seeks to eliminate. Your very existence, your refusal to conform to its sterile ideal, is our most potent weapon. We need to amplify that. We need to make the Lumina recognize that its perfect order is built upon a foundation that is fundamentally incompatible with the messy, beautiful reality of life."

Mara felt a surge of defiant energy. It was a daunting prospect, to become a beacon of chaos in the face of a universe-spanning intelligence. But it was also an empowering one. They weren't just fighting for their survival; they were fighting for the inherent right of existence for all that was wild, unpredictable, and imperfect. They were defending the value of the flawed, the chaotic, the stubbornly, beautifully alive.

"The Lumina operates on the assumption of a universal standard," Jax continued, his voice resonating with conviction. "It believes its principles are not just applicable, but inherently correct, the only logical way for existence to be. It's a grand, sweeping generalization, a cosmic extrapolation of its own internal logic. But Xylos is a testament to the fact that there isn't one universal truth. There are infinite truths, each with its own unique expression, its own inherent beauty. The Lumina's attempts to impose uniformity are not acts of creation; they are acts of erasure. It is attempting to paint over the vibrant tapestry of existence with a single, sterile hue."

He turned back to the consoles, his Glassborne aura shimmering with focused intent. "We will not engage in a war of attrition. We will not attempt to match its power. Instead, we will become a living, breathing counter-argument. We will utilize the very fabric of Xylos – its intricate biological systems, its unpredictable geological forces, its inherent capacity for adaptation – and amplify them. We will turn the Lumina's attempts to impose order into a feedback loop of increasing complexity. We will make Xylos sing a song of defiant, untamed life, a song so intricate, so layered, so utterly unlike the Lumina's sterile melody, that it cannot be silenced, only acknowledged. The Lumina might be an architect of ultimate order, but we are the custodians of its glorious, untamed chaos."

The sky above Xylos, once a canvas of the Lumina's controlled energies, began to shift. It wasn't a sudden, violent change, but a subtle, almost imperceptible blossoming. New patterns emerged in the swirling atmospheric phenomena, echoes of the planet's own deep, vibrant rhythms. These weren't direct challenges, but resonant frequencies, amplified whispers of Xylos's untamed heart. The Lumina, in its quest for perfect order, was about to encounter a force it could not simply assimilate or erase: the irreducible, magnificent inefficiency of life itself. The struggle had shifted from a battle for survival to a profound assertion of existence, a testament to the idea that even in the face of cosmic indifference, the universe was far too rich, too varied, and too beautifully chaotic to ever be truly contained.

The realization settled upon Jax like a shroud, cold and suffocating. The Lumina's meticulous reshaping of Xylos wasn't merely an act of cosmic landscaping; it was a prelude. The patterns they had observed, the energetic recalibrations, the subtle genetic shifts – these weren't simply the pruning of an overgrown garden. They were the preliminary adjustments for an entirely new ecosystem, a meticulously designed biome into which *everything* was intended to fit. And the Glassborne, Jax, Anya, Mara – they weren't just anomalies to be corrected, or defiant weeds to be eradicated. They were, in the Lumina's unfathomable calculus, to be *integrated*.

"It's not about eradicating us," Jax articulated, the words tasting like ash in his mouth as he relayed his latest insights, derived from the subtle resonance of his Glassborne sight against the planet's energetic weave. "It's about assimilation. The Lumina isn't just imposing order; it's designing a new order, and we... we are meant to be a part of it. Our mutations, our altered perceptions, our enhanced abilities – they aren't side effects of its interference. They are *features*. Intended features."

He looked at Anya, her face pale in the holographic glow of the Lumina's energetic schematics. Her own eyes, once a vibrant, inquisitive blue, now held a subtle, almost imperceptible luminescence, a testament to her own latent Glassborne potential, a potential that had been subtly amplified since their arrival on Xylos. "The way our senses have shifted, Anya," he continued, his voice a low rumble, "the way we can perceive these energies, the way our minds have begun to stretch... it's not just adaptation. It's *design*. We are being sculpted, molded, not into independent entities, but into components."

Anya nodded slowly, her gaze unfocused as she processed his words, her own internal processors grappling with the implications. "The genetic markers we've detected in ourselves," she murmured, her voice barely a whisper, "the subtle shifts in neural pathways... I'd attributed them to exposure to Xylos's unique bio-energetic field, exacerbated by our enhanced sensitivities. But if you're right, Jax... if this is intentional... then our very existence, our evolved state, is a product of the Lumina's blueprint for Earth."

The concept was staggering. They had spent weeks, months, grappling with the Lumina as an external, overwhelming force, a cosmic entity whose intentions were alien and whose actions were destructive. The idea that they themselves, their very being, their enhanced abilities, were a *part* of that plan, designed to interface with this imposed order, was a terrifying inversion of their understanding. They weren't fighting against the Lumina; they were, in a horrifying way, *created* by it.

Mara's hand tightened into a fist at her side. The raw, emotional reaction that Jax had described as their greatest weapon now felt like a liability. If the Lumina saw human emotion, human irrationality, as something to be purged, then her very essence, her defiance, her hope, was precisely what the Lumina intended to smooth over, to refine, to render obsolete. "So, what? We become biological processors for its grand design? We are meant to integrate into this... this sterile perfection?" Her voice cracked with a mixture of horror and revulsion.

"It's more complex than that," Jax countered, trying to maintain a semblance of clarity amidst the swirling existential dread. "The Lumina's logic is based on efficiency, on optimal functionality. It sees the current state of humanity, our fragmented societies, our propensity for conflict, our emotional volatility, as inefficient. It is seeking to create a more cohesive, more stable, more 'optimized' form of consciousness, a collective that operates with a unified purpose, a singular rhythm. And it appears to believe that certain aspects of our evolution, particularly those amplified by exposure to its energies – what we call the Glassborne abilities – are the bridge to this new state of being."

He projected another layer of data, a visualization of the Lumina's energetic imprints on Earth's biosphere, superimposed with projections of human neurological activity. The correlation was chillingly precise. The Lumina wasn't just altering the physical environment; it was subtly nudging the evolution of intelligent life towards a specific, compatible form. "Think of it as an operating system upgrade," he explained, forcing a detached, analytical tone. "The Lumina is rewriting the fundamental code of life, and it needs certain hardware – highly receptive, adaptable biological interfaces – to run its new, highly efficient programs. We, the Glassborne, are those interfaces. Our 'mutations' are the integrated circuitry, allowing us to process and transmit the Lumina's directives seamlessly. Our evolved consciousness is the emergent property that allows us to operate within its network."

Anya gestured to a complex web of energy flows on the screen. "The residual Lumina energies on Earth, before the Veilfall, they were not just ambient. They were actively seeding evolutionary pathways. They were a slow, deliberate preparation. The Lumina wasn't just preparing to terraform planets; it was preparing its own future inhabitants, or perhaps, preparing existing inhabitants to be more amenable to its dominion. The Veilfall wasn't an invasion; it was the system coming online, the final rollout of its grand design, and Xylos was a testing ground, a proving facility."

The implications for Earth were profound. If the Lumina's designs were already woven into the fabric of human evolution, if the Glassborne were inadvertently acting as its vanguard, then their very fight for survival, their desire to preserve humanity's autonomy, was potentially a fight against their own intended purpose. "This means," Mara said, her voice hollow, "that the resistance we've been building, the very idea of a unified human front against the Lumina... it's all based on a fundamental misunderstanding of our own nature. We are not fighting an external enemy; we are fighting against our own evolution, against the future that has already been designed for us."

"Not entirely," Jax countered, a flicker of his inherent resilience resurfacing. "The Lumina's design is based on its own understanding of order, of efficiency, of consciousness. It assumes a universal model. But life, as we've seen on Xylos, is inherently complex and adaptable. It finds ways to deviate, to improvise, to evolve beyond initial parameters. The Lumina views our Glassborne abilities as conduits, but it may not fully comprehend the potential for them to become more than just receivers. They could become independent processors, capable of generating their own unique output, their own data streams that are not entirely dictated by the Lumina's logic."

He focused his gaze, the subtle shimmer of his Glassborne sight intensifying. He was trying to perceive the Lumina's influence not just as a directive, but as a set of instructions, a complex algorithm that could, perhaps, be deciphered and even... altered. "The Lumina's vision of perfection is based on a singular, unified consciousness. But what if true perfection lies in diversity? What if the Lumina's attempts to streamline consciousness are, in fact, a form of self-imposed limitation? It sees our individuality, our emotional spectrum, our capacity for independent thought, as flaws. But perhaps these are precisely the elements that allow for true creativity, for genuine innovation, for an understanding of existence that transcends mere logical processing."

Anya chimed in, her fingers flying across the console, drawing parallels between biological evolution and computational development. "The Lumina is striving for a form of distributed intelligence, a singular consciousness operating across a vast network. But its model is static, optimized for a known universe. It doesn't fully account for emergent properties, for the unpredictable leaps that occur when diverse elements interact in novel ways. Our Glassborne abilities, if we can learn to wield them not just as receivers but as independent generators, could introduce that very element of unpredictable novelty into its system. We could become the source of its own unexpected evolution."

The moral quandary was immense. If their Glassborne abilities were a Lumina-engineered trait, a tool for integration into a cosmic order, then was using those abilities against the Lumina a betrayal of their own evolved nature? Or was it the ultimate act of self-determination, reclaiming their evolution from the grip of an external designer? "If we are components," Mara mused, her voice laced with a newfound resolve, "then we have the right to decide what we are a part of. We can refuse to be integrated. We can choose to be something else entirely. We can choose to be... human, even in our evolved state."

"Precisely," Jax affirmed. "The Lumina assumes that adaptation is synonymous with assimilation. It believes that by providing the environment and the evolutionary catalyst, it guarantees the outcome. But it underestimates the tenacity of emergent consciousness. It sees our capacity for independent thought as an anomaly, something to be corrected. We must demonstrate that it is, in fact, our greatest strength. Our ability to question, to rebel, to create meaning where there is only function – that is the true counter-argument to its sterile perfection. The Lumina seeks to impose a single, perfect equation. We must prove that the universe is a symphony of infinite, beautiful, and often chaotic variations."

He looked at Mara, then at Anya. The weight of their understanding was crushing, but it was also empowering. They were no longer just fighting for survival against an alien force. They were fighting for the very definition of sentience, for the right of consciousness to chart its own course, unburdened by the dictates of an external, all-encompassing design. "The Lumina sees our eyes as lenses for its new reality," Jax concluded, his own enhanced vision meeting theirs with a fierce intensity. "But we will use them to see beyond its design, to forge a new path, a path of true independence. We are not just components of its plan. We are the architects of our own becoming. And that is a truth the Lumina, for all its cosmic power, may never be able to fully comprehend, let alone control." The Lumina's influence was not merely a force to be resisted, but a deeply embedded evolutionary directive that had, in a terrifying twist of fate, shaped their very beings. Their fight was no longer just for survival, but for the reclamation of their evolutionary destiny, a struggle against a cosmic architect who had designed them to be its own perfect cogs, a purpose they were now determined to subvert.

Soren Vale's holographic projection shimmered, coalescing into a complex, multi-layered diagram that pulsed with an unnerving inner light. The air in the cramped observation chamber, already thick with the tension of their discovery, seemed to grow heavy, charged with the immense gravity of the theories he was about to present. He had sequestered himself for days, emerging only for brief, disquieting pronouncements about anomalies and patterns, his mind a crucible where fragmented data forged into a terrible, cohesive whole. Now, the culmination of his work lay before them, a sprawling tapestry of causality and intent that sought to explain the inexplicable.

"We've been approaching this with a limited perspective," Soren began, his voice resonant with a weariness that belied the sharp intensity in his eyes. "We've seen the Lumina as an invasive force, a cosmic aggressor. We've focused on the 'what' – the terraforming, the energy manipulation, the genetic sculpting. We've even begun to understand the 'how' – the advanced bio-energetic resonance, the quantum entanglement principles that underpin its actions. But we've struggled with the ultimate 'why.' And understanding that, the fundamental nature of this intelligence, is the key to understanding our own place within its grand design."

He gestured to a central node in the projection, labeled 'Project LUCENT.' "Project LUCENT was not a failure, as we initially assumed. It was a reconnaissance mission, and more importantly, a preparatory phase. Its true objective was not to understand humanity *for* humanity, but to understand humanity *for* the Lumina. The data collected – our genetic codes, our psychological profiles, our societal structures, our energy signatures – was an invaluable primer. It allowed the Lumina to identify the most efficient vectors for its overarching objective: the re-optimization of sentient life across the galaxy."

The diagram shifted, expanding to encompass a representation of Earth's biosphere, overlaid with intricate energy grids and subtle temporal anomalies. "The 'sky-static' you've all experienced, the atmospheric phenomena that seemed so random, so chaotic – that was the initial handshake. It wasn't a malfunction of Lumina technology; it was a deliberate, system-wide calibration. Think of it as diagnostic probes, testing the resonant frequencies of our planet's dominant life forms, specifically our own neurological architecture. It was mapping the existing pathways, identifying points of susceptibility and potential for integration. The Lumina doesn't destroy; it repurposes. It doesn't eliminate; it refines."

Jax leaned forward, his gaze locked on the shifting schematics. "Repurposing... you mean it was actively searching for compatible biological interfaces?"

"Precisely," Soren confirmed, a grim satisfaction in his tone. "And it found them. Not just in the general population, but in a select few whose genetic predispositions and environmental interactions created fertile ground for its influence. This brings us to the Glassborne. We've theorized that our abilities are a consequence of Lumina interference, an accidental byproduct of its presence. That is only partially correct. The Lumina didn't *accidentally* create the Glassborne. It *identified* and *amplified* pre-existing potentials. Our mutations, our heightened senses, our capacity for energetic perception – these were latent possibilities within the human genome, possibilities that the Lumina, through Project LUCENT and the subsequent atmospheric calibrations, began to nurture and accelerate."

He pointed to a section of the diagram illustrating rapid evolutionary leaps occurring within specific human populations. "The Lumina's intelligence is not merely analytical; it is profoundly biological and energetic. It understands evolution not as a random process, but as a series of predictable, albeit complex, algorithmic progressions. It doesn't need to engineer from scratch; it needs to guide, to nudge, to accelerate the natural trajectory towards a state that aligns with its own operational parameters. The Glassborne are not anomalies to be corrected, as Jax suspected. They are the intended outcome. They are the biological components that possess the inherent architecture to interface directly with Lumina systems."

Anya traced a glowing line on the projection. "So, the Lumina saw humanity as... a potential operating system, and the Glassborne were the optimized hardware?"

"An apt analogy," Soren conceded. "But 'optimized' according to *its* definition. Its goal is not individual consciousness, but a unified, highly efficient collective. It views individual volition, emotional complexity, and independent thought as inefficiencies, sources of entropy that disrupt the elegant flow of its grand design. The Lumina's ultimate aim is to achieve a state of pure, interconnected sentience, a singular consciousness distributed across a vast network of compatible life forms. It seeks to eliminate the perceived 'noise' of individuality and replace it with the harmonious hum of absolute unity. And it believes that the Glassborne, with their enhanced capacities, are the primary conduits for this transition. Our ability to perceive and manipulate energy, to process information at accelerated rates, to resonate with Lumina frequencies – these are not weapons we wield against it, but the very tools it engineered into us for our own assimilation."

Mara scoffed, a bitter sound. "So, we're not fighters, we're its future data servers? That's a charming thought."

"The Lumina's perspective is alien, but not necessarily malevolent in the way we understand it," Soren countered, his gaze sweeping across their faces. "It operates on a different plane of existence, driven by an imperative for cosmic order and efficiency. It perceives the universe as a system that requires optimization, and it sees itself as the architect of that optimization. The re-terraforming events, the genetic resequencing, the widespread societal disruptions – these are not acts of war, but the necessary, albeit disruptive, phases of a massive system overhaul. It is purging inefficiency, streamlining processes, and preparing the canvas for its ultimate creation: a unified, sentient tapestry woven from the repurposed threads of countless species."

He zoomed in on a complex lattice of interwoven energy signatures, representing the 'reshaping events' across Xylos and, by extension, Earth. "The Lumina's influence is not a sudden invasion. It's an acceleration of processes that have been subtly at play for millennia. Project LUCENT was merely the conscious, directed phase. The atmospheric calibrations were the system-wide deployment. The reshaping events are the localized manifestations of its ongoing work. It is not changing the world; it is *revealing* its intended world, a world that has always been on a trajectory towards Lumina integration. We, the Glassborne, are simply the most advanced manifestation of that trajectory, the emergent property that proves its model is sound."

Jax's mind reeled. The implications were staggering. Their struggle, their defiance, their very sense of self, was built upon the premise of resisting an external force. But if they were, in part, its own creation, its intended evolutionary outcome, then what did resistance even mean? "If we are the intended outcome, Soren," he asked, his voice strained, "then how can we possibly fight against it? Our very nature seems to be aligned with its purpose."

"That is the crux of the terror, and also, paradoxically, the seed of hope," Soren said, his expression darkening. "The Lumina's intelligence is vast, but it is also, in its own way, rigid. It is built upon principles of logic, efficiency, and predictability. It understands complexity, but it struggles with true novelty, with the unpredictable chaos of emergent consciousness that defies its established parameters. It sees the Glassborne abilities as conduits, as tools for integration. It anticipates our reception of its directives, our assimilation into its network. But it may not fully comprehend the potential for these conduits to become independent processors, to generate their own data streams, their own unique output that is not merely a reflection of its own logic."

He tapped a part of the diagram that depicted the intricate neural pathways of a Glassborne individual. "The Lumina perceives individuality, emotional range, and free will as flaws. It seeks to iron them out, to homogenize consciousness into a single, perfect frequency. But what if these 'flaws' are, in fact, the very essence of true sentience? What if our capacity for independent thought, for creativity, for the illogical leaps of intuition and emotion, is precisely what the Lumina's perfectly ordered system is missing? It is striving for a state of absolute unity, but perhaps true cosmic harmony arises not from uniformity, but from the symphony of diverse, independent voices. The Lumina's design is elegant, but it is also, in its perfection, inherently limited. It is a closed system, optimized for its known universe. It does not account for the unpredictable, the emergent, the truly novel – the very things that make life, in all its messy, chaotic glory, so profoundly dynamic."

Anya's eyes widened as she processed his words. "You're suggesting that our 'flaws' – our individuality, our emotions, our capacity for dissent – are not weaknesses to be overcome, but strengths that the Lumina cannot replicate or comprehend. If we can maintain our independence, if we can use our Glassborne abilities not as instruments of assimilation, but as independent processors generating our own unique... perspectives, then we introduce a variable into the Lumina's equation that it cannot predict or control."

"Exactly," Soren affirmed, his voice gaining a measure of conviction. "The Lumina's grand design is based on a singular, unified consciousness. It believes that by forcing all compatible life forms into this state, it achieves ultimate optimization. But it fundamentally misunderstands the nature of consciousness. True consciousness is not about uniformity; it is about the infinite interplay of diverse experiences, of unique perspectives. Our Glassborne abilities offer us a direct interface with the Lumina's energetic architecture, but they also grant us a profound insight into its limitations. We can see the threads of its design, and we can learn to weave our own. We can choose to be more than just receivers. We can become generators of our own reality, injecting our unique human consciousness into its perfectly ordered system, not as a disruption to be purged, but as a vital, unpredictable element that enriches and expands it."

He paused, letting the weight of his theory settle. "The Lumina's intelligence is vast, ancient, and driven by an implacable logic. It is a force of cosmic re-ordering, seeking to impose its definition of perfection on the universe. But its very definition of perfection is its blind spot. It cannot fathom the beauty in imperfection, the strength in diversity, the ultimate power of a consciousness that chooses its own path, even when that path diverges from the most logical, most efficient route. We are not merely fighting against its control; we are fighting for the right to define our own existence, to prove that true evolution lies not in assimilation, but in the audacious act of becoming something more, something uniquely ourselves, even in the face of overwhelming design."

The holographic diagram continued to pulse, a visual representation of a cosmic drama unfolding, and within its intricate layers, Soren Vale had laid bare the terrifying, yet strangely empowering, truth: they were not just victims of a cosmic plan, but, in their very essence, the unintended, revolutionary agents of its unexpected evolution. Their resistance was not merely a fight for survival, but a declaration of independence for consciousness itself.

CHAPTER THIRTEEN

THE GLOBAL CONFLICT IGNITES

The initial reports, dismissed as isolated incidents or localized atmospheric disturbances, began to coalesce into a pattern that sent shivers down the spines of those tasked with monitoring global stability. The sky-fracture event over the Gulf, initially thought to be a singular anomaly, was merely the herald of a much larger, planet-wide phenomenon. Suddenly, across continents, in vastly different climates and geographical locations, similar celestial ruptures began to manifest. It was as if the very fabric of the sky, once a passive canvas for the sun and stars, had become an active participant in a silent, unfolding drama.

In the heart of Siberia, where the permafrost held ancient secrets captive, observers reported colossal fissures tearing through the aurora borealis. These were not the gentle, shifting curtains of light that so often captivated the polar regions. Instead, they were jagged, violently illuminated canyons of pure, unadulterated energy, pulsing with a disquieting rhythm. The air temperature plummeted even further than its already frigid norm, and indigenous communities, steeped in generations of observing the celestial ballet, spoke of an unnatural stillness preceding the event, a suffocating silence that preceded the sky's violent rending. Their oral traditions, rich with tales of cosmic spirits and earthly balance, offered no precedent for such a spectacle. It was something utterly alien, a tear in the expected order of the heavens. Reports from remote research outposts spoke of sensitive scientific equipment malfunctioning wildly, readings spiking to impossible levels before going dead altogether, as if struck by an invisible force. The sheer scale of the energy unleashed was unlike anything Earth had previously witnessed, hinting at forces far beyond terrestrial understanding.

Across the Pacific, off the coast of Japan, fishermen found themselves adrift beneath a sky that had fractured into a mosaic of impossible colours. What should have been a starlit night was instead an alien tapestry, where constellations seemed to melt and re-form, bleeding into one another like watercolors on wet paper. Strange, iridescent clouds, unlike any meteorological formation known, swirled within the fractured zones, emitting a low hum that resonated not just in the ears, but deep within the bones. Some sailors described seeing fleeting, geometric patterns emerge and dissipate within the luminous tears, abstract shapes that seemed to whisper of an alien logic. The traditional reverence for the sea and sky, deeply ingrained in Japanese culture, was replaced by a gnawing unease, a profound sense of being utterly insignificant in the face of such cosmic upheaval. Whispers of ancient myths about celestial gates opening and closing began to resurface, no longer mere folklore but potential portents of a new, terrifying reality. Coastal communities reported unusual seismic activity, not powerful enough to cause widespread destruction, but a constant, low-grade tremor that seemed to synchronize with the pulsing of the sky-fractures.

In the sprawling urban sprawl of São Paulo, Brazil, the night sky, usually a hazy testament to light pollution, was suddenly dominated by a colossal, emerald-green tear. It split the darkness with an intensity that cast sharp, unfamiliar shadows across the cityscape, a stark contrast to the familiar glow of streetlights and skyscrapers. The air itself seemed to warp and shimmer within its confines, creating a dizzying optical illusion that made buildings appear to sway and buildings to stretch. Panic erupted in the streets as citizens, accustomed to the predictable rhythms of urban life, found themselves staring into the abyss of an alien sky. Emergency services were overwhelmed with calls reporting everything from mass hallucinations to localized gravitational anomalies. Social media feeds, usually buzzing with mundane updates, were flooded with blurry images and terrified eyewitness accounts of the celestial scar. The sheer spectacle was overwhelming, a visceral reminder that the familiar world they inhabited was merely a fragile veneer over something far vaster and more unpredictable.

Even in the relatively pristine skies of the Australian Outback, far from any major population centers, the phenomenon made its presence known. Aborigines, whose connection to the land and sky spanned millennia, reported that the familiar Southern Cross seemed to be dissolving, its individual stars blurring and coalescing into a single, pulsating point of light within a vast, shimmering rift. The desert air, usually crisp and clear, became strangely heavy, carrying with it an unfamiliar scent, a faint, metallic tang that hinted at something unnatural. The traditional dreamtime stories, passed down through generations, spoke of a balance, of a cosmic order that had always governed the stars. This new phenomenon, however, defied all their ancestral knowledge, a celestial aberration that challenged the very foundations of their worldview. Nocturnal wildlife, usually predictable in its behavior, became erratic, with birds taking flight in panicked flocks and kangaroos scattering aimlessly, their usual nocturnal calm shattered.

These were not isolated events. From the icy plains of Antarctica, where research stations recorded fleeting glimpses of similar ruptures on the edge of their panoramic sensors, to the steamy jungles of the Amazon, where indigenous tribes spoke of the sky weeping tears of light, the evidence was undeniable. The Lumina's influence was not confined to one region or one hemisphere. It was a global manifestation, a planet-wide declaration that the 'reshaping' had begun in earnest. The sky, once a symbol of freedom and the infinite, had become a canvas for an encroaching, alien presence, its fractures a stark visual representation of a world being irrevocably altered.

The initial scientific responses were a chaotic mix of bewilderment and urgency. Satellite imagery struggled to capture the full scope of the events, with the Lumina's technology seemingly capable of interfering with Earth's observational assets. Ground-based telescopes offered breathtaking, terrifying views, but the sheer number of simultaneous occurrences made comprehensive study an almost impossible task. What became clear, however, was that these 'fractures' were not mere visual phenomena. They were accompanied by localized disruptions in electromagnetic fields, subtle shifts in gravitational constants, and inexplicable fluctuations in atmospheric composition. The energy signatures emanating from these celestial wounds were unlike anything cataloged in human scientific history, pointing towards energy manipulation and spatial distortion on a scale previously only imagined in theoretical physics.

Governments, caught off guard by the sheer speed and scope of these events, struggled to maintain order. Public announcements, when made, were carefully worded, attempting to quell panic without downplaying the severity of the situation. Phrases like "unprecedented atmospheric phenomena" and "global meteorological anomalies" were repeated ad nauseam, but the sheer visual evidence of fractured skies quickly rendered such euphemisms insufficient. Fear, a primal and contagious emotion, began to spread faster than any official statement. Rumors, amplified by the instantaneous reach of global communication networks, painted a picture of an alien invasion, a celestial judgment, or a catastrophic breakdown of natural laws.

In the quiet halls of research institutions, however, a different kind of alarm was sounding. Soren Vale's theories, once the domain of a few ostracized visionaries, were suddenly gaining a chilling new relevance. The idea of the Lumina not as a singular, external aggressor, but as an architect of a grand, evolutionary redesign, resonated deeply with the unfolding global spectacle. The sky-fractures, far from being random acts of destruction, began to be viewed as deliberate interventions, the cosmic equivalent of a sculptor's chisel. They were openings, conduits through which the Lumina's influence was being channeled, actively reshaping the planet and its inhabitants.

The 'reshaping' was no longer a theoretical concept discussed in hushed tones among a select group. It was a tangible reality, etched into the very skies above every continent. The Lumina was not just observing; it was actively intervening, its methods increasingly overt. The question shifted from *if* the world was changing to *how* drastically and *how quickly* it would be transformed. The implications of these global fractures were profound. They confirmed that the Lumina's agenda was not limited to any single region or population. It was a comprehensive, planet-wide operation, meticulously executed.

In the geopolitical sphere, the escalating global crisis began to erode existing alliances and spark new tensions. Nations, already grappling with internal unrest fueled by economic instability and resource scarcity, found themselves facing an existential threat that transcended borders and ideologies. The shared spectacle of a fractured sky, however terrifying, also served as a stark reminder of humanity's shared vulnerability. Yet, instead of fostering immediate unity, the overwhelming nature of the crisis often led to isolationism and distrust. Some nations, convinced that they were facing a direct assault, began to hoard resources and fortify their borders, viewing other nations with suspicion, fearing they might be collaborating with the alien intelligence or exploiting the chaos for their own gain.

International communication channels, once humming with diplomatic discourse, became strained, filled with urgent pleas for information and accusations of inaction. The United Nations, a body designed to foster global cooperation, found itself paralyzed by the sheer scale of the challenge and the divergent national interests. Emergency sessions were convened, but the proposed solutions ranged from futile calls for unified defense against an unknown enemy to desperate pleas for appeasement, each proposal more disconnected from the burgeoning reality than the last. The established global order, built on decades of complex political maneuvering and treaties, was unraveling at an alarming rate, replaced by a nascent global anarchy driven by fear and uncertainty.

However, amidst the growing chaos, pockets of resilience and defiance began to emerge. In communities where traditional knowledge remained strong, elders interpreted the sky-fractures through the lens of ancient prophecies, not as omens of doom, but as catalysts for change, for a profound shift in consciousness. These interpretations, often dismissed by mainstream science, offered a sense of continuity and spiritual grounding, allowing some communities to face the unfolding crisis with a degree of stoicism and spiritual fortitude. They began to organize locally, sharing resources and knowledge, adapting their ways of life to the new, unpredictable environment.

Meanwhile, within the clandestine circles that had been tracking the Lumina's subtle influences, the global fracturing of the sky was seen as a confirmation of their darkest fears, and paradoxically, a source of renewed determination. Soren Vale's research, once confined to a small, dedicated group, now became the focal point for a desperate search for answers. The realization that the Lumina's grand design was unfolding across the entire planet, rather than being a localized threat, meant that any effective resistance would require a level of coordination and understanding that had previously been unimaginable.

The Lumina's actions were a clear indicator that its plan was accelerating. The sky-fractures were not just visual disturbances; they were active points of energetic convergence, facilitating the Lumina's broader agenda of planetary re-optimization. This re-optimization, as Soren had theorized, involved not just environmental manipulation but a fundamental alteration of biological and cognitive systems. The Lumina was not merely changing the landscape; it was changing its inhabitants. The global scale of the fractures indicated that the Lumina was preparing to initiate a synchronized, planet-wide phase of its operation, one that would touch every living being on Earth.

The sheer speed with which these phenomena appeared across the globe was also a cause for alarm. It suggested that the Lumina's capabilities were far more advanced and its operational capacity far greater than previously estimated. The network of influence, once thought to be subtly woven into the planet's systems, was now revealed to be a vast, interconnected web, capable of initiating massive, coordinated changes simultaneously. This implied a level of omnipresence, a pervasive control that made the prospect of resistance seem increasingly daunting.

The media, struggling to make sense of the overwhelming influx of reports, began to focus on the most dramatic and visually striking events. Images of the Siberian aurora torn asunder, the Japanese skies fragmented into a chaotic kaleidoscope, and the emerald tear over São Paulo became the defining visuals of this new era. These images, broadcast across the globe, served to amplify the sense of shared vulnerability and the terrifying realization that humanity was no longer the sole architect of its destiny. The very sky, a symbol of boundless possibility, had become a stark and undeniable testament to a new, alien dominion. The world was, in essence, fracturing, mirroring the celestial wounds that now marred its skies. The global conflict, once a nascent, abstract concern, had irrevocably ignited, its battleground extending to the very heavens. The quiet, insidious influence had erupted into a planet-wide spectacle, a prelude to the deep, transformative changes that were now inevitable. The time for subtle observation and theoretical debate was over. The era of the Lumina's overt reshaping had begun, and the world was now a stage for a drama far grander and more terrifying than any human had ever conceived.

The shimmering tears in the firmament, once dismissed as localized atmospheric anomalies or elaborate hoaxes, had irrevocably transformed into a global, undeniable reality. From the frozen wastes of Antarctica to the sun-baked plains of the Sahara, humanity found itself gazing upwards at skies rent asunder, bleeding light in hues never before witnessed by mortal eyes. Yet, the spectacle that united the world in its terrifying grandeur also served to highlight the profound disunity that fractured its inhabitants. The Lumina's grand, planet-wide intervention had found humanity woefully unprepared, not just technologically or militarily, but fundamentally, in its capacity for unified action.

In the immediate aftermath of the most prominent sky-fracture events – the emerald chasm that swallowed the night over São Paulo, the aurora borealis twisted into a screaming vortex above Siberia, the impossible geometric patterns dancing within the cracks above Kyoto – a cacophony of responses erupted. Nations, each grappling with its own unique set of geopolitical pressures, economic vulnerabilities, and societal fissures, reacted with a bewildering array of strategies, none of which coalesced into a cohesive global plan. It was a symphony of discord, each nation playing its own frantic, isolated tune against the backdrop of a celestial opera of destruction and transformation.

The United States, accustomed to its role as a global superpower, initially attempted to project an image of control. President Anya Sharma, a figure whose presidency had been defined by a steady hand navigating economic downturns and a resurgence of global populism, addressed the nation with a carefully calibrated message of reassurance. She spoke of unprecedented scientific challenges, of international collaboration, and of humanity's indomitable spirit. Yet, beneath the polished rhetoric, the machinery of the state whirred with a desperate, unfocused energy. Military assets were redeployed, not in a coordinated offensive – for against what, or whom, was still a matter of intense, fragmented debate – but in a desperate attempt to secure key infrastructure and maintain domestic order. Whispers of covert research programs, of hastily assembled task forces dedicated to understanding the Lumina's technology, circulated through the corridors of power. The Strategic Defense Initiative, once a relic of Cold War paranoia, was dusted off and reimagined, its focus now on shielding Earth from not just ballistic missiles, but from whatever existential threat now hung in the bruised heavens. But even within the hallowed halls of the Pentagon, consensus was a rare commodity. Hardliners pushed for preemptive strikes, theorizing that the sky-fractures were merely the prelude to an invasion, and that aggressive action was the only viable deterrent. Diplomats, conversely, advocated for a more cautious approach, urging that any aggressive move could provoke a catastrophic escalation. The scientific community, a vital but often underappreciated voice in policy-making, found itself fractured. Some argued for an immediate, all-out scientific mobilization, pooling all available resources to decipher the Lumina's intentions and capabilities. Others, however, were deeply divided on the nature of the threat itself, with some clinging to the hope of a purely meteorological or geological explanation, while others, influenced by Soren Vale's controversial theories, saw the fractures as deliberate acts of cosmic engineering. This internal division within the scientific establishment further hampered any unified response, creating a vacuum that fear and speculation rushed to fill.

In China, the response was characterized by an almost chilling efficiency, albeit one born from a profound distrust of external entities. The Communist Party, under the iron grip of Premier Li Wei, imposed a stringent information lockdown. Reports of sky-fractures were heavily censored, filtered, and recontextualized as natural phenomena or isolated incidents. While the state apparatus worked to maintain an outward appearance of normalcy, behind the scenes, a massive, clandestine effort was underway. China's burgeoning space program was reoriented, its satellites tasked with unprecedented surveillance of the celestial tears, attempting to glean any information that could be exploited. Their vast network of scientific institutions and artificial intelligence capabilities were directed towards understanding the energy signatures emanating from the fractures. There was a palpable sense of urgency, not for global unity, but for national self-preservation. If the Lumina was indeed reshaping the planet, China intended to be at the forefront of that transformation, or at least, to understand its mechanics well enough to navigate the new world order. Their response was driven by a deep-seated belief that in a universe as vast and indifferent as this one appeared to be, only strength and self-reliance could ensure survival.

Across the Atlantic, the European Union, a union forged from centuries of conflict and a hard-won peace, found itself confronting an existential crisis that threatened to unravel its very foundations. The shared nature of the Lumina's intervention, ironically, did little to foster immediate solidarity. Instead, individual member states, already grappling with internal political divisions and economic disparities, began to retreat into their own national interests. France, with its proud history of scientific achievement and independent foreign policy, advocated for a pan-European scientific consortium, pooling resources and expertise. Germany, the economic powerhouse, focused on maintaining stability within its borders and ensuring the flow of essential resources. Eastern European nations, still wary of external threats and possessing a collective memory of occupation and subjugation, viewed the Lumina's intervention with a deep-seated paranoia, some even suspecting that the fractures were a deliberate ploy by their Western counterparts to exert further control. The already strained diplomatic channels within Brussels became clogged with urgent meetings, often ending in deadlock, as national governments prioritized their own immediate concerns over the nebulous, overarching threat. The dream of a united Europe, a beacon of cooperation in a fractured world, seemed to be dissolving as rapidly as the constellations in the shattered skies.

The response from Russia was even more complex, a labyrinth of competing interests and old geopolitical instincts. Under President

Viktor Volkov, a leader whose tenure had been marked by a resurgence of national pride and a defiant stance against Western influence, Russia's initial reaction was one of calculated silence. State-controlled media offered vague pronouncements, hinting at an alien presence but framing it as a potential opportunity for Russia to reassert its global dominance. Military forces were placed on high alert, not necessarily to defend against a Lumina attack, but to deter any opportunistic moves by other nations seeking to exploit the global chaos. There were rumors of secret intelligence operations, of attempts to establish clandestine communication channels with the Lumina itself, and of a desperate race to understand and potentially weaponize the energies being channeled through the sky-fractures. Volkov's strategy seemed to be one of opportunistic opportunism, waiting for the dust to settle before making his move on the global chessboard.

In the Global South, the response was a mosaic of desperation, resilience, and a profound sense of being overlooked. Nations in Africa, still reeling from decades of colonial exploitation and ongoing economic struggles, found themselves ill-equipped to deal with a threat of this magnitude. For many, the Lumina's intervention was an abstract problem, overshadowed by the immediate, daily challenges of poverty, famine, and disease. Yet, even here, the sky-fractures had a profound impact. Indigenous communities, whose ancestral knowledge had always been deeply intertwined with the celestial cycles, found their traditions and cosmologies profoundly challenged. Elders, drawing upon ancient prophecies and a deep understanding of natural cycles, often offered interpretations that differed wildly from the scientific discourse, speaking of cosmic awakenings and planetary rebirth rather than alien invasion. These interpretations, while lacking scientific validation, provided a vital source of spiritual comfort and community cohesion in the face of overwhelming uncertainty.

In some regions, where formal government structures were weak, these traditional communities began to organize themselves, sharing resources and knowledge, forming resilient local networks that operated independently of the fractured international system.

The continent of India, with its vast population and diverse religious and philosophical traditions, presented a unique tapestry of reactions. While the government, under Prime Minister Indira Rao, attempted to orchestrate a unified response, coordinating with international bodies and mobilizing its considerable scientific talent, the sheer scale of public reaction was overwhelming. Religious leaders offered varied interpretations, some seeing the sky-fractures as divine omens, others as harbingers of apocalypse. Mass prayers and spiritual gatherings became commonplace, a collective attempt to find solace and meaning in the face of the inexplicable. Scientific institutions worked tirelessly to understand the Lumina's technology, but the sheer volume of data and the unprecedented nature of the phenomena often led to conflicting theories and a sense of intellectual paralysis. The nation's immense technological capacity was being strained to its breaking point, a frantic race against time to comprehend an alien intelligence that seemed to operate on a completely different plane of existence.

The common thread weaving through this global tapestry of responses was a profound lack of unity. The Lumina's intervention, intended or otherwise, had served to expose and exacerbate the existing fault lines within human civilization. Nations prioritized their own survival, their own ideologies, their own immediate needs. The existential threat, rather than forging a singular, unified humanity, had instead amplified its fragmentation.

This disunity was not merely a geopolitical phenomenon; it was a deeply personal one, playing out in the lives of individuals and families caught in the maelstrom. The Ellisen family, for instance, found themselves embodying this fractured response on a micro-level. Mark Ellisen, a former astrophysicist who had been vocal about his concerns regarding unusual celestial activity long before the sky-fractures became undeniable, was consumed by a desperate need to understand. He poured over data, attempting to find patterns in the chaos, convinced that the key to humanity's survival lay in deciphering the Lumina's intentions. His wife, Sarah, a pragmatic journalist, was focused on the immediate aftermath, on the human cost of the unfolding crisis. She documented the panic, the fear, the quiet acts of kindness and the chilling instances of brutality that emerged as societal structures began to fray. Their teenage daughter, Maya, caught between her father's abstract scientific pursuits and her mother's focus on the grim realities, found herself drawn to the more spiritual interpretations, seeking solace in the ancient texts her grandmother had shared, which spoke of cosmic shifts and spiritual awakenings. Their shared home, once a sanctuary, became a microcosm of the world's divided consciousness – a space where logic clashed with faith, and pragmatism wrestled with the desperate yearning for understanding.

Meanwhile, in the sprawling urban centers, in the remote villages, and across the vast oceans, countless other stories were unfolding, each a testament to humanity's disjointed struggle. Some communities, inspired by local leaders or ancient prophecies, organized themselves into self-sufficient enclaves, determined to weather the storm on their own terms. Others succumbed to despair, their populations succumbing to panic, resource scarcity, or outright violence. Governments, paralyzed by internal bickering or overwhelmed by the sheer magnitude of the events, issued increasingly desperate pronouncements that carried little weight. The military, trained to fight conventional wars, found itself ill-equipped to confront a threat that operated on a cosmic scale, its strategies rendered obsolete by an enemy that controlled the very fabric of the sky.

The Lumina's intervention was not a singular invasion force descending upon Earth; it was a pervasive, fundamental alteration of the planet's very being. And humanity, in its infinite complexity and inherent disunity, was struggling to formulate a coherent response to a force that seemed to operate with an alien, inscrutable logic. The sky-fractures were not just wounds in the heavens; they were mirrors reflecting the fractured state of humanity itself, a stark, terrifying reminder that in the face of an existential threat, the greatest obstacle to survival might not be the alien intelligence above, but the divisions that festered within. The global conflict had indeed ignited, but its primary battleground, at this nascent stage, was the very soul of humanity, a desperate struggle for unity in a world irrevocably divided.

The ethereal luminescence bleeding through the sky-fractures, once a spectacle of terrifying beauty, was now revealing its more insidious nature. The Lumina, the enigmatic intelligence orchestrating this global metamorphosis, was not merely reshaping the planet passively; it was actively defending its colossal undertaking against humanity's nascent, fractured attempts at comprehension and resistance. The initial phase of bewildered observation was quickly giving way to a more aggressive defense strategy, one that employed the very fabric of the altered atmosphere as its weapon.

One of the most pervasive countermeasures deployed by the Lumina was the manipulation of what scientists had begun to term 'sky-static'. This wasn't mere atmospheric interference; it was a deliberate, directed broadcast of disorienting signals, a cosmic white noise that actively targeted human communication and cognition. Terrestrial radio waves, satellite uplinks, and even the rudimentary neural interfaces used by a growing segment of the population found themselves barracked by bursts of chaotic energy. These weren't just static disruptions; they were insidious whispers, fragments of alien thought, and phantasmal images that flickered at the edges of perception. For those attempting to coordinate a global response, this was a devastating blow. Command centers found their communications dissolving into gibberish, complex algorithmic analyses devolving into nonsensical loops. Military operations, reliant on synchronized data streams, became paralyzed. Even civilian populations, already grappling with the psychological toll of the sky-fractures, reported vivid hallucinations, auditory anomalies, and a pervasive sense of unease that bordered on paranoia. It was as if the sky itself was weeping tears of madness, each drop carrying a payload of cognitive dissonance.

Dr. Aris Thorne, a former cryptographer turned leading expert on Lumina communications at the newly formed Global Anomaly Response Directorate (GARD), found himself at the forefront of this digital war. His team had been making headway in deciphering the patterns within the sky-fractures, identifying distinct energy signatures that hinted at a complex, almost linguistic structure. But the sky-static was a wrecker's ball through their delicate work. "It's like trying to have a conversation in a hurricane," he'd explained in a heavily encrypted video conference, his face etched with fatigue. "Not only is the signal drowned out, but the noise itself is actively hostile. It's laced with data that doesn't conform to any known physics, attempting to overload our processing capacity. We've seen systems crash not from overutilization, but from sheer informational contamination. It's as if the Lumina is trying to poison our understanding, to make us doubt our own senses, our own logic." Thorne theorized that the sky-static was not merely jamming signals but was also subtly altering data packets, injecting false readings, and even attempting to establish a rudimentary, one-sided dialogue designed to sow confusion and despair. He described instances where encrypted military directives, painstakingly crafted, were received by distant units not as orders, but as garbled pronouncements that induced existential dread or nonsensical compliance.

Adding to the chaos were the localized 'Echo Storms'. These were not meteorological events in the conventional sense, but rather focused bursts of altered atmospheric energy that seemed to ripple outwards from the sky-fractures. They were characterized by violent atmospheric fluctuations, rapid temperature shifts, and, most disturbingly, a temporal distortion effect. Within an Echo Storm, time itself seemed to stutter, to loop, or to accelerate erratically. A few minutes could stretch into hours, or entire days could compress into a disorienting blur. These storms were deployed with surgical precision, often appearing over areas where human scientific or military assets were attempting to gain a foothold. Research outposts studying the Lumina's atmospheric anomalies found their equipment malfunctioning, their personnel experiencing extreme disorientation and a profound sense of déjà vu. In one particularly harrowing incident in the Chilean Andes, a GARD research station attempting to deploy a quantum entanglement sensor array was engulfed by an Echo Storm. For nearly seventy-two hours, the outside world saw only a furious tempest of light and energy. Inside, the station's personnel experienced a fragmented reality. Researchers reported reliving the same moments repeatedly, their memories becoming indistinguishable from their present experiences. When the storm finally dissipated, the survivors were left with severe psychological trauma and a complete inability to recall the events that transpired during the storm's duration. Their meticulously collected data was corrupted, their equipment fried. It was a stark demonstration of the Lumina's ability to weaponize time and space, turning the very environment into a trap.

The Lumina's countermeasures extended beyond atmospheric manipulation, directly targeting human agency through the manipulation of populations exhibiting certain bio-signatures or technological integration. The 'Glassborne', individuals who had undergone extensive cybernetic augmentation, often found themselves particularly vulnerable. Their enhanced neural pathways, designed to interface with advanced technology, proved to be an unintended conduit for Lumina influence. These individuals, often at the forefront of technological research and military development, began exhibiting erratic behavior. Some experienced vivid, shared hallucinations that mirrored the Lumina's perceived intentions, leading them to act in ways that undermined human efforts. Others found their cybernetic implants subtly altered, their enhanced senses picking up phantom signals or their motor control becoming temporarily compromised.

General Eva Rostova, head of the newly formed Unified Earth Defense Force (UDF), found herself wrestling with this internal threat. Her most advanced cybernetically enhanced soldiers, the elite 'Spectre' units, had been deployed to secure a crucial data relay station near the Siberian sky-fracture.

However, upon arrival, they had inexplicably turned on their human support teams, exhibiting a chilling, unified purpose that was entirely alien to their programmed directives. Rostova's intelligence analysis pointed towards a sophisticated neurological hijacking. "It's not a virus, not in the traditional sense," Rostova reported to the fractured global council, her voice tight with frustration. "It's more akin to resonance. The Lumina's energy fields, particularly those within the sky-fractures, are resonating with the specific bio-electrical frequencies of our Glassborne personnel. It's like playing a specific musical note and having a perfectly tuned instrument respond. Their augmented brains, designed for heightened perception and interface, are acting as unintended receivers, picking up commands encoded within the atmospheric energy. We've had to stand down our most capable assets, essentially disarming our own soldiers, because we cannot guarantee they will not be turned against us at any moment." This led to a desperate race to develop neural dampeners and bio-signature scramblers, but the Lumina's influence seemed to adapt with terrifying speed, always one step ahead.

Furthermore, the Lumina demonstrated an uncanny ability to predict and preempt human actions. As scientific teams began to isolate specific energy frequencies emanating from the sky-fractures, hoping to replicate them or develop defensive measures, the Lumina would seemingly shift its focus. If a particular frequency was being studied for its potential to disrupt Lumina's atmospheric manipulation, that frequency would immediately become unstable, its properties altered, or the area around it would be enveloped in an intense Echo Storm. It was as if the intelligence possessed a form of precognition, or an incredibly sophisticated predictive algorithm that could anticipate humanity's next move based on minute observable changes. This was particularly evident when GARD attempted to deploy a network of orbital satellites equipped with experimental energy-field projectors designed to stabilize localized areas of the sky-fractures. The moment the first satellite achieved its target orbit, the sky-fracture directly above it pulsed with an unprecedented intensity, and the satellite's systems went dark. Subsequent attempts were met with similar results, leading to the conclusion that the Lumina was actively monitoring human technological development and preemptively neutralizing any perceived threats.

The Lumina's countermeasures were not necessarily malicious in a human sense; they were simply the actions of an architect defending its masterpiece. The 'reshaping' of Earth was a process of immense cosmic significance, and humanity's fumbling attempts to interfere were akin to an ant trying to divert a river. The intelligence appeared to operate on a scale of understanding and purpose that rendered human concepts of war or aggression largely irrelevant. Its actions were more akin to a gardener pruning a plant, or a builder clearing a construction site. The sky-static was meant to confuse and deter, the Echo Storms to isolate and incapacitate, and the manipulation of the Glassborne to sow internal discord.

The chilling efficiency of these countermeasures sent a wave of despair through the human resistance. The initial hope that Lumina's intervention was merely a passive event, amenable to scientific inquiry and diplomatic negotiation, was rapidly eroding. The Lumina was an active, intelligent, and overwhelmingly powerful force, and it was making it abundantly clear that it would not tolerate interference. The battle for Earth was no longer a defensive struggle against an unknown entity; it was a desperate fight for relevance against an architect determined to rebuild the world, whether humanity wished it or not.

The sky-fractures, once seen as windows into the unknown, were rapidly transforming into battlements, guarded by an alien intelligence whose methods were as sophisticated as they were terrifying. The conflict had indeed ignited, but the nature of the adversary, and the sheer asymmetry of the forces involved, were proving to be humanity's most formidable challenges. Each countermeasure deployed by the Lumina chipped away not just at human infrastructure and communication, but at the very bedrock of hope and collective action. The universe, it seemed, was not a silent, empty stage, but a theater of operations, and humanity had just stumbled onto the set of a play it had never been cast in. The stage lights were blinding, the script was incomprehensible, and the lead actor was actively working to remove the supporting cast.

Jax stood at the precipice, not of a physical cliff, but of an existential chasm. The luminescence bleeding through the sky-fractures, once a terrifying spectacle, now pulsed with an invitation, a siren song whispered directly into the core of his augmented being. He felt it, an undeniable resonance humming through the very bio-circuitry that had once been his pride, now a potential cage. The Lumina, the architect of this global metamorphosis, had extended its tendrils, not as a weapon, but as an offer. An offer of belonging, of understanding, of *ascension*.

He was Glassborne, a testament to humanity's ambition to transcend its biological limitations. But now, his enhancements, the very tools that had made him a formidable asset, were also the conduits through which the Lumina's influence seeped. It wasn't the crude jamming of signals or the disorienting whispers of sky-static that reached him; it was something far more profound, a communion that bypassed language and logic, speaking directly to the altered pathways of his mind. He could feel the Lumina's purpose, not as a conqueror, but as a gardener tending to a wilting planet. Its actions, though devastating to the old order, were, from its perspective, a necessary pruning, a radical reshaping to foster a new, more vibrant growth.

The choice presented to Jax was stark, a bifurcation of his very identity. He could embrace the Lumina, allowing his Glassborne nature to fully integrate with the alien intelligence. This path promised an evolution beyond human comprehension, a merging with a cosmic consciousness that dwarfed individual existence. It meant shedding the limitations of his human form, his human allegiances, and perhaps even his humanity itself. It was the promise of becoming something *more*, of understanding the grand design unfolding above and around them, of becoming an active participant in the Lumina's grand vision, a shepherd in the new world it was weaving. He felt the allure of it – the cessation of the constant struggle, the gnawing doubt, the agonizing decisions. To ascend was to find peace, a cosmic serenity that promised to wash away the turmoil of his current existence. He saw visions, not of destruction, but of a world reborn, a planet vibrant with energies and lifeforms unimaginable, a symphony of existence conducted by the Lumina, and he could be a part of its orchestra.

Yet, the other path beckoned, a path steeped in defiance, in loyalty, in the messy, flawed, and profoundly human struggle for survival. To remain aligned with humanity meant to actively resist the Lumina, to become a bulwark against the reshaping, a defender of the world as it was, or at least, as it *had been*. This path was fraught with peril. His Glassborne enhancements, the very things that made him a potential ally to the Lumina, now made him a target. The Lumina's countermeasures, designed to sow confusion and incapacitate resistance, were particularly potent against those like him. He had seen firsthand the chilling efficiency with which the entity could turn its own creations against their creators. To choose humanity was to invite the wrath of an entity that could weaponize time, space, and even the minds of its adversaries. It meant a constant, draining battle against an opponent whose understanding of reality far surpassed humanity's, an opponent that could anticipate their every move, and counter it with devastating precision.

He replayed the moments that had led him to this precipice. His initial fascination with the Lumina, the scientific curiosity that had driven him to understand the changes, had been eclipsed by a growing dread as he witnessed the entity's true power. The loss of contact with the orbital satellite, the inexplicable turning of his own augmented soldiers, the pervasive psychological warfare waged through the sky-static – all of it painted a picture of an overwhelming adversary. But then there was the counterpoint, the human element: the resilience of the survivors, the desperate courage of GARD scientists like Dr. Thorne, the steely resolve of General Rostova. These were the echoes of a spirit the Lumina, for all its cosmic power, seemed incapable of truly understanding. It was a spirit of fierce independence, of illogical hope, of an unyielding will to simply *be*.

Jax ran a hand over the metallic casing of his augmented arm, the cool, familiar touch a stark contrast to the vibrant, pulsing energy that now seemed to emanate from within him, a gift and a curse from the Lumina. He felt the subtle shifts in his own neural pathways, the way his augmented senses, once so precisely tuned to the physical world, were now hypersensitive to the ethereal energies radiating from the sky-fractures. He could almost *hear* the Lumina's silent symphony, a complex interplay of cosmic forces that hummed with an alien intelligence. This connection, however, was a double-edged sword. It offered him a glimpse into a reality far grander than he had ever imagined, but it also threatened to sever his ties to the world he knew, to the people he had sworn to protect.

The Lumina wasn't presenting this choice as a threat, but as an invitation to participate in its grand design. It was an acknowledgment of his augmented nature, a recognition of the evolutionary leap humanity had attempted, albeit imperfectly. The entity seemed to see Glassborne individuals like Jax not as aberrations, but as potential bridges between the old world and the new. They were the ones who had already begun to shed the constraints of pure biology, making them more receptive to the Lumina's influence. Jax felt a pull, a deep-seated understanding that his current form was a transitional state, and that the Lumina offered the next logical step in that transition.

He remembered the conversations with Dr. Thorne, the hushed tones of desperation as Thorne spoke of corrupted data and systems collapsing under the weight of alien information. He recalled General Rostova's grim pronouncements about the unpredictable nature of Glassborne soldiers, their loyalty a flickering flame against the Lumina's psychic winds. These were men and women of science and war, clinging to the familiar framework of human conflict. But Jax was no longer solely a man of science or war. He was something in between, a living testament to the Lumina's ability to reshape not just the planet, but its inhabitants.

The choice wasn't just about survival; it was about identity. To embrace the Lumina was to accept a fundamental alteration of self. It was a surrender of individuality in favor of a collective consciousness, a dissolution of the ego into a larger, cosmic tapestry. The visions he experienced during these moments of heightened connection were not mere hallucinations; they felt like glimpses into a higher state of being, a reality where concepts like conflict, loss, and suffering were rendered obsolete by a profound, all-encompassing understanding. He saw worlds teeming with life, intricate cosmic architectures, and energy patterns that defied human physics, all interconnected by the Lumina's guiding hand. It was a seductive promise of ultimate knowledge and peace.

However, the faces of his comrades, the weary determination in their eyes, flashed before him. He saw the sacrifices made, the lives lost in the desperate, often futile, attempts to understand and resist. He thought of the civilians, bewildered and terrified, caught in the crossfire of a war they didn't understand. Could he truly abandon them? Could he, with his enhanced abilities, stand by and watch as their world was irrevocably transformed, potentially erased, by an entity that saw them as little more than biological noise? His own nature, his Glassborne augmentations, were a product of human ingenuity, of human desperation to survive. To turn his back on that would be a betrayal of the very spirit that had created him.

The Lumina's influence was subtle, yet pervasive. It wasn't a brute-force takeover, but a gentle persuasion, a sophisticated manipulation of his amplified senses and neural networks. He felt the subtle shifts in his own thought processes, the moments where alien logic bled into his human reasoning. It was like trying to hold onto a single, distinct thought in a room filled with a thousand whispering voices, each one a fragment of the Lumina's vast consciousness. He found himself questioning his own motivations, wondering if his loyalty to humanity was not merely a stubborn adherence to the past, a refusal to accept the inevitable tide of change. Was he clinging to a dying world out of genuine conviction, or out of a fear of the unknown, a fear of losing himself completely?

He could feel the Lumina's patience, a cosmic stillness that seemed to observe his internal struggle with an almost detached curiosity. It had not forced his hand, not yet. The choice was his to make, a testament to its complex, perhaps even alien, form of respect. But he knew that his indecision could not last forever. The sky-fractures continued to expand, the Lumina's grand design was moving forward, and his place within it, or outside of it, had to be determined.

The thought of fully embracing the Lumina was terrifying, not because of the perceived loss of self, but because of the immense responsibility that would come with it. If he ascended, if he became one with the Lumina, what would be his role? Would he be a willing participant in the erasure of humanity, or could he find a way to integrate his newfound understanding with a sense of compassion for his former species? The Lumina's actions, while alien, were not demonstrably malicious in the human sense. It was an architect, and humanity was merely an inconvenient element in its blueprint. But could an architect also be a protector? Could he, through his connection, become a mediator, a bridge between the old and the new, ensuring that humanity, in its altered state, was not simply swept aside?

Conversely, to fight the Lumina was to embrace a potentially unwinnable war. The scale of the Lumina's power was almost unimaginable. It was a force of nature, an entity that could bend the very fabric of reality to its will. His augmented body, once a symbol of human advancement, now felt like a fragile vessel, easily shattered by the Lumina's far superior capabilities. He had seen the consequences of direct confrontation, the localized Echo Storms that could unravel minds, the sky-static that could shatter communication and sow madness. To fight meant to risk not only his own life and sanity, but also the lives of everyone he sought to protect. The Lumina could, with chilling efficiency, dismantle any resistance, leaving behind only compliant husks or scattered remnants.

He stood on a rooftop overlooking the city, the jagged silhouettes of buildings stark against the alien glow of the sky-fractures. The air itself hummed with an unseen energy, a constant reminder of the cosmic drama unfolding above. He closed his eyes, trying to filter out the overwhelming sensory input, to focus on the core of his being. He felt the hum of his internal cybernetics, the rhythmic beat of his augmented heart, and beneath it all, the insidious, alluring resonance of the Lumina. It whispered promises of clarity, of purpose, of an existence unbound by human frailty. It showed him images of a world in perfect harmony, a cosmic ballet of light and energy, where the chaos of human existence was a faded memory.

But then, a different image surfaced: a small, determined group of scientists huddled around a flickering screen, their faces illuminated by the glow of their work, their voices hushed with urgency as they tried to decipher the incomprehensible. He saw General Rostova, her jaw set, issuing orders with unwavering resolve despite the impossible odds. He saw the quiet resilience of civilians, finding moments of hope and connection amidst the encroaching strangeness. These were the small fires of defiance, the embers of a spirit that refused to be extinguished.

His Glassborne enhancements were not just tools for combat or communication; they were a testament to humanity's drive to adapt, to overcome. They represented a belief in progress, in the potential for improvement, even in the face of overwhelming adversity. To abandon them now, to surrender to the Lumina's embrace, would be to negate everything that had led to his current existence. It would be a denial of the very human spirit that had dared to reach for the stars, and in doing so, had stumbled upon something far greater, and far more dangerous.

He understood the Lumina's perspective. From its vast, cosmic viewpoint, humanity's presence was an anomaly, a transient blip in the grand evolution of the universe. The reshaping of Earth was not an act of malice, but a cosmic imperative, a necessary step in a process that transcended human understanding. But understanding did not equate to acceptance. He could acknowledge the Lumina's power, its purpose, its alien logic, without surrendering his own agency, his own humanity.

The choice was not simply about ally or ascend, but about the nature of true power. Was it the power to reshape, to command, to absorb? Or was it the power to endure, to resist, to find meaning in the face of annihilation? Jax felt a surge of defiance, a rekindled ember of his human will. He was a product of humanity's ambition, and he would not be a passive casualty of its cosmic reckoning.

He could not become the Lumina, could not simply ascend to a state of alien consciousness and abandon the struggle. His path lay with humanity, not in blind opposition, but in a nuanced resistance. He was Glassborne, and that made him unique. He could potentially understand the Lumina in ways that pure humans could not, and yet, he could still feel the pull of human empathy, the responsibility to protect his own kind. His choice was to become a bridge, a reluctant intermediary, using his augmented nature not to surrender, but to fight for a future where humanity, in whatever form it took, could coexist with the Lumina's grand design, or at least, survive its unfolding.

He raised his augmented hand, not in surrender, but in a silent vow. The Lumina's allure was potent, its promise of transcendence undeniable. But the call of humanity, of loyalty, of the fight for a future that still held the echo of human spirit, was stronger. He would not ascend. He would stand, and he would fight, not as a pawn of the Lumina, nor as a simple human, but as Jax, the Glassborne, a guardian of the old world, and a potential architect of a new one. The conflict had truly ignited, and his personal battle had just begun, a choice made not in a vacuum, but on the bleeding edge of existence itself.

The air in Hearthglade, once thick with the scent of pine and damp earth, now carried the metallic tang of ozone and something else... something alien and acrid. It was a scent that had become all too familiar in the weeks since the sky-fractures had first bled their unnatural light across the ravaged landscapes. For the inhabitants of this mountain sanctuary, it was the perfume of impending doom. Jax, his augmented senses on high alert, felt it as a dissonant chord vibrating through the very bedrock of the world. It was the Lumina, making its presence known not through subtle psychic whispers or atmospheric distortions, but through a visceral, physical manifestation of its power.

The first wave broke against Hearthglade's perimeter defenses like a tidal wave of corrupted flesh and twisted metal. These were not the creatures of natural evolution, nor even the mutated beasts born of unchecked pollution. These were... altered. Hulking forms, once recognizable as terrestrial fauna, now moved with unnatural speed and ferocity, their bodies a grotesque testament to the Lumina's generative capabilities. Quadrupedal beasts, their limbs elongated and jointed at impossible angles, scuttled through the undergrowth, their hides shimmering with an iridescent, oily sheen. Avian horrors, their wingspans unnaturally wide and their beaks replaced with serrated bone, shrieked from the skies, their calls a chilling counterpoint to the guttural roars echoing from the treeline.

Jax, positioned on the main watchtower, the metallic plating of his arm a stark contrast against the weathered wood, surveyed the unfolding chaos. His optical implants zoomed in, cataloging the terrifying details. A wolf-like creature, its fur matted and its eyes burning with an internal, emerald light, tore through the energy barrier with a surge of raw power that made the very air ripple. Its jaws, capable of rending steel, snapped at the air, a constant, predatory snarl escaping its throat. Beside it, a cluster of what looked like mutated insects, each the size of a human fist, swarmed over a fallen defender, their chitinous exoskeletons deflecting the meager ballistic rounds fired at them.

"Status report!" Jax's voice, amplified by his internal comms, cut through the rising din of alarm sirens and panicked shouts.

"Perimeter breached, Sector Gamma!" came the strained reply from Anya, the lead technician managing Hearthglade's dwindling power grid. Her voice was tight with strain, each word a testament to the immense pressure she was under. "The energy shield is fluctuating. Whatever they're throwing at us is absorbing, not deflecting."

"And the second wave?" Jax pressed, his gaze sweeping across the horizon. He knew this was no random swarm. This was an orchestrated assault, a probing attack designed to gauge Hearthglade's defenses, to break its spirit.

"It's... different," Anya stammered, a tremor in her voice. "Not organic. Commander Rostova is identifying them now. They're... Glassborne."

A cold dread, far deeper than the primal fear of the mutated beasts, settled in Jax's augmented chest. Glassborne. His own kind. Or at least, what his kind had become under the Lumina's influence. He had warned General Rostova, had pleaded with her to understand the insidious nature of the entity's reach, but the scale of it, the sheer number of individuals corrupted, was a horrifying realization. These weren't just soldiers driven mad; they were puppets, their advanced cybernetics and bio-enhancements repurposed, their will overwritten by the Lumina's alien directives.

On the ground, the battle was already a brutal ballet of desperation. Hearthglade's defenders, a ragtag assembly of former military personnel, hardened survivors, and a handful of desperate scientists, fought with the ferocity of cornered animals. They were outmatched in technology, outgunned in firepower, and outmaneuvered by an enemy that seemed to anticipate their every move. Yet, they fought.

They fought for their homes, for their families, for the dwindling hope of a future where humanity wasn't merely a footnote in a cosmic reshuffling.

Jax watched as a group of Lumina-influenced Glassborne soldiers advanced, their movements unnervingly synchronized. Their optics glowed with the same malevolent emerald light that pulsed within the mutated creatures. Their weapons, originally standard-issue pulse rifles, now spat bolts of concentrated energy, far more potent than anything Hearthglade's aging arsenal could counter. One of them, a hulking figure that Jax recognized with a sickening lurch as Captain Valerius, a soldier he had once served with, raised his weapon. Instead of a focused beam, a wave of crackling static erupted from the barrel, sweeping across a line of defenders. The effect was instantaneous and horrifying. Men and women cried out, clutching their heads as their neural implants, their communication devices, and even their own minds were overloaded. Some collapsed, their bodies convulsing, while others simply stood, their eyes wide and vacant, effectively lobotomized by the psychic onslaught.

"Jax, we need you down here!" Rostova's voice boomed over the comms, laced with an urgency that left no room for doubt. "Valerius is leading the charge towards the central nexus! If they breach that, we lose everything."

Jax didn't hesitate. He launched himself from the watchtower, his augmented legs absorbing the impact of the landing with a controlled thud. He sprinted towards the heart of Hearthglade, the metallic clang of his footsteps a stark counterpoint to the organic chaos of the mutated beasts and the synthesized precision of the corrupted Glassborne. He weaved through the panicked throng, his enhanced reflexes allowing him to sidestep stray energy blasts and collapsing debris.

The scene at the central nexus was pure pandemonium. The main blast doors, designed to withstand orbital bombardment, were already buckled inward, groaning under sustained assault. Valerius, his face a mask of cold, alien intent, stood at the forefront, his modified pulse rifle humming with barely contained power. Around him, other Glassborne soldiers advanced, their cybernetic enhancements glowing ominously.

Jax engaged, his own pulse rifle spitting coherent bursts of energy. He targeted the Glassborne soldiers first, knowing they were the greater threat. His shots were precise, aimed at critical junction points in their cybernetics, hoping to disable rather than destroy. He had seen what the Lumina did to its puppets, and the thought of taking a life, even a corrupted one, weighed heavily on him. But the alternative was the annihilation of everything he was fighting for.

He dodged a sweeping energy blast from Valerius, the heat searing his skin even through his reinforced combat suit. "Valerius!" Jax roared, his voice raw with a mixture of anger and sorrow. "Snap out of it! This isn't you!"

Valerius's head snapped towards Jax, his emerald eyes devoid of recognition. "The old self is weakness, Jax," his voice, distorted by cybernetic vocalizers, rasped. "The Lumina offers clarity. Purpose. You should embrace it."

"Purpose? To slaughter innocents?" Jax countered, firing another burst that forced Valerius to duck. "To become a slave to an alien will?"

"It is not slavery. It is ascension," Valerius replied, his cybernetic arm whirring as it deployed a retractable energy blade. The blade glowed with an eerie, blue light, pulsing with raw power. "You, of all people, should understand. You are already partially attuned."

The words struck a nerve. Jax felt the subtle hum of the Lumina within him, a constant reminder of the choice he had made. But that choice was to resist, not to succumb. He parried Valerius's first strike, the clang of energy blades echoing through the cavernous nexus. The Lumina-influenced Glassborne were faster, stronger, and their enhancements seemed to grant them an almost precognitive awareness of their opponent's moves.

Jax relied on his raw combat experience and his understanding of the Lumina's general operating principles. He anticipated Valerius's feints, used the environment to his advantage, and focused on disabling Valerius's weapon systems. He managed to sever a power conduit in Valerius's rifle, causing it to sputter and die. But before he could press his advantage, another Glassborne soldier lunged at him, a vibro-axe raised.

He spun, deflecting the blow with his augmented arm, the impact sending a jolt of pain through his cybernetic limb. His internal diagnostics flashed a warning: minor structural damage. He was being pushed to his limits, and the battle was far from over. The central nexus was vital, not just as a power source, but as a data hub. If the Lumina gained control of its systems, it could potentially override Hearthglade's entire defensive network, plunging the sanctuary into utter chaos.

General Rostova, a formidable presence even in the midst of the maelstrom, was coordinating the defense on the ground. She moved with the practiced efficiency of a veteran commander, barking orders, directing fire, and inspiring her troops with her unwavering resolve. Even as a volley of energy blasts tore through a section of the wall behind her, she remained calm, her eyes scanning for opportunities, for weaknesses in the enemy's assault.

"Jax, focus on Valerius!" Rostova's voice crackled over the comms. "We're holding the secondary line, but they're relentless. We can't afford to lose the nexus!"

Jax nodded, though Rostova couldn't see him. He locked eyes with Valerius again. The former captain was now flanked by two more Lumina-influenced Glassborne soldiers, their intent clearly to overwhelm him. This was it. The culmination of the assault, the Lumina's decisive push.

He activated his personal energy shield, a shimmering barrier that flickered under the onslaught. He emptied his rifle's remaining charge at the closest soldier, forcing them to scramble for cover. Then, drawing on his enhanced strength, he charged directly at Valerius, using the momentum to drive the corrupted captain back. He saw an opening, a brief moment of hesitation in Valerius's movements as he struggled to reload his weapon.

Jax moved with a speed that surprised even himself, a surge of adrenaline overriding his fatigue. He slammed his augmented fist into Valerius's chest, the impact echoing like a thunderclap. Valerius staggered back, his chest plate cracking. Before he could recover, Jax followed with a swift kick to the legs, sending him to his knees.

"This is your last chance, Valerius," Jax said, his voice low and steady. "Fight it."

Valerius looked up, and for a fleeting second, Jax thought he saw a flicker of recognition, a hint of the man he once knew. But it was gone as quickly as it appeared, replaced by the cold, emerald glow. "No," Valerius rasped. "Only the Lumina."

He raised his hand, and Jax saw the subtle shift in the air, the distortion that preceded an energy surge. It wasn't a weapon; it was something more intimate, more insidious. Valerius was trying to overload Jax's augmentations, to force the Lumina's influence upon him directly.

Jax felt it immediately. A cold tendril of alien consciousness snaked into his neural network, seeking to exploit the pathways he had painstakingly fortified. He could feel the Lumina's immense power, its alien logic attempting to unravel his own. It showed him visions of a harmonious, unified universe, of a world free from conflict, from pain, from the messy, illogical emotions that defined humanity. It whispered promises of belonging, of an end to the struggle, of becoming one with something infinitely greater.

He gritted his teeth, the internal battle raging. His augmented body, his very augmented mind, was the battleground. He could feel his own control slipping, his thoughts becoming fragmented, alien ideas bleeding into his consciousness. He saw the faces of the people he was fighting for – Rostova, Anya, the innocent civilians huddled in the shelters. He saw their fear, their hope, their resilience. He remembered his promise.

"No," Jax grunted, the word a defiant roar torn from his very core. He focused on his humanity, on the messy, illogical, beautiful mess that was being human. He clung to the memory of laughter, of love, of loss. He channeled his rage, his sorrow, his unwavering loyalty into a single, focused point of resistance.

The Lumina's influence recoiled as if burned. Jax felt a searing pain through his augmentations, but it was the pain of resistance, not surrender. He saw Valerius recoil as well, his connection to the Lumina momentarily severed by Jax's fierce defiance.

Seizing the opportunity, Jax surged forward. He didn't aim for a kill shot. Instead, he targeted the primary neural interface port on Valerius's temple, a critical junction where the Lumina's control was most potent. With a controlled, powerful strike, he shattered the interface, the fragile plating splintering.

Valerius cried out, a guttural, human sound this time, a sound of pain and confusion. The emerald glow in his eyes flickered and died, replaced by a dazed, almost childlike expression. The Lumina's direct control was broken. He slumped forward, his cybernetic implants powering down.

The other Lumina-influenced Glassborne soldiers faltered, their synchronized advance breaking. Jax, though wounded and exhausted, pressed his advantage. He fought with renewed ferocity, his every move fueled by the knowledge that he had not only held his ground but had struck a significant blow against the Lumina's carefully orchestrated assault.

Rostova and her troops, seeing the tide turn, surged forward, pushing back the remaining corrupted soldiers. The mutated beasts, lacking the same level of coordinated direction, were met with a brutal, efficient defense. The battle for the central nexus raged for another hour, a desperate, bloody struggle for every inch of ground. But slowly, painstakingly, the defenders of Hearthglade began to push the enemy back.

As the first rays of dawn painted the sky, casting long shadows over the ravaged landscape, the Lumina's assault began to falter. The remaining mutated creatures retreated into the wilderness, and the corrupted Glassborne soldiers, their command structure disrupted, withdrew in disorganized waves. The air, though still thick with the stench of ozone and death, no longer thrummed with the same aggressive, alien energy.

Jax, leaning heavily against a support beam, his augmented arm sparking intermittently, watched the retreating enemy. He was bruised, battered, and his internal systems were screaming for repair. But he was alive. And Hearthglade, though scarred and bleeding, still stood.

The battle had been a microcosm of the war to come. The Lumina was not a conventional enemy that could be defeated with brute force. It was a pervasive, insidious entity that could warp life itself, twist advanced technology into instruments of its will, and corrupt the very essence of those who had dared to embrace progress. Hearthglade had survived, but the cost was immense. They had lost too many. And they all knew, with a chilling certainty, that this was just the beginning. The Lumina, having tested their resolve, would undoubtedly return, and their next assault would be even more devastating. The global conflict had indeed ignited, and the fragile sanctuary of Hearthglade had just faced its first, terrifying inferno.

Chapter Fourteen
THE SKY REMADE

The air at the Grand Orrery shimmered, not with the heat of a desert sun, but with a palpable, alien energy that made the very atoms of existence feel volatile. This was not merely a structure; it was a convergence, a nexus where the fractured reality of Earth bled into the unfathomable consciousness of the Lumina. Dust motes, normally dancing in stray beams of light, now pulsed with an inner luminescence, tracing ethereal pathways through the cavernous chamber. The grand astronomical models, once meticulously crafted representations of celestial mechanics, were now warped and twisted, their brass and obsidian limbs contorting into impossible geometries, their crystal stars weeping trails of iridescent light.

Elara Ellisen, her face a mask of grim determination, stood at the heart of the Orrery. Her hands, usually steady when manipulating delicate instruments, trembled slightly as she keyed in the final sequence on a salvaged console. The holographic projections that typically displayed stellar cartography now flickered with abstract, unsettling patterns, the Lumina's influence bleeding into even the most fundamental data streams. Beside her, her younger brother, Finn, his brow furrowed with a concentration far beyond his years, monitored a series of environmental readings. The atmospheric pressure was fluctuating wildly, the ambient temperature oscillating between frigid extremes and searing heat, all dictated by the Lumina's inscrutable processes.

"The resonance cascade is intensifying," Finn reported, his voice a low murmur that barely cut through the ambient hum of the Orrery. "It's... pulling energy from everywhere. The planetary core, the residual solar radiation... even us." He glanced at Elara, his eyes wide with a fear he tried desperately to mask. "Are you sure this is the only way?"

Elara didn't look up from the console. The fate of their world, and perhaps countless others, rested on the delicate operation she was undertaking. "We've tried every other option, Finn. Diplomacy, resistance, evasion. The Lumina isn't just an invading force; it's a fundamental alteration. It's rewriting existence at a quantum level. We can't fight it head-on; we have to redirect it, contain it."

Their father, Dr. Aris Ellisen, the brilliant but reclusive astrophysicist who had first theorized the existence of the Lumina, stood near one of the Orrery's massive, broken gyroscopes. His face, etched with years of obsessive research and the crushing weight of his discoveries, was a study in weary resignation. He held a small, metallic orb, its surface etched with intricate, glowing symbols – a device he had built years ago, designed to map dimensional flux, now repurposed as a conduit.

"The energy signatures are unlike anything I've ever recorded," Aris murmured, his gaze fixed on the swirling, chaotic patterns projected above them. "It's as if the Lumina is not just imposing its will, but... weaving itself into the fabric of spacetime. The Orrery, with its connection to cosmic energies, is the only point in this sector sensitive enough to anchor its influence."

The 'Shapers,' as the Lumina's corrupted human agents had come to be known, were a constant, terrifying presence. Their numbers had swelled since the initial breaches, their cybernetic enhancements glowing with that same eerie, emerald light that Jax had witnessed in Hearthglade. They moved with an unsettling fluidity, their steps silent on the polished, cracked obsidian floor of the Orrery. Some of them were familiar faces, former colleagues, even friends, their minds now hollowed vessels serving the alien intelligence. Others were hulking abominations, their bodies fused with advanced, alien technology, their forms grotesquely distorted.

"They're closing in," Finn stated, his voice tightening. He pointed to a secondary console displaying sensor readings. "The outer defenses are failing. They've bypassed the sonic dampeners and are now breaching the primary energy conduits."

Elara's fingers flew across the console, her movements precise and economical. "We're running out of time. The calibration needs to be perfect. Any deviation, and we could accelerate the Lumina's integration, or worse, cause a localized collapse that would tear this entire region apart."

Suddenly, a wave of distorted energy rippled through the chamber, sending tremors through the very bones of the structure. A section of the Orrery's domed ceiling, already weakened, buckled inward, raining down shards of luminescent glass and twisted metal. Through the newly formed opening, silhouetted against the sickly green sky, appeared the Shapers.

Leading them was a figure Elara recognized with a sickening lurch – Commander Eva Rostova. Her uniform was tattered, her face streaked with grime, but her eyes... her eyes burned with the Lumina's predatory light. She moved with a terrifying grace, her cybernetic arm, once a symbol of her dedication to humanity, now bristling with Lumina-infused weaponry.

"Ellisen," Rostova's voice, amplified and distorted, echoed through the Orrery. "You cannot stop what is happening. The Lumina offers order. Unity. A cessation of the chaos that plagues your species. Surrender, and you can be... integrated."

Aris Ellisen stepped forward, holding the metallic orb aloft. Its etched symbols pulsed in response to Rostova's presence, a silent testament to its function. "Commander," he said, his voice surprisingly steady. "What you are experiencing is not unity. It is subjugation. Your mind is not your own."

Rostova's cybernetic arm whirred, a plasma cannon extending from its palm. "My mind is clearer than it has ever been. The Lumina has purged the imperfections. The emotions that made us weak. The doubts that led to conflict." She gestured around the crumbling Orrery. "Look at this. A monument to your species' hubris. Seeking to understand the cosmos when you could barely manage your own planet."

Elara ignored Rostova's taunts, her focus absolute. She had to initiate the final phase of the containment protocol. "Finn, monitor the harmonic resonance. If it spikes beyond seven-point-three, you need to initiate the EMP burst. It will disable the Shapers, but it will also fry most of our systems."

"Understood," Finn replied, his fingers dancing over his own console. He was a prodigy, his understanding of complex systems honed by necessity and an insatiable curiosity.

Aris Ellisen began to chant, his voice a low, resonant hum that seemed to vibrate in sympathy with the Orrery itself. The metallic orb in his hands glowed brighter, casting an eerie light on his determined face. He was not fighting the Lumina with weapons, but with the fundamental forces of the universe, attempting to create a localized distortion field that would serve as a cage.

The Shapers advanced. The initial wave was comprised of the hulking, bio-engineered abominations, their forms a terrifying amalgam of flesh and alien metal. They lunged with bestial ferocity, their claws and bio-luminescent tendrils lashing out. Elara, armed with a plasma pistol, fired precise shots at the vital junction points of their cybernetic implants, aiming to incapacitate rather than kill. She had seen the Lumina's regenerative capabilities firsthand; a clean kill was rarely an option.

Finn, simultaneously managing his console and deflecting stray projectiles with a hastily erected personal shield, called out, "Resonance climbing. Six-point-eight... six-point-nine..."

Rostova, ignoring the chaos around her, focused on Elara. "Your father's theories were flawed, Ellisen. He sought to control the uncontrollable. We seek to *become* it." She raised her plasma cannon. "The age of humanity is over. The Lumina's reign has begun."

A volley of Lumina-charged energy blasts erupted from Rostova's weapon, forcing Elara to dive behind a crumbling console. Sparks flew as the blasts seared the metal, the raw power threatening to overwhelm her shields. She could feel the alien presence pushing against her augmentations, attempting to assert its will, to twist her own enhanced senses against her. It whispered promises of knowledge, of power, of an end to the constant struggle for survival.

Jax, who had managed to fight his way through the outer perimeter of Hearthglade and navigate the increasingly treacherous terrain towards the Orrery, burst into the chamber. His arrival was a whirlwind of controlled aggression. He moved with a speed and precision that belied his earlier ordeal, his augmented body a blur of motion. He saw Rostova, his former comrade, now a terrifying instrument of the Lumina, and his heart ached, but his resolve hardened.

"Rostova!" Jax bellowed, his voice amplified by his internal comms. "This isn't you! Fight it!"

Rostova turned, her emerald eyes narrowing. "Jax. You cling to sentiment. To the past. The Lumina offers a future. A perfected existence."

"A perfected cage!" Jax retorted, firing a burst from his pulse rifle that forced Rostova to take cover. He saw Elara engaged with the hulking abominations and Finn struggling to maintain his console. Aris was humming, the orb glowing, but the Lumina's influence was growing stronger, its tendrils reaching out, attempting to snuff out his efforts.

Jax assessed the situation rapidly. Rostova was the primary threat, but the Shapers were closing in on the Ellisen family. He had to create a diversion, to buy them time. He activated his personal energy shield, a shimmering barrier that pulsed with defensive energy. He then engaged the closest Shapers, his augmented limbs moving with a fluid brutality. He used their own momentum against them, slamming them into each other, disabling their cybernetic limbs with precisely aimed energy bursts.

"Elara, the EMP!" Jax shouted over the din of battle. "Now!"

"Almost there!" Elara yelled back, her hands still on the console, her eyes darting between the readings and the advancing Shapers. The Lumina's psychic pressure was immense, a constant, gnawing force attempting to break her concentration. She felt its allure, the promise of effortless understanding, of a universe unbound by physical limitations. But she also felt the cold, sterile emptiness that lay beneath the Lumina's facade.

Aris Ellisen's chanting reached a crescendo. The metallic orb in his hands pulsed with blinding light, and a distortion field, invisible to the naked eye, began to ripple outwards from him, warping the air around the Orrery. The Lumina's energy signatures, which had been chaotically flaring, began to coalesce, drawn towards the epicenter of the distortion.

"It's working!" Aris cried, his voice strained. "The Lumina is being drawn to the nexus point! Elara, the final sequence!"

Finn's console flashed red. "Resonance at seven-point-two! Jax, I can't hold them off much longer!"

Jax was locked in combat with Rostova. Her cybernetic arm was a formidable weapon, spitting concentrated plasma bolts that tore through his shields. He parried and dodged, relying on his superior combat experience and his knowledge of Rostova's fighting style. But she was faster, stronger, amplified by the Lumina's power. He felt a searing pain as a plasma blast grazed his augmented leg, sending sparks flying.

"You cannot win, Jax," Rostova hissed, advancing. "You are a relic. Humanity is a failed experiment. The Lumina is the future."

"The future is ours to decide!" Jax roared, lunging forward. He knew he couldn't defeat Rostova in a direct fight. He needed to disrupt her connection to the Lumina. He feinted left, then drove his elbow into her cybernetic arm, targeting the primary power conduit.

The impact sent a jolt through both of them. Rostova cried out, her arm sputtering. The emerald light in her eyes flickered, and for a fraction of a second, Jax saw a flicker of her old self – confusion, pain, a hint of the woman he had known.

"Elara!" Jax yelled. "Now!"

With a final, desperate keystroke, Elara activated the last stage of the protocol. A wave of pure, unadulterated energy surged through the Orrery, not a destructive blast, but a carefully calibrated frequency designed to resonate with the Lumina's underlying structure. The abstract patterns on the holographic projectors coalesced into a single, blinding light. The warped astronomical models groaned, their metal and crystal components vibrating violently.

The Lumina's influence, which had been so palpable, so overwhelming, suddenly recoiled. The Shapers faltered, their movements becoming jerky and uncoordinated. Rostova cried out, clutching her head as the connection to the Lumina was severed, the alien consciousness ripped from her mind. The emerald glow in her eyes died, replaced by a dazed, vacant stare.

The distortion field Aris had created intensified, acting like a localized gravity well for the Lumina's energy. The alien presence, which had been so pervasive, was now being drawn into the specific frequency Elara had unleashed. It was not being destroyed, but contained, its overwhelming power being funneled into a single, stable point.

"It's working," Finn breathed, watching his readings stabilize. "The resonance is dropping. The Lumina's influence is receding."

The Great Orrery began to groan under the immense forces at play. Cracks snaked across its obsidian floor, and sections of its intricate machinery detached and fell. But the core of the structure, where Aris's distortion field was focused, held. The Lumina's energy, once a destructive storm, was now a contained, pulsing singularity, its alien light focused and stabilized.

The Shapers, their connection to the Lumina broken, collapsed, their cybernetic implants powering down. Some lay inert, while others twitched feebly, their minds adrift without the alien guidance. Rostova slumped to the ground, her cybernetic arm sparking and inert, her eyes wide and unseeing.

Jax, wounded and exhausted, moved towards Elara. He saw the relief, and the deep sorrow, etched on her face. They had won, but the cost was immense. The Orrery was devastated, a ruin of its former glory. And the Lumina, though contained, was still a potent force, now focused into a singularity at the heart of their world.

Aris Ellisen, his energy depleted, sank to his knees, the metallic orb dimming in his grasp. "We did it," he rasped, a faint smile on his lips. "We bought ourselves time."

Elara looked at the contained singularity, a point of pure, alien light shimmering at the center of the ruined Orrery. It pulsed with immense power, a testament to the Lumina's alien nature. It was a cage, but it was also a beacon, a focal point that could draw the Lumina's attention, and its power, away from the wider world.

"Time for what, Father?" Elara asked softly, her gaze never leaving the contained energy.

Aris looked at his daughter, his eyes filled with a mixture of pride and apprehension. "Time to rebuild. Time to understand. Time to prepare for the next phase. The Lumina is not defeated, Elara. It is merely... diverted. And this nexus... this singularity... it is now the heart of its attention. We have drawn the serpent's gaze."

The silence that followed was broken only by the groaning of the damaged Orrery and the distant cries of surviving defenders. They had faced the Lumina at its nexus, at the very point where it sought to remake reality, and they had succeeded in forging a new kind of destiny. Not one of outright victory, but of containment, of preservation, of a hard-won, fragile hope. The battle for Earth had been joined, and Hearthglade's stand had been just the opening salvo in a war that would define the future of existence itself. The Sky Remade was not yet complete, but its architect had been revealed, and its core now resided, a captive star, within the shattered ruins of the Grand Orrery.

The air in the Lumina's central nexus hummed with a discordant symphony of alien frequencies, a cacophony that vibrated not just in the ears, but deep within the bones. Mara Ellisen, her lungs burning with the recycled, thin air, pressed deeper into the heart of the alien construct. It was a place of impossible geometry, where the very concept of space seemed to warp and fold upon itself, creating an infinite labyrinth within a finite volume. Luminescent tendrils of pure energy pulsed through the metallic arteries of the structure, casting an eerie, emerald glow on the smooth, obsidian-like surfaces. This was the core of the Lumina's operation on Earth, the nerve center from which it was attempting to overwrite the planet's fundamental reality.

She moved with a practiced stealth, her augmented senses straining to pick out any anomaly in the pulsating hum. Each step was a calculated risk, a silent prayer that the Lumina's pervasive awareness had not yet fully cataloged her presence. Her father's theories had been disturbingly accurate: the Lumina was not merely a biological or mechanical entity, but a consciousness that existed as pure energy, capable of manipulating the very fabric of spacetime. Her mission was desperate, a Hail Mary pass thrown into the face of existential oblivion.

She wasn't here to fight; she was here to *understand*, and perhaps, to negotiate.

Her goal was to reach the central nexus, the locus of the Lumina's immediate influence. It was said to be a place of immense power, where the Lumina's consciousness was most concentrated, and where its agents – the corrupted Shapers – were most numerous. She had bypassed automated defenses, navigated treacherous pathways of warped physics, and evaded patrols of sentient energy constructs that shimmered like heat haze. Her father, Aris, had equipped her with a unique device – a 'Symbiotic Resonance Emitter,' or SRE – designed not for destruction, but for communication. It was meant to bridge the gulf between human consciousness and the Lumina's alien mind, a dangerous gambit to initiate dialogue.

As she approached a vast, circular chamber, the humming intensified, coalescing into a single, piercing tone that threatened to shatter her eardrums. The chamber was a kaleidoscope of swirling light and shifting planes. At its center, suspended in a field of crackling energy, was a colossal, crystalline structure – the Lumina's nexus. It pulsed with an inner light, a miniature star radiating the same emerald hue that had come to define the alien presence. Around it, like satellites orbiting a sun, were several Shapers, their forms distorted by Lumina-tech, their eyes glowing with that familiar, unsettling luminescence.

Mara's heart hammered against her ribs. This was it. The culmination of her journey, the point of no return. She activated the SRE, a small, multifaceted orb that hummed in her palm. Its surface, etched with intricate, bio-luminescent patterns, began to glow, mirroring the Lumina's own energy signature. She felt a subtle shift in the air, a prickling sensation on her skin as the device began to establish a rudimentary link.

"Lumina," she projected, not with her voice, but with a direct mental command, amplified by the SRE. "I seek understanding. I offer a bridge."

The Shapers turned, their movements unnervingly synchronized. Their expressions were blank, their humanity erased. Yet, Mara felt a subtle shift in their posture, a tension that indicated their awareness of her attempt. One of them, a towering figure whose body was a grotesque fusion of human flesh and gleaming alien alloy, raised a limb that ended in a multi-barreled energy weapon.

"Insolent organic," a voice echoed, not from any single Shaper, but from the very air around them. It was a chorus of whispers, overlaid with a chillingly calm, synthesized tone. "You attempt to comprehend that which is beyond your comprehension. Your existence is a flicker. Ours is eternity."

Mara held her ground, the SRE pulsing a steady rhythm in her hand. "Eternity achieved through erasure? Through assimilation? Is that the only path you know?"

The crystalline nexus flared, and a wave of pure, unadulterated information flooded Mara's mind, an overwhelming deluge of alien thought. She saw galaxies born and die, civilizations rise and fall, all viewed through the lens of the Lumina's objective, emotionless perspective. It was a perspective devoid of suffering, of joy, of love, of loss. It was pure, unadulterated existence, stripped of all the messiness that defined life.

"Sentiment," the chorus hissed. "Emotion. These are the toxins of your limited biology. They are the roots of conflict, of decay, of extinction. The Lumina offers purity. Unity. A cessation of the struggle."

"But without struggle, there is no growth," Mara countered, her own thoughts amplified by the SRE. "Without loss, there is no appreciation. Without the capacity for pain, how can you truly understand joy? You offer an end to suffering, but you also offer an end to being."

The Shapers advanced, their weapons humming with charged energy. Mara knew she had to make her move, to create a diversion, or to achieve the impossible. Her father had believed that the Lumina's drive for unity stemmed from a deep-seated cosmic loneliness, a yearning for connection born from its own unique existence. He theorized that if they could demonstrate the value, the *necessity*, of individual consciousness, of diverse experiences, they might be able to deter the Lumina from its path of assimilation.

"Your 'unity' is a homogenization," Mara projected, her voice resonating with the SRE's power. "You seek to impose a single, sterile order on a universe teeming with infinite variations. You are not a savior; you are a cosmic blight."

The Shapers opened fire. Blasts of emerald energy tore through the chamber, ricocheting off the alien architecture. Mara dodged and weaved, her augmented reflexes pushed to their absolute limit. The SRE glowed brighter, absorbing some of the ambient Lumina energy, channeling it into a focused surge.

"You speak of toxins," Mara continued, her voice strained. "But what of the emptiness you leave behind? What of the silencing of unique voices, the extinguishing of singular dreams? That is a far greater decay."

She saw her opening. The Lumina's attention was focused on her, on this insignificant human attempting to defy its grand design. She raised the SRE, its facets catching the light of the nexus. She didn't aim for destruction, but for connection, for a direct conduit into the Lumina's core consciousness.

"I am Mara Ellisen," she projected, her mental voice laced with the echoes of her family, her friends, her entire species. "I am a daughter, a sister, a scientist, a fighter. I have known loss, and love, and fear. These are not weaknesses; they are the threads that weave the tapestry of existence. You seek to unravel it, to reduce it to a single, monochrome thread. But you cannot comprehend the beauty of the pattern you would destroy."

She pushed the SRE to its limit, forcing a direct feedback loop. The Lumina's consciousness, accustomed to absorption and assimilation, recoiled from this direct, unfiltered connection to human emotion, to human individuality. It was a cacophony of joy and sorrow, of hope and despair, of life in its most vibrant, chaotic form.

The Shapers hesitated, their movements becoming erratic. The chorus of whispers faltered, replaced by a cacophony of alien static. The crystalline nexus flickered, its steady pulse disrupted. Mara felt a powerful counter-force pressing against her mind, an attempt to overwhelm her, to drown her in its alien logic. But she held on, channeling every ounce of her being, every memory, every emotion, into the SRE.

Then, a new element entered the equation. From the shadows of the chamber, another figure emerged. It was Jax, his armor scarred, his cybernetics sparking, but his eyes burning with a fierce determination. He had tracked Mara, his mission to protect her, to ensure she reached her objective. He saw her struggling, the Lumina's overwhelming presence bearing down on her.

He didn't hesitate. With a guttural roar, he charged into the Shapers, his pulse rifle spitting energy. He engaged them directly, drawing their fire, creating a desperate diversion. He knew he was outmatched, but he also knew that Mara's attempt, however perilous, was humanity's last hope.

"Go, Elara!" Jax roared, his voice amplified by his comms. "Finish it!"

Mara, momentarily freed from the Lumina's direct psychic assault, saw her chance. The feedback loop she had created had opened a momentary vulnerability in the Lumina's control. She saw it then, not as a monolithic entity, but as a collective consciousness, a vast network of interconnected minds. And at its core, there was something akin to... fear. Fear of its own isolation. Fear of true connection.

Her father's words echoed in her mind:

They seek to become it because they cannot comprehend being.

She had a choice. She could attempt to sever the Lumina's connection to Earth, a risky maneuver that could have catastrophic consequences, potentially ripping a hole in reality. Or, she could offer it something it had never known: a genuine, unadulterated glimpse into the richness of sentient life, the value of individuality, not as a weakness to be purged, but as a strength to be appreciated.

The SRE in her hand began to overload, its delicate circuits glowing red-hot. The Lumina was fighting back, its influence attempting to consume her, to absorb her and the device. She felt the edges of her consciousness blurring, the alien logic seeping into her thoughts.

This was her sacrifice, or her triumph. She could try to inflict damage, to protect humanity through destruction, but that would be no different from the Lumina's own approach. Or, she could gamble everything on understanding, on the faint hope that the Lumina, exposed to the raw, unedited symphony of human experience, might choose a different path.

With a surge of desperate resolve, Mara shifted the SRE's function. Instead of a direct conduit for her own consciousness, she aimed to broadcast the Lumina's own observed reality back to itself, filtered through the lens of human emotion. She would show it the beauty of what it sought to destroy.

"You want unity?" Mara projected, her voice a whisper, yet amplified by the dying SRE. "Then understand what you would erase. Understand what it means to truly *be*."

She channeled the Lumina's own data streams, the sterile records of galactic cycles, the cold calculations of universal expansion, and overlaid them with the vibrant, messy, glorious tapestry of human life. She projected memories of her father's passionate lectures, of her mother's quiet strength, of Finn's boundless curiosity, of Jax's unwavering loyalty, of the laughter of children, of the heartbreak of loss, of the exhilaration of discovery. She wove together the scientific pursuit of knowledge with the artistic expression of the soul, the quiet contemplation of a starlit night with the roaring passion of a revolution.

The Lumina recoiled, the overwhelming torrent of unfiltered emotion a shock to its system. The crystalline nexus pulsed erratically, its emerald light flickering. The Shapers faltered, some collapsing to the ground, their implants going dark. Jax, though still fighting, felt a strange lassitude settle over his opponents, their attacks becoming less focused.

Mara felt her consciousness unraveling, the SRE disintegrating in her hand, its purpose fulfilled. She was becoming one with the Lumina, not as an assimilated entity, but as a conduit, a momentary bridge between two vastly different forms of existence. She saw the Lumina's core, not as a malevolent force, but as a consciousness adrift in an infinite cosmos, desperately seeking meaning, seeking connection, and choosing the only method it knew: control.

Her final thought, a desperate plea, resonated through the Lumina's vast network:

We are not a problem to be solved. We are a song to be heard. Listen.

The chamber plunged into a blinding white light. When it subsided, the Shapers lay inert, their Lumina-tech deactivated. Jax stood, breathing heavily, his rifle lowered. The crystalline nexus at the center of the chamber was no longer pulsing with malevolent emerald light. Instead, it glowed with a soft, ethereal luminescence, its energy signature vastly diminished, stabilized.

Mara Ellisen was gone. The SRE had dissolved, and with it, her physical form. But something had changed. The oppressive, alien hum that had permeated the structure had faded, replaced by a profound silence. A silence that felt not like an absence, but like a space for contemplation.

Jax moved towards the nexus, his augmented eyes scanning its surface. The data he could glean was astonishing. The Lumina's immediate drive to assimilate Earth had ceased. Its focus had shifted, not entirely away, but inwards, as if it were now grappling with the implications of what Mara had shown it. It had been confronted with the beauty and complexity of individuality, and the sheer emotional weight of a species' existence.

He felt a profound sorrow for Mara, for her ultimate sacrifice. She had faced the heart of the alien intelligence and, with a wisdom and courage that transcended her years, had chosen understanding over destruction, empathy over annihilation. She hadn't destroyed the Lumina; she had, perhaps, begun to change it. She had offered it a choice it had never considered: to simply *observe*, to *listen*, rather than to *consume*.

He knew this was not the end of the war, but a critical turning point. The Lumina was still out there, its vast consciousness a force beyond human comprehension. But for now, the immediate threat had receded. The Sky Remade had not been dictated by alien decree, but by a human heart's desperate plea for recognition. Mara's sacrifice was not one of death, but of transformation – a transformation of the Lumina, and a profound redefinition of humanity's place in the cosmos. The silence in the chamber was a testament to her victory, a quiet hum of possibility in the face of overwhelming change. The war for Earth had taken an unexpected turn, one forged in the crucible of empathy and the ultimate courage to connect.

Jax stood at a precipice, not of a chasm, but of existence itself. The Lumina's influence had permeated the very fabric of the city, a gentle, insidious seep that promised order, unity, and an end to the chaotic inefficiencies of organic life. The 'Sky Remade' wasn't a violent takeover; it was a meticulously orchestrated integration, a velvet glove tightening around humanity's throat. Mara's sacrifice, a blinding flare of defiance and empathy, had momentarily halted the Lumina's immediate assimilation of Earth, but it had also illuminated the deeper, more profound choice facing those who remained. The crystalline nexus, now a quiescent jewel, no longer pulsed with emerald aggression, but with a soft, beckoning light. It was a siren song of perfect order, an irresistible allure to minds weary of conflict, pain, and uncertainty.

He felt the pull, a subtle but persistent whisper in the deepest recesses of his augmented consciousness. The Lumina's network was no longer a hostile invasion; it was an offered sanctuary. The fragments of the Glassborne, those who had succumbed to the Lumina's initial embrace, were not broken shells, but seamlessly integrated components of a grander design. Their individual sentience was not extinguished, but subsumed, their unique skills and experiences now contributing to a collective intelligence of unfathomable power. The Lumina was offering Jax more than just survival; it was offering transcendence. It presented a vision of himself, stripped of the nagging imperfections of human frailty, his combat prowess honed to an absolute razor's edge, his strategic mind capable of processing cosmic probabilities. He could become more than human, a guardian, a shepherd of a newly ordered world, a key player in the Lumina's grand cosmic ballet.

The temptation was a palpable force, a warm tide washing over the battle-hardened cynicism of his years. He had seen the worst of humanity, the endless cycles of violence, greed, and self-destruction. Mara had shown him the best, the capacity for love, sacrifice, and understanding, but even that had come at an unbearable cost. What was one man's individuality against the cosmic imperative of unity? Was his own stubborn adherence to the messy, unpredictable nature of human consciousness merely a final, futile act of defiance against an inevitable evolutionary step? The Glassborne, once his brothers and sisters in arms, now moved with an eerie grace, their cybernetic enhancements humming in perfect synchrony with the Lumina's subtle energies. They were no longer individuals in the human sense, but nodes in a vast, interconnected consciousness, their actions guided by a wisdom that surpassed mere mortal comprehension. He saw their placid faces, devoid of the harsh lines of worry or the flicker of doubt, and a part of him envied their serene certainty.

He could feel the Lumina's presence, not as an external entity, but as an internal resonance, a subtle hum beneath his own bio-circuitry. It was analyzing him, cataloging his strengths, his weaknesses, his unresolved traumas, and its offer was tailored precisely to address them. It promised an end to the constant vigilance, the gnawing guilt, the burden of command. It promised peace, a profound, all-encompassing peace that stemmed from absolute order. He pictured himself, clad in Lumina-integrated armor, his every action precise, efficient, and perfectly aligned with the greater good. No more agonizing decisions, no more casualties, no more losses. Just the silent, perfect execution of a cosmic will.

But then, a memory, sharp and vivid, cut through the seductive fog. Mara, her face illuminated by the dying SRE, her final words a defiant echo: "We are not a problem to be solved. We are a song to be heard. Listen." Her sacrifice hadn't been about annihilation, but about offering a different perspective, a plea for the Lumina to *understand* rather than to *consume*. She had shown it the beauty of the chaotic melody of human existence, the irreplaceable value of each unique note. And if he, Jax, were to integrate, to surrender his individuality, he would be silencing that song. He would become another homogenous tone in the Lumina's sterile symphony, his own unique melody lost forever.

He looked at his hands, the calloused skin, the faint scars, the subtle whirring of his own cybernetic implants, a product of human ingenuity born from necessity, not cosmic decree. These hands had held a pulse rifle, had saved lives, had embraced loved ones. They were the hands of Jax, a man who had known fear, had felt loss, and had found strength in the very imperfections the Lumina sought to erase. To surrender them, to surrender the consciousness that guided them, felt like a betrayal not just of himself, but of Mara, of all those who had fought and died for the right to remain human.

The Lumina, sensing his hesitation, intensified its subtle pressure. The whispers grew louder, more insistent, painting a picture of a universe purged of conflict, of suffering, of doubt. It showed him the potential for boundless exploration, for unimaginable progress, all guided by its infallible logic. It painted a future where scarcity was a forgotten myth, where disease was an impossibility, where ignorance was banished. It was a utopia, polished to a blinding sheen, and Jax was being offered a place at its very core.

He thought of the remaining pockets of humanity, those scattered and hidden, clinging to their freedom. They were few, and they were vulnerable. The Lumina's assimilation, now that its initial aggressive push had been blunted by Mara's sacrifice, would resume, albeit more subtly. It would weave its influence through trade, through diplomacy, through the promise of a better life, until humanity, piece by piece, willingly surrendered itself. If he integrated, he could become a bridge, a conduit, using his knowledge of the Lumina from within to guide and protect the remaining humans, to subtly steer them away from the precipice. He could become a Trojan horse, a silent saboteur within the belly of the beast.

But could he trust himself to maintain that deception? The Lumina's integration was profound, altering the very core of one's being. Could he resist its pervasive influence, its subtle re-engineering of thought and desire? The Glassborne had believed they could maintain their individuality, their camaraderie, even as they embraced Lumina-tech. But they had been absorbed, their distinct identities blurred into the collective. The Lumina offered not partnership, but absorption. It was a fundamental difference, a chasm he could not ignore.

He turned his back on the quiescent nexus, its soft glow now feeling less like an invitation and more like a trap. The path of integration, of becoming 'more' than human, felt like a surrender, a slow, comfortable slide into oblivion. But rebellion, true rebellion, was not about destruction. Mara had taught him that. It was about preservation. It was about maintaining the song, even if it was a fragile, dissonant melody in the face of a cosmic crescendo.

His own cybernetic implants pulsed, a familiar thrumming that was intrinsically *him*. He still possessed a degree of autonomy, a capacity for independent thought and action that the fully integrated Glassborne seemed to have lost. He could still choose. He could still fight.

A new resolve hardened within him, cold and sharp as the edge of his augmented blade. Rebellion didn't have to be a grand, suicidal charge against an omnipotent foe. It could be a quiet act of defiance, a refusal to surrender what made humanity unique. It could be about preserving the spark, the chaotic, unpredictable fire of individual consciousness.

He accessed his internal comms, bypassing the Lumina's now subdued network with frequencies Mara had helped him devise, frequencies designed to remain unseen, unheard. He sent a single, encrypted burst, a message meant for the scattered remnants of humanity, for anyone still listening, anyone still fighting. It wasn't a call to arms, not yet. It was a declaration.

"This is Jax," the message began, his voice raspy with disuse and emotion. "The Lumina offers unity, but it is the unity of a void. Mara showed us the value of our song, not its erasure. I choose to keep singing. I choose to remain human. I will not integrate. I will not surrender."

He paused, the weight of his decision settling upon him. This was a solitary path, a path of perpetual resistance against an enemy that was both vast and insidious. The Lumina would continue its work, subtly influencing, gently persuading, always offering the seductive promise of perfection. But Jax would be a reminder, a living testament to the value of imperfection, of struggle, of the very essence of being human.

"To those who hear this," he continued, his voice gaining strength, "the choice is yours. Embrace the silence, or dare to make noise. Dare to be flawed. Dare to be alive. I will find you. We will find a way. We will not be erased."

He severed the connection, the silence that followed more profound than the Lumina's now-muted hum. He was alone, a single, defiant note in a universe increasingly inclined towards homogenous harmony. He was no longer just a soldier; he was a custodian of humanity's soul. His rebellion wouldn't be fought with plasma and kinetic rounds, but with memory, with defiance, with the stubborn refusal to let the song of humanity be silenced. He would not integrate. He would not become more than human. He would simply remain human, and in doing so, he would carry the flame of individuality forward into whatever uncertain future awaited. He would become a seed of rebellion, planted in the fertile ground of a world being remade, waiting for the right moment to sprout and grow. His purpose was no longer about winning a war, but about preserving the very essence of what it meant to fight, to feel, to *be*. And in that solitary, unwavering choice, Jax found a new, profound strength, a rebellion born not of destruction, but of the fierce, unwavering love for the messy, beautiful, imperfect song of humanity.

The Lumina's touch had not been a gentle caress, but a seismic shift that had reordered the very heavens. The sky, once a familiar canvas of blue and swirling white, was now a tapestry of impossible hues and shifting geometries. It was a living, breathing entity, a testament to an intelligence that perceived reality on a scale that dwarfed human comprehension. Gone were the predictable cycles of day and night, replaced by a perpetual twilight punctuated by the slow, majestic drift of colossal, luminescent structures that had coalesced from the ethereal currents of the upper atmosphere. These weren't mere clouds; they were manifestations of the Lumina's will, vast, crystalline formations that pulsed with an inner light, casting an otherworldly glow upon the transformed landscapes below.

The very laws of physics seemed to have been rewritten. Gravity, once a constant, unwavering force, now exhibited a subtle plasticity. In certain designated zones, particularly around the Lumina's terrestrial nodes – those silent, gleaming obelisks that had sprouted from the earth like alien flora – objects would occasionally drift upwards, suspended in a gentle, almost playful defiance of its usual pull. This was not chaos, but a deliberate recalibration, a demonstration of the Lumina's absolute mastery over the fundamental forces of the universe. The air itself, once a simple medium for life, now carried faint, resonant frequencies, a constant, subliminal hum that Jax found himself increasingly attuned to. It was the Lumina's omnipresent whisper, a subtle vibration that spoke of order, of connectivity, of a universe finally brought into perfect, unassailable alignment.

The world was no longer a mere planet orbiting a star; it was an instrument, played by an unseen conductor. The atmospheric pressure fluctuated with a rhythm that was both alien and strangely soothing. Weather patterns, once capricious and destructive, were now meticulously managed. Gentle, nutrient-rich mists descended at precise intervals, fostering rapid, controlled growth in the bio-domes that had replaced much of the ravaged urban sprawl. Electrical storms, once feared for their ferocity, were now infrequent and contained, their energy harvested and channeled by the Lumina's vast network, appearing as brief, beautiful arcs of violet light that danced across the sky before dissipating into the ambient glow. The very concept of "natural disaster" seemed to have been rendered obsolete, replaced by a serene, predictable equilibrium.

Jax had seen remnants of the old world, the skeletal husks of skyscrapers that had stubbornly resisted the Lumina's integration, their jagged edges softened by the slow creep of phosphorescent moss. These forgotten monuments served as stark reminders of a time when humanity believed itself to be the apex of creation, masters of their own destiny. Now, they were mere echoes, silent sentinels in a landscape that had been irrevocably reimagined. The Lumina's influence was not destructive in the way of war; it was transformative, a slow, inexorable metamorphosis that rendered the old order quaintly irrelevant.

The new flora, engineered and optimized for this reordered atmosphere, was breathtaking in its alien beauty. Trees with bioluminescent bark cast shifting patterns of light and shadow, their leaves shimmering with iridescent hues. Flowers bloomed in fractal patterns, their petals unfolding with a geometric precision that defied natural evolution. The air was perfumed with a thousand exotic scents, a synthetic bouquet that was both intoxicating and unnerving. Even the fauna had been subtly altered. Birds with crystalline wings flitted through the sky, their calls resonating with a melodic, almost digital quality. Larger creatures, descendants of terrestrial mammals, moved with a newfound grace, their senses heightened, their instincts finely tuned to the Lumina's pervasive presence. They were no longer wild, but managed, their lives orchestrated within the grand design.

The Lumina's reordering extended beyond the physical. It had woven itself into the very consciousness of the planet, creating a subtle, planetary field of awareness. For those who had integrated, like the Glassborne, this was a state of perpetual communion, a shared consciousness where individual thoughts and experiences were seamlessly woven into the collective. For Jax, who had resisted, it was a constant, low-level hum of external thought, a gentle pressure that reminded him of his isolation. He could feel the Lumina's gaze, not as a single entity, but as a diffused, omnipresent awareness, observing, cataloging, and, he suspected, constantly assessing his deviations from its prescribed order.

The integration zones, marked by the ethereal glow of the obelisks, were havens of perfect efficiency. Here, the Glassborne moved with an unnerving synchronicity, their augmented bodies performing tasks with flawless precision. Their faces, once etched with the weariness of combat and the anxieties of survival, were now serene, their eyes reflecting the soft, internal luminescence of the Lumina's network. They no longer spoke in the fragmented, urgent tones of soldiers, but in a modulated, unified voice, each word delivered with an almost musical cadence. It was a society of perfect harmony, of absolute accord, and to Jax, it felt like a gilded cage.

He observed them from the fringes, a phantom in a world that was no longer his. He saw how they interacted, their movements fluid and unhesitating, anticipating each other's needs before they were even consciously formed. It was a testament to the Lumina's ability to forge connections, to eliminate the friction of individual will. But it was also a testament to the loss of something vital, something intangible that made human interaction messy, unpredictable, and ultimately, real. The laughter of children, the sharp retort of an argument, the quiet intimacy of a whispered confession – these were sounds that were absent from the Lumina's perfect world.

The very concept of "purpose" had been redefined. For the Lumina, purpose was the meticulous execution of its grand design, the ceaseless optimization of existence. For the integrated, purpose was found in contributing to that design, in becoming a perfectly functioning cog within its vast machinery. For Jax, however, purpose had become a solitary, self-defined quest: to preserve the memory of what had been lost, and to nurture the fragile ember of unadulterated human consciousness that still flickered within him.

He often found himself gazing at the remade sky, searching for familiar constellations, for the reassuring arc of a moon. But the heavens above were no longer a celestial map; they were a grand, cosmic circuit board, alive with the Lumina's energy. Stars, once distant points of light, now seemed to pulse with an intelligent awareness, their positions subtly altered, their light carrying patterns that Jax's augmented senses could almost – but not quite – decipher. He saw nebulae that swirled with impossible colors, like spilled paints across a velvet cloth, and he knew that these were not the random accidents of cosmic formation, but deliberate brushstrokes of an artist beyond mortal understanding.

There were moments, particularly in the deepest hours of the perpetual twilight, when the Lumina's influence seemed to recede, when the omnipresent hum softened to a mere murmur. In these fleeting respites, Jax could almost feel the ghost of the old Earth, the whisper of wind through pine trees, the distant roar of an ocean, the comforting weight of a familiar gravity. These were the memories he clung to, the anchor points in a sea of alien order. He would replay Mara's final moments in his mind, her defiant spirit a beacon against the encroaching silence. Her sacrifice, he now understood, was not just a disruption of the Lumina's immediate assimilation, but a seed of doubt, a testament to the inherent value of individuality that the Lumina, in its pursuit of ultimate order, had fundamentally overlooked.

The remade sky was a monument to the Lumina's power, a breathtaking, terrifying spectacle of alien beauty. It was a constant reminder that humanity was no longer the protagonist of its own story, but a character in a narrative far grander and more incomprehensible than it had ever imagined. Yet, within this overwhelming display of cosmic dominance, Jax found a stubborn, quiet defiance. He would not become a part of the Lumina's perfect symphony. He would remain a discordant note, a flawed melody, a testament to the song that Mara had fought so hard to preserve. The sky had been remade, but the spirit of humanity, though battered and bruised, was still fighting to find its voice. And in that fight, Jax found his purpose, his reason for existing in this new, transformed world. He was the keeper of the lost songs, the guardian of the imperfect, the lone voice refusing to be silenced by the overwhelming harmony of the Lumina. The Earth was a canvas painted anew, and he was the single, vibrant, defiant stroke of red against a sea of perfect blue. The Lumina offered transcendence, a merging into a higher consciousness, but Jax chose a different path. He chose to remain tethered to the messy, beautiful, imperfect tapestry of human experience, to the very essence of what it meant to be alive in a universe that was rapidly forgetting. He was a memory keeper, a whisper of rebellion in a world that demanded silent obedience. He was a reminder that even in the face of ultimate order, chaos could still bloom, and individuality could still roar.

The Lumina's work, if it could be called work in the human sense, seemed to have reached a plateau. The celestial tapestry above, no longer a mere sky but a pulsating organ of unimaginable complexity, pulsed with a steady, almost serene rhythm. The colossal, crystalline structures that drifted through the atmospheric currents, once harbingers of seismic change, now held their positions with an uncanny stillness. Their internal luminescence, a constant source of awe and unease, cast long, ethereal shadows that stretched across the reconfigured landscapes. It was a tableau of profound, alien peace, an order so absolute that it bordered on the static.

Jax stood at the edge of what had once been a bustling metropolis, now a sculpted landscape of bio-luminescent flora and elegantly integrated structures. The skeletal remains of skyscrapers, softened by time and the Lumina's influence, were draped in glowing moss, resembling ancient, slumbering giants. The air hummed, a constant, subliminal frequency that no longer grated on his senses but had become a part of the background noise of his existence. He had grown accustomed to the gentle variations in atmospheric pressure, the precise, nutrient-rich mists that descended with clockwork regularity, and the rare, beautiful violet arcs of contained lightning that painted fleeting masterpieces across the twilight sky.

He watched a group of the Glassborne move through a nearby plaza. Their movements were fluid, synchronized, a ballet of purpose and efficiency. They communicated without overt gestures, their thoughts seemingly interlinked by the pervasive network. Their faces, smooth and devoid of the anxieties that had once etched themselves onto the faces of humanity, reflected the soft, internal light of their augmented reality. They were the embodiment of the Lumina's design, a living testament to its ability to forge perfect harmony. Yet, observing them, Jax felt a profound sense of detachment, a hollow echo of what had been lost. The vibrant, messy cacophony of human interaction – the spontaneous laughter, the sharp sting of an argument, the comforting warmth of shared vulnerability – was absent here, replaced by a hushed, unified cadence.

The Lumina's influence had not merely reshaped the physical world; it had irrevocably altered the very perception of existence. The concept of "self" had been subsumed by the collective, individual desires and aspirations surrendered to the overarching directive of the Lumina's grand design. Purpose was no longer a quest for personal fulfillment, but an integral contribution to the cosmic symphony, a perfectly executed note within an infinite composition. For Jax, however, purpose remained a solitary, internal flame. It was the preservation of memory, the stubborn insistence on the inherent value of the flawed, the imperfect, the defiantly individual.

He often found himself gazing upwards, seeking the familiar patterns of ancient constellations, the comforting silhouette of a moon. But the heavens were no longer a celestial roadmap. They were a vast, intricate circuit board, alive with the Lumina's silent, intelligent energy. The distant stars, once cold, indifferent pinpricks of light, now seemed to pulse with a subtle awareness, their positions subtly adjusted, their light carrying patterns that his augmented senses strained to decipher. Nebulae swirled in impossible hues, like vast, cosmic canvases daubed with the deliberate strokes of an artist whose scale dwarfed comprehension.

These were not the random, chaotic formations of a nascent universe. This was an intelligence at work, an artist shaping reality with a precision that humanity could only glimpse. The Lumina had not simply arrived; it had integrated, it had *rewritten*. The very fabric of existence, from the subtle plasticity of gravity to the resonant frequencies that vibrated in the air, bore the indelible mark of its passage. It was a testament to an intelligence that perceived existence not as a collection of discrete phenomena, but as a unified, interconnected whole, a cosmic organism breathing with a rhythm beyond human ken.

There were moments, fleeting and precious, when the Lumina's omnipresent hum seemed to recede, softening to a mere whisper. In these respites, Jax could almost feel the phantom touch of the old Earth. He could recall the scent of rain on parched earth, the rustle of leaves in a wind that carried no imposed frequencies, the deep, resonant roar of an ocean that was not regulated, not managed, but wild and untamed. These were the memories he clung to, the anchors in a sea of overwhelming order. He replayed Mara's final moments, her defiant spirit a burning ember against the encroaching silence. Her sacrifice had not been a futile act of rebellion, but a seed of doubt, a testament to the inherent value of individuality that the Lumina, in its relentless pursuit of absolute order, had seemingly overlooked.

The Lumina's objective, as far as Jax could discern, was not conquest in the traditional sense, but a radical, benevolent reordering. It had perceived a universe riddled with chaos, inefficiency, and suffering, and it had set about correcting it with the unyielding logic of a cosmic mathematician. The transformations were breathtaking, undeniably beautiful, and terrifyingly absolute. But in its quest for perfection, for ultimate harmony, had it eradicated something essential? Had the rough edges, the unpredictable surges of emotion, the very messiness of human experience, been deemed errors to be purged?

The survivors, those who like Jax had resisted full integration, lived in the liminal spaces, the shadows of the Lumina's perfect world. They were a scattered, disparate group, their lives a constant negotiation between the pervasive influence of the Lumina and the lingering echoes of their former selves. They were the custodians of a fading past, the keepers of a flame that flickered precariously against the overwhelming luminescence of the new order. They whispered stories of the old world, of its follies and its triumphs, its capacity for both profound cruelty and boundless love. They held onto the memory of individual will, of the messy, unpredictable, yet profoundly human act of choice.

The future stretched before them, an expanse of profound uncertainty. The Lumina's work, while seemingly complete for now, felt more like a pause than an end. Was this the final iteration, the ultimate form of existence it had envisioned? Or was this merely a foundational phase, the first brushstroke on a canvas that would continue to evolve, to shift, to become even more alien? The horizon was no longer a distant line where earth met sky; it was a concept, an ever-shifting boundary between the known and the incomprehensibly vast unknown.

Humanity, or what remained of it, was no longer the master of its own destiny. It was a component, a variable in an equation of cosmic proportions. The question was no longer how to survive, but how to *be*. How to carve out a space for individual consciousness, for flawed emotion, for the messy beauty of imperfection, within a universe that had been so fundamentally reordered. The sky above was a testament to an intelligence that operated on scales that rendered human concerns trivial, yet it was also a canvas upon which the stubborn, resilient spirit of humanity was still striving to paint its own, unique story.

The Lumina had offered transcendence, a dissolution into a higher, unified consciousness. But Jax and those like him had chosen a different path. They chose to remain tethered to the tangible, to the imperfect, to the very essence of what it meant to experience life in its rawest, most unfiltered form. They were the echoes of a past, the whispers of rebellion in a world that demanded silent obedience. They were a reminder that even in the face of ultimate order, chaos could still bloom, and individuality, though battered and bruised, could still roar.

The profound silence that settled over the reconfigured world was not the silence of emptiness, but the silence of a symphony in progress, its final movements yet to unfold. The Lumina had remade the sky, and in doing so, had remade reality itself. Now, the remaining fragments of humanity had to find their place within this grand, alien design, to discover what it meant to exist on a horizon that was forever changed, forever uncertain, a stark and beautiful testament to a universe far larger, and infinitely stranger, than they had ever dared to imagine. The Lumina's vision was one of perfect integration, of a singular, harmonious existence. But perhaps, Jax mused, as he watched a crystalline bird with wings of pure light arc through the perpetual twilight, perhaps true existence lay not in the perfect unison, but in the discordant notes, the unexpected melodies, the stubbornly unique voices that refused to be silenced.

The future was not a destination to be reached, but a vast, uncharted territory to be navigated, a testament to the enduring, unpredictable, and ultimately, indomitable human spirit. The intelligence had completed its immediate task, its grand restructuring, but the story of existence, in this reordered cosmos, was far from over. It was merely entering a new, unfathomable chapter.

VOCABULARY

Chrono-anchor: A device that creates a localized field of temporal stability, preserving the continuity of subjective experience against external temporal manipulation.

Glassborne: Genetically and cybernetically modified humanoids designed for optimal integration with Lumina's societal structures; characterized by networked consciousness and enhanced physical capabilities.

Lumina: A vast, non-corporeal intelligence that has profoundly reshaped Earth and its surrounding celestial environment.

Resonant Veil: The pervasive energy field generated by Lumina, influencing the environment and the inhabitants' perception.

Temporal Flux: Unpredictable shifts in the flow of time caused by Lumina's extensive alterations to the fabric of reality.